W9-BDR-529

Machinery Gone Mad . . .

There was a scraping sound behind them. One of the gnome controllers, the one that welded furnace tops, was peering through the gap in the welding screen frame. Two red lights in the front turned toward Warren, and the controller cocked to one side. It shook from side to side in pantomimed disgust and turned majestically away, striding on pipe legs to the nearest metal bench.

The controller from Shipping reared up as far as its legs would allow and let go with an ear-splitting screech like a steam whistle.

In the silence that followed, Antony bellowed, "Ev-erybody out, now!"

The automated equipment stepped away from its posts. A blowtorch waved evilly at Hammer Houlihan; a discarded rotary saw blade at the end of a pipe arm hummed at Benny Behind.

They all headed for the doors like Thoroughbreds out of a starting gate . . .

THE GNOMEWRENCH IN THE PEOPLEWORKS

Nick O'Donohoe

ACE BOOKS, NEW YORK

THE GNOMEWRENCH IN THE PEOPLEWORKS

An Ace Book / published by arrangement with
the author

PRINTING HISTORY
Ace mass-market edition / August 2000

All rights reserved.
Copyright © 2000 by Nick O'Donohoe.
Cover art by Walter Velez.
This book may not be reproduced in whole or in part,
by mimeograph or any other means, without permission.
For information address: The Berkley Publishing Group,
a division of Penguin Putnam Inc.,
375 Hudson Street, New York, New York 10014.

The Penguin Putnam Inc. World Wide Web site address is
http://www.penguinputnam.com

Check out the Ace Science Fiction & Fantasy newsletter
and much more on the Internet at Club PPI!

ISBN: 0-441-00760-0

ACE®
Ace Books are published
by The Berkley Publishing Group,
a division of Penguin Putnam Inc.,
375 Hudson Street, New York, New York 10014.
ACE and the ''A'' design are trademarks
belonging to Penguin Putnam Inc.

PRINTED IN THE UNITED STATES OF AMERICA

10 9 8 7 6 5 4 3 2 1

ACKNOWLEDGMENTS

My research sources for this novel included Richard Rhodes's *The Making of the Atomic Bomb* and Doris Kearns Goodwins's *No Ordinary Time*. The first won a National Book Award, the second a Pulitzer Prize; if I were to try to make either of these fine writers take the rap for my inaccuracies, the world would laugh. I may as well own up now and admit that any mistakes were mine.

The same holds for my use of *Delivered from Evil*, by Robert Leckie.

Thanks also to the Providence Public Library for its newspaper archives. As for the Cranston Public Library, I owe it a great deal of gratitude and overdue book fines equivalent to the sticker price of a mid-eighties Toyota Tercel.

Thanks to the Island Fencing Academy, most especially to Ben and Jill for their fencing instruction, which somehow made its way into this book. Again, any mistakes are mine.

Thanks once again to my agent, Don Maass; to my editor, Ginjer Buchanan, and to my wife and front-line editor, Lynn Anne Evans. Thanks to all the friends and relatives who have patiently listened as I talked my way through scenes and dialogue. Thanks to the good folks at C. I. Hayes, the industrial furnace company where I formerly worked, for their contributions to this book. Hayes was a fine place to work, and has a proud history dating back through arming the country for two world wars.

My mother, Beth Larson O'Donohoe, was a steady sounding board and resource through the writing of this book. It is dedicated to her with love.

ONE

GRADY CAVANAUGH STOOD in a cave, with bats and stalactites and torchlight. He was holding a home-made metal sword and his cane, trying to fight one-handed.

Something with a twisted, scaly arm lunged forward and slashed at a dwarf—my God, it was Antony—in front of Grady. The blade was part of the arm. Grady realized, without being sure how he knew it, that the attacker was a gnome.

The blade slashed into the dwarf, who dropped quietly down and died. Grady had lost his best friend.

At Grady's left, Susan Rocci waved a second home-made steel-and-electrical-tape sword. She stepped forward as Grady had, parrying the gnome arms that stabbed at them out of shadows.

Then Grady's brother Kevin and his father stepped forward. Kevin was in an Army uniform but unarmed. His father was in trousers from a navy uniform but was wearing only an undershirt. He held a range pole for surveying and stared in confusion at the battle. He was terribly tan.

Two identical gnome arms lunged forward, and a

grinning face came out of the gloom, bloody teeth smiling wide enough to dislocate a normal jaw. Grady shouted, "Klaus, no!" and tried to leap in front of the oncoming blades, but his leg collapsed under him and he fell sprawling in front of his father and Kevin. Grady jerked his head around, watching as the thrusts hit home. He saw the spurt of blood from each of their chests, ending in an arc onto his face. He tasted the salt—

And thumped onto the bed, waking up. His pillow was thrown across the room, and he had torn the top bedsheet. His mouth did taste of blood; he had bitten his lip. He stared wildly around the room, trying to sort out the dream and assess what was real and what was not. He had been in a cave full of gnomes and dwarves. . . .

Grady sagged back, relieved. Kevin was in the European Theater, Dad somewhere in the Pacific. They wouldn't come back until their parts in the war were over. They had never even been in the Dwarfworks, where Antony and Susan and he had battled the gnomes. And Antony and Susan were still alive.

But so were Klaus and the gnomes. It was an odd dream, he reflected, in which the fears were fantasy but the monsters were real.

He dressed, though his alarm wouldn't go off for half an hour. From previous nights, he knew better than to try to go back to sleep.

As he rode his bike to his sister-in-law's, he noted the fullness of the buds on the trees. At this hour there was more energy on the spring tree branches than there was on the streets. Providence was waking up, but weekday traffic would stay light as long as gas rationing stayed in effect.

Mary greeted him at the door, leaning out balanced on one foot in her nightgown and robe. "Did you hear the news?"

"Let me guess." He swung off the bike, spinning his

canetip down with the poise of a swordsman—which was hardly surprising. "Hitler and Churchill kissed and made up."

She stuck her tongue out. "The Allies are rolling across Germany. Everyone says it's just a matter of time before Berlin falls."

Grady pointed out, "It's just a matter of time before I starve to death."

"Not in this house." She gestured to the table.

His coffee cup was full, there was a pitcher of syrup, and his plate was stacked high with pancakes. A good swamp Yankee would hold out for johnnycakes.

Grady was a good Rhode Islander but not a good swamp Yankee. He dove on the pancakes and wolfed them down. "So," he mumbled around the pancakes, "what else did you hear?"

"Not for nothing," Mary said, mocking Grady's own way of saying it, "they're gonna hit Berlin like Dempsey hit Tunney. Soon."

Grady shook his head in wonder, but somehow his fork always found his mouth. "If the Nazis had any brains, they'd surrender."

"If they had any brains," Mary said bitterly, "they wouldn't have started a war." She pointed to Julie, who was peering around the door frame as though suddenly shy, holding herself up by the frame. "She's never known anything but the war."

"Be glad she's in Rhode Island and not in England." Grady mopped up syrup with toast, wishing wistfully that Mary had fried some eggs for him. Still, he'd been the one who'd insisted on limiting eggs to every other day for him. What was the point of giving Mary his ration stamps and cards if he ate all the meats, fats, and dairy products? "Not for nothing, Julie looks like she's ready to run across the room."

"She's close," Mary admitted proudly. "Yesterday she

made it all the way across, holding on to things. She took a couple of steps by herself."

"No, sir."

"Absolutely." Mary added because she couldn't help it, "I'd kinda hoped Kevin would be home to see this part."

Grady nodded but said nothing. They'd all hoped Kevin would be home from Europe by now, even Grady's father—who, himself, had shipped out for the Pacific with the SeaBees fewer than four months ago.

He gave her a peck on the cheek good-bye and hurried to work. It wouldn't do for a sales engineer to be late. These days there were more than enough contracts and proposals at Plimstubb, and he took credit for a great deal of that.

He skidded to a stop in the parking lot, leaned his bike against the building, and whipped his cane out of the basket. He raised it in a swordsman's flourish to the dark brick building. "We who are about to die, salute you." Then he rested some of his weight on the cane and walked in the EMPLOYEES ONLY door.

It opened on the shop floor. Grady surveyed it with satisfaction. Compared to the scary emptiness during the fall of 1944, this year the shop floor had heat treating furnaces half-assembled every fifteen feet. One of the welders, Kenny "Flash" Layman, grinned at him. "Here to sell more furnaces?"

Grady said, "You bet, Kenny," and patted his shoulder. He patted it slowly and gently, not wanting to make Kenny nervous. Kenny, an irascible man in his fifties, didn't react well to quick motion. His nickname did not come from his speed or agility but because of his complaints about his vision as a result of welding with his mask up.

Grady looked at the shop floor in satisfaction. For once, things were going well. The brake shear, under Betty's control, was loudly snapping off metal plates.

He could see lights from three welders and four cutting torches; the snarl of grinding work was deafening; at the other end of the plant someone, probably Hammer Houlihan, was pounding on a metal frame with a lead-head hammer. The paint station emitted a slow, steady hiss that sounded sinister but promised high production. Life was good.

Grady felt less than good. He had a hard morning ahead. He waved in the general direction of the shop floor and headed for the door to the offices. He glanced left and right to ensure that nobody was looking and leaned against the entryway, rubbing his eyes tiredly.

Susan said, "Give up prizefighting. It doesn't agree with you."

Tired as he was, he smiled at the sound of her voice. "Tell me about it." He lit a cigarette for her. Lately they'd met every morning for a quick smoke. "How's engineering?"

"Fine. I'm working, Tom Garneaux's placing bets." Garneaux, an engineer in his fifties, seemed able to complete his work without ever appearing to do anything constructive. "So who were you boxing?"

"My bed. I had a bad dream."

He told her enough of it to matter, glad there was someone he could talk to about the Dwarfworks and about Klaus and the gnomes. Susan listened impatiently, which didn't surprise Grady, then asked, "Was I in your dream?"

"You're in all of them," he said cheerfully.

She laughed, looking more like Betty Grable than ever. She punched his arm and strode away, half-running. Grady watched her as his smile faded.

From his pocket he took a small purple crystal—a gift from a friend in the Dwarfworks—and pointed it toward Susan. To his delight, there was a faint glow. "A little love," he said softly.

He pointed it toward himself, with the grace to turn

his head away. Even so, the violet flash was strong enough to bring tears to his eyes.

Opening the door to his own office, he threw his cane at the coathook and watched with satisfaction as the cane rocked into place. Throwing his cane had proven a useful skill.

He looked at his desk with some satisfaction. You couldn't call it neat, but it was organized, with stacks of proposals. The two major stacks and one small stack had science fiction magazines on them. Only Grady knew the significance of the stacks.

He blew a kiss to the Betty Grable pin-up above his desk, courtesy of Tom Garneaux and his sources. Tom said Grady wasn't fooling anybody, but at least it looked like he only had a crush on a movie star.

He turned to his desk and lifted the copy of *Amazing*. He had never thought of himself as an organized person, but the exigencies of the war had required him to ensure that the requests for quotation and the follow-up correspondence that came to his office reflected some sort of order.

First he called Radio Corporation of America. Plimstubb's conveyor furnaces could meet their specs for glass-to-metal sealing for vacuum tubes. The engineer at the other end of the phone, a high-voiced man named Lee Jerrolds, said anxiously, "Can we get it real soon?" He added earnestly and breathlessly, "It's for the war," as though that were a deep, dark secret.

"Absolutely you'll get it by the date we promised," Grady said. "Sometimes our shipments get bumped on account of troop trains on the East Coast—"

"Oh, of course!" he squeaked. Clearly he hadn't thought of that. "But as soon after that as you can, right? Because we"—he stopped hastily—"because we need it," he finished lamely.

Grady said gently, "I promise, I'll make sure it goes out fast. Contracts for the war do."

They said pleasant good-byes and Grady hung up, bemused. Grady was in his mid-twenties, and it was the first time he had spoken to an engineer younger than himself who had the authority to buy anything bigger than a fountain pen.

He looked at the next item down and did a double take, grinning as he called. The voice at the other end said briskly, "Renfrew."

"Cavanaugh," Grady said with mock firmness. "Subject: opening day. Subtopic: bets for the season. I say the Cardinals in the pennant race again."

"It's too early," Renfrew protested. "Pick an opening-day game and we'll bet. No fooling, Grady, how are you?"

"Great, great. Listen, I just want to run down some contracts. . . ."

They spoke carefully in contract numbers only about the navy, the army, the air corps, and one private contract for Thomson Aircraft that had an AA priority and that Renfrew followed as zealously as he did his own contracts.

After ten minutes, Grady took a breath. "Satisfied with how things are going?"

"Very," Renfrew said. "Like you'd say to me, the joint is jumping."

"Fats Waller would've said that," Grady corrected. "I just sing along." He hummed as he lifted a copy of *Astounding* with a single folder underneath it. "Here's a final contract." He looked at the number on it and the single designation MANHATTAN. "I'll skip reading about it. You know which one it is."

"Of course I do," Renfrew said unhappily. "I also know who's gonna call me about it. Honest to God, he's what Boris Karloff would be if Karloff were skinnier and scarier."

"Agreed." Grady read the latest letter in the folder:

To: Grady Cavanaugh, Plimstubb Furnaces

From: Drake Stode

Subject: High-temperature furnace

1. *I am glad to hear that the hearth materials arrived already. Test them as soon as possible.
   Your source has improved upon any lead time
   I know of for these materials. At some point we
   should discuss this, but not now.*

Grady cringed. So far he had managed to avoid discussing the source of those materials with Stode. There
was almost no chance that would last forever. The letter
went on:

2. *You were three days late with your last report
   on furnace assembly. All reports on this equipment must be up to date. Failure to do this will
   require me to inspect onsite and verify assembly stages. I wish to avoid this.*

Grady fervently wished to avoid a visit from Stode,
too. Renfrew wished to avoid it as well. Stode was characterized by efficiency, intelligence, perception, and a
presence that made everyone around him profoundly uncomfortable.
The letter concluded:

3. *You have promised that you will deliver the furnace on schedule. As before, however, you
   stated in your letter that the movement of troop
   trains on the East Coast might delay or prevent
   delivery of the equipment on completion.*

Be advised, once again, that if you will provide a firm date for the readiness of the equipment, I will divert troop trains on the East Coast.

Yours,
Drake Stode

The letter contained a reference number for the contract and a memo entry stating: MANHATTAN. Grady looked at it unhappily before tucking it in a blue file folder for the furnace.

Now it was time for the last stack. Grady braced himself and lifted the copy of *Weird Tales*.

Below it lay a stack of requests for quotation best characterized by their range and difference. Some were paper, some parchment, some foolscap. One was a piece of leather disturbingly like human skin, stretched on a wooden framework and marked at the edges with stick figures drawn in dried blood. Grady stared at them helplessly, unsure of every last thing about them—including how they were arrived on his desk.

Grady read the top RFQ, which was written in silver on black parchment.

To the makers of industrial furnaces, known as Plimstubb in Rhode Island,

We ask this of you, mindful of all those who share the sea for our border, and the sea grass for the safety of our shores. May the Emerald Lady live in charity with you, as with us, and may she cherish all those you lose to the cold depths of her kingdom in peace and in war.

Grady blinked. He was reminded of "The Navy Hymn," which spoke of "those in peril on the sea." He tried not to think of his father, who with any luck was onshore somewhere in the Pacific. The letter continued:

> *We request a forge that can create bracelets of health. If we provide the sand from a beach walked on only by women, and use said sand to provide a casting in a vessel touched only by the blind, said forge must provide final processing of a gold coat on the bracelets generated from those castings. . . .*

Grady read on unhappily. At the end he made a note to himself: CONFIRM TEMPERATURE UNIFOR-MITY REQUIREMENTS, ATMOSPHERE PURITY. He added hastily, "PURITY" MEANING IN THIS CASE ABSENCE OF WATER AND OXYGEN. He set the note aside hastily and glanced at his calendar.

Reassuringly, it told him that it was still 1945 and summer was coming. The baseball season would come even sooner; FDR had insisted that wartime baseball was good for morale. Heartened, Grady went back to the pile. He read four more proposals, shaking his head nearly the entire time. Two of the proposals were on parch-ment, one on papyrus, one on a flat plate made from a turtle shell.

Two of them were for rings—one for wishes, one for healing. Grady, glad of a realm where he had some ex-perience, scrawled, "Sure, why not?" across each of them. He tried not to listen to the part of his mind that fretted there might be a reason why not. The turtle-shell proposal asked for an iron ax to divide the waters of the world. Grady stared at it for a long time before he drew a large question mark on it, something he could have done when he first looked at it.

Another one was for a singing sword. Grady was un-sure why singing would be a good quality in a sword. He himself was in a choir, and except for a wartime shortage of tenors, the conductor didn't seem to find singing a good quality in Grady. He read the specs dubiously and refiled it without answer for now.

Two more were for bracelets, which apparently were popular items for attack and defense. One ring rendered the wearer invulnerable. The equipment had to be built and the gold heated in places where no injury had ever been done. Grady sketched a thoughtful note to that one; he was accustomed to wars being overseas, and it occurred to him that there must be many places on the planet where no one had been injured. He resolved to look in *National Geographic* and make a list.

The other bracelet reversed all blows onto the attacker, provided the user told no lies while wearing it. Grady had been in sales long enough to know that he could no longer safely test that item himself; he made a note to that effect.

The final new proposal, on parchment in a dark, wedge-shaped lettering, was on a starkly laid-out page: "We request a batch or cabinet furnace in which we may heat the precious metals for a Cloak of Invisibility. The metals are to be drawn into thread under a new moon and woven into an overall fabric in such a way that they distort light. The furnace provider is in no way responsible for the weaving of the thread, but for the imparting of light diversion to the metal threads. . . ."

Grady read on, his eyes glazing over. He scribbled a cautious note, not entirely sure what he was guaranteeing he could or couldn't do.

He read with concern the note at the bottom, which was handwritten with what looked like a quill pen: "Please. You in America, you cannot know the need Hitler has given us to hide ourselves."

Grady wrote a memo to himself: "Accept this one if we can." He had no idea how Plimstubb could.

Finally he needed to get away for a moment; he went to the office next door. There Tom Blaine, in Research, was using asbestos gloves to hold a ceramic crucible steaming with something molten. He was wearing welder's goggles. Bill Riley, watching from a safe distance, nodded to Grady and smiled.

The air smelled of clams.

Tom whipped off the goggles and held the crucible forward, smiling. "Want some chowder?"

"No, thanks."

"For true, we got enough for you and anyone else. Good stuff. Sure you don't want a cup or a bowl?"

"I'm sure." Grady reconsidered. "A cup. Listen, don't set this place on fire, okay?"

Blaine shook his head gloomily. "That's what everyone says. Plimstubb is more afraid of being set on fire by accident than it is of being on fire for any project."

"I'll bet." Grady hesitated, then blurted out, "Listen, Tom. What if you could bring in new projects for Plimstubb but they'd be strange, I mean Ripley's Believe-It-or-Not strange. Would you do it?"

"Hmm." Blaine did his best to sound noncommittal instead of negative. "I'd have to say it depended on the projects. I've seen a lot of things I would never bring in here as projects—and Plimstubb built them. Then again, I've seen projects I thought were the easiest thing in the world the do—and Plimstubb backed out of them without so much as saying 'boo.' "

"We could take on something new," Bill Riley said. Bill believed in Tom and himself, in Plimstubb, in genius and victory. Grady, in his weakest moments, envied Bill.

"If we know enough about it," Tom said cautiously, and for once he was right.

Grady went back to his office and tucked the unusual proposals back under the copies of *Weird Tales*. Happy to have that over with, he walked out front to check with the receptionist, Talia Baghrati, and see if there were any messages.

At the receptionist's station he stopped. The cords to the switchboard hung down, swinging freely and uselessly. Talia's head was lolled backward; her eyes rolled back in her head until only the whites showed.

Grady assumed, not unreasonably, that Talia had knocked back a few quick ones before work. He stepped to the door of the receptionist's area, wondering how to revive her and marveling that all that cloying perfume smell covered any hint of booze on her breath.

Then he noticed that she was typing, far faster and more accurately than she ever had while awake.

He read, fascinated, as the paper rolled upward out of the typewriter:

TO: PLIMSTUBB (INDUSTRIAL FURNACE
    SALES)
FROM: JOTUNHEIM INDUSTRIAL WORKS

"Holy jumping Jesus H. Christmas."

Grady swung around at the voice. Joey Cataldo leaned past to touch Talia. "Say, is she all right? If you ask the Old Spaniard, she doesn't look not so pretty good." His eyes were round with worry.

"Hi, Joe. She'll be fine. She just"—he struggled to find something reassuring and finished lamely—"sometimes she gets like this when she types."

"That's too bad," he said seriously. "You know mostly I think she looks like a million in old bills." He put a hand on Grady's shoulder. "If she has any real trouble, you call me."

Grady patted his hand. "I will, but don't worry. I'll keep an eye on her." He watched thoughtfully as Joe left. The older man was widowed, and so was Talia. Given time . . .

He chuckled, daydreaming happily about a wedding

between Joey and Talia, and the conversation at the reception. Lately Grady enjoyed thinking of people in love.

The letter was nearly done. He scanned it quickly, over her shoulder.

> *Your company name was forwarded to us by one of your recent business associates. Please excuse this means of correspondence, but it is very rapid, and, if your associate said anything at all about us, you will understand that we would find coming to you in person awkward.*

Grady frowned at that. He had learned lately that there were way too many reasons why a customer might find showing up in person awkward. Not all of them had to do with the difficulties of wartime travel.

> *Attached please find several pages of our specifications. Because of the particular climate in which we work (north of Greenland's southernmost tip) and because of our natures, we find processing with heat exceedingly difficult—particularly the handling of the parts themselves. Design of the cooling sections is exceedingly important.*

Talia's breath was coming in short, anxious puffs, with white clouds hanging in the warm indoor air. Grady wrapped her protectively in his suit jacket.

> *We are willing to pay for additional insulation if that is necessary to avoid your equipment giving off heat into the processing area, which is unacceptable for us.*
> *We are grateful for the time you can spend on this project, and would appreciate anything you could do to shorten the normal span of time be-*

*tween proposal and product. We understand that
at the moment you are on a wartime footing. We
sympathize, but would remind you that we are always on a wartime footing.*

*Best regards,
Fridtjof Njus
Jotunheim
President (Acquisitions and Processing,
Posthumous)*

Grady read the signature block five times, trying to
decide which noun "posthumous" went with. He gave
up and left Talia, typing dreamily away, the corner of
her tongue now sagging slightly out of her mouth.

He sat on the reception counter in reception, watching
Talia install a second sheet of paper and methodically
type a table of available utilities (water, nitrogen, hydrogen, electricity, and something called aether) at a loca-
tion in the Arctic Circle. He returned to his office,
shaking his head.

A voice in his office said,
GRADY CAVANAUGH.
He looked around, but no one was there. He looked
at his phone; it hadn't rung.
KNOW ME, GRADY CAVANAUGH.
Grady was a good enough Catholic, and a busy
enough Catholic who occasionally skipped Mass, to feel
immediately guilty at voices from the air. "What do you
want?" he said, and amended hastily, "What can I do
for you?"
YOU MUST SPEAK WITH US.
"Glad to." He croaked, "Is this a personal matter, or
business?"
BUSINESS.
Grady's relief was only momentary. The voice went

on, seemingly from everywhere in the building, THERE
WILL BE WARS AND RUMORS OF WARS. FOR
THIS WE MUST PREPARE. MAKE STRAIGHT A
PATH IN YOUR BUSINESS, AND PROVIDE US
WITH THE TOOLS OF THE LORD.

Grady swallowed. He had been part of providing repair furnaces for navy vessels, barrel-hardening equipment for Remington Arms, and a high-temperature,
special-alloys furnace for the committee that had rede-
signed the Mustang fighter plane. He had been proud of
all that. However, he was dubious about what this voice,
which was either more than one person or one person
on a greater and more individual level than he had ever
imagined, would need for weapons production equipment. "Where do you want to meet?"

ON THE MOUNTAIN.

That stopped him. "Rhode Island doesn't have mountains." He added, in a feeble attempt at humor, "That's
why they call us Flatlanders in New England."

COME TO YOUR HIGHEST PLACE. WE SHALL
MEET YOU. REJOICE.

Grady, feeling there was something imperious in that
last REJOICE, said, "I will. Shall. Will."

Silence followed. Gradually he realized that he had
been standing with his hands clasped over each other,
knuckles clenched until they were white.

He stopped at Tom Garneaux's desk. Tom had a piece
of tightly pressed fiber insulation, a sample of high-
temperature and very expensive material, on his desk.
He had drawn a crude target on it and was flipping a
jackknife into it, poising the blade point on his index
finger before each snap. Tom was in his fifties but
showed the enthusiasms of a twelve-year-old.

Grady watched for a moment. "Where'd the sample
come from?"

"From a vendor. I thought of taking it home with a

half-dozen hearth tiles to make a path through my victory garden, but that would be wrong." Garneaux finished without a pause or a change of expression, "What the hell, I still may. What can I do for you?"

"I'm not sure yet. What's the highest point in Rhode Island?"

Tom reached into a desk drawer—one of the left-hand ones, since the right-hand ones were full of menus—and took out a battered almanac. He turned it to the back, thumbed through the middle, and read reverently, "Highest Places in the United States." He pulled his glasses down on his nose, straining at the small print. "Rhode Island—Jerimoth Hill. Eight hundred and ten feet, approximately. Is something bothering you? 'Cause that looked way too important for a geography question."

Grady glanced behind them. To Grady's relief, Warren Hastings wasn't in. Grady said flatly, "I am in way over my head."

"Swim till you touch bottom," Tom said agreeably. He was engrossed in an eight-variable calculus equation that looked impressively obscure until Grady recognized the variables as horses and the solution, reached three times, as win, place, and show.

"No, I mean it. Not for nothing, you have no idea how weird some of our customers are."

Garneaux's eyes narrowed. "Some of his?" He jerked his head toward the office of Warren Hastings, head of sales.

"Oh, God, no." Grady shuddered. "Nothing like that. These are honest—I think."

"Good for you. I sock away bail money, but not enough for my friends."

Grady was flattered to be Tom's friend; Tom was easily thirty years Grady's senior.

Tom went on, "Let me guess. Your friend Antony found these yahoos."

"Sort of. It's a trade agreement." He took a deep

breath. "Tom, you've never asked about the Dwar——
about Antony's factory."

"You've never asked how I made my money before
I became an engineer." He raised a warning finger.
"Don't."

"It's a deal." Grady went on, "So should I call him
and ask for help?"

"Do you trust him?"

"More than I trust"—he glanced over his shoulder at
Warren Hastings' office—"some of the other people in
sales here."

"That goes without saying." Tom said shrewdly, "So,
are you afraid Antony won't think you can do your job?"

"No. Of course not. Not at all." Grady finished, "A
little. Remember, we're still trying to sell to him."

"And would he yell for help if he thought you could
help him?"

"Sure. But he's—" Grady bit off saying "older." Antony looked younger, though he was in his seventies.
"More experienced."

"Then get experience. There's no better teacher." He
thumped his desk. A menu from a steak place in New-
port drifted off the desk; Tom caught it reverently and
put it back. "In the meantime, make a phone call and
take the second-best teacher you can have: advice from
a friend."

Grady said, relieved, "Sure." He grinned at Tom.
"Two friends, actually. Thanks."

Garneaux, already absorbed in one-person mumblety-
peg again, said absently, "Enjoy your climb."

Grady should have returned to his desk, but found
himself at Susan's instead. That had been happening a
lot lately. He barely glanced at the pictures of Einstein
and of Marie Curie. His gaze lingered momentarily on
the third picture: Susan's father, Vince, beside a fighter
plane named *Sassy Suzie*. Not long ago, Vince had died
in combat in the Pacific. Susan, who lived alone with

her mother, sounded angry nearly all the time.

Grady glanced at her desk, which was littered with design folders, sketches waiting for draftsmen to turn them into blueprints, and a slide rule. There was also a copy of the publications *Nature* and *The Physical Review*. Grady thought guiltily about the science fiction magazines on his own desk. Maybe he should learn more about physics, if only to have something more to talk about with Susan.

She still hadn't looked up. She was sketching a loading table on a conveyor furnace design and making soft muttering noises to herself. She erased a series of dimensions from the conveyor belt calculations and reached without looking for the slide rule.

Grady moved it over another foot. She reached farther and farther, finally looking up when her hand stopped in an ashtray half full of cigarette butts with lipstick stains on them.

He leaned on her desk and said deadpan, "Getting any work done on the war contracts?"

She glared at him. "Of course I am! What do you think I—oh. That was a joke."

Tom Garneaux called amiably from his desk, "You never would have made it in vaudeville, kid."

"That's a fact," Susan said in Tom's general direction, but she was looking back down at her work. "I'll need a bigger drive for the second Thomson Aircraft furnace. The load table's bigger, that makes the belt longer, and I haven't figured the tension yet but I know it'll be greater—"

"Well, there's already enough tension around here." He said casually, "I'm meeting a potential customer in a few minutes."

Her head snapped up sharply. "Another war contract?" She narrowed her eyes when he didn't reply. "Yes or no?"

"I honestly don't know." He added, "And I don't

think *Thomas Register* will list this guy's plant."

"Ahh." Now he had her full attention. "One of *those* customers."

"You know it. Honest to God, when I started here I felt like I didn't know anything about metal processing. Now I feel that way again. How can I promise a working piece of equipment when I don't understand the product it makes?"

Susan pointed out, "We did that for Drake Stode. We're doing it again now."

"That's different." He lowered his voice. "Whatever Stode's going to make with it will obey natural laws."

"Are you sure?" But he was glad to see her smiling again.

"Don't start with Schrödinger's cat again. I hate that."

"If you hate that, think what you'd make of Heisenberg."

"Who?"

"He wrote a proof of something called the Uncertainty Principle. You can know where a subatomic particle is or its velocity, but never both at once."

"Why do you like these guys? They only say that you can't know things." Right now Grady's life had enough uncertainty.

Susan frowned at him, but it wasn't her usual anger or arrogance. "I like them because they tell the truth." She rolled her chair back from her desk, her head resting under the portrait of her father. "They pointed out the uncertainty that's there, that's all."

Gray left without responding. Their lives were different. Just now he was glad that his brother's and his father's futures weren't as certain as Vince Rocci's.

The walk to his office was fast. Sometimes he kidded himself that his foot was getting better. Actually, he was too busy to dawdle. He tossed his cane onto the coat rack, barely watching it settle to a stop on the hook, and looked around cautiously before opening his right-hand drawer. He removed a plain sheet of paper, folded it in half at the middle, and scribbled a quick note.

He signed it with a flourish, held the note by the fold as though it were a paper airplane, and threw it forward overhand. The paper fluttered out his office door and beyond, gaining altitude as it flapped.

Grady didn't even bother opening a window. The note would find its own way out.

After a twenty-mile drive on back roads lined with budding apple trees, Grady hopped a barbed-wire fence, struggled upward through scrub oak, maples, and underbrush, and finally found himself, panting, at the top of a disappointingly modest, rounded hilltop. There were a few scattered slate rocks, a grassy clearing between the trees with new shoots peeping among the dried clumps of last season, and a bush. Grady brushed twigs from his too-long hair and muttered, "At least the bush isn't burning."

A blinding white column of light appeared in front of him.

REMOVE YOUR SHOES AND APPROACH.

Grady did so, praying that he was not about to be told to lead the Irish out of Rhode Island.

REJOICE, the light repeated, FOR YOU HAVE BEEN CHOSEN TO DESIGN AN ENGINE FOR FIRING AND QUENCHING THE SWORDS OF THE SERAPHIM.

The white column raised an arm and drew an even brighter shaft of light, brandishing it proudly.

Blinking and squinting, Grady said, "Could you be more specific?" and added humbly, "Please." He wasn't sure how to address this customer.

The column of light chanted in a manner reminiscent of the responsorials at Mass. Grady scribbled frantically, interrupting once to say, "We'll need specific materials,

sizes, maximum heats, and load weights so we can size
the quench tank." He interrupted shortly thereafter to say
plaintively, "Do the prints have to be measured in cu-
bits?"

Grady ate a gloomy lunch at Haven Brothers diner
downtown, barely noticing the hot dogs. Afterward he
sneaked quietly in the employees' back door on his return, but it did him no good. A voice rang out from near
the receptionist's area.

"Cavanaugh." Warren's voice had no love in it whatsoever. "You were meeting with someone."

There was no hiding. "A customer."

"I assumed, or you'd be in trouble." He smiled. Warren smiled more at trouble than any human Grady had
ever met, though not as much as some nonhumans did.
"How did the meeting go?"

He waved a sheet of scribbled numbers. "I got the
customer's specs."

Warren shook his head, and not a hair of his perfect
haircut went out of place. "I'm more curious about the
customer's mood. That's more important than specs."

Which wasn't true in their line of work. Grady wondered what someone flying a B-29 whose parts came
from Plimstubb equipment would think of the customer's mood being more important than, say, the quality of annealed bolts in his landing suspension. Aloud
he said, "The customer was all right."

Warren raised an eyebrow. " 'All right?' "

"Good." He considered. "In fact, I'd have to say very
good." He moved to go, lifting his cane.

Warren grabbed Grady by the sleeve, and if he realized how badly he threw Grady off balance, he didn't
care. "You're thinking of calling your little friends to
help, aren't you?"

Grady seriously considered lying, but couldn't think
of a way to make the lie stick forever. At some point

he'd need Warren's involvement. "Of course."

Warren let go of him. "Good for you."

Grady was astonished. One of his friends—he would never, ever think of them as "little friends"—had put a sword to Warren and backed him against a wall not long ago. One of them also had forced Warren into giving Grady his job back in sales at Plimstubb. "I'll get on it right away."

"Do that." But he added casually and far too smoothly, "Don't forget that I'll be coming with you."

Grady chewed his lip before saying, "Didn't you agree that I'd represent Plimstubb in any dealings with—"

"In any sales to them, yes. But I'm your manager; I'd still have to sign off on the sale. And this is hardly a furnace sale, is it?"

Once, less than a year ago, Grady had been tricked into a bad business deal by someone clever and evil. At that time he had sworn he would be careful that it never happened again.

"All right," Grady said finally, "but I'll drive."

That afternoon the phone rang. Grady looked around to be sure it was the real telephone before lifting the receiver gingerly out of the cradle. "Plimstubb. Grady Cavanaugh."

"Got your note already," Antony said breezily.

"You're kidding."

"Air mail. Good news travels fast. You sound spooked, kid," came the easy voice from the other end of the wire.

" 'Spooked' is exactly right," Grady said with relief. "Antony, we've got to talk."

"We're talking now."

"You know what I mean. I can't keep you talking that long at a pay"—he glanced around furtively—"at your office phone."

"Fair enough." Antony paused. "So, your place or mine?"

"Yours," Grady said flatly. He knew that Antony wasn't that comfortable at Plimstubb.

"Then come up to see us." He added dryly, "Kirsten would love a visit from you."

Grady winced. He hadn't been at his best with Kirsten. "I won't be coming alone."

"You know we'd love to see Susan."

Grady cupped his hand around the mouthpiece and said as quietly as he could, "She'll come, but I wasn't talking about her."

Antony was silent for long enough that Grady said, "Are you still there?"

"Hastings." The name fell from Antony's lips with the flat thud of a dropped brick. "Do you have to bring that bum?"

"I do. He's my boss." Grady added, knowing it was reckless to speak so at work, "And if only he were just a bum, he wouldn't be so much trouble."

"You've got me there." Antony sighed loudly. "Okay, kid, bring your troubles back to us again."

"You brought your troubles to us," Grady pointed out. "You looked us up."

"Maybe we're both to blame a little," Antony said quickly. He took a deep, shuddering breath. "Bring the heartless bastard. Is that accurate enough?"

"Add 'scheming' and you're dead on target." He looked at the pinup of Betty Grable looking coyly over her shoulder. At the moment he could picture Betty looking over her shoulder because something dark was sneaking up on her. "Listen, we'll all keep an eye on him this time, and on—your big friends." He felt a little like Warren calling the dwarves "little friends," but Grady didn't say the word "gnomes" out loud at Plimstubb. Or at all.

"Let's hope they don't find out—no, that's no good, is it? I have to tell them."

Now the silence was on Grady's end. He rolled a big rubber eraser over his fingers, listening to the irregular thump-thump-thump as it fell on one side, then the other. Grady said, "I wouldn't keep anything from them."

"Except friends. See you Friday, kid."

Antony hung up. He was standing on the seat of a phone booth in the parking lot of the Schuylkill Diner. It was midafternoon, the shadows were getting long, and every last one of them looked as though it had claws. He hurried back down the road, running into a culvert without ducking. He did not emerge on the other side of the road. Neither, in fact, did the culvert.

Grady hung up. A shadow skittered across his desk. He ducked before looking up.

A moth had wandered in and was dancing its crazy, fatal dance of love around the overhead electric light. The moth's shadow fell across the picture of Betty Grable. Grady moved instinctively to shield the picture.

Then he went to tell Susan—and Warren—that they were going.

TWO

THE DAY OF the trip to the Dwarfworks was sunny and clear, with a promise of the warmth to come in a few months. Even by the seacoast, there was no fog. The drive through Connecticut to New York felt shorter than Grady remembered. Warren was driving it at wartime speeds, but it seemed to go by quickly, possibly because Grady was anticipating every turn and curve.

They crossed the Hudson near one of their own customers, Hudson Drill, and turned off the main road into the hills. They turned off that road onto what looked like a farm driveway. Before they were out of the car, Grady saw that underneath the vines that hid it, the great front door of the plant was open for them.

Inside, the Dwarfworks looked organized, operational, and orderly. Iron hearths walked into and out of forges. Dwarves pounded metal on anvils, or held long-handled ore puddlers in fires and chanted to time the melting. In the corner, a Plimstubb CR-8-12-27, its legs shortened to accommodate the height of the dwarves, ran a conveyor belt full of automobile parts into and out of a red-hot heating chamber.

But there were dents and burn marks on the furnace,

and some of the smiths' hammers had nicks from parrying blades. The walking hearths were skittish and
stayed near shelter, and some of the stalactites had fresh
scars where something had sliced through the stone.

Worst of all was a cold hearth, with lovingly polished
tongs and tools leaning against the empty workbench.
Grady stared at it, swallowing and remembering a solemn dwarf named Bernhard, who had watched the dwarf
children so worriedly and had died for one of them so
readily.

Kirsten ran up to them, her short legs nearly parallel to
the floor. "Welcome!" She leaped up, graceful as any
ballerina, and kissed Grady's cheek. Once back on the
floor, she stretched an arm around Susan's waist and
hugged her tightly enough to make Susan gasp.

She stepped back then and regarded Warren. "Mr.
Hastings. Negotiations will be in Pieter's office in a few
minutes. Perhaps you would like to wait there."

He frowned. "I thought I'd take a look around." He
glanced toward the dark tunnel labeled GNOMENGE-
SELLSCHAFT. "After all, if I have a few minutes—"

"I'll escort you to Pieter's office," Kirsten said firmly.
She reached up to take his elbow, seemingly touching
him lightly.

But Warren grimaced and stumbled forward as Kirsten propelled him. He snapped over his shoulder, "Stay
out of trouble, Cavanaugh."

From behind Grady, Antony said in disgust, " 'Stay
out of trouble.' And that from him."

Grady shrugged, shaking hands with him. "I still need
the job, or I'd be long gone. When Kevin and my dad
come home—"

Antony caught the bitter look on Susan's face. "Sure,
sure. In the meantime, it's good to have you back"—he
forced a grin—"under quieter circumstances." He nodded to Susan, thought better of it, and kissed her.

The two of them were engulfed by a shadow. Grady looked up, startled, and moved to defend them, then broke into a grin. "Sonny!"

The black man was dressed in work pants, a long-sleeved denim shirt, and suspenders, and he was grinning wider than anyone without the mouth of a gnome could. " 'Don't call me by name, 'cause I just might come.' "

Grady grabbed his hand. "Bessie Smith?"

"Nope. Me. Been writing some." He put a hand on Grady's shoulder and squeezed, hard enough that he could have picked Grady up if he had wanted. "How you been?"

"Good."

A tiny laughing flash ran past Grady and leaped at Sonny. He caught her and held her, laughing. Grady said, "Hi, Katrina."

The dwarf child waved, hugging Sonny tightly. Grady looked at the black man and at Katrina. He was glad that Katrina had someone strong to turn to, but he couldn't help but feel jealous.

Kirsten walked back toward them, still with Warren at her elbow. Behind her was a gangling, misshapen figure, his rough flesh reshaping constantly.

Until that moment, Grady had never realized that gnomes could have taken pleasant forms if they wished. So far, none of them Grady had met had ever wished.

He nodded. "Heinrich."

The gnome nodded, purposely letting his forehead slump over as he did. "A pleasure to renegotiate with you."

Warren said sharply, "I'll be doing the bargaining, thank you."

"Even more of a pleasure," Heinrich said smoothly. Grady looked unhappy and so, he noticed, did Antony.

Susan, ignoring them both, walked over and stared at the floor. It was unmarked except for a tiny, fresh chip where something heavy had been dropped. "This is where he died," she said.

Grady knelt and looked at the chip mark. "Bernhard." He had known the quiet dwarf, watched him guard the dwarf children, and had been unable to stop him from being killed. "There's not even a sign he was here."

"There never is," Antony said. "When one of us dies, we don't leave a thing for humans to find."

Which might have been rude, Grady reflected, but he had his reasons. "Do the children miss him?"

"They're getting over it." Antony stared across the forges to the cold hearth, left standing for now. "The rest of us . . . I used to kid him," he said quietly. "I used to try to make him laugh, or make Katrina and the little boys chase him, and I'd do anything just to break up that little frown he always wore." He shook his head, angrily wiping his eyes. "I guess we all lose somebody if we live long enough."

Warren looked completely indifferent. Antony stared at him a moment and then said with complete contempt, "Maybe we should get to the bargaining table."

The table was cold stone. At one end sat Warren, at the other a twisted figure with claws and fangs: Heinrich. He had pulled in all appendages, sitting with immense dignity and only occasionally snapping, fangs extended, at a moth that fluttered around one of the torches in the room.

At the end of the table, Pieter, his beard immaculate for the occasion, leaned forward in his tall chair and nodded to Grady, smiling. "So good to see you again, boy. Your work, does it go well? I know you work hard; you did for me."

"Yes, sir." Grady smiled. Praise from Pieter meant more than anything; he had been a good boss but a demanding one. "It goes well. Except for a few things, which I brought with me."

Pieter gestured at Grady's cane. "So the trouble you had, it will not heal?"

"Nah," Grady said. "It's with me for life." He added, "I did a stupid thing in college, fencing. That's why I'm not in the army or the navy." He said it casually, as though he hadn't felt guilty about it every day since December of 1941.

The old dwarf said curtly, "Then I am glad it happened." He gave a sidelong glance at Antony, who winced. "Fighting and dying for people you have never met, what sense is that making?"

"Sometimes people have to," Grady said tactfully. His father was in the Pacific, and his brother, for all he knew, was just outside Berlin.

"Perhaps it is so." Pieter looked around the table, his eyes resting affectionately on Kirsten and Antony. "There are so few of us, perhaps I forget how people can worry for a flag or a country." He put his hands on the table, suddenly all business. "And now, what did you come here with?" He wagged a finger, mock-seriously. "Because I know you, boy, you bring problems to the table."

"In this case, it's my problem and not yours." Grady spread the proposals immediately. "I can't make heads or tails of these. Maybe you can help me."

Warren shook his head in disgust. Grady flushed, knowing he'd given away any bargaining advantage by admitting weakness. Still, he said stubbornly, "We need to know which ones we can take safely. Can you help us?"

Pieter said firmly, "We owe the boy Grady, and for that reason Plimstubb." He looked directly at Warren. "If we owe you something in person, say so now."

Warren said without flinching, "I make deals in which weak people back down."

After a moment, Pieter nodded. "You do. After we decide if that is good or bad, we will tell you." To Antony he said, "Is there any good in the requests they have so far?"

"Oh, yeah." Antony stared at the requests for proposal hungrily. They weren't the best, but they had come from the four corners of the earth. "But there are traps, too."

Pieter said sharply, "Tell me one."

Antony frowned at the first RFQ, then turned to Grady. "A singing sword?" he said incredulously.

Grady said with a laugh, "That one sounded crazy to me, too."

"You don't know the half of it." Antony tossed the order aside. "Singing swords have to be quenched in the blood of a virgin. Can you imagine trying to guarantee the process?"

Grady was about to break the silence that followed by chuckling when Warren said, "Yes, I can."

They turned to look at him—Susan, Grady, and Antony in confusion, Kirsten with complete loathing. "I should have known you'd think of that."

Klaus nodded slowly. "Very clever." He stretched a bony index finger until it was the length of a ruler. "But where will you find a supply of infants?"

Susan put her hand to her mouth, then pulled the hand down quickly, glancing at Grady to see if he had noticed. Grady had, but just now he wanted to hear Warren's reply.

It was predictable. "Not our problem." His smile was narrow and cold, self-satisfied. "We tell them what they can do. It isn't our fault if they don't do it."

"Or if they do," Susan said quietly. "An adult might live after losing that much blood, but not a baby."

Grady reached across the table and tore the sword RFQ in half. "So we're forgetting that one," he said easily, ignoring Warren's face. "What about the lantern for the lost?"

Antony shuddered. "Eyeballs in the heating mechanism. Cows or pigs will do. You can set up processing if you're near a slaughterhouse, but otherwise . . ." He looked at their faces and said defensively, "What did you expect? Haven't you figured it out yet?"

Predictably it was Susan who nodded thoughtfully. "It's like conservation of matter or conservation of energy. Magic costs."

"Now you get it, kiddo." Antony pointed to the contracts. "Some of them cost blood, some cost flesh, some cost something precious, like your firstborn or your first love. Others are more reasonable."

Grady nodded as though he already knew that. Actually, he had already suspected it, which was why he was here. "Let's talk about some of these proposals," he said, and added casually, "and about the cost." He sorted through the remaining proposals hastily and judiciously. He didn't want to ask about the feasibility of creating loving cups that would ensure the fidelity of the dead. "All right, here's one last proposal, and I'll admit"—he glanced at Warren and ignored his frown—"I don't know enough to accept this one, even though I want to." He tossed the proposal down the table.

Pieter picked it up immediately and read it, his lips moving slowly in English. "You want to, boy?" He meant no offense to Grady; Pieter was well over two centuries old.

Grady took no offense. "I do. I don't know." He slapped the table. "Nothing that I learned to become an engineer helps me on this one, but I worked for you, Pieter"—he stumbled over the dwarf's first name, even though it was their tradition not to use titles—"and I really feel we can do this one."

"And you're right." Pieter regarded him affectionately, and it meant a surprising amount to Grady. "We taught you well, down in your stomach, where the answers matter. You can do this one, and so can we."

"Come on." Grady was frankly astonished. "It's from"—he glanced down—"Budapest. It's for a cloak of invisibility."

"And how are they made?" Pieter asked, smiling at Grady.

"Well, it's funny you should ask, because the request lays out every detail of making one. Gold thread—lucky it wasn't silver, because I've been amazed how hard it's become to get silver or copper. The light of a new moon. Well, sure, there's one of those every month. The song of a happy woman." Grady avoided Susan's eyes. "That's the toughest, but as long as you're willing to spend some time making a woman happy, even that's not hard."

Antony muttered, "Well, I guess." The others at the table turned to him and he amended hastily, "I guess you're right about that."

Pieter nodded, reading the proposal slowly and carefully. "And they want it for this war you and our Antony think is so important to the world." He shook his head, smiling exasperatedly at Antony. "You can't wait, Antony? Every so much you must join a human war. It is only yesterday, I am thinking, you ran off to join the war with the biplanes in Europe?"

Antony said exasperatedly, "Boss, that was more than a quarter century ago."

Pieter nodded curtly and indifferently. "Even so." He glanced at the table. "This proposal makes the cost small, even though the cost of the war is large."

Grady said to Antony, "You used this as an example to me of why magic can't win a war. Suppose you're wearing a cloak of invisibility and a grenade hits. Now you're invisible and dead."

Antony shook his head. "They think they have a use for it. For several of them. I can't argue."

Heinrich flipped the proposal with a thick finger. "If the Magyar think this contract will reduce the suffering

caused by the war, why not let them have their dreams?
It harms no one, and it doesn't change the truth." He
nodded amiably at Grady. "And you, cripple—if you
think of a way in which the good from the Gnomengesellschaft will benefit your people, let us know."

Antony tensed. Heinrich had been there at the last
victory—and Grady had bought it, partly through a
bluff.

Heinrich went on, "Probably, even if the contract
should endanger you, we would only wait until you grew
faint and weak. Certainly we would never acknowledge
any tiny success you had, and never"—he glowered—
"any paltry victory that you won against us, by passion
and by resistance. At any rate, we have no objection
against a contract that will do little good and will do ill
to other humans." Heinrich shrugged, letting his shoulders ripple toward the cavern ceiling. "Of course we
approve such a foolish venture."

The room was silent. Finally Grady said easily, "Then
we accept with pleasure. I can't help but feel that you
wouldn't admit your motives on a contract unless you
were trying to discourage us."

After a frozen moment, Heinrich nodded. "From here
I will be more subtle."

Warren, watching Grady angrily, said hastily, "I
agree. Careful contracts are the best."

Heinrich shrugged. "That is between you and Klaus—
or has been in the past." He added, "It seems a shame
that your people do not add scars in memory of failed
contracts."

Susan snorted. Warren said with forced amusement,
"Oh, we have our ways of remembering."

Heinrich stared at him for a moment, then nodded
slowly. "It seems I have underestimated shame." He
shook his head, letting it wobble to and fro for effect.
"Before we attempt to draft an agreement about these
small metals processing contracts—and I grant you,

these contracts are too small to involve the Gnomenge-sellschaft—is there any other matter that concerns this table?"

"I could name a few." All heads turned toward Antony. He swallowed and finished, "There are things I don't get about metalwork."

Pieter frowned, clearly unhappy that Antony admitted a weakness.

Grady gaped. "You? You've been working with metals—"

"Before your father was born, sure. And some of us here"—he consciously avoided looking at Pieter—"have worked at a forge longer than America was a country." Antony added dryly, "But wars tend to spark technical improvements, and the United States has had a few wars."

Susan said suddenly, "Ironclads and the Civil War. Tanks, artillery, and World War I—"

"The Great War," he interrupted. To Antony it would always be the Big One.

Even Warren nodded. "And now, special alloys and lightweight steels for aircraft." He gestured easily. "Answer his questions, Cavanaugh."

Grady tensed. Warren was giving him a chance to fail, and Warren was looking for a chance to fire him. "I'll do my best. What do you want to know about?"

"Case hardening."

Grady relaxed. "I thought you'd ask something tough. You add carbon to the outside of a metal object—the outside is the 'case'—and the carbon makes the metal harder."

Antony looked even more puzzled. "And that's all you want, is to make the metal harder? In that case, why do you need case hardening? Why can't you just tell the metal to get harder?"

"Beats me," Grady said frankly. "I mean, we can't because we don't know how to. Maybe you could, but—

listen, could you tell the part only to get hard around the outside?"

Antony blinked. "Of course not. It's just a part. You have to talk to the metal, not the part."

"And if you do that, the whole part hardens, right? That's no good; the part will be brittle. Antony, you know something about this. Remember the ax of anger? It lends strength to the arm?"

Susan blinked, looking at Grady oddly.

"The Berserker weapon, sure. We made them for the Norwegians. You were in on the tail end of the order." Antony's eyes snapped wide open. "That was what all the soot was about?"

Grady nodded vigorously. "We rubbed the ashes of heroes all over the blades. Now, maybe carbon migration was only the physical part, and there was something important about their being heroes—but the carbon hardened the metal near the surface." He added, momentarily distracted, "Did the Berserkers come and pick the axes up in person?"

Antony said feelingly. "One did. Ever wonder what somebody is like who fights naked in the snow at twenty below, and charges in battle biting the front of his shield?"

Grady said, "Do they really—"

"Kid, you can't imagine."

Grady shut up. "It does occur to me," Kirsten said suddenly, "that you two contain the answers to each of your problems."

Grady and Antony looked at each other. Grady had known that coming here, Antony had known it inviting him. It was all a question of how to find the answers. She continued, "Grady worked here half-time and we learned a great deal." She didn't blush, but she did avoid Grady's eyes. "Perhaps we would both benefit if Antony worked half-time at Plimstubb Furnaces."

The silence that followed was overwhelming. The

idea alone was frightening to the dwarves. Antony, at least, had done it once before, for the sake of the War to Save Democracy, and for a personal interest or two.

Sonny broke his silence. "Antony," he said worriedly, "I know you're tough, and I know you've been out in the world before. Still—it can wear on you. That's all I've got to say." He avoided looking at Susan and Grady, but folded his arms and stared straight at Warren, who bristled.

Grady said carefully, "Most of us would take care of him, Sonny."

"Most is a lot," he said firmly. "Most ain't all, and having a good heart won't make it all."

Antony grinned, hoping he didn't look nervous. "I've had worse offers, Sonny. Sure I'm willing to go, if we get some help out of it for the Dwarfworks no matter what. Maybe I'll learn everything we need to know about metalwork, but it's good to know that if I go, we all get what we wanted." He looked around the table earnestly.

Grady steeled himself, ready to argue for Antony's proposal. Grady believed in what he was here for, but as much as that he believed in Antony.

Pieter said before any of them were ready for an answer, "Antony, you will go and learn." He pointed toward Grady. "You, boy, you will see that he is as safe as he needs to be. As safe as you can make him, against his will." He flashed a smile, the skin crinkling around his eyes. "That is all I need."

"You'll have it," Grady said. He added, because for Pieter he had to, "And I promise I'll be more help than you expected."

Pieter laughed and said with real affection, "You were, from the first." Grady, his ears turning red, swore that he would see that Antony came to no harm at all.

"Then that's all settled," Warren said smoothly. "We'll provide work on odd weeks for Antony van der

Woeden, and in exchange he will review the proposals we find—unusual." He scribbled on a sheet of paper. "A memo of understanding should cover it."

Heinrich nodded. "It will. Sadly, we have no debate about the rules covering such a contract."

Grady tensed. Once before he had been duped into bargaining under the gnomes' rules, and once he had prevailed and signed a contract under normal law. "What is the threshold?"

"The rules are complex," Pieter said slowly. "One thing that is not so complex is that both sides must tell each other when the threshold has been reached. We will make sure you know."

"Thanks," Grady said with relief. He would try never to sell another major piece of equipment to the Dwarfworks until they paid off their debt to the gnomes.

"One moment." Heinrich stretched an arm forward smoothly, the length of the table. The arm twisted in midflight, ulna and radius corkscrewing as the clawed hand at the end spread like a raven's wings until there was more than a foot span from thumbnail to fingertip. The hand wrapped itself around Warren Hastings' throat, the fingers and thumb passing each other and meeting again at his Adam's apple.

Warren neither moved nor looked afraid. Grady was silently impressed. The dwarves and humans were silent as Heinrich spoke, softly but not gently. "The first time you came here, you struck a bargain with Klaus."

Warren opened his mouth. Heinrich held up a warning index finger the length of a kitchen knife. "Granted, there was no proof—but we knew. You fell vulnerable to your colleagues," he nodded curtly to Susan and Grady, "as your partner Klaus fell vulnerable to us. From us at least, you received no punishment. Does that make you feel clever?"

He tilted a fingernail to Warren's jugular. Warren stayed still and said nothing.

Heinrich sighed. "Wise silence. I wish you had been foolish . . . it may intrigue you to know that one of my colleagues is returning to his former duties as of today. His punishment should be longer, but we have use of his bargaining skills."

Heinrich turned his head a full 180 degrees. "Klaus!"

Of those around the table, only Kirsten and Warren did not react. Pieter, for his part, frowned. The rest drew back from the table with revulsion and pity.

A gnome entered, limping. Two of his fingers were missing, and his right ear dangled by the merest thread of flesh. His lower lip had a tear in it, and a scar half an inch deep zigzagged down his right cheek as though someone had poured hot lead down a wax sculpture. The scar continued onto his body and spread like the delta of some great river, dispersing into dozens of small cicatrices. The gnome stood just inside the door and stared at them, saying nothing, waiting.

"You may wonder," Heinrich said dryly, "why I would trust Klaus in my organization after so great a failure. I assure you, trust has nothing to do with it.

"Still," he said, looking the scarred gnome up and down, "he has shown remarkable tenacity in hanging on to his present rank and position against all odds."

Klaus inclined his head slightly.

Heinrich continued thoughtfully, "I cannot help but wonder how he would fare against me."

"I have been too busy lately to wonder that," Klaus said. His voice was rasping, as though his throat were raw and sore.

Heinrich smiled—a gnome's smile, the lips parting far enough and wide enough that it seemed only needle-sharp fangs kept his head attached. "Very honest. Once, of course, you had more free time." He scowled and rapped the table with scaly knuckles. "Now that you will have leisure again, I advise that you not wonder recklessly."

Klaus turned to stare at Grady, and the gnome's dull eyes glowed again. "I will have enough thoughts to fill my time."

Heinrich nodded vigorously. "Good. Good." He said to the assembled company, "One thing all those who deal with us admit: we have a strong work ethic."

"I'll bet you make the trains run on time," Susan muttered.

Heinrich ignored her. "I will now turn these proceedings over to my colleague." He pointed at Klaus and chanted in a singsong voice.

The hairs on Grady's neck stood up, and the sheets of paper on the table clung to its surface. Blue sparks glowed on Kirsten's sword, Warren's rings, and on every piece of metal in the room.

Gradually fewer and fewer sparks shone anywhere but near Klaus. Those nearest him grew brighter and brighter until his body was a blue, coruscating mass. His arms and legs twitched and danced, and his face was a rictus of pain.

Suddenly his entire body relaxed, sagging back in his chair until it seemed he would pour under the table. Before that could happen, he sat up, testing each of his arms in turn and then his legs. His missing fingers grew back. His ear reattached fully to his head. His face . . .

"What's this?" Heinrich arched an eyebrow until it was nearly on top of his head. "What's this?"

Staring at the humans, Klaus touched the scar on his right cheek. "I decided to keep a reminder."

Heinrich beamed. "Excellent choice. I knew you had a head for business. Think of your recent troubles as an opportunity for growth. It toughened you. It did you some good."

Klaus turned to him slowly. "Is it a growth opportunity you greatly desire?"

Heinrich waved a fluid limb carelessly. "Not at present. There's too much to do. I'm glad to have you back on the team. And I'm sure that the others will respect your leadership abilities even more."

Klaus smiled for the first time, a grin that was the more horrible on a gnome for being narrow and showing no teeth. "I can ensure that." He turned one last time to Grady. "I look forward to your next visit. Perhaps we'll meet then, informally."

With that he turned and left. A bat swooped low over him. His arm rippled loosely and effortlessly overhead. The bat shrieked briefly and was still.

Pieter said, "I'll just go to watch him with an eye." He left. Warren followed; Grady suspected that Warren left partly because he wanted to make a deal with Klaus, but also because all the other managers had.

Sonny winked at them. "Don't you think that crowd needs one honest eye?" He followed, casually but also alertly.

After they were gone, Grady wordlessly lit a Lucky Strike each for himself and for Susan, who took hers and sagged in her chair. "Wow. Are you two sure this is a good idea?"

Grady quoted Antony. "Change is good for me. And I am not afraid."

Antony, grinning, said in Grady's accent, "Optimism and confidence."

Kirsten said seriously to Grady, "Watch Klaus. He wants to destroy you."

Grady, surprised, said, "Well, sure."

Kirsten smiled crookedly. "I apologize if I've underestimated you. Sometimes it seems that you are more trusting than you should be." She looked pointedly at Grady.

He blushed. He had made more than a few mistakes as an apprentice at the Dwarfworks.

Kirsten let him off the hook by turning to Susan. "Susan, you did very well improvising a sword the last time you were here."

Susan nodded briefly, flattered but seeming to expect praise.

Her jaw dropped as Kirsten said firmly, "Next time be trained on the weapons in advance." She laid two foils on the table. They were heavier than normal human foils, with blunt edges and a bead formed on the point. They were longer than the dwarves' own weapons.

They were the same length as the sword Grady had practiced with when he worked inside the Nieuw Amsterdam Dwarfworks.

Susan looked down at the weapons, then across at Grady. "He'll be teaching me?"

"Unless you prove a poor student," Kirsten answered with no change of expression. "In that case I will ask Antony to take over, though your height differences would require extra care and attention during lessons. Also—" but she did smile at Antony as he said it— "Antony has fought with swords, guns, and hammers. I think that he prefers to carry a hammer."

She set her hands on the table, palms down. "In my absence, Grady is the best teacher you could have. Do you think you can take advantage of his skills?"

"I'll do my best," Susan said a little sharply. She took the foils.

Grady tried not to smile; Kirsten had deftly converted Susan's ego from resisting Grady's tutelage to proving that she could learn from him. A good warrior, he reflected, would make a great salesman.

"You know," Susan said tentatively, "my life is full of outside work. I work at bandage rolling, blood drives, bond rallies—I could only do this at work."

"We can practice before work, in the mornings," Grady said. "We meet then anyway."

Antony looked speculatively at Susan but said nothing.

Sonny appeared out of nowhere, saying with emphasis, "Warren's ready to go home, so I guess everything's all right."

"Thanks for the warning," Susan said, and then added with sudden realization, "You've done this kind of thing before, watching for danger, haven't you?"

"The parishes of Louisiana weren't so bad," Sonny said in a seeming non sequitur, but added, "You should watch everything you say. Everything."

"Thanks a lot." Grady looked at Sonny, who was older and who had been very kind to Grady when he had needed it. "You give Katrina a kiss for me."

Sonny laughed out loud. "I'll give her a couple." He waved and left. Grady looked across the cavern, expecting Warren.

Instead, Klaus came out of the darkness, a new confidence in his stride. He stood in front of Grady, scaly arms folded, confident and challenging.

Susan said without a single tremor in her voice, "Welcome back to the business world."

"Oh, I never left." He reached a long finger up to his scar. "Fear, pain, cicatrices—it's all business."

He turned to Grady. "All right, it's not all business. I remember an occasion on which you bested me. One day I will try to recoup my losses for that occasion." He extended his arm only slightly, scraping talons across the stone with a sound like scratching a blackboard. "On that day, outrun me."

Grady stood his ground. "On that day, I'll turn and fight."

Klaus shook his head, letting his elongated jaw swing left to right like the beak of a vulture surveying the dead below. "Not at all, not if you need to outrun me to protect someone else." Without warning he extended his arm and touched Susan on the chin, dragging a fingernail down her neck and chest before she could step back. "So good to see you again."

Grady, furious, spun his cane at Klaus's arm, which,

suddenly rubbery, sagged out of his way and wriggled snakelike across the floor as it contracted out of reach. Grady, too angry to feel ridiculous, pointed his cane like a sword at the gnome. "I beat you once."

Klaus frowned. "Injudicious of you to remind me." He touched the scar on his face. "And I have all the reminder I need. Know this: I don't intend to forget. And I am aware that I swore not to hurt you physically— unless, of course, you or a coworker should break your own agreements with us."

With that he spun and strode into the shadows.

Grady exhaled. Kirsten looked concerned and so, to Antony's surprise, did Susan.

The good-byes were short and very sweet. Susan hugged Antony, clearly not wanting to let go. "I wish I felt as sure of myself as you do."

He leaped up and kissed her when she let go. "And I wish I felt as sure of myself as you think I do. Kiddo, we all pretend. Make sure you pretend hard enough to matter."

Kirsten nodded. "It's not like poker, where they call it a bluff. Instead, we all do our best, and then a little better than we think we can." She hugged Susan, then turned. "And Grady? Train Susan, and train with Antony. It won't be as good as training with me, but it's the best you can do." She leaped up and stroked his cheek softly, but landed facing away from him and strode off toward Pieter's office.

Antony, watching her, sighed. "God, kid, I wish I could figure out how to do to her what you do without wanting to. You make it look easy."

"You'll get your chance." Grady looked after her as well. "How long have you two, how long have you—"

"How long have I been courting her?" He shrugged. "Since before the Great War. Seriously since 1912, somewhere in there. It takes patience."

"I guess," Susan said. She stole a look at Grady and looked away quickly.

Antony, grinning, didn't miss it.

Grady didn't either. The drive back to Rhode Island would be long, but full of daydreams.

A moment later, Warren returned, glaring right and left. "I'm pleased that our business has gone so well, but it's time to return to work." He leaned on the last word, as though today had been recreation.

Grady and Susan moved resignedly to the car. Antony said, "Take care, kid. I'm looking forward to working at Plimstubb."

Grady held his hand up. It still had a gold ring on it with a braided dragon design. "Remember telling me to be careful what I wished for?"

Antony, ready to say something self-confident about knowing exactly what he was doing, shut up. He remembered a moment during the Great War, stepping forward to volunteer at Fort Snelling in Minnesota, in which he had thought he knew exactly what would happen to him if he flew a biplane over France. He hadn't even been close.

Grady waited until they were on the road to ask Warren, "What did you agree to?"

Warren sailed around a corner, enjoying the discomfort of his passengers as they swung against the doors. "A kind of technological advance for our in-house equipment. They have better controllers here. . . ." For a moment Warren seemed like an engineer instead of a manager. "The things they can do . . ." he said wistfully.

He shook his head vigorously. "Not all contracts are your province, Cavanaugh."

"I know that." At Plimstubb, a privately held company, a great many contracts were confidential. "But your first dealing with the gnomes . . ." he let the sentence trail off.

Warren said sharply, "That was our first meeting. Now I know the customer better."

"He knows you better, too," Susan pointed out.

He smiled at her, wolfishly enough that she checked the neckline of her dress. "I have years of skill behind my bargaining."

Grady considered pointing out that none of them knew how old Klaus was, but didn't bother. Warren wasn't likely to listen.

Instead he reached a hand forward. "Let's see the contract."

Warren passed it back, too happily for Grady's taste. He and Susan each scanned it. Grady squinted at the small print he knew would be there: "The company does not extend its warranty to theft, damage from inappropriate use, or malfunction due to malice."

Appended to it was a new clause: "This applies specifically to technology that is used beyond the purchaser's plant, particularly for resale or for incorporation on other equipment. This contract grants the use of Gnomengesellschaft components solely inside the plant of the purchaser."

Grady said flatly, "Klaus thinks this is a loophole. He's out to get you."

Warren raised an eyebrow. "You mean that he's out to get us."

Susan snickered. "That's true, if you mean he's out to get both you and Grady."

Warren turned to her coldly. She said defensively, "I'm just trying to be accurate."

Grady said, "It's true." Warren turned his attention reluctantly to Grady, who went on, "He wants to get me because I shamed him in front of his own people. He wants to get you because . . ."

He trailed off, trying to find a tactful way to put it. Finally he said, "He wants to get you because you kept yourself from being the fall guy in his last contract, no matter how hard he worked to make you one."

Warren brightened. "That's true." He frowned. "On the other hand, this is a good contract for Plimstubb. The object of a good contract is to leave the other person paying more than he thought for less than he thought."

Susan said, "Silly me. I thought contracts were how two people exchanged real goods for real services."

Warren smiled down at her. She hastily buttoned an additional button on her dress when she noticed how far down he was smiling. "That, young lady," he said patronizingly, "is why you merely design things and I sell things."

They fell into silence. Grady, who had hoped to spend the trip daydreaming about Susan, instead spent it worrying about what Warren thought was badly written about the contract, and why Klaus would write a bad contract intentionally. The answers Grady came up with all made him nervous.

THREE

T HE MORNINGS WERE still chilly, but the sun promised better things to come. Often it was in the seventies by midafternoon, though breezes off Narragansett
Bay could still take that below sixty. These days Grady
and Susan took a morning cigarette together outdoors
instead of at their desks or elsewhere in the plant.

On this particular morning, Susan was waiting for him
outdoors. She had taken both swords with her. She
brought them out now. "First lesson." She picked up one
of them, pointing it at Grady with her body leaning toward him, her weight unbalanced.

"Uh-uh." Grady flipped his cane around, hooking the
crosspiece of the sword, and pulled. She stumbled forward, and he touched her above the breast and below
the throat with a single finger. "Now you know why we
start with footwork."

But her flesh felt warm and smooth under his finger,
and she blushed as she recovered her footing. The lessons would be even more awkward because she knew
that Grady was in love with her.

Grady said quickly, "Set the sword aside and put up
your hand, palm up, elbow roughly a hand length from

your body . . . shoulder height on the fingertips . . . that's good. Now hold your rear hand as though you're holding a lantern in a duel." A thought struck him. "Did you ever take ballet?"

"When I was little," she said, and added defensively, "Ma made me."

"Terrific, because I can't show you all the footwork perfectly." He gestured with his cane. "I think they call it first position, with the feet at right angles. Put your lead foot toward me. First we'll learn the ready position, then you'll walk into the *en garde* . . ."

The first lesson took fifteen minutes. By the end of it, Susan was accustoming herself to a balanced stance. She and Grady moved back and forth in the parking lot, fingertips touching, like lovers in an MGM musical.

At the end, she was out of breath. "When do I start with the sword?"

"You'll hold it once next lesson, but you'll learn some more footwork. How to cross your feet advancing or retreating, how to lunge and advance-lunge, and finally a leaping lunge." He grimaced. "I may have to sketch that one for you; I can only do it with the cane, and it doesn't look the same at all."

She nodded. "I'll learn it." Susan was nothing if not confident. As they went inside to go to work, she smiled at him over her shoulder. "I guess I'll get used to fencing with you."

"Hey, you made me sing with you." Grady, an enthusiastic but untrained singer, had joined the Providence Choral Society. The conductor shouted at him, insulted him, and wrung his hands over him, but needed him too badly to do anything drastic.

She smiled. "It's good to know I can make a guy sing." Grady tactfully said nothing as she lit two cigarettes and held out one for him. He liked the gesture until she said, "Smoke fast or take it with you. Chester Traub is in early, and he wants to see you."

Grady whistled. Chester was the treasurer, and passionately careful about money. If he was that anxious to see Grady, that meant either that one of Grady's sales was in trouble . . .

Or Grady himself was in trouble. He considered that possibility unhappily and raised his cigarette in salute to Susan.

Chester was reading *Variety* when Grady knocked at his door. Chester was devoted to the movies, not simply as a fan but also as someone who could tell you what was spent on every new picture, and sometimes what should have been spent. He looked up, startled. "Come on in, kid."

He gestured. "Here, sit down." Chester self-consciously swept a small stack of movie magazines off the chair.

Grady, a copy of *Astounding* tucked in his back pocket, smiled patronizingly. "Is there something I can do for you?"

"Not you, really." Chester handed a sheaf of papers to him. "It's about your friend Antony who's coming to work here."

"Antony." Grady stared at the papers as though they might burst into flame any second.

"Antony van der Woeden." Chester raised an eyebrow, and suddenly he didn't look embarrassed or unsure at all. "Last employer, service record if any."

Grady wondered frantically what Chester would make of Antony's service in World War I. If you went by Antony's face, he had been born after the war ended. "Gee, do you really need all that?"

"Didn't used to. Now, with the war contracts, you now how it is." He scanned the papers, though he clearly knew what they said. "It's just the usual stuff before he starts a new job. Some references, some identification . . . is there something I should know?"

"No. I mean, sure. He should tell you where he comes

from." Grady tugged the paperwork out of Chester's hands, trying to look casually at it. "I'll ask him to fill it out."

Chester said back, too casually, "I'll look forward to that." Grady tottered out, stunned that he'd forgotten such a simple detail.

It took Grady five minutes to guess what he had to do and half an hour more to get his nerve up. When he arrived in front of Garneaux's desk, the engineer was cackling gleefully into the phone, "That's why they call it a horse race, Rocco." Tom hung up and wrote a figure on a memo pad. Grady, impressed, noted that the figure had three zeros behind it.

"Tom?"

Garneaux turned. "You've got a problem," he said flatly.

"You know it."

Tom looked him up and down and said softly, "Always remember that I have friends I can go to who will get you out of any problem at all." He held up a warning finger. "Once you owe them something, you're theirs. And those guys never forget. Be sure you need that before you say anything."

"I'll remember, and thanks," Grady said, intrigued. He knew Tom had done some rum-running during Prohibition, and he knew enough about Rhode Island to understand that either Tom owed favors to someone or that someone who was still making money owed big favors to Tom. For Tom's sake he hoped it was the latter. "But right now I need something smaller, but still tough for me to do."

"Ask. Is it something for family—or for Susan?" Tom grinned at him shamelessly. "Like the SeaBees say, 'Can do.' "

"Actually it's something for work, and for Antony."

"Dutch?" Garneaux looked delighted. "He's all right.

Say, what a time we had in Boston. Remember?"

Grady remembered leaving Boston before they could be arrested. "It was something, all right." Leaving out essential details such as the magical elements of the Dwarfworks and the existence of the gnomes, Grady sketched out the problem, finishing, "So I have a friend who's working here and can't prove where he's worked or that he's a citizen or anything."

"But he's older than he looks, and he flew in the Great War."

Grady said, puzzled, "World War I, sure. I didn't realize you'd picked that up—"

"Credit me. I pay attention." Tom punched him on the arm. "Just for his service time, I'll get him papers. Passport, driver's license, citizenship, you name it."

"Thanks," Grady said, nonplussed. Garneaux's patriotism always seemed to thunder in out of nowhere, like the Lone Ranger saving the day.

Tom Garneaux barely heard him. "Better yet, we get him papers that show him as a displaced person, fresh out of Poland or the Netherlands. No way to trace it, for now. I can do all that in a heartbeat."

"Yeah, out of Amsterdam would be perfect."

"Sure." Garneaux stared into space, and Grady could swear that Garneaux's eyes misted over. "There he was, defending his homeland, and suddenly all these paratroopers drop out of the sky. In the fighting, maybe it's the Nazis and maybe it's the defenders, the dikes are blown and the whole damn world is flooded. The Germans were bad, but the Dutch never had an enemy like the sea . . . sure, I can get some papers for him."

"Thanks," Grady said, relieved. "How can you do all that?"

Garneaux winked. "Years of practice. This is nothing. The hard part is getting all that for someone the police already know." He went back to looking over a racing sheet as though Grady weren't there at all.

Grady reflected that there was more to being a grown-up than he had ever considered when he was a child.

Telephoning wasn't enough; for this one he went face-to-face.

His arrival in the Dwarfworks was more explosive than he had expected. The last time he had come to the cave, he had been with Susan and also with someone universally despised. It was a formal occasion. This time, nobody cared who saw what they did.

Antony shook his hand and pounded his back. Kirsten hugged him tightly, holding him off the ground. Pieter waited until they were done and put a callused hand on Grady's chest. "So how is one of my good workers?"

Grady had been ostracized here, been abused and been beaten unconscious. Still, for one second he regretted leaving. "I'm fine, Pieter," he said affectionately.

He walked over and shook hands with Sonny LeTour, who was filling out a production form and smiling. Sonny grabbed his hand and squeezed it tighter than a vise. "Grady, how are you?"

"Fine." Grady looked around. "I figured Katrina would be here—"

Katrina dashed out from behind Sonny's legs and hugged Grady so hard around the knees that he nearly toppled backward. He barely caught himself on his cane, then bent forward and hugged her back. "I figured she was your friend now."

"She is." Sonny shook his head, smiling. "But she didn't forget."

Grady hadn't either. He patted the little girl and doubled over, kissing the top of her head. When he straightened up he saw that the dwarves were looking at him in amusement. Grady blushed, wondering if he would always stay this good at blushing.

Pieter said abruptly, "You have come to make your dealings with Antony, boy?"

Grady nodded. Pieter went on, "Best you do that alone. I know you two, you talk better to each other when the Old One is away." He chuckled, but his smile faded as he looked at Antony. "You," he said gruffly. "Antony, you be sure to do what this one tells you. I know by my heart he will keep you from harm."

But he looked back sharply at Grady, who said, "Of course I will."

Pieter spread his arms, palms up. "Then we know." He finished, because he couldn't help himself, "But you have care when you walk in that world. Not every man is as good as our Grady, you know that."

Antony nodded. "I know that, boss. I promise I'll be careful." He added, "Besides, it'll be good for me. Change is good for me—"

"Yah, yah, and you are not afraid. Antony, sometimes I wish to hell you had more fear." He turned toward his office. "Come say your good-bye before you are taking the truck." He walked away.

Antony watched him go and said shakily, "His English goes all to hell when he's upset."

Grady said awkwardly, "He's only worried for you."

Kirsten said sharply, "Of course he is."

They looked at each other. All three of them knew that Pieter's mother and nearly every dwarf in the Netherlands had been hunted on horseback and killed by humans when Pieter was an infant.

"On some days you'll work with me," Grady said.

"I can do that," Antony said confidently. Inside he was feeling relief.

"The first day, and most of the other days, you'll work in the shop, on War Department contracts."

"Oh," Antony said unhappily.

Kirsten said quickly, "Is something bothering you?"

"Not much. Not really." He swallowed. "So, how's Roy Burgess these days?"

"He's still the foreman." There was no way around saying it. "He can be hard to work for."

"You've done it?"

"I have." Grady added frankly, "It wasn't great. The other guys in the shop helped me out, and they'll help you. Most of them."

Kirsten folded her arms. "Good. If they don't, I want to know."

Grady and Antony both grinned. Kirsten had met Roy Burgess. The meeting hadn't gone well—for Roy.

She tilted her head up and stared into Grady's eyes. "What about work papers? Does Antony need any?"

"He'll have them. They'll say he's worked for Nieuw Amsterdam Metalworks for a couple years and was a refugee before that ... Antony?" This was as hard as talking to Garneaux had been. "I think—Garneaux knows you're not what you say you are."

Kirsten's eyebrows nearly disappeared into her blond hair. Antony shrugged. "I never said I was anything."

"You know what I mean. He knows—okay, he guesses—that you're not human. Is that a problem?"

Antony considered and said slowly, "Not if he knows, no. If he tells somebody else, that's a problem."

"He never would," Grady said immediately.

Antony grinned crookedly at him. "How do you know?"

There was no good answer to that. "I just know, that's all."

"I believe you," he said seriously. "It's like me and Curly Larson."

Grady said dubiously, "You've always described him as being one step ahead of being thrown in jail."

"That's true. But I knew I could trust him." Antony said with tactful vagueness, "And Tom Garneaux reminds me of Curly sometimes. Did I ever tell you how Curly and I were in one of the first bombings of an airfield?"

Relaxing, Kirsten rolled her eyes and left. Grady shook his head resignedly. He knew enough of Antony to know that the story was coming no matter what he said.

Besides, the ones he hadn't heard yet were fascinating.

Antony settled back against the rocks, his eyes focusing on the ceiling as he remembered. "Let's see . . . it was winter in France. I'd thought nothing could be cold after New York, but I'd always been underground in the Catskills, out of the wind. Here we were in the barracks, and whoever had run them up wasn't worried about little subtleties like insulation or filling in cracks. When the wind blew, every candle outside of a glass chimney wavered, if it didn't go sideways." He shivered suddenly. "And it seemed to me that at night in winter, the wind always blew.

"Anyway, this night the candles were smoking but staying lit, so it couldn't have been too bad. We were wrapped in brown wool blankets, sitting around the stove. We fought about everything else, but that stove was sacred; we all fed it wood. About half of us were smoking pipes and drinking coffee, wishing the officers would leave so we could pour something else into the coffee. Anyway, we heard a plane overhead, buzzing and coughing around. Curly said it was a Fokker, but I thought it was smaller; back then we went by the sound of the motor as much as by the silhouette. None of us worried about it; some idiot was flying around at sunset, doing reconnaissance. What else were planes for?

"Then the explosion came." Antony leaned forward. "There was a thud that we could feel in our chests and in the slap to the soles of our feet, even before the outside wall fell down and Curly was thrown out of his chair. My first thought was, *Sacred Sun, that plane nearly crashed on us*. Then there was another explosion, and my next thought was, *That's not right,* but I couldn't think why. Then I'd remembered that I'd only heard one plane, so there could only be one crash."

Grady nodded. "Makes sense."

"That's because you have time to think, kid. Remember, I'd seen my best friend thrown off his feet, and I didn't know why. We ran outside—we weren't sure that life was safer outside, but at least we could see what was going on. The next thing I saw was Koudelka, this Bohemian kid from Iowa, out on the airfield. He was a big boy, muscles all over him from throwing feed sacks around in a seed-and-feed store in some town called Protivin. He had a tripod machine gun cradled in his arms and he was holding the barrel straight up, firing into the sky and crying. Later I figured out he was scared. He fired straight up until the ammo belt ran out. Smoke was coming from his shirt before he quit. I still couldn't figure out what he was doing."

Grady frowned; he couldn't either.

Antony watched his face and said with amusement, "Kid, there weren't any antiaircraft guns yet. The guy in the sky was bombing us, dropping artillery shells out of the cockpit and seeing what he could hit. He didn't have any target system, but we didn't have any way to fight back."

Grady thought about it and shivered. "How did it end?"

Antony shrugged. "The bomber couldn't hit anything and neither could we. Eventually he ran out of shells and flew home. Maybe he made it back to his own airfield and maybe not; planes in those days crashed more than they landed." He stared straight ahead, remembering. "But we looked around the craters on the airfield and repaired the one broken wall, and we knew that everything was different. Not just our airfield, or our war, everything."

He looked Antony in the eye. "Back in the thirties, when Franco bombed Guernica, everybody was shocked.

Then when Hitler bombed Coventry, everybody was angry but not so many were shocked. This spring the Allies fire-bombed Dresden and burned civilians, but nobody much wept over here in America. Me, I knew it was all coming from the moment I saw a shell land next to us on the airfield."

Feeling uncomfortable, Grady changed the subject. "Whatever happened to Curly?"

"Last I heard from the army, he was AWOL from France," Antony said, chuckling. "Of course, that's been a while. I got a card from him from New York City, while I was still in France. The army wanted to ship him back to France before they'd let him go home. He said he wasn't going. I'll bet he made it back to Iowa all the same." He shook his head, chuckling again. "Shook as he was, he was mad as hell about that bombing. We'd been playing poker, you see, and he'd gone over that stove still clutching three queens and two deuces. Afterward nobody'd let him collect on the hand, because the cards had been out of sight in his shirt pocket."

"What did he do during the bombing?"

"Dragged me out of the barracks, rolled two planes off the field where they'd be safe, and shot at the Hun—excuse me, at the Germans—with a forty-five." Antony said levelly, "He was the only one of us who kept his head. The point is, sometimes the people you wonder about are the people you should trust the most."

Grady nodded, impressed. Only later did he realize that Antony had said nothing at all about where Curly Larson was today.

He changed the subject. "It's good that you came; we have our first joint customer coming in to talk about processing."

Grady raised an eyebrow. "The cloak of invisibility?"

"Yep. Want to stay and meet him?"

"Sure." But he braced himself. Some of the Dwarf-works' customers were strange. A few were outright dangerous. From time to time he glanced nervously toward the cavern door.

Antony noticed, and chuckled to himself. Aloud he said, "This one may surprise you."

"When will he show up?"

"After lunch."

Lunch was wonderful, a chicken pie with pearl onions and cut-up potatoes and carrots. Grady sat with Sonny at a higher table than the one the dwarves used, and there was a bench his size. He remembered, but did not remark on, the times when the dwarves had taken away that table and bench, leaving him to crouch over his food and his work.

Sonny asked for news about everybody at the plant. Grady relayed everything he could remember and added, "Sonny? Do you think there's any chance that Joey Cataldo is sweet on Talia Baghrati?"

Sonny laughed, a great, booming sound that made everyone smile. "Do you think there's any chance he's not?" He waved a finger at Grady. "You make sure you tell me when he gets the sand to ask her out."

Grady said around a forkful of chicken and gravy, "Actually, Antony can fill you in, starting from here."

"True enough," Antony said casually, but didn't look either of them in the eye.

Grady realized for the first time how nervous Antony was about working at Plimstubb. Grady thought of his own first days at the Nieuw Amsterdam Dwarfworks and wondered how anyone from here could be afraid of a factory in Providence.

After dinner Grady played with Katrina, chatted with Kirsten until she said apologetically but firmly that she had work to do, and generally fidgeted.

At three minutes to two he asked Antony, "Do I need a garlic necklace?"

"If you had, Kirsten would have decked you out in it. Relax, kid."

"I'll try. By the way, you said once that a cloak of invisibility didn't matter during a war with grenades."

Antony shrugged. "Not everybody feels that way, I guess."

Grady lunged forward and grabbed his shoulder. "Don't give me that. You believe in what he's doing or in what he thinks he can do. "What's the customer—" But before he could finish there came a soft knock at the cavern door. If they hadn't been listening for it, they would have missed it.

"Heads up." Antony brushed his hand off and opened the door.

The customer came slowly in. He wore a battered dark hat. His coat, the same color but thicker, was just as battered, as though the fabric had been dented by a thousand small impacts. He strode carefully into the cavern.

For a moment Grady squinted, trying to see something that wasn't there. Confused, he tried to understand what he was looking for.

The man with the mustache sagged against a pillar, wiping his face with a soiled handkerchief. Images came to Grady, from Movietone and the *March of Time* and *National Geographic*, and he realized what was missing: the bags, badly and hurriedly wrapped, carried for miles by hand even though the bearers were exhausted. This man was a refugee.

Grady had heard this sort of man, complete with a drooping mustache, called a "Mustache Pete." Just now all he saw was the sorrow and the loneliness of looking around for something familiar that would never again be there.

He strode forward. "Welcome to the Nieuw Amsterdam Dwarfworks. I'm Grady Cavanaugh from Plimstubb Furnaces; we work with the Dwarfworks wherever we can. Did you come from Europe?"

"Europe?" In his mouth even the word sounded foreign. "Part of Europe, yes. I was from Poland. I did very special machining . . . do you remember the Stuka?"

"Of course." Grady had seen newsreel after newsreel of German airplanes diving and stitching bullet holes, damage, and carnage into the landscape below the planes.

"I knew them too well. What about the Messerschmitt? Did you know that?"

"I've heard of it," Grady said guardedly. He really didn't know much about the German jet plane beyond frustration that Allied engineers hadn't come up with it first.

Stanislaw tapped his own chest. "Well, I'm here to see that not many people hear of it."

Grady nodded. "I see. What was your name again? The man hadn't mentioned it."

"Stanislaw." He regarded Grady with large, sad eyes. "In this country I am always Stan."

Grady said, "What's your last name?"

He shrugged. "Soozhielinski. Do not try."

Grady stuck his hand out again. "A pleasure to do business, Mr. Soozhielinski. What can we do for you?"

Stanislaw regarded him dubiously. "I am not sure if you can. You do not speak or look like you belong here."

"I agree," Grady said seriously. "But then, you don't speak or look like most of the people in America, and you belong here."

Stanislaw raised a brushy eyebrow and said dryly, "Now it is you who doesn't speak or look like most of the people in America." He sat down. "I have friends still in Poland. They are machinists, like me . . . well, not as good, but a little like me."

Grady began to suspect that Stan had a sense of humor.

"The Germans needed machinists, so my friends were

taken to Germany. They sent notes to me. I will not tell you how. I have told everyone I can in the government about the notes. They thank me very much, and maybe they listen."

Now Grady was alert. "I'll"—he gestured toward Antony—"we'll listen."

"All right. Did you ever hear of an American named Robert Goddard?"

Antony looked blank. Grady said, "I've read his name." He didn't mention that it was in letters and columns from *Astounding* and *Amazing*. "He did things with rockets. He once said that someday a rocket could go to the moon."

"And no one in America listened. So instead the next rockets were German, and the V-1s and V-2s went to London." He leaned forward. "Some of my friends worked at a place called Peenemünde. It will close any day, or perhaps it has. But even if it has, the Germans have things we must destroy before the end of the war."

"Things to do with rockets?" Antony said blankly. Grady felt a sudden chill.

Stanislaw nodded and said bluntly, "I made a request for an oven that will make twenty cloaks to make us unseen. Twenty of us can make sure that plant does nothing for Germany."

Antony shook his head. "Sir, understand, to build the metals oven you want, we'd have to get materials, make plans, build it, and ship it. Believe me, the war will be over before you get it."

"No, it won't," Grady said firmly. Their heads turned. "Antony, I'll get the parts. I'll scrounge, I'll grab, but we'll get the parts."

"And I will pay five thousand dollars," Stanislaw said flatly. "One thousand today, one thousand when I receive the oven, three thousand when it is running overseas."

"It has to get across the Atlantic safely."

Stanislaw spread his hands. "So do I. All right. Make the furnace, make one working cloak in it, and I will pay for the cloak and"—He grimaced—"one-half the furnace."

"Done." Grady looked at the proposal again. "The cloaks use woven gold. We may have trouble finding that much gold—"

"*You* may, not me," Antony said, grinning. "Kid, I can get the gold in a week. Are you sure you can build a furnace to do what he wants?"

Grady made a mental note to teach Antony not to ask embarrassing questions in front of customers. "Antony, we've worked with gold for decades. You heat it to the required temperature and the customer draws it into wire. That's his responsibility—yours, in this case—but we can heat it, no trouble at all." He raised an eyebrow at Antony. "And I'll bet that if I asked you whether you could handle the charm process"—he leaned into the next few words—"and I asked you in front of the customer, you'd tell me that as long as the gold was hot enough, the next stage wouldn't be a problem."

Antony flinched, realizing how tactless he'd been. "No trouble at all. And I know you can heat the gold to the right temperature."

He added, "I already did a sample here."

Stanislaw said cautiously, "Of the gold?"

Antony held up a purple fabric interwoven with gold. The gold sparkled more than was normal. "Of the cloak." He ignored Grady's raised eyebrow. "We already have a Plimstubb furnace. I modified the processing cycle for one run and heated up the gold." He gestured to an already battered conveyor furnace near the main electrical box. Flames were coming out of one end of the furnace—hydrogen heated to more than fourteen hundred degrees Fahrenheit.

He passed the fabric to Stanislaw, who turned it over and over in his work-hardened hands. Grady edged forward, watching him, and said out of the corner of his mouth, "You left out some processing details."

Antony said back the same way, "Okay, we heated it up on a forge afterward to get it even hotter. It takes way longer than Stan wants us to take. You know you can do it in a furnace, right?"

Grady said "Absolutely" as Stanislaw, satisfied with the fabric, swung it over his shoulders and was gone.

Antony and Grady ran forward frantically. No one was there—but three feet above the ground, a blue line of thread swung back and forth, as though it were dancing in the sunlight.

Stan reappeared, holding the cloak. "Can I take this one now?"

Antony looked at Grady, who shook his head. "Stan, it's a thing we call a benchmark. We have one working cloak, and we use it to measure how well each of the others work."

Stanislaw shrugged. "One alone would be little use. Hurry with the others, then. I will go back to Europe to tell my friends. I will return in one month for the furnace."

"It'll be ready." They shook hands. Stan's grip was firm, but his knuckles were knobby and scarred, showing his age. Grady thought for a moment of his own father and said impulsively to Stanislaw, "You seem pretty old to go to the war."

Stanislaw regarded him solemnly. When his smile came, it was like a crack crossing a monument. "Then it is good that the war came for me, isn't it?"

That did it. Grady said firmly, "I'll bet we can find a way to get you back to Europe." He turned to Antony. "Can't we?"

Antony looked at him unhappily.

Grady, his chest tightening, said, "Some other way, maybe?"

Antony somberly handed him a shipping manifesto, dated for today. Grady shivered involuntarily.

The drive from New York through Connecticut was much shorter than he remembered the first time. Perhaps that was the familiarity with the gradual dwindling of cities and factories, the fading behind him of the last farmhouse, the bumpy ride over mud and log roads into the salt marshes until he stopped at a single time-darkened pier. Grady got out of his car, absently glad that he hadn't broken an axle.

He and Antony unloaded four wooden crates. Stan offered to help, but they wouldn't let him. The two of them carefully moved the crates to the end of the pier, as far away from land as possible.

After that, none of them spoke. Grady stared across the marsh toward the sea, and it seemed to him that the sunlight had turned weak and watery.

A moment later he was sure of it. A breeze from inland, with cold air from Canada, brought a front of clouds. Streamers of mist curled up from the water—something Grady associated more with wind from the sea. The streamers tore and drifted seaward on the breeze. . . .

They broke apart on the spit of a ship, pulling away from the wood as if consciously from an unclean thing. The wood was dark with age, pitted with damage from salt and years at sea.

The ship tacked against the wind, and for a moment the eye sockets of the thing that served for a figurehead fell on Grady and on Stanislaw, who crossed himself.

Grady said to him as the ship approached, "You don't have to do this—"

"I do," Stanislaw said firmly, "or I wouldn't."

The ship stopped, not touching the dock. Empty-eyed sailors appeared on deck in the uniforms of a dozen nations, some of the nations long gone in wars and treaties. The sailors lowered a black gangplank and stepped well back.

A blond man with ice-blue eyes strode down the gangplank, looking to the left and right but never hesitating. He wore dark clothes, but his jacket was open as though the air were not suddenly cold. He stepped onto the dock, which seemed to shudder, and Vandervecken, captain of the *Flying Dutchman,* was kneeling in front of Grady, checking the new cargo. He looked up into Grady's eyes. Grady exhaled shakily. "Captain."

Vandervecken nodded at the voice. "We have dealt before." He gestured at the boxes. "Cargo for Denmark. So, this time the little men are afraid to come?"

Antony stepped from behind Grady. "I'm here, Captain." He added to himself, *and you bet I'm afraid.* He leaned forward, shipping papers and money in his fist. His hand was beside Grady's waist.

Grady took the shipping papers hastily and held them as far forward as he could, letting go of them as Vandervecken stepped forward to take them.

There was a soft crackle as the damp wood between them froze. Vandervecken looked Grady in the eye. "So, I do not take you on as passenger or crew to Rhode Island, do I?"

Grady shook his head from side to side carefully, afraid that his muscles would go numb. "No, sir, Captain."

Vandervecken gave a small, empty laugh. "You have learned to say 'Captain' to me, after last time."

He thumped Grady's chest and indifferently watched Grady's sudden labored breathing. "Well, you do not sail this time, then. But there is always room. For now, you have for me a passenger I guess." He nodded to Stanislaw, who clutched his carpetbag and nodded back.

Vandervecken took a carpenter's pencil from his pocket and scrawled something on one the papers. "Then we should go." He walked up the steaming gangplank, which crackled under his feet.

"He's willing to take you to Europe," Grady said earnestly. "I guess there's a little good in all of us."

"He will be paid," Stanislaw said. His dark eyes looked with pity on Grady. "And someday you will learn that in some of us, there is no good at all."

From the deck, Vandervecken laughed without mirth. Perhaps he had heard them. He gestured toward them, and a cattail between the shore and the boat sagged as frost accumulated on it. "Aboard!" he shouted at Stanislaw. "Now. I never wait."

Stanislaw strode on board with no visible fear and without looking back. The gangplank shuddered back onto the ship, and the wind shifted to come from the sea as the *Flying Dutchman* tacked toward the sea, against the wind as always.

Grady shivered and turned back to the car. Antony was already in the truck, driving away as quickly as the road would allow.

Antony was waiting in the Plimstubb parking lot, standing beside the truck.

Grady said, "You could have gone in."

Antony nodded. "I could have." He added lightly, "I thought I ought to wait for you."

Grady thought of Roy Burgess and said immediately, "Good idea."

A small group gathered when Grady and Antony walked in. Joey Cataldo peered in friendly confusion at Antony. Benny "Behind" Blaws, known for dropping his trousers at nearly any opportunity, crouched down to look Antony in the eye. Hammer Houlihan, the Hose of Tralee, snorted and said, "Welcome back to the circus, Dutch."

Roy Burgess tucked in his pocket the work order he'd

been reading. "You." He caught himself. "You back to buy another furnace?"

Grady said formally, "Roy, you remember Antony van der Woeden. He's training for sales, but he'll be working part-time here on the floor."

"Ahhh." Roy looked at Antony again, as though he were suddenly new.

Grady didn't like the look. "You know, Roy, he was a customer before this—"

"I remember," Roy said huskily. "You have a phone call."

Grady looked confused. "Wouldn't Talia have left a message?" She wouldn't necessarily have remembered to, but there was a good chance.

"How the hell would I know? You got a phone call. Go check on it." Roy frowned. "Or is business so good that Sales doesn't follow up on calls?"

It might have to do with Garneaux's work on Antony's behalf. Grady exited hastily, with an apologetic backward glance at Antony. The dwarf winked at Grady, watched the shop door close, and sighed, alone in the lion's den at last.

The rest of the shop had formed a circle around Antony. Their faces reminded him of the spectators at a bare-knuckle fight he had watched in a bar in Paris. Only Betty, on the edge of the circle, looked openly sympathetic.

Antony realized as Roy turned around, grinning, that there had never been a telephone call for Grady.

"Good to see you, you short little shit." Roy patted the top of Antony's head, hard enough to hurt. "Life was different when you were a client, but now you're right under my thumb." He thumped his thumb on Antony's scalp. "So to speak."

"Sure hope you washed your hands since FDR became president," Antony muttered, and said in mock embarrassment, "Gosh, I'm sorry. Was that disrespectful? So where's my work?"

Benny "Behind" Blaws chuckled. Antony moved to the edge of the circle. To his relief, it parted for him. He looked around at the untended and strange machinery, and for a moment he was tempted to move inside the circle and take his chances away from the machinery.

Roy glared at Benny and turned back to Antony. "We'll just see if you can learn fast enough to keep your job." He gestured at the grinding wheel. "Care to try it?"

Antony winced. He'd seen it throwing sparks from a chunk of steel the last time he was in Plimstubb. The wheel was fixed to a bench Antony could reach by holding his arms the height of his head. Eight hours of that and he'd feel like he was crippled. If he didn't know how to use the wheel, he might really be crippled.

Still—"Sure, I can do that. Who's going to teach me?"

Roy shrugged. "Who has the time? Good luck." He added, turning away, "Don't lose a finger your first day."

Benny chuckled again and gestured, left-handed. Antony realized with a chill that one of Benny's fingers was gone to the first knuckle joint.

Joey Cataldo blocked Roy's way with a broom. "Sorry," he said apologetically. "But I got to know where to work next. I want to clean up over there, but you know me, I can't tell my ass from your elbow unless I check with you first."

Roy rubbed his eyes. "Joey, you're doing it again."

Joey looked around in innocent frustration. "What? What? Don't tell me I said something nice about you again?"

Roy barked, "Just go sweep where it's needed." He stomped away as Joey half-saluted.

Once Roy was gone, Joey Cataldo offered his hand to Antony, bending just enough to put it at the right height without being patronizing. "It's good to see you here. We're a little handed of short workers now."

Antony sorted through that and replied, "It's good to be here." He took Joey's hand, grateful for the friend- ship.

"It really always is, except for some times. Listen, I gotta sweep. I'll start by the grinder." He moved a bat- tered wooden stool from under a tool bench, casually carrying it over and setting it in front of the bench with the grinder. "You mind some advice while you use the grinder for the first time?"

Antony laughed out loud. *"Gracias, señor."* He hopped on the bench.

Grady met Antony at the shop door at five o'clock; the shop was back on extra hours. Antony was setting up his workbench. He needed a stool to reach it.

Grady said, "So how did it go?"

"Not badly," Antony said. "I made friends for my- self."

"Big surprise," Grady said, grinning. "Any other problems?"

"I can't believe how much paperwork you people keep. Can't you just remember what you've done?"

Grady considered. "I wish we could," he said finally, "but people change jobs—not so much here, but most places—and plans change and inventions happen. Be- sides, it's good to know what we've done, in case we change our minds about what we should do." He added delicately, "Is that your biggest complaint about your first day at work?"

Antony considered his answer and finally said care- fully, "I'm not complaining about anything. I guess Roy Burgess is unhappy about my being hired."

"Actually," Grady said grimly, "he's been praying for this situation since you first met him. You had what my dad would call a smart mouth when you and Roy first met."

Antony grinned. "I let him off easy. Think back and see if you don't agree."

Grady thought back. The tips of his ears turned red, and he changed the subject. "Tom Garneaux helped me take care of most of your luggage. We stuck labels on it as though it had been through the port a couple years back." He had driven downtown with Tom Garneaux. Grady had been confused by all the paperwork, particularly when a public official mentioned fines but was unclear what he meant or how payment would find its way to the U.S. judicial system. Tom Garneaux had looked pityingly at Grady, some folded bills had exchanged hands, and Antony was officially a displaced person from the Netherlands, complete with backdated documents.

"Any trouble?"

"Nothing Tom and I—okay, Tom—couldn't handle. Listen, I'm sorry that some people are like this—"

"Don't be," Antony said sharply. "It's something humans do naturally to each other. They do it when they feel bad and need a pick-me-up. They do it when they feel good, and superior to anyone else. They do it when they feel neutral, just to feel something. They do it whenever they feel like it."

He went back to polishing his new workbench, teetering on the footstool Joey had given him.

Watching him and the awkwardness of the footstool, Grady remembered his own time in the Dwarfworks. For a while he had been hated. Every time he built a workbench the right height, someone stole it. No one spoke to him at dinner. No one let children play with him. Every single night of that period, he went home alone and lay down wishing he wouldn't have to wake up and return to work. Near the end of it, he wound up in a fistfight with Antony, who had beaten Grady unconscious.

All he said to Antony was, "I know how that could hurt."

Antony spun his head toward Grady, and for a moment Antony was feeling what he had when Kirsten, the woman Antony loved, was pining for Grady. "Anything that happened to you at the Dwarfworks happened for a reason."

"Of course," Grady said, and for a moment he was back in a world of loneliness and abuse. "Guys like you always have a reason."

The next moment he was sorry. "Listen, Antony, I'm just saying that these things happen and the tough job is to get through them. You come back to my house for dinner tonight and we'll set up your room. I've got an extra key for you in case you need it."

Antony looked stubborn. Grady said almost pleadingly, "You'll be in my brother Kevin's room."

Antony was stunned. After a moment he said only, "Thanks. This is kind."

"I owe you," Grady said simply. He said to change the subject, "So, do you and Curly keep in touch?"

Antony said curtly, "He writes." He didn't trust himself to say more.

Grady was intrigued enough to want to pursue the subject, but saw that it bothered Antony. He dropped it, instead making small talk about dinner and sleeping arrangements.

Dinner that night was strained; Antony was finding the atmosphere at Plimstubb difficult. Grady was good at keeping small talk going, and the talk engrossing, but Antony was aware that he was once again sleeping away from the Dwarfworks. When he lay in his bed—Kevin Cavanaugh's bed—he stretched his arms and legs out, feeling how huge and strange the mattress was. He listened to the sporadic traffic and the occasional train whistle in the night. It seemed to him that he could hear the rustle and thud of human habitation in all directions, smothering every bird call, every rustling tree branch, every natural sound that would have reassured him.

He rose and stared out the window. The moon was full, and he could see row on row of frame houses, penning him in like pickets of a fence. The doors and windows were huge, to match the people inside them.

Antony went back to Kevin's bed and turned his face to the wall, bitterly lonely. "Change is good for me," he said softly, but he did not believe it anymore.

FOUR

IT WAS THE second week in April. To no one's particular surprise, the Germans were still falling back as the Allies advanced. Grady spent the better part of Monday morning sketching a preliminary design for the furnace to produce cloaks of invisibility. He spent longer on the specifications. On the last page, he tallied the budget for materials.

When he was done, he reread the last page thoughtfully, tapping a pencil. It was a habit he'd picked up from Susan, one he'd initially found annoying. He sighed and pocketed the sheets, heading for Engineering.

Susan looked at Grady's plans casually, then blankly. "A test model?"

"Well, sure." But he felt uncomfortable even as he said it.

"And if you can't sell it, who pays for it?"

"I'm kind of hoping it'll be cheap."

"That's no answer."

"Real cheap," he said heavily.

Susan glowered at him. "Did you ever notice how nobody in Sales ever figures in enough money to make a project easy to build?"

He smiled brightly at her. "Gee, isn't it swell that you're all such great engineers, and can build it anyway?" He dodged Susan's thrown pencil.

"Oo-kay." She ducked her head, muttering, and, predictably, began tapping another pencil. Grady left, feeling more confident.

Half an hour later, Susan called him. "Which would you rather have: a good-looking test furnace, or one that was free?"

"Free?"

"Calm down. Meet me in Research and Development."

It was forty feet from his desk, but Susan made it from Engineering, across the plant, before he could get there. She was holding a sloppier sketch than Grady's, but it had hard dimensions and an accompanying wiring sketch. She had given Tom Blaine, the gloomy swamp Yankee in R&D, a bill of materials. His head was bent over it dubiously until his bushy beard brushed the paper and it looked as though his pipe might set fire to it.

She tapped the list with a manicured nail. "How close can you come to this design with spare parts and scrap?"

He shook his head. "I can come close—make some substitutions here, fudge a dimension there—but I can't swear it'll work."

"Of course it will," Bill Riley called confidently from his desk. Bill was as wiry and optimistic as Tom was stocky and pessimistic. Between them they had fine-tuned most of the Plimstubb electric furnace designs over the past decade. "Let's get started."

Tom and Bill walked out to the shop—and past. Susan and Grady followed, bemused, as they walked to the trash bins outside Roy Burgess's office windows.

Susan peered over the edge of one. "Can you really get anything good out of that?" She sniffed and grimaced. "Oh, murder."

"Not out of that one," Tom explained. "That's paper

trash, plus people's lunches. We don't empty it half often enough." He glanced at a panhandler in the driveway. He was bearded and disheveled, and he was watching them hopefully. "I sure hope he hasn't been hanging around to eat from this."

"Who hasn't?" Antony, appearing from nowhere, raised himself up over the edge of the trash bin and lowered himself back down hastily. "Whew! I hope you didn't lose anything in there."

"I'd tell you what we're doing here," Grady said, "but I have no idea."

Tom and Bill had hauled a footstool to the other trash bin. Tom was doubled over it, saying almost cheerfully to Bill, "Read to me from the bill of materials."

He obediently read, "Eight feet of one-half-inch pipe."

"Will three-quarter-inch do?" Irregular lengths of pipe sailed over his shoulder to land in the parking lot.

"Sure, but the flow will be slower unless you up the pressure." Bill dodged as a handful of pipe unions nearly landed on his shoes.

"Fine. Next."

"Twelve feet of hot-rolled steel, one-quarter-inch thick, two-inch channel—okay, it says all that, but what it means is 'something for the legs.' Any more pipe?"

"Something for the legs, right." Four five-foot lengths of pipe in varying sizes, all corroded and bent, slid out beside Tom's right shoulder and clanged against the other pipe. "We can fasten a heat chamber on with U-bolts if we can find something—whoa."

"Whatcha got?" Susan asked eagerly. Grady and Antony were still staring, appalled, at the rusty junk accumulating on the parking lot.

"The mother lode. Bill, Dutch, hoist yourselves up and help with this."

Bill and Antony each scrambled up the side of the bin. Shortly, they were lowering a blackened steel wire cage the size of an icebox. They exercised the care they might have lavished on a jade statue.

"I completely forgot about this thing," Tom said reverently. "Remember it? From a vacuum furnace we made for Remington."

Bill poked at the discolored ruins of a piece of insulation pinned to the inside of the cage. "We called it the blue bomber."

"And bomb it did," Tom said with morose satisfaction. "The insulation kept falling apart—something to do with gases from their process, I guess—and we gave up on it. Talked them into four little bean-pot vacuum furnaces instead. Ran the same loads almost as cheaply." He poked at the steel wires, some of which were bent and discolored by heat. "Lucky thing this didn't end up on a scrap heap."

"Lucky how?" Antony wanted to know.

Tom grinned down at him. "That's right, you've never seen one of these." He hopped down from the footstool. "It's nothing but a frame to hold the insulation between the heating elements and the steel walls of the heating chamber." He turned to Grady. "Ever wonder how we can build a steel furnace to heat steel?"

After a second, Grady said, "I should have."

"Yep." That was Bill, taking the story up. "We wondered. Actually, Mr. Plimstubb wondered, and he asked us as people wanted higher and higher processing temperatures. He had the idea, and we designed it—from the hot work out.

"First you have the load to be treated." He gestured with his hands as though they held a small tray of work. "Make sure it's spread out enough to distribute the heat, but dense enough so that you get the maximum amount of processed work in each load. Next, you put the heating elements to heat the work. You put them all over: top, bottom, sides. That's why the work trays are screens and mesh baskets, to let in the heat from all angles."

He held up a warning finger. "Now you insulate, so that the furnace doesn't melt itself." He gestured to the frame cage. "Finally, you slide that into the furnace, and you run water through the jacket of the heating chamber so that the steel on the heat chamber never gets very hot at all. Got that?"

"You bet," Antony said, and his head was spinning with new ideas. Except for one new Plimstubb furnace, there was no heat-treating equipment more modern in the Dwarfworks than a brick kiln. "Wait! Wait!"

He ran inside to the loading dock. "I know they're somewhere—bingo." He held up an irregular block of asbestos brick insulation, left as scrap. "There's a whole stack of these waiting to be dumped. They're none of them the same shape—"

"They wouldn't be," Tom Blaine said. "They're the leftovers stacked behind the cutting saw, scrap from odd blocks." Tom regarded the piece in Antony's hand almost affectionately. "If you fit them inside the cage and lay a couple pieces of broken hearth tile on top of the brick, we'll have a furnace—"

"Except for the heating elements and the transformer." Susan immediately looked sorry she had spoken; still, Grady reflected, it had to be said.

Bill shrugged. "There's plenty of waste wire around here. It's short lengths, mostly, but I'll bet we can wire in a couple of heating elements—"

"Four on each side," Susan said flatly.

He raised an eyebrow. "Three on a side, if you're lucky. That's all we can pull out of the stockroom without Roy complaining that we're wasting money."

Susan was ready to protest. Grady nudged her, Antony coughed, and she subsided, saying glumly, "Okay, but it'll never work."

"Of course it'll work," Bill said confidently. He used the same tone he did when encouraging one of Tom

Blaine's designs; any doubts Grady had about the feasibility of the test furnace vanished.

Assembling the furnace barely took an afternoon. Sometimes Grady was appalled at how little precision was involved—they bolted a frame for the legs out of steel scrap and U-bolts, not bothering to match the scrap lengths—but sometimes it felt like an adventure, letting the materials determine the design. Installing the insulated brick turned into a jigsaw puzzle, with the object being to require as little brick cutting as possible.

They had a piece of luck on the transformer. There was one in obsolete inventory from a mistake on a furnace order in 1943. Fortunately, the engineer who had made the expensive mistake, Brian Kelleher, had enlisted in the navy at about the same time Susan's father had enlisted. Grady put the transformer on one of the rolling carts scattered throughout the plant and rolled it to the furnace. "Isn't this great?"

Susan agreed. "We're lucky it didn't end up on Tom Garneaux's hot-water heater." Tom Garneaux's house and yard had hearth-tile garden paths, a Honeywell controller as a furnace thermostat, and a fourteen-foot, high-temperature alloy steel flagpole. Garneaux refused to discuss where these things had come from.

Hooking the transformer up to a current source took five minutes. Connecting the wires to the heating elements and tying them in to the lowest setting on the transformer took an additional twenty. At a little after four, Tom Blaine sat back on his heels and wiped his sweating, balding forehead and scratched his beard absently, shifting his pipe back and forth as he scratched. "That's it," he said.

Grady looked, amazed, at the ramshackle construct in front of them. The legs were different sizes, though the heating chamber was level. The stained and irregular insulation showed through the wire heating cage that held it in place. The furnace door was a piece of scrap with a file-drawer handle bolted onto it. The door slid through tracks made from scraps on the steel shelf.

But it was a furnace, a working one with any luck, and Grady had helped build it in less than a day.

Roy Burgess, on an end-of-day plant inspection, regarded it scornfully. "What the hell is that?"

"A heat treating furnace we built in one day, Roy." Grady added innocently, "Can your guys do that?"

"If my guys put together a piece of shit like this, they'd be fired. Who's gonna buy this?"

Susan patted it. "It's Frankenstein's furnace. We'll sell it to someone stitched together out of corpses."

Immediately she looked uncomfortable. So did Grady. Their business with the Gnomengesellschaft and with the Dwarfworks had shown them that the range of customers out there was far wider than either of them could imagine.

"Want to watch the grand moment, Roy?" Tom Blaine said casually, and Grady recognized from the edge in his voice that somewhere during the afternoon he'd begun to take the design personally. Tom flipped the fork switch that gave current to the elements.

Roy leaned forward expectantly, but there was no buzzing to indicate an overload and no ozone smell to indicate a wiring problem. They watched the furnace, waiting.

After a few minutes they saw the first of the steam from the brick. "It's drying," Tom said unnecessarily. "Leave it at low heat overnight, maybe three or four hundred degrees, if you want to save the brickwork."

"The brickwork's good for fourteen hundred degrees Fahrenheit," Susan objected.

Grady, who had worked in the Service Department a month before, said dryly, "The water in it is only good for two hundred and twelve degrees Fahrenheit."

Susan shut up. Expanding steam in pockets inside the

brickwork could blow the bricks apart if it happened quickly enough.

"How soon will it be ready to start processing?" Antony asked.

Bill pursed his lips. "I'll raise it another five hundred degrees in the morning," he said thoughtfully. "It's a puny little thing, so I'm betting that'll be enough to dry even the outer layer in two hours. What are you processing in there?"

Now there was no way around it. "Gold," Grady said quietly.

Tom whistled. "That explains the atmosphere line. I'll hook that up to a tank at midmorning, see if we can force the air out of the brickwork." He said thoughtfully, "We'll spike it with a little hydrogen, too, see if we can clean up the last of the oxygen inside there." He shook his head dubiously. "Nominally it'll be ready to go to fourteen hundred degrees by lunch time tomorrow, but I wouldn't guarantee it'll work."

"It'll work," Bill said.

Antony wrote a memo and let it go on the southerly winds before going back to Grady's house that night.

On Tuesday morning, Grady awoke to find Antony gone. Grady shrugged, left a note in case Antony returned, and then left for breakfast.

Grady barely got to his office when Antony showed up in Grady's office carrying a small wooden crate. The crate was fairly small, but Antony's face was purple. Grady automatically stood and held out his hands to take it.

"No!" Antony said, puffing. Grady backed off. Antony walked stiff-legged to the desk and set the crate down. The desk creaked.

Antony exhaled. "Fresh from New York. Want to see it?" With a single motion he ripped the lid off. Grady blinked at the sudden burst of light reflected off his desk lamp.

He put a hand on the metal bar, then used both hands and wrenched away the straw packing. "Like you'd say, Sacred Sun." He didn't want to say the words he had in mind. "What's this for?" But he knew.

Antony stretched; carrying the crate from the truck alone had been taxing. "Want to take it out to the shop with me?"

"For the cloak—wait." He hefted the gold bar. "That's a hell of a lot more than you need for one cloak."

"Check the specs. It's what you need for two dozen cloaks." Antony added unnecessarily, "It's a hell of a lot of gold."

Grady took his sport coat off and laid it reverently over the box. "We'll take it out during lunch break."

"Gee, kid, don't you trust the people you work with?" But Antony was relieved. "See if Tom and Bill can cut the power around eleven and open the door, let it cool some before we go out."

When the shop floor stopped for lunch, the area near the loading dock was deserted. Grady and Antony put the gold on a work tray built for another furnace. This tray was merely stainless steel, for "low temperature" applications under fifteen hundred degrees. They used a steel rod to push the tray down an inclined board into the furnace. They moved quickly, but the furnace end of the board was smoking before they finished. Grady was ready to slam the furnace door shut when Antony said, "Wait."

He whispered strange-sounding words to the gold before closing the door. Grady thought he heard a beautiful, clear voice like a boy soprano's answer from inside the furnace.

When Grady closed the switch that brought electricity to the furnace, Antony reached into one pocket of his coveralls and removed a small bag. Looking either way furtively, he leaped easily up to the top of the furnace.

"Hurry," Grady said immediately. "We don't insulate the tops that much—"

Antony nodded, shifting his feet back as he quickly poured the contents of the bag down the vent stack of the furnace. He leaped off, landing on the floor and rolling like a parachutist. *Of course he did,* Grady thought belatedly. *He's a pilot; he's used a parachute.*

"Let's check it in a few hours," Antony said. For once he was visibly nervous as he checked from side to side for Roy Burgess. "Tell me how it's coming out."

"Bet on it," Grady promised. The metal block in the furnace would already be heating, getting brighter as it became purer, surface contamination burning away. Grady had learned from his work on jewelry furnaces that gold was a miraculous metal, one that could return to purity after the most corrupting of treatments. Grady and Antony could go back to their normal work without worry while they waited for the furnace, and Antony's charms and interventions, to change gold into the stuff of invisible cloaks. Grady didn't trust magic, and Antony was uncertain about engineering, but for both of them, gold was the metal of faith.

Grady shut the furnace heat off at three o'clock. At four he opened the front door partway, feeling guilty that his reason for waiting until four was not revealing to most of the shop workers how much gold was available in the shop.

The block of gold blazed at them in the afternoon sun. Any impurities on the surface had burned away, and it seemed to Grady that whatever Antony had introduced to the furnace had made the gold even shinier, as though light bounced away from it.

They slid the work tray onto a board again. Antony quickly wrapped the cooling metal in blue cloth, partly to insulate his hands, partly to hide the gold from the shop, and partly to introduce the cloth immediately to the gold.

The cloth immediately became hazy, allowing a glimpse, as though through fog, of the gold underneath.

Susan gasped, but Grady sighed loudly. "Not good enough."

"No, it's perfect," Antony said earnestly. "The mist is just the exhalation from the gold. The metal wants to stay pure."

Hammer Houlihan, on overtime, slouched by and looked suspiciously their way. He was followed by Benny Behind. Grady said, "If that's so, it's the only thing in this shop that does. Bring me a finished product when you can."

Antony said, "Two days from now." He grinned and picked up the cloth and the brick, laying them quickly on one of the rolling work carts. On the way out the door he turned to Grady and said in awe, "Do you realize how long this would have taken my people? High-temperature work is really something."

On Thursday, Grady was at his desk, engrossed in re-sponse letters. No, glass-to-metal sealing couldn't be done more cheaply; temperature uniformity was every-thing. (That letter wasn't to RCA, but to a competitor who had heard of the process already.) Yes, "green rot" in heating elements could be countered, usually by rais-ing the temperature but also by running more atmo-sphere. Sorry, adding extra depth to the layer of carbon on steel to harden the surface was still an uncertain pro-cess; Plimstubb would be looking into it, however, and would provide equipment for such a process the moment they could.

Grady looked at each of the letters a final time before signing them. It was a ritual: Check the spelling of the customer's name, check the application and the address, check all the sentences. He reached out for his pen—

The pen rose off Grady's desk, hovering a foot in front of him. When he reached for it, the pen drifted quickly out of reach and settled on the bookcase.

Now a back issue of *Weird Tales* rose off the shelf, stood upright, and danced in the air mockingly. Grady moved cautiously toward it and, with a sudden slash of his cane, knocked it to the floor. It lay inert.

Behind it he saw a blue flicker, like the afterimage from a welding spark. He also heard a chuckle.

He said tentatively, "Antony?"

"Good guess, kiddo." Antony appeared, holding a cloak in his hands. "It only took half a day. Pretty good, huh?"

"I'll say." Grady touched it, fascinated. The cloth felt soft and yielding, the gold unnaturally warm. He wrapped himself in it and stepped to one side quietly. Antony never shifted his eyes, thinking that Grady was still beside the desk.

A letter opener rose and twisted in the air directly in front of Antony, who backed away hastily. "Sacred Sun!"

Grady laughed, removing the cloak. "It's one thing to know it works, and another to see it."

"Or not to see it." Antony grinned awkwardly, embarrassed at how easily he'd been startled. "Let's put that away."

Grady set it aside reluctantly. There was so much fun to be had in a place like Plimstubb Furnaces with a cloak like that. "Are you sure you don't want to visit Roy Burgess?"

There were some great answers to that. Antony said only, "Not now."

" 'Not now'? When, and what are you going to do?"

"Wait and see." Antony put the cloak in the duffel he had brought with him. "Or not see. Let's skip it and head home."

Grady, startled, checked his watch. It was after five.

Part of him was absurdly pleased that Antony would consider the Cavanaugh house home.

Fewer than two hours later, Grady and Antony were cleaning up after an early supper. Grady washed and handed the dishes down to Antony, who had cleaned out the washtub in the basement and now used it to rinse dishes for drying. He dunked a plate, spun it expertly on one hand while passing a cloth over it, and slipped it effortlessly onto the stack on the kitchen table. Except for the dwarf's serious expression, Grady was reminded of doing dishes with Kevin when the Cavanaugh boys were younger and just learning to pitch in on housework.

The knock startled Grady but not Antony, who lost his seriousness for a moment and said, "Get that, will-ya?" Grady, dishtowel over his shoulder, opened the door.

It was Susan, hollow-eyed and in shock. She said nothing, and Grady was suddenly terrified.

She moved her lips, licked them, tested them, and said suddenly in an awkward, little-girl voice, "The president's dead," and began crying.

Too numb to speak, Grady held her.

They went to Mary's and sat. Julie was asleep on Mary's lap, but she ended up in turns on Grady's, Antony's, and even Susan's laps before nestling in the arms of her beloved Auntie Rose. They sat around the radio, listening to tributes and eulogies, but nothing did anything to take away the empty shock of the moment. FDR was gone.

They heard a broadcast, maybe a recording by then, of the White House announcement. At a little after seven o'clock, Harry Truman had become president. Grady tried to imagine Truman, a short, natty, but fairly nondescript man with a frank, blunt way of speaking, as the president. It didn't seem right, like a child walking around in an adult's shoes.

Susan dropped Antony and Grady off, hugged them both, and started sniffling again. Grady held her as long as he could, wishing there was something he could do. She held on to him for a long time before smiling weakly and returning to her car.

Antony, watching, gave the ghost of a grin and punched Grady's arm. "Your arms are good for her," he said. "The time's gonna come—" he froze, looking at the door.

A folded sheet of paper, trimmed in black, hung upside down like a bat from the door knocker.

Grady snatched it up and read quickly. The text was ostensibly polite, but terse:

Dear Mr. Cavanaugh,

I have received information concerning the death of Franklin Delano Roosevelt. Words cannot express my feelings concerning your grief at this time.

"Words cannot express . . ." Grady, well aware of how much Klaus hated him, could well imagine the gnome's feelings. Gnomes enjoyed human suffering. He read on:

The death of Roosevelt must surely feel like the death of a beloved parent. Those of you who have lost parents in the Pacific, or who have the potential of doing so, must be doubly affected by this national sorrow.

Grady glanced involuntarily into the house. His mother's furniture, unchanged by his father, was still unharmed. The scars of Grady's and Kevin's play growing up were still on the woodwork and on the walls, some of it hidden behind the furniture. Everything in the house seemed safe and unchangeable.

Grady finished the letter:

At times like this, one cannot help but think of family. Be advised that I have not ceased, in this crisis, to think of you, of Miss Rocci, and of your relatives. Please accept my expression of sympathy for the passing of a father figure, and I hope that you will appreciate my thoughts of you should anything additional happen to another father figure, to a father, or to your families.

Warmest regards,
Klaus

Grady reread it twice, appreciating more deeply each time Klaus's relish for human loss and suffering. Finally, Antony nudged Grady gently and in exchange received the letter. He read it carefully and said in a cautiously neutral voice, "We knew this about Klaus."

"He knows where I live." Grady added, his voice trembling, "He knows where my father is."

"We know where he is, kid." Antony heard the confidence in his own voice and remembered, from his flight training in Princeton before the Great War, an army instructor who said confidently, "Remember, you'll always come down." He didn't share that remark with Grady.

Grady took the letter back and said helplessly, "I've been sleeping with my door unlocked."

"Don't." Antony opened the front door and stepped in. "Like your people say, don't you know there's a war on?"

"I know there is now." Grady went inside, but paused and held the letter at arm's length. When he let go of it, it vanished into the night air, skittering just under the tree limbs before disappearing.

That night, whenever Grady quit worrying about Klaus, he remembered that Roosevelt was dead. When he went to bed, for the first time in many nights he left his cane on the covers where he could touch it in the night. Part of him felt helpless and without support.

The following Monday was filled with eulogies for Roosevelt, but the Yankees-Senators game that was to open the season and was to have been dedicated to Roosevelt was canceled because of rain. Grady, reading the sports page on Tuesday morning, felt glumly that it was an omen. Even Julie tugging on his hands couldn't cheer him.

FIVE

A LONG WITH THE rest of the country, Grady put the
death of FDR behind him while he waited for the
death of Hitler and of the war.

The baseball season opened, a day late, with two
games in New York City: Yankees–Red Sox and Dodg-
ers–Philadelphia. Fiorello LaGuardia threw out the first
ball, and perhaps that inspired the Yankees, who won,
8–4, with the help of two homers from some right fielder
named Derry. Grady thought gloomily that it might be
an omen for the Sox' season.

Grady subsequently noted with interest that three Ne-
groes were trying out for the Red Sox, and the team had
exhibited interest in two. One of them, Sam Jethroe, had
been Negro American League batting champion last
year. The other had played college baseball and was
fresh out of the army. Grady shrugged. They might do
all right with this Jethroe player, but taking this other
kid—Jackie Robinson—would be a gamble.

He sighed moodily. Earlier in the year, Grady had
seen a newspaper article that said that as of January '45,
fifty-four hundred of the fifty-eight hundred American
pro ballplayers at the time of Pearl Harbor were in the

armed forces. He could see why managers would be looking for miracles from Robinson and the other Negro ballplayers, but they'd all be glad when players like Ted Williams got out of uniform and into a baseball uniform.

Shoot, he'd be glad when everybody he knew got out of a uniform.

The fencing lessons went well, and went quickly. Grady taught Susan the basics as slowly as she would allow him to. "Lunge with your arm first, your legs next. That's it—don't lean forward, keep your weight distributed—"

She sighed loudly. "When do I get to *hit* somebody?"

"Soon. Since you'll be hitting me, I want to be sure you do it right." They worked on parries. "Slight movement to the side. No, much less than that; you want the other person's blade to barely miss you."

"You're kidding." She cut her wild swing in half; it was still too large.

"I kid you not, kiddo. Because when you follow the parry with a riposte—and always follow a parry with a riposte; you're fighting the opponent, not his sword— you want your weapon to be as close to his target area as possible." He demonstrated. "Lunge at me. I catch your blade on the forte of mine, down by the hilt, and I slide up with a wall of steel between me and you— now I lunge." It was a flip of the hand and a straightening of the arm, no movement of his legs or torso at all. "And I've got you, just when you thought you could get me."

"No, you've killed me." She pulled her weapon back and looked at him seriously. "That's what this is about, isn't it? Kirsten's afraid I'll need to know this for a battle."

"She thinks you should know it," Grady said carefully. "I don't know that Kirsten's ever afraid. Listen, Susan, if it makes you safer, I'm all for it."

He added with a grin, "And on the bright side, someday it'll make your mom nuts that you play with swords."

That got an answering grin and Susan, whose fencing up to now had been fueled mainly by anger, began to work for control. It appalled Susan that Grady remained better than she. It wasn't just his prior experience; he had a genuine talent for it.

Still, she was getting better rapidly. And Grady could sympathize with someone who longed to be in combat; these days combat was on everyone's mind even more than usual.

On April 25, Allied forces had met with Soviet Army troops. They were seventy-five miles from Berlin. During the rest of April and the first week in May, Grady broke the rule about listening to radio news broadcasts in front of Mary. He even put on the news at breakfast in Mary's house. Mary didn't mind; she was obsessed with the notion that the war was about to end and Kevin would come home safely.

Grady and she (and on every other week, Antony) sat at breakfast, listening to the latest reports out of Europe and arguing spiritedly about how soon the troops would be in Berlin. It was clear that the war in Europe would be over in weeks, not months.

On the other hand, every second day the newspaper published guardedly confident statements about the marines on Okinawa. Grady was beginning to read those articles as carefully as he read sales correspondence from field representatives, and he knew when he was seeing false confidence in both. He thought of his father and was not sure, even with Kevin in Europe, that he would think of the surrender of Germany as that big a day.

Tom Garneaux kept the radio on all day all the time. Grady realized how stressed Tom must be when he saw how much work he was doing, one ear leaned toward the radio and waiting for a bulletin. For the first time in

Garneaux's life, he was restlessly doing far more design work than his job required. Grady quietly spirited Garneaux's quirky visions to Research and Development, where Tom Blaine boisterously announced that the designs would never work and quietly proceeded to ensure that they would.

Around the first of May, Garneaux waltzed through the shop and said casually, "The Italians killed Mussolini."

"Good for them," Betty called out. She had taken to singing patriotic songs loudly and tunelessly to the rhythm of the clanking brake shear.

"About damn time," Hammer Houlihan muttered. "Now if someone would just shoot Hitler, we could finish the whole sorry mess up."

"You bet," Grady said heartily on his way through, but wondered guiltily how many people he would wish dead, just to be sure his father came straight home.

Grady was in Engineering at about nine o'clock in the morning on May 8 when every fire whistle in earshot went off. They were followed by police sirens. A cop car dashed by on Promenade Street, the sign hung out of the driver's windows unreadable.

The announcer at WPRO said, "We interrupt this broadcast for the following news bulletin. Flash . . ."

They all knew what it said, but they all listened. They heard German and American names in a context they had dreamed of and prayed for but that seemed unexpected when it came. Grady listened to the fast-paced voice, explaining in telegraph style what the German High Command had agreed to after the suicide of Hitler, and he tried with all his heart to imagine peace.

Tom Garneaux slammed his fist on his desk. "Kids, let's go downtown."

Tom drove. His car was an elderly Studebaker, but it clearly had more punch than any car Grady had been in; probably the engine was oversized, a substitution made during Prohibition. Grady, in the backseat, held on to the armrest as they took corners.

They screeched to a halt in front of the Cathedral of Saints Peter and Paul downtown. It was full, every pew jammed. Grady suspected that every church in the state, possibly in the nation, was the same way: people sitting or kneeling with folded hands and praying for relatives, for friends, for complete strangers who had died alien and alone and who now, suddenly, deserved the blessings of God.

They exited to a world of chaos. Garneaux could no more have moved his car than he could have made it fly; a crowd in their twenties was standing on it, waving American flags. A cop nearby looked at them and said automatically, "No cars into or out of Providence."

Garneaux shrugged and said, "Let's get some lunch." He rubbed his hands together. "A real lunch."

The first three places they tried were closed. A voluble, happy man with a loosened tie told them that the staff was probably out partying. "I heard somebody say three-quarters of Brown and Sharpe walked right off their jobs, hones' to God! Ain't nobody working today."

He wandered unsteadily off, and Grady said thoughtfully, "What do you think we'll all be like by nightfall?"

Susan said grimly, "I'll be pretty hungry."

Garneaux patted her hand. "Not a chance, sweetheart." He led them down a side street toward Westminster.

They never made Westminster. Instead, they ate in a French restaurant, with five courses and a man who treated Garneaux as though he were God himself. The courses were unbelievable: a light bisque, a fish filet decorated with capers and almonds, a beef filet that was clearly in violation of meat rationing. Garneaux presided over the courses, pointing to the excellencies of the presentation and apologizing for the necessities of the war— which were barely observed.

Coffee came out, with a treasured bottle of cognac from before the war—possibly from before Prohibition, though more likely Garneaux had brought it over for the restaurant and was now receiving his just reward. Garneaux raised his glass and wept through the after-dinner toast, praising democracy and eulogizing those who had died in the war. Susan kissed him and cried on his shoulder, and Grady was suddenly, fervently, sick of the war.

He managed to feel better when they moved through the streets downtown and it seemed as though every woman in Providence wanted to dance with him, game leg or no, just to celebrate the return of the men they really wanted. Grady agreed with their sentiments, shouting loudly, and wondered what reporters searching deeply enough would find in his and Garneaux's actions.

The bars were all closed; the state wasn't taking any chances. Despite that, a group of patriots or business sharpers had erected a corner stand on sawhorses, selling drinks with nearly no markup. Grady bought scotch and sodas for the three of them, for once not worrying about the cost.

The man who poured the drinks nodded vacantly at Grady but nearly went across the table at Garneaux. "Tommy! Is this your crowd?" He hastily stuffed Grady's money back in Grady's shirt pocket. "This one's on me. No lie, you were always smarter than I was—look at this street. Until the bulls close in, we've got the sweetest deal we've had since—"

Garneaux, rolling his eyes toward Susan and Grady, put a finger to his lips. Susan held a slightly unsteady hand out to the man behind the counter. "Mr. Pug Brady, what a pleasure."

"That's right, we met once at Rhodes on the Pawtuxet." He shook her hand, then with an apologetic glance at Grady kissed the hand. "I told you then a friend of Black Tom's gets special treatment."

"And should," Garneaux said easily. "Say, I guess

we'd better not distract you from business."

As they moved away, Grady said lightly, "War prof-
iteering?"

"Never," Garneaux said firmly. "There's some profit
in it, of course, but I just knew that people would want
a drink today." He beamed at Grady. "Don't you?"

Grady, who had been convinced previously that this
day would mean nothing to him, realized that he didn't
want a thing.

The following day was like the worst hangover Grady
had ever had, though his head felt fine. He woke, staring
around the empty house with its shut rooms and sheets
over the furniture, and he knew it wasn't time to open
it yet.

He rode his bike down the street slowly and thoughtfully. There were still blue-star homes wherever at least
one householder was in the armed forces and still, God
help them, gold-star homes marking where a household
had lost someone to the war. Milk delivery was still
every other day, split up by where people's last names
stood in the alphabet, and there were still steel pennies
around, to save copper for other uses. The celebration
yesterday was for a victory, not for the end of a war.

Grady skidded to a stop in the Plimstubb parking lot,
staring at the Employees Only door. There was a white
note tucked into the doorframe and fluttering in the
breeze.

There was no breeze.

It tugged and pulled, trapped by someone's hasty
slamming entrance. Grady freed it, catching it as it fluttered downward, exhausted.

The note was from Antony to Grady and said simply,
"Stanislaw says the contract for the cloak furnace is canceled."

Grady tucked the note between the knuckles of his
cane handle and strode rapidly to Warren's office.

• • •

Warren Hastings barely reacted. He refolded the note and calmly passed it back to Grady. "Is this the first time you've had a customer back out on a deal?"

Grady considered lying. "Well, sure."

"Get used to it." Warren leaned against the wall, facing Grady. "Customers cheat. They lie. They back out of contracts, and the first thing you know, you're trying to explain how the monthly gross for last month has to be corrected lower. Nobody wants that. At that moment, there are plenty of fingers longing to point at someone that's not them."

From another boss, that speech would sound comforting—but Warren was smiling too much, unblinkingly watching Grady, who resolved not to show any anxiety. "What happens then?"

"Plenty. And you'd better get used to that, too. I don't have to tell you how insecure wartime contracts are now"—he frowned—"except that I've always had to tell you." He paused for effect. "Tell me, are the rest of your contracts related to the Dwarfworks"—he said it with disdain, as the FBI might have talked of Al Capone earlier—"secure? Are they at a stage where, if canceled, they would show a profit?"

Of course they weren't. Warren knew that. Grady struggled helplessly to find a response that wouldn't leave him vulnerable for firing. "Right now the layout for any of the Dwarfworks projects"—he thought of Mr. Fahdi and Mr. Fahrouk, two mysterious men from the Middle East "—has the potential to lose money if canceled, yes. Even the ones that you signed on."

Warren tapped a pen on the desk and said firmly, "That I signed on after listening to your advice. Never forget that. I won't."

"Fine. You won't." Grady was sweating, thinking of his family, but he was also angry. "They're all projects in the early stages. For almost any project that cancels

early on, the company outlay exceeds the profit we
would make if the jobs died later. That's true of any
project you could name—"

"Right now I'm naming yours, Cavanaugh." He was
enjoying this hugely. "That's because none of my customers canceled. One of yours did. Do you think any of
the others will?"

"They could," he admitted. "They haven't said they
would."

"Nobody ever says they might until they do." Warren
frowned. "I don't have to say what happens to you if
you lose another contract this year."

Grady looked him in the eye and said, "I find another
job."

For a moment, Warren glared. Then, to Grady's aston-
ishment, he chuckled. "Good for you. You needed
toughening. All the same, I'll fire you, and if I have
anything to say about it, you'll never get another sales
job at a furnace company if you foul up one more contract."

Which was unkind, since Grady had never fouled up
a contract. In fact, he had watched helplessly while Warren had signed a bad contract, and had been blamed and
penalized by Warren for the mistake. He looked into
Warren's smug, pitying face and wished for any other
boss at all: for Jiggs or for Mr. Dithers, Dagwood Bum-
stead's raging boss from the funny papers, just so he had
someone who would give him guidance. Sometimes he
felt like a thief on the street, learning his trade from
strangers.

Grady said only, "How are we doing for new work?"

Warren snorted. "Still booming. Too much war work,
though—and remember: Customers back out of things.
The war's end is going to teach you a lot about that."
He opened a manila file and tried to tuck the memo into
it. The paper struggled frantically. Warren, eyes wider
and nostrils flared, stapled the memo to the file and

stuffed the struggling paper away. Grady could only watch.

He left Warren's office and went to the shop, hoping to let off steam to Antony. He looked from side to side, not finding Antony. Then he saw Benny Behind scratching his crotch and grinning. Grady followed his gaze.

Antony's workbench was on jury-rigged metal stilts, its flat surface a full eighteen inches above any other bench in the shop. Antony, face impassive, was tottering on a short ladder, assembling atmosphere piping for a gas generator. He nodded to Grady but did not speak.

Grady turned away, bumping into Roy Burgess.

Roy steadied him. "How do you like the new workbench?" Roy looked at it thoughtfully, as though seeing it for the first time. "You know, I thought I told those boys to take a foot and a half off the height of that bench, not put it on." He shrugged. "It must be one of those errors the engineers make."

"And the shop never makes one, right? When are you going to fix it?"

Roy raised an eyebrow at Grady's tone. Grady jerked a thumb at the workbench. "You're riding him pretty hard."

Roy scowled at Grady. "Do I tell you how to run Sales? Do I?" Which was unfair. Roy told anyone who would listen how Sales should be run, every workday of the year. At production meetings he spread his calloused hands and explained with grief and self-pity how the shop would never be able to finish X project—whatever the most crucial project was at the moment—on schedule because of lapses in the sales quote, incompetence in the design, or laxness in purchasing.

Grady only said, "What do you know about Antony?"

"He's short. He's easy to kid." Roy added grudgingly, "And his work's good. And he's never, even once, complained about what's happened to him here."

Grady nodded vigorously. "Exactly. And he won't

complain. And I sure hope you don't, if you keep riding
him and something happens to you."

Roy's face darkened. "This is my castle."

"Did I say it wasn't? But every castle has a jester.
Just don't be surprised if anything that happens to him
comes back to haunt the person who did it. I'm not saying that would include you, of course."

"Of course." But Roy chewed his lip as Grady walked
away. Grady hoped, for Antony's sake, that Grady had
made enough of an impression to slow Roy down at the
very least.

Later Grady sneaked into Warren's office and copied the
information from the stapled Dwarfworks memo onto
another sheet of paper. After that he used his penknife
to pry the Dwarfworks memo free carefully, then stapled
the copy in its place. The original memo sat on Grady's
palm, fluttering anxiously.

He stroked it while glancing at Warren's desk and
froze, reading a telephone message from Talia Baghrati
to Warren: "Your boxes from New York were delivered
today." Somewhere in the building, probably in shipping, were a number of gnome controllers.

The memo in Grady's hand rose suddenly and flew
off strongly toward the southern end of the plant. Grady
followed it and coaxed it out the door. It spiraled once
in an eddy of air by the doorway, then rose quickly. He
watched it fly away, wishing that he could outstrip his
own problems as easily.

SIX

IT WAS A beautiful day in mid-May, one of those rare and gorgeous days in New England when there are no clouds and when the opening of the leaves on the elm and maple trees is suddenly striking. Days like that breed agreeability, even romance.

When Grady arrived and went up front to check his messages, Joey Cataldo was standing at the reception area, grinning. "Actually, I'm fifty-seven years old as the hills."

Talia Baghrati clasped her hands. "Really? You don't look a day over the hill."

He chuckled, embarrassed. "You're just saying that to get under my good side." He turned away, nearly knocking down Grady. "Sorry." He reached out with a steadying hand.

"I'm fine, Joey." He glanced back at Talia. "I don't mean to interrupt—"

"No, no. That's okay. We're done for." He sneaked a peek at Talia himself and burst out in a whisper like the valve on a pressure cooker, "She's sweeter than flies caught with honey."

"I believe you." Grady, leaning on his cane, watched

him nearly skip back to the shop. For a moment he thought with real regret, *Even people more than twice my age can skip when they're in love.* He shook his head, returning to the present, and asked Talia, "Do I have any calls?"

"All that you want," she said, smiling vacantly. She was winding the phone cord around her index finger and staring into space.

"I mean, did anyone call me?" he asked gently.

"Oh!" She looked at him. "I'm sorry. I'm not thinking straightaway—"

He looked solemn. "Sometimes that happens in the spring. Do I have any messages?"

"Not phone messages, no."

Sometimes talking to Talia took a great deal of patience. "Do I have any other messages?"

"One from Mr. Renfrew."

Grady stiffened. Bob Renfrew, in his midthirties, was the local supervisor for government contracts. He was a fellow Red Sox fan, though he cynically and consistently bet against them, and he was, on the latest government contract, the most nervous person Grady had ever met.

She looked around for it, found it, dropped it under the switchboard, and shrugged helplessly.

Grady considered stooping for it, but he would have to roll Talia's chair away from the board. Among her chair, the switchboard plug-in wires, and his cane, the logistics were discouraging. "What's the message?"

Talia leaned forward dangerously, clutching the switchboard desk as her chair threatened to roll out from under her. She moved her lips and said carefully and slowly, " 'I'm waiting for you in the lobby.' "

Grady made record time through the lobby door.

Renfrew leaped up, his baby face wide-eyed with worry. Grady said, red-faced, "I'm sorry if you were waiting long."

"Sure. I mean, no. Listen," he said, half-pushing

Grady toward one of the lobby chairs, "we have to t-lk."

"This isn't baseball talk, is it?" He wanted Ren? v to relax.

For a second it worked as Renfrew frowned and shook his head. "Not the way this season's going. Seems to me there are more errors than runs . . . I want players like DiMaggio back."

Grady punched his arm lightly. "Talk to Washington. Win the war."

"I talked to Washington," Renfrew said grimly. "Or at least to Stode."

Grady shrugged. "He should be happy. I've sent him regular reports."

"The reports he likes—all right, he says they're 'satisfactory,' which is as good as you're going to get. But he wants to know more about where the materials come from."

Grady felt his own chest grow tight. "He should be glad I could find them. Molybdenum isn't exactly lying around outside."

"That's what bothers him. He told me to look over the plant, talk to you, look for records, the usual." Renfrew spread his hands. "Who knows why he asks things? He's always looking for fifth columnists, you know? That's his job."

"Sure." Grady tried dubiously to imagine proving clearance for a centuries-old factory of dwarves with no paperwork for the war. This was not going to be easy if Stode pushed it.

Renfrew added encouragingly, "But he warned me not to scare you off the contract."

"Nice of you to tell me. I hope G-men don't operate this way when they look for spies."

"I'm not looking for a spy," Renfrew said frankly. "I'm asking questions of a guy who doesn't scare me at all because I was asked to by a guy who scares the hell out of me. Grady, what are you building? Why is it so important that he won't shut it down when he doesn't trust you?"

"Tell you what." Grady patted his shoulder. "Let's walk the shop floor together, check the prints, check with Purchasing, and give you enough to go on."

"Sure." He hesitated. "Grady? I hope you can give me the whole morning. I've been straight with you, and in exchange I want to see everything I can."

"You've got it."

They started with the equipment. The frame for the legs was already in place, the piping assembled on a nearby bench. Beside the bench was the metal shell of the heating chamber, with openings in it for water and for power terminals to the heating elements.

Renfrew poked at it dubiously. "This is vital to the war effort?" Flash, who had welded on it, glared at him but said nothing.

"It looks better assembled," Grady said, nettled. He pointed to the holes for the terminals. "We seal that up, put in heating elements, and we can take it up to more than forty-five hundred degrees Fahrenheit."

"And the steel will take that?"

"Not really. The steel is insulated inside. And, as you know, it has a moly hearth." Grady walked over to another bench and pointed with pride to the *pièce de résistance*, the centerpiece of the furnace.

Renfrew looked at it, fascinated. The moly shone, and the work was flawless. He picked it up.

Grady flinched. "Carefully. If you drop that stuff it breaks like glass, and we have to start over." He finished, "And I'm not telling Stode."

Renfrew set it down as gently as he would have a newborn. Still, he asked politely, "Can you tell me where it came from?"

"I can do better than that." He cupped his hands around his mouth and shouted, "Antony?!"

A voice called, "Call me Dutch here!"

"It's business!" Grady shouted back. "Come on over here!"

Antony showed up inside of twenty seconds. Grady waited a moment for Renfrew to do a double take at Antony's height, then waded in. "Bob, this is Antony van der Woeden, a worker from the Nieuw Amsterdam Metalworks. Antony"—he put a slight edge in his voice—"this is Bob Renfrew, who supervises government contracts."

"Sure, the guy we did the hearths for." He shook hands. "You need some more? We'll do our best."

"Good to meet you." Renfrew was clearly feeling better. "Actually, all I wanted to do was ask you—"

"You. Shorty." Their heads turned as Roy Burgess came over. "What are you doing over here? Nothing to do?"

Antony gestured at Renfrew. "The customer had a question—"

"Then get a salesman to answer it. You get back to work." He smacked Antony on the backside. "You're a little behind."

Grady bit his lip. Renfrew stared in disgust. Antony, keeping his thoughts to himself for now, said, "Nice meeting you, Bob. I hope you liked the hearth." He trotted back to his own bench.

Grady said apologetically, "You know, Bob, shops can be kind of rough—"

"I know," Renfrew said crisply. He wasn't all that tall himself. "But at least it's not a fifth-column problem. Antony just has a son of a bitch for a boss." He added, unwillingly, "And it's his problem."

Grady said feelingly, "If I could do anything—"

"Don't." Renfrew was startlingly firm, a different person on this issue. "Antony solves it for himself or he can't do this kind of work. Let him solve it his own way."

"I will." Grady, intrigued, regarded Renfrew. "You know, people give me a hard time out here because of"—he considered saying "my leg" and said instead, raising it for show—"my cane."

"And you wanted somebody outside helping with that?"

"What?" Grady was suddenly disoriented. "No, never."

"I've worked with a lot of contracts. Some of them made money, some didn't. The key is, listen to the needs of the people who have to sign with you." He stared fixedly at Grady. "And never, never try to solve their problems before they sign."

"Okay. Sure." Grady added, not self-pityingly but thoughtfully, "But they always come with problems."

Renfrew nodded. "And if you know what they are, you're able to work with them."

It was a second before Grady realized that Renfrew was talking about the Stode contract. "Well, now you know," he said. Grady moved Renfrew to Susan's desk to talk about contract details, feeling faintly guilty that he'd been counting on Roy Burgess to shut down any tough questioning of Antony. He was even guiltier that he'd always underestimated Renfrew.

Shortly Grady realized that he should have worried more about Susan; she had no sense of how to handle customers. They spread all the prints on a table in Engineering, so they could move from piping to wiring to insulation and proprietary assembly prints. Grady thought wistfully about the EGAD prints, the Elf-Gnome Assisted Design prints on which a miniature work crew built a tiny version of the finished product while you watched. The tiny workers were nasty and ill-tempered, but watching them required less imagination than did visualizing a finished product from two-dimensional drawings.

Susan, on the other hand, had too much imagination.

"You're worried about this job, aren't you?" she said to Renfrew as she traced wiring numbers with a restless index finger.

"A little, sure. I'm not that worried—"

"You should be." She pointed to the right-hand end points of a wiring schematic. "See this? Wire numbers eight through twenty-two. They feed into your temperature controller."

"Sure," Renfrew said, sounding anything but sure.

Susan folded her arms. "Show me the controllers."

Renfrew licked his lips nervously. Grady moved in to save him. "C'mon, Susan, they'll be on the other end of the wires. The first wires, up top, they're on the over-temperature controller." He said to Renfrew, casually, "You know. It shuts the whole thing down if the temperature shoots too high—if the other controller fails, or the control thermocouple fails and forgets to shut things off. And the wire connects to a terminal on the over-temperature controller."

Renfrew nodded. Susan said, "And the controller for the heat?"

"It comes out right—no, wait. Okay, that's T-two, that's the thermocouple to the main controller, and that's wired to number four." But the number-four wire ended in a blank, connected to nothing. "Okay, let's check the vacuum switch, which tells how low the pressure has gone, and it won't turn on the heat through the controller until the pressure's down to five hundred microns . . ."

The vacuum switch wasn't connected to anything either.

"I sketched these prints," Susan said flatly, "and there was a controller there when I sketched it. It was from Wheelco," she added, as though that made it even more real.

"Let's check the purchase orders." Grady opened the folder and sifted through them. "Here's an over-temperature controller from Wheelco, here are the two thermocouples—here are two spare thermocouples; you guys sure order enough spare parts. . . ."

He trailed off. There was no order for a second controller.

Susan pointed to the signature block on the print. The latest entry said only "Revised," no date, and the initials "W.H."

"Warren Hastings," Grady said resignedly. "Okay, so either he changed this or Stode called him and changed it."

Renfrew shook his head vigorously. "Stode wanted to work only through you."

"Well, I want to kiss Betty Grable, but you'll notice I don't," Grady retorted. He saw Garneaux, out in the shop for once, grinning at him and at Susan, and he wished he'd picked another actress. "Warren runs the show here, and he's taken over this furnace. This could be something the two of them have cooked up. I'll ask Warren when he's back."

"That's all I can ask for." Renfrew stood up, checking his watch. "Thanks for your time. I guess there's nothing to worry about."

"I wouldn't say—"Susan began, but shut up as Grady put the tip of his cane on her left foot and leaned on it.

"Of course we won't," Grady said. "We wouldn't say anything about this visit."

Grady returned after walking Renfrew out. "No controller?" he said wonderingly.

"That's the least of the troubles with this job." She waved the purchase order and accompanying paperwork at Grady. "No destination, no start-up service, no on-site acceptance. Grady, what are they doing?"

"Something secret," he said defensively and not too convincingly. "So they don't tell us what's going on. Do you know anything about keeping secrets?"

"I've kept some in physics," she said defensively.

"Why would physics have secrets?"

"Because it's going to change the world," she said bluntly. "Also, it's all changing so fast. So much of physics is new since I was born. And the past ten years . . . did I tell you that when I was at Columbia I met the Italian physicist Enrico Fermi? He won a Nobel Prize before coming to Columbia."

"So you met a guy who won the Nobel Prize." That was so far out of Grady's normal life that he wasn't sure how to react. "What did you learn from him?"

Susan frowned. "Not much, except for his classroom work. I audited it, since I wasn't a graduate student. Other than that, I didn't see much of him; he was busy with some project. But he liked me." She dimpled. "He called me Suzie."

"Maybe he thought you were cute. Did he tell you what he was doing?"

She looked shocked. "Of course not. Some of what he was doing was secret even before we entered the war." She said, with forced casualness, "So I went around him and learned that Dr. Fermi was trying to start a chain reaction in a device built partly of graphite bricks."

Grady was seriously impressed. Physics was impressive, but espionage was beyond him. "How did you find out?"

Susan half-ducked her head and muttered.

Grady strained to hear. "What?"

Blushing, Susan said more loudly, "I dated a football player."

Grady gaped at her. She added defensively, "Bull Branciewiecz. A fullback. He weighed nearly two twenty-five, but he was shy, and kind of sweet." She added absently with an awe that annoyed Grady no end, "And big."

From his desk, Tom Garneaux sang in a husky tenor, " 'Freddie the Freshman, the freshest kid in town.' " Susan glared at him, but dropped her eyes when Garneaux grinned at her.

"Okay," Grady said, "you were going out with a football player. If I work hard at it and train, I can imagine that. What does that have to do with Enrico Fermi?"

Susan rolled her eyes. "Well, you wouldn't expect a bunch of scientists to carry all that uranium by themselves."

"What uranium?"

"Uranium oxide. Big cans full of it, to build something Dr. Fermi called a pile." She waved her hands, sketching out something about the size of her desk. Grady frequently wondered if she could talk at all while sitting on her hands. "Anyway, one night Bull broke a date and said he couldn't tell me why. I made him tell me, of course—"

"Of course."

She ignored him. "It turned out he was carrying uranium. So I made him tell me where, and it turned out to be Schermerhorn Hall, and I snuck in to watch." She frowned. "That evening was a dud."

Grady wondered, uncharitably, how many evenings spent with Bull had been duds. "What were they trying to do?"

"I told you, a chain reaction, you dope. They wanted to get atoms to split other atoms." She sketched some numbers on her desk: 2-4-8-16-32-64-128-256-512. . . ."

Grady stopped her pencil. "I get the idea."

"No, you don't," she said solemnly. "Nobody ever does. That's in the first millionth of a second. Keep going until you've got a figure with seven zeros in the first second or so. Then you've got the idea."

Grady said, fascinated, "So, did he do it?"

"No," she admitted grudgingly. "But he learned enough to be pretty sure that he could." She sighed. "The next thing I heard was that he was going to the University of Chicago."

"So that ended that."

She looked at him pityingly. "So I called my father and said I was transferring to Chicago."

"He went along with that?"

"Not at first." She smiled a little wistfully, as she often did when talking of her father. "He always said I could talk him into anything." She shook her head quickly, returning to the present. "My timing was perfect. I went out to Chicago early on purpose, went to the science building, and asked if Dr. Fermi had said where to deliver the extra boxes."

"What extra boxes?" Grady said helplessly.

"There weren't any extra boxes. I just wanted his new address. I got there and, talk about luck, there was still a delivery truck and they were still moving in. Dr. Fermi and his wife were surrounded by boxes. So I said hello, and he introduced me to his wife, Laura, and then he left and I helped her unpack. She was nice." Susan added with distaste, "She said the university—or the government, she wasn't clear—made them watch a film about foreigners and espionage. Why do people think like that?"

Grady said, "Don't you know there's a war on?"

"All right, I've heard that a thousand times. I still don't think they had to do that to Dr. Fermi and his wife. Well, I saw Laura Fermi a few times after that, but I still had to figure out what he was doing on campus. Since I knew what he was doing—"

Grady, completely lost, said, "What was he doing?"

"Creating a chain reaction: Haven't you been listening? And I knew from what I'd read and what I'd heard in classes that he'd have to use uranium again, and it's heavy. So"—and she had the grace to blush—"I checked to see if the University of Chicago had a football team—"

Tom Garneaux said solemnly, "I'm detecting an ugly pattern here."

She ignored him. "But this time the physicists must have hired workers outside. Security was tighter than it had been at Columbia."

"So what did you do?"

"I used my brain." She tapped her forehead with one finger. "Dr. Fermi needed a building with plenty of room in it, one that was taking deliveries from big trucks. For security, it had to be one that wasn't in use for something else—and universities are always short of space, even in wartime. So I started looking for buildings that had been closed down." She thumped the desk. "Sure enough, there were notices posted that the squash courts were closed until further notice."

"So you found Dr. Fermi's project. Was it as big as you thought?"

"Bigger." She smiled proudly. "I was right: It was important. They built this big structure of graphite bricks, with cadmium rods sticking through it to absorb neutrons and control the reaction, and when it really got going they pulled the rods out."

Grady was beginning to feel the energy of the project. "And did they ever pull the rods out?"

"Once. I was there for it. I wasn't supposed to be, but I'd found a way in—"

Grady said, a little bitterly, "Who did you date for that?"

"Nobody," she said, hurt. "I just found a way." She smiled, back in the moment. "And there I was, way above the floor where there was this huge pile of graphite bricks, and wires coming out in every direction, and they started pulling the rods out and letting the chain reaction happen—"

"Letting it happen?"

"Oh, yes," she said seriously. "When you get that much uranium-two-thirty-five in one place, it wants the reaction to happen."

She sounded to Grady like Antony talking about metals processing. "So what happened next?"

"A high-pitched whine from a Geiger counter—from a machine that detects radiation. And the other instruments made it clear that the pile had gone critical, had created a chain reaction that sustained itself." She was staring at the ceiling, drifting back to the moment. "If Dr. Fermi and the others hadn't stopped it, Chicago would have seen more energy unleashed than any place on the planet."

Grady shuddered. If Susan were telling the truth, who thought it was a swell idea to do an experiment like this in Chicago? "So what happened next? Did you just get out the way you came?"

Susan blushed. "I got caught. I guess I made some noise trying to leave. Two guys in suits and ties, no lab coats, grabbed me and brought me down to the squash court floor." She smiled, the hero worship full in her face. "But Dr. Fermi told them, 'It's all right,' and he raised his glass and said, 'Suzie, come here and have some of the wine.'" She finished triumphantly, "So I did. I helped toast the first chain reaction on earth."

Grady reflected that wherever Susan had gone up to now, she had found someone to spoil her. "Then what?"

She sighed loudly. "Then he left Chicago, and so did I. I wrote him a couple of times, care of the University of Chicago, with a 'please forward' message on the envelope. I never heard from him."

After a polite silence, Grady admitted, "I still don't see why that's important."

Susan's look could have frozen Narragansett Bay in place. "All right. If nothing else will work, I'll give you some figures."

Grady quailed. He was nowhere near as fond of math as Susan was.

She caught him. "And just to be sure you get the

picture, I'll translate them into kilowatts and into pounds—maybe tons—of TNT."

Grady's ears pricked up at that. At the beginning of the war, Plimstubb had created furnaces for two-thousand-pound bombs. He knew what a ton of TNT was, and was vaguely aware of what it could do to a building.

She did some rapid calculations and showed him a number. It made no sense. She must have missed a decimal point somewhere. He ignored the number and said slowly, "So you thought this experiment of yours could win the war."

She chuckled. "I thought this experiment of Dr. Fermi's could change the planet." She dropped her head down to her work. Clearly, the discussion was over.

On his way out of Engineering, Grady said politely to Tom Garneaux, "Did you catch all that?"

Garneaux said easily, "I ignored all that jazz about physics, but I heard the part about the football player. Kid, she's got a soft heart behind that hard patter she throws out. Reach in and touch it."

"Easier said than done," Grady said bitterly. "You think that thing she described on the Chicago squash court had shielding?"

But Garneaux only chuckled. "Women aren't made of bricks—though, come to think of it, I knew a woman built like a brick—"

He continued with a seemingly pointless but fairly entertaining anecdote, at the end of which they both laughed. Garneaux wrapped his hand around Grady's on top of the cane. "Do you get the idea? They aren't really brick. They want us to touch their hearts. Never quit trying."

"I won't," Grady found himself saying. Tom Garneaux had been a bootlegger, a gambler, and, Grady suspected, a thoroughgoing scoundrel—but Grady listened

to his advice the way he had to his father's words before
his father shipped out for the Pacific.

Garneaux waved a stubby finger. "See that you don't.
Seems to me you spend half your time talking about
atoms, and the other half reading moonshine about the
future."

Grady was halfway back to his office before Garneaux's last comment, rattling around in Grady's brain,
produced a chain reaction of its own. Grady grabbed a
pen and scribbled as rapidly as he could, creating a character named Sally Panheim, beautiful but worried physicist, and Cliff Walker, brilliant and athletic engineer.
Their romance revolved around the creation of an explosive atomic weapon that would win the war.

The story involved no evil Japanese, no villainous
fifth column. Instead, the enemy was the land invasion
of Japan, which would slay millions of Americans need-
lessly. Grady wrote it freehand, barely crossing out a
word.

He looked up after an hour and a half, feeling guilty
that he wrote it on company time. He used the rest of
the afternoon to bat out proposals for drill furnaces, an-
nealing furnaces, and one atmosphere-oil quench furnace
for heavy industry. He mailed them out proudly, feeling
that the acceptance of any of them would (a) make up
for the time he had wasted and (b) win the war.

Late in the day he was interrupted by a phone message: "There are two people waiting for Mr. Hastings. I
can't reach him."

Grady stared at the phone. The voice had an eager
warmth he did not associate with Talia.

Two Arabs, both elegant in conservative suits, were
waiting in the lobby. Talia was smiling and holding a
hand of the tall one, and her eyes were full with tears.
Grady remembered them well, though he had met them
only once. "Mr. Faroukh, Mr. Fahdi. It's a pleasure to
see you." He wondered what was up. As far as he knew,

they hadn't signed on a furnace the last time they were in.

Mr. Faroukh bowed, still seeming tall. "Always it will be our pleasure." He said to Talia, "Please excuse us, dear lady."

"Excuse me, too," Grady said, and added with a grin, " 'dear lady.' "

Talia laughed, sniffling, and waved a hand at him. It kicked up a wave of perfume that nearly choked him, and he turned toward Mr. Faroukh and Mr. Fahdi. "So, what brings you here?"

"A purchase," Mr. Fahdi said. He was short and round-bodied and seemed eager to make friends.

"The fulfillment of a previous promise," Mr. Faroukh said. "We have a contract with your Mr. Hastings, to make final and sign." His dark eyes looked down at Grady. "I think that he did not tell you."

Grady nodded. "You are very respected customers, and he insists on caring for you himself."

Mr. Faroukh laughed, but without ridicule; he had a hand on Grady's shoulder. "That may be true," he said graciously, "but I think I would feel better if you were the person with whom we made the contract. Excuse me."

He left Grady and Mr. Fahdi waiting in the lobby. Grady said to Mr. Fahdi, "If you want to go with him, I can amuse myself here."

"Oh, no," he replied eagerly. "I will enjoy talking to you. We travel so much, and still it seems we meet so few people. And my friend Mr. Faroukh will do well alone, negotiating." He held up a finger for emphasis, raising one of his dark eyebrows. "He is very intelligent. More than brilliant. He is—"

"A genius?" Grady said politely.

Mr. Fahdi looked at him, disturbed, and then started to chuckle. "You are very clever."

Grady smiled back. Inside he felt strange, though he

had suspected the truth the last time the two men had visited.

"But you like jokes." Mr. Fahdi looked back and forth as though he were going to admit to a crime. "Tell me. There is a show on the radio, *Jack Benny*. I will tell you the jokes. Can you explain them to me?"

For what seemed like an hour, Grady explained the natures of Jack, Rochester, Dennis Day, and the many sounds of Mel Blanc. Mr. Fahdi leaned forward, smiling and nodding and listening to every word, never so much as chuckling. Grady added more gestures, more punch lines, even Rochester's low, rasping voice.

When Grady stopped, exhausted, Mr. Fahdi patted his knee. "Thank you, my friend. The next time I hear Mr. Benny, I am sure I will laugh."

"I sure hope so," Grady said frankly.

Mr. Faroukh returned with Warren Hastings and two copies of a contract. "Here you are, Cavanaugh," Warren said smugly but without malice. Grady knew immediately it was a good deal for Plimstubb.

"Anything I can do?" Grady said.

Warren waved a negligent hand. "Witness the signings, keep a copy, see our guests out. I'm afraid I have a phone call." He left with cursory handshakes and good-byes for the customers.

Grady watched with distaste. Now that the customers had signed a contract, they had no importance to Warren—and this was the time when their importance should just be beginning.

Mr. Faroukh, watching him go, smiled slightly. "No carpet you can buy will ever fly as fast as the rug merchant you paid."

"Pity," Grady said, but he might have been speaking about the rugs. "I hope the contract is all right with you now." He scanned down the top copy. "That's funny."

Mr. Fahdi said fretfully, "When your people say that, no one laughs."

"It's nothing. The control description is different than I remembered." In fact, it was generic.

Mr. Faroukh said ruefully, "The price is different as well. But we derive more capabilities from the equipment, so your Mr. Hastings promised, and if it does as he says, it is well worth the price."

"That's that, then." Grady handed the contract back to them, hiding his unease. Warren had promised them that their controller would record temperature, read old records, and correct temperature errors in future runs. As far as Grady knew, that was impossible. He wouldn't put it past Warren to cheat foreigners, but he hated to think that men as nice as Mr. Faroukh and Mr. Fahdi were being cheated.

Also, it was probably dangerous to do so.

The two men signed both copies of the contract, one under the other, with beautiful liquid signatures. Grady compared it to Warren's cramped scrawl. "Wow."

Mr. Fahdi said, amused, "It comes of writing in Arabic for so many years."

Grady decided not to ask how many. He kept one copy of the contract and walked them to the door.

The two men took an affectionate farewell of Talia Baghrati, who began to cry again and excused herself. Grady opened the door for them and paused, looking at the curb. "I assumed you would drive here."

"I had hoped we would," Mr. Fahdi said regretfully. "I love the car."

"We had to hurry, my friend. I promise, next time you may drive me." He bowed, and a dark bronze oil lamp fell out of the breast of his suit and thunked onto the carpet of the reception area.

Grady stooped quickly and picked up the lamp.

It was like the moment in the movie theater when the projector froze, and everyone knew that the scene in front of them would melt and burn in moments. Mr. Faroukh held his hands forward pleadingly in silence.

Mr. Fahdi held his arms sideways, trying to shield his friend.

After a moment, Mr. Faroukh said, "You know you could rub the lamp." Mr. Fahdi looked appalled.

Grady looked at the dark lamp in his hands, feeling the time-worn curves of the lamp and knowing what it might mean to rub it. In this part of the war, power and wishes seemed wonderful and tempting things.

But he said slowly, "I don't think it's good business to do that. Also, I don't think it's right to do that to good friends of Talia Baghrati." He set it carefully on a chair.

Mr. Faroukh sat down shakily beside it, wiping his forehead with an immaculate white handkerchief. "God is great." He said to Grady, "Do you wish her well?"

Grady said frankly, "Of course I do." He considered what else to say. "She's been kind to me."

"No," Mr. Faroukh said, moving protectively beside his friend. "I think that you have been kind to her. Very well." He picked up the lamp and moved it inside his coat. Strangely, there was no bulge. "I thank you," he nodded, bowing his head, "and I will bless this summer, for you and for those around you."

Instead of thanking him, Grady said, "How far does that blessing extend?"

"Oh." Mr. Faroukh moved over him, his dark eyes luminous with sympathy and pity. "If our blessings could extend so far over so many, do you think this part of your war would happen? But we pray for you, and for your brothers and sisters in Japan, and we wait to know God's mercy."

Grady nodded, not sure what that meant. He watched as they walked out the front door, and a moment later he stepped out himself and looked both ways. They were nowhere in sight.

•   •   •

The following noon he borrowed Talia's L. C. Smith typewriter and pounded out a revision of his story, pausing only for bites of a ham sandwich he barely tasted. In midafternoon he finished typing. At ten minutes to five he dashed off a short cover letter to the editor of *Amazing*, shoved it and the story in an envelope, and bought postage from Chester Traub to send the story off.

He returned home with a sense of work well done. Only later did it occur to him that he had done nothing about Renfrew's worries.

SEVEN

THE FOLLOWING MORNING Grady came in, had the usual demanding but otherwise pleasant fencing lesson with Susan, tossed his cane onto the coathook by his desk, and went straight to work on proposals. He sent one to Hughes Aircraft, based on a furnace model the aircraft industry was particularly fond of for processing stainless steel. He wrote another to one of Antony's customers, proposing a tiny "bean-pot" furnace, little more than a circular heating chamber with a lid on it, for melting impurities out of a neck chain to cure asthma. He also wrote a carefully worded letter of regret to a Mr. Jabroux of New Orleans, expressing regret but declining to build a furnace to create manacles for zombies. He had barely needed Antony's advice to turn that one down.

It reminded him and he wrote a brief, cheerful note to Zoltán on the back of a postcard of Providence. He had met Zoltán when Grady worked at the Dwarfworks, and they had gotten along well. Of the dwarves, Kirsten especially had disapproved of the friendship, but Grady liked Zoltán and, after all, it wasn't Zoltán's fault he was dead. Undead.

Grady mailed his correspondence and walked to Warren's office to check in with him. It wasn't something he enjoyed doing, but he had to do it once a day even so.

Warren's office was dark and locked. Grady was ready to leave when a sharp voice said, "Looking for me?"

Warren was in coveralls, and his hands were dirty. He had actual grease on them, and one previously manicured fingernail was torn. But he looked happy, in the way design engineers get when they've left their desks and gotten back to fiddling with hardware: rewiring, adding unions and tees and nipples to piping, adjusting the tightness of drive chains, and calling to someone at the other end of a machine, "Try 'er again."

Grady had never seen Warren like this. For a moment he thought sadly that this was the boss he could have liked and respected.

That vanished as Warren said smugly, "To get it done right, do it yourself."

"Actually, Warren, the guys out in the shop are pretty good at what they do."

"Really?" Warren regarded him with cold amusement. "Well, this wasn't what they do."

"Then what is it?"

"A few adjustments to shop equipment, courtesy of my—business acquaintance, Klaus."

One of the standing jokes in any shop was to take a piece of cold steel, in warm weather, and hold it on the back of someone's neck until he shivered. Grady felt as though someone had wrapped his entire spine in a sweat-beaded, icewater pipe.

Not noticing, Warren said proudly, "Go out and look." Grady went as hurriedly as he could to the shop.

A sliding box attached to a welding rod was rolling slowly across the top of a furnace heating chamber, fol-

lowing a chalk line like a spider moving up silk. Behind
it, curving down like the tail on a stingray, a metal arm
held a welding rod on the chalk line. The rod sparked
steadily, leaving behind a ruler-straight weld on the furnace roof.

Flash, his cap on backward (to fit under his welding
mask) and cut-off cigar in his mouth (ditto), leaned on
the opposite side of the furnace with Hammer Houlihan,
staring fascinatedly. Flash was looking directly into the
welding arc, blinking frequently. "Did you ever see anything more impressive?"

"Not with my pants on," Hammer replied.

Grady moved on to the steel rack, where the brake
sheer thumped methodically, cutting rectangles for the
heat chamber sides and thin strips to cover slots in the
sides.

No one was running the shear. In front of it, a black
box on a steel tripod rested on two ratcheted arms that
extended toward the brake shear. At the end of each arm,
pincers clamped onto a plate of quarter-inch steel.

Betty, her overalls immaculate for once, watched the
whole process from the far shelves of the steel rack.
Grady shouted to her over the clank of the metal, "Isn't
it great?"

She pulled even farther away from the brake shear,
never taking her eyes off of it. "Uh-huh."

Grady tried again, wondering why he felt obligated
to. "You've gotta admit, it's better than risking your
hands pushing the steel in." He watched the long, vi-
cious horizontal line of the other shear rising, dropping,
biting with a thud through steel and spitting a strip of
scrap out the back onto the floor. "At least nobody loses
a finger in it this way."

She said quietly, "Bets?" and moved to the other side
of the steel rack. Grady gave up and moved on.

In Wiring he found an eight-armed controller with
wire cutters at the ends of two arms, looking remark-

ably like a spider crab. It measured the lengths of wire between two pincered claws, then cut the wire with a quick stroke of the wire cutters. Grady was reminded uneasily of a picture he had seen in a college art textbook: the three fates—Clothos, Atropos, and Lachesis—spinning, measuring, and cutting the thread of a human life.

The last controller had a mouth. It was formed of half-inch pipe, with a lidded opening at the rear and a compressed air hose plugged onto a nipple just above the lid. It rolled along the floor on long, shaky legs, straddling wooden shipping crates. One by one, a skinny arm fed nails point first through the rear opening, the lid closed, and the controller spat the nails into the crate with a sound like a short, sharp bark.

Grady watched it seal up a box of metal heating elements, replacements headed by rail to Thomson Aircraft. He watched as Roy Burgess rolled the controller gingerly over to the next box, a low, flat carton of thermocouples bound for a plant in Altoona. It seemed to Grady that the controller needed remarkably little assistance.

The controller squatted and spat, rhythmically nailing another lid on a box the size of a child's coffin.

Roy walked briskly past Grady with a cursory nod and headed for a spare tire where, Grady recalled, there was a dusty bottle of cheap whiskey stashed. Grady watched him going, thinking that he didn't trust the controllers either.

He heard a rustle in shipping and turned his head quickly. The box was all nailed and the controller had stopped, facing the windows to Grady's left—but he had the nagging feeling that it had been watching him and had turned away too quickly for him to catch it.

For once, he was relieved to go back to Warren's office.

"Well?" Warren said proudly. "What do you think?"

Grady shook his head. "It's like something from science fiction."

Warren chuckled, and it was clear to Grady that Warren was glad of having someone who could share the moment. "Robot. We're in the first factory to use robots."

"Sure." Some images that had been nagging at Grady fell into place: clanking metal men carrying struggling women, mostly blond, around spaceships and strange planets. He must have seen a hundred magazine covers on that theme. He felt absurdly relieved that none of the women had looked like Susan.

He couldn't help asking, "What I don't get is, why bother? We're not an assembly line factory, we're a job shop. We custom-design industrial furnaces, and we can ship a hundred fifty a year, two hundred fifty with overtime work—my God." It made appalling amounts of sense. "People's overtime."

"Plimstubb's overtime." Warren's smile was back to being smug. "I can cut back the hours in shipping, welding, wiring, and fabrication starting Monday. In five workdays I'll pay for one of the controllers. In a month I'll have paid for the investment—and I can cut costs on the furnaces, and start selling even more."

Grady said, "Too bad you can't put them directly on the equipment we sell, if they're that cheap."

"Isn't it?" Warren agreed, but his eyes looked suddenly distant and amused. "Don't worry, Cavanaugh, I've got other deals going with friend Klaus; I won't miss any opportunities." He chuckled. "It's too bad for him he doesn't know the bargain he's given me."

In his mind, Grady saw himself sprawled on the cavern floor of the Dwarfworks, disgraced in front of everyone there. Antony was helping him up and handing him his cane, saying, "Remember, kid, if you think

you're running ahead of a gnome, you've forgotten
something."

Grady went back to his office, wondering unhappily
what Warren had forgotten.

EIGHT

G RADY AND ANTONY both ate breakfast at Mary's
when Antony was in town, at her insistence. Antony
always felt as though he should apologize for his work
clothes, which were stained even when freshly laun-
dered. Mary never seemed to notice or mind. He took
great care, since he couldn't offer ration cards, to drop
off smoked ham or freshly dressed chicken, or perhaps
newly churned butter, at the first of every week that he
returned to Rhode Island.

He and Grady only crossed paths at Mary's for half
an hour. Antony had to excuse himself while Grady was
still eating and leave for work. The shop side of Plimstubb began an hour earlier than Grady's job, took only
half an hour for lunch break, and closed at three-thirty.

On this particular day, Antony left five minutes earlier
than usual. Grady, savoring his coffee, raised an eyebrow. "In a hurry to see Roy Burgess?"

"Please. I've just eaten." He winked. "In a hurry to
see a friend." He left, whistling.

When Grady arrived and entered through the employees' door, he saw Tom Garneaux leaving the shop, a
paper bag under his arm. Garneaux stopped short to

avoid bumping Grady, and the bag clinked and gurgled.

Grady said, "It's a bit early in the day."

"Drop by later," Garneaux agreed. "It's from Dutch."

"What did he do that for?" Grady asked uneasily, with visions of Rip van Winkle and twenty-year naps.

He winked, looking momentarily like Antony. "I did him a favor." He glided easily back to Engineering, whistling "Little Brown Jug."

Grady searched hastily for Antony. He found the dwarf on tiptoe, cleaning ground-level windows. Below him, Joey Cataldo crawled on his hands and knees, sweeping the floor with a brush and a dustpan.

Grady sighed. "What now?"

Antony grinned. "I got my friend Joe in trouble."

"No, no," Joe said earnestly. "I hit Roy's fan all by myself."

Grady turned back to Antony. "And he told you to clean windows?"

"Just the bottom tier." He smiled crookedly. "With a bucket and a rag, no long-handled mop available—and strangely, no ladders available, either."

Joe raised the brush and dustpan. "No brooms. He said I have to use this. I wish I could switch with Dutch."

That had probably appealed to Roy's sense of humor, Grady thought glumly. Joe was one of the tallest workers in the shop. Moreover, this was the kind of labor that waited until a plant was slow—and there was still a war on, for God's sake. He said quietly, "Where's Roy?"

"Don't bother him," Joey said wide-eyed. "He's lying like a sleeping dog."

"I wasn't gonna bother him, I just wanted to know where he was." Grady walked as quickly as he could to Shipping and then to Wiring, returning with two poles and a roll of insulating tape. "Roy, tape the brush on the end of this and it's almost a regular broom. Antony, bunch up the rag and tape it on the end of this pole."

"And if Roy wakes up—"

"Tear the tape off and work the old way. Or face it out; after all, you've done what he said."

Antony nodded approvingly. "Nice. You're getting better at recognizing loopholes."

"I've had to be," Grady said frankly. Contracts since he met the gnomes and the dwarves were far more complicated and much riskier.

Antony nodded. "Well, use the loopholes to do good things."

While Joe assembled his 'instant broom,' Grady said softly to Antony, "Speaking of doing good things, I see you gave some beer to Tom Garneaux."

"I sure did." Antony saw Grady's expression. "Relax, kid. This is the good stuff. He'll wake up tomorrow morning early, and he won't even have a hangover." He punched Grady gently on the lower arm. "It's good for him. Good for you, if you want some."

"I'll pass this time." The dwarves had once tried to put Grady to sleep for twenty years with a drink of beer.

"Your choice," Antony said easily. "Anyway, Tom's a good guy. I may ask him to help me with a small project."

"You and Tom?" Grady started to ask, then caught himself. Antony and Tom had a number of things in common. One was a love of practical jokes on people who richly deserved punishment. "If I don't ask, will you still make sure I get to see the result when the time comes?"

"You got it." He finished taping the rag onto the stick, whirled the homemade mop deftly in the water, and returned to washing windows. "Thanks for helping us out this morning. Say, did I ever tell you how Curly Larson and I got home from Europe?"

"Did you go together?"

"Nope. I met him in New York afterward." Antony said with a grin, "I flew."

"No."

"Yep." Antony added, "It sounds tougher than it was. The weather was good, there wasn't much wind, and I don't weigh much."

"You flew in an army plane?"

Antony was suddenly sorry he had brought it up. "Not exactly. I had something I'd made up out of junked parts. I had a lot of parts to pick from by the end of the war; we'd all crashed a lot. And I had a lot of help." He finished uncomfortably, "Anyway, that's how I got home, France to New York."

"And Curly?"

"Went AWOL from Paris, took a train to Calais, where they were loading the tenders that took troops onto the ships. Curly looked until he found a tender that was being run by a corporal—Curly was a major by now, believe it or not—and when the corporal read a list of names for boarding, he swore at the kid and chewed him out for not having Curly's name on the list of soldiers headed to New York. The kid apologized and let Curly onto the ship."

"So Curly was AWOL going to New York," Grady said musingly. "Were you?"

Antony was silent a while, finally saying, "Kid, it's not like it is now. I'd fought, and we'd won, and I wanted to go home."

Grady nodded, thinking only how much his brother Kevin probably wanted to come home now.

Antony startled him by asking, "If your brother showed up AWOL from Europe, would you turn him in now?"

"Of course not." Grady added honestly, "I'd sure chew him out, though. He'd have no business doing that, and him with a wife and child."

"Fair enough." Antony pointed a stubby finger at Grady. "Just remember, though: He'd be doing it to get home to them. Everybody has somebody they want to

come home to." He thought of Kirsten and smiled, looking up to see Grady watching him and grinning. "Okay,
you caught me. But you see my point."

"I hope Kevin doesn't," Grady said feelingly. "I have
a feeling he'd be easier to catch than you were. So, did
Curly Larson get in any trouble?"

"Him?" Antony laughed affectionately. "I always saw
him get out of it, too. Know how he got home from
New York to the Midwest?"

"No clue."

Antony folded his hands, remembering. "We went to
see the Yankees. I really did see the Babe, back when
he was still the Sultan of Swat. But anyway, we met in
Times Square and took the train out to the game. He
offered his seat to an old man—"

"You've never made him sound like a gentleman."

"He always was," Antony said seriously. "Besides, the
old guy was with a pretty girl. So anyway, we went to
the game, and the Babe was everything we'd both heard.
He hit three out of the park, and he made everything
look easy but running the bases. But the old guy insisted
on telling us how the game worked and what was going
on. I had to laugh—Curly had played ball in Iowa, even
seen the White Sox in Chicago before going to the
war—but he shook the old guy's hand maybe two dozen
times and hung on every word. I thought he was over-
doing.

"Of course, I wasn't the one planning on going out
with the girl. And even Curly had no way of knowing
that her godfather was Secretary of War Baker."

Grady was getting a feel for these stories. "The old
guy, or his best friend?"

"Who'd believe that?" Antony said, hurt. "The old
guy was her grandfather. He'd shelled out big bucks to
get Wilson elected, and he was part of the money behind
Baker's appointment as well." He raised a busy eyebrow. "Bear in mind that Curly knew none of this when

he offered the seat to the old guy on the train."

"But he never passed up an opportunity." Grady was starting to wish he could meet Curly Larson.

"Maybe. Or maybe he was a nice guy inside. Sometimes it pays to be nice, kid." He shook his head, coming back to the present. "Anyway, he saw the girl a few more times—"

"Naw."

"—And one weekend she said to him, 'Mr. Larson, if you could have anything from the army, what would it be?' and he said, 'Send me back to the Midwest.' "

"And he got sent back."

"Oh, no." Antony shook his head violently. "He went back to barracks in New York, where the army had stuck him. He got into a poker game. Luckily, he won. Then he got into a crap game, with dice thrown onto an army blanket stretched flat as a Neuport out of gas—well, flat as they come. And he was hot, and he came up with a pile, and then somebody came into the barracks and said tiredly, "Larson, you son of—" He cut off politely.

"We'll fill in the blanks," Susan said, as she walked up, but it was clear she was hooked on the story. "What happened next?"

"Next," Antony said heavily, "the U.S. Army transferred Curly Larson to Camp Dodge near Des Moines. He arrived in New York AWOL, but he left hundreds of dollars richer with an honorable discharge and a promotion. That was Curly."

"So what's the moral?" Grady fixed Antony with a steely glare, or at least the best he could do. "I know you. There's always a moral."

"I hope that's kind of a loose term." Antony paused—mostly for effect, since this was why he'd told the story in the first place—and said, "Always remember, kid: Do right by people—you always seem to—but always keep pushing for your own dreams, too. I know you. Your dreams will always do right by people."

"Did they do right by Curly? Did he get where he wanted to go?"

"Huh? Oh, sure." Antony changed the subject. "I'd better quit gabbing here, before Roy comes back."

Grady nodded sadly and left. Antony watched him go, glad that he'd been able to distract Grady from the subject of the airplane.

Grady moved on to check on the furnace for Stode. It was coming together quickly. The heating chamber was assembled and the insulation in place inside its metal cage. The railings to slide the cage down were welded into the heating chamber. The piping, nearly complete, was attached to the vacuum pump. The intake piping rested on a wooden trestle, ready for fitting to the opening on the heating chamber. The flanges that would mate together, on the pipe and on the outside of the heating chamber, had been machined mirror-smooth.

But the control panel still had a hole in it where the controller would go. Grady opened the rear door of the control panel and stared, disheartened, at the array of unconnected wires dangling uselessly from the thermocouple and vacuum switch connections, among others. He checked the print. There was a penciled note on it, in block caps: SEE WARREN HASTINGS. He set the print down, unconsciously wiping his fingers on his trousers.

A radio on a shop bench blared as he passed, playing music Grady didn't recognize. No one was nearby to listen. He turned it off and, for good measure, unplugged it.

Before he got back inside the office, the radio was blaring strange music again. He didn't see who had turned it on, but clearly someone must have. He shrugged and went in.

Before he could check his messages, Talia said firmly to Grady, "Watch out for the snakes."

"Snakes?"

Talia gestured shakily at the floor under Grady's desk. "Electric snakes."

Grady wondered uneasily if Talia's drinking had finally caught up with her.

He patted her shoulder. "I haven't seen 'em, Talia, but if I do, I'll watch out for them. I'll even tell them to keep away from you—"

She pulled away irritably. "Don't talk to me with that voice, like butter wouldn't melt you. I'm old enough to be spinning in your mother's grave. I saw them." She was shivering and near tears. "I saw them, and they were real!"

"All right. I believe you." But he couldn't help adding, "Talia, I haven't seen any of them, and I walk through the plant a lot."

"Maybe you don't see as well as I do," she snapped. "Remember, I see"—she caught herself. "I can see other things."

Grady considered. "You're talking about Mr. Fahdi and Mr. Faroukh—"

"I am talking about other things," she said evasively. "You know how you people say, 'Bless your eyes'? When I was a girl, someone did." She smiled, remembering, but the smile vanished quickly. "And I saw electric snakes."

"Are you sure you just didn't see electrical wires?"

"Yes—no. I don't know," she said helplessly. "But if they were wires, why should they move like that? And don't try to tell me they didn't move." She waved a finger at him in warning. "That was as plain as the nose on your face." She peered at him and finished, "Plainer."

She vanished into the women's room before Grady could ask what that last remark meant.

Even on good days, dictating letters to Talia could involve extensive explanations and backtracking. Grady borrowed her typewriter again and answered the day's mail quickly and efficiently. Yes, Plimstubb could build a conveyor furnace that would heat rivets in a reducing atmosphere (nitrogen and hydrogen) and drop them quickly into an oil quench for hardening. No, Grady couldn't guarantee that the oil would not catch fire, but Plimstubb would tell the customer how to minimize the hazard. He sketched a cross section for the letter, of a bucket of oil, a long-handled screen basket to catch the parts as they dropped into the oil, and a safety nitrogen line to purge the air out of the bucket if it should catch on fire. As an afterthought, he put an extended, insulated handle on the buckettop so the workers could shut the bucket and smother the fire that way.

Yes, Plimstubb could provide a dissociated ammonia generator that would heat ammonia past 1,650 degrees Fahrenheit and "crack" NH_3 into three parts hydrogen to one part nitrogen. Yes, for an additional fee Plimstubb would provide a gas dryer that used a catalyst to pull water out of gas before it was used for heat treating. No, neither unit needed excessive electrical power. (He then more forthrightly added the power requirements, after planting the idea that it was not excessive.)

Yes (Grady wrote more hesitantly), Plimstubb was willing to bid on contracts involving metalwork for unbreakable shields. This would involve a batch tempering furnace and would process two to four shields hung vertically, parallel to each other (see sketch) below a convection fan. No, Plimstubb did not itself inscribe the Runes of Power, nor did it guarantee complete invulnerability to users due to constant technological innovation in the field of warfare. (Grady toyed with drawing a warrior stepping on a land mine but wisely decided that it was bad for sales.) However, Plimstubb had engaged a trustworthy business partner who would write the guarantee and its limits for that particular process and its applications.

He reviewed three letters, winced and retyped one, and signed and mailed them, keeping the carbons for his files. Afterward, curious about what Talia had said earlier, he went back to the shop.

He had wanted to ask Antony if he'd seen anything unusual, but Antony was nowhere around. Joe Cataldo said, "Roy found something special for him, garbage detail," and walked away shaking his head.

Grady, by himself, inspected the shop. The windows were clean, the floor well swept. Grady was pleased that it looked orderly, busy, and completely ordinary.

A voice behind him said loudly, "Are you praying?"

He turned. "No, just thinking how good it is to see the place busy and—Benny?"

Benny Behind was wearing a tie. He was sober, his hair was combed, and he smelled faintly of aftershave.

Benny nodded piously to Grady. "God be with you. Heaven keep you from your wicked habits, which include gambling on sports, drinking beer and spirits, a strong lust for women . . ." He continued with a level of detail that Grady felt was overly zealous.

"God does his best, Benny." Grady searched for a single familiar topic of conversation with the Benny Behind that he knew and finally said awkwardly, "You know, the last time I spoke to you, your entire attitude about sin was more liberal."

"Hallelujah!" Benny shouted fervently. "I thank my God that He has seen fit to cleanse me of my evil ways, spawned"—he glanced around furtively—"in this hellhole of a factory." He added more naturally, "I mean, I always thought I worked in a hellhole, but this was divine proof, I ain't shittin'. Excuse me, I ain't lyin'."

" 'Divine proof'?" Grady was still trying to adjust to a pious Benny Blaws. "By the way, what's that red mark on your cheek?"

"The mark of a scarlet woman," Benny Behind said darkly. "I told Betty Quist about the judgment awaiting her for her sins—maybe I shouldn't have made some guesses about what her sins were—and she slapped me. Tough woman," he said admiringly, "but my point is made. Look at how nervous she is, how jumpy she's become. She knows, all right."

Benny dropped his voice as though afraid of being overheard. "There are demons in this plant. Wicked, hell-spawn on creaking legs, crawling under the workbenches of sinners."

Grady tried to understand. "Are you talking about electric snakes?"

"No, no. What are you, crazy?" Benny looked at him scornfully. "Who the hell ever heard of electric snakes?" He added, "No, these are like mechanical rats. But they're demons, all right. They seek our downfall. I want to please them," he said inconsistently. "No, wait. I want to purge them."

"Castor oil might work," Hammer Houlihan said solemnly. He was wiping his hands on a formerly red rag.

"Godless heathen!" Benny bellowed. "Look at you and Grady, wallowing in your sinful Irish ways."

Grady wondered absently what sinful Irish ways he and Hammer Houlihan shared.

Houlihan turned bright purple, but Benny was already walking away, nose in the air, shouting about the wicked and probably drunken panhandler who had been mooching in front of Plimstubb lately.

Grady watched him go. "You know, I think I liked him better when he was walking around picking fights and dropping his pants."

"I know I did," Hammer grunted. "I'd rather trade punches with him than sing psalms with him."

"Amen. Hammer, do you feel as though everybody around here who was the least bit screwy just keeps getting screwier?"

Hammer Houlihan regarded him sourly. "Is it a contest? Because your girlfriend is pulling up on the outside, with only a couple of lengths between her and Benny Behind going into the straightaway."

"She's not my girlfriend."

"Maybe she's not as crazy as I thought." He shook his head. "She's pushing on her little pet project, though, and your SOB—"

"Who?"

"Sweet Old Boss. Hastings. He's going to take her in hand if she keeps it up." He grinned, not kindly. "If I were her, I'd keep away from those hands."

Grady was at her desk moments later. "Did you have a fight with Warren Hastings?"

She sniffed. "Not much of one. He has some kind of project going overseas—"

"For Mr. Fahdi and Mr. Faroukh, yes."

"Well, it's not a wartime project, and he pulled workers away from the furnace for Stode. So I made them go back."

Grady's head was swimming. "You can't."

She smiled triumphantly. "I did. And when Warren tried to take them back, I told him that furnace was more important than any of his pet projects."

"You *what?* Susan, he's a vice president here."

"He's a lot of things." But she avoided his eyes. "That furnace is more important."

"You don't know that."

"I'll bet on it." She looked up now. "You're a betting man. Want to take that one against me?"

Long ago, Grady had been warned never to bet against someone who knows more about the bet than you do. He shook his head and wandered away through Engineering.

Tom Garneaux, for once, was bent studiously over his desk. Grady hurried forward silently, and was rewarded when Garneaux hastily covered thermal calculations for brick insulation with the sports page describing (and assessing odds for) the coming weekend's boxing matches.

Grady said, "Why is it so embarrassing to admit you do work for Plimstubb?"

Garneaux said evasively, "Who said I admitted I did work here?"

There were a couple of hours of the workday left. Grady shrugged and went to the files for blueprints.

The drawers had been rearranged again, with a folder of new prints in place of the ones for Stode's furnace. Grady leafed through them, completely confused.

A second later, Tom Garneaux was leaning over him, saying, "Are you okay, kid?"

Grady shook his head. "Sorry. I must be seeing things." He glanced down. "Nope, I'm not. What are these, anyway?"

"Say, look at that." Garneaux turned the prints one by one: footprint, framework, wiring, hydrogen piping, master bill of materials. "I wonder how Plimstubb got a set of these."

"Set of what?"

"Prints for the Hindenburg. Look at this." With distaste he held out a pencil rendering of a landing complete with a German flag, its swastika waving proudly. "Look at how sharp the drawing is, though. It's like it was done by a machine."

Grady looked at the next print in the folder: the zeppelin in flames, tiny figures plummeting out of it to their deaths at the bottom of the print. It was a pencil sketch as well, but it reminded Grady uneasily of the Elf-Gnome Assisted Design prints, the EGAD drawings on which tiny figures built the equipment represented by the drawing.

In these prints, not just the design but also the tragedy was planned.

"I wonder why we have these," Garneaux said thoughtfully. "Did we supply parts before the war, or maybe a furnace to temper the girders? Can't be. I was here then. Wow, just the thought makes you sick."

"You bet," Grady said weakly. He looked at the other prints in the folder. There were beautiful, detailed pencil renderings of the framework for the *Titanic*. Behind that was a layout sketch and bill of materials for an iceberg. "Listen, help me close this folder, will you? I'd lift it myself but . . ." he gestured feebly with his cane.

"Glad to." Garneaux lifted the heavy folder back into the cabinet. "Beats me why we store junk like this. Maybe after the war it'll be worth something."

"Maybe." Grady wandered back to his office and, eventually, home. He made a note that said, "Check rest of prints and find sources," but he hoped he could put it off until he had spoken to Antony. He also wanted to ask Antony about strange goings-on in the shop.

Grady had forgotten that it was Friday; Antony had driven back to the Dwarfworks after work. That night Grady missed him mightily. Grady called Susan and spoke about a range of foolish topics (Bogart vs. Edward G. Robinson; *Detective Comics* and the Batman; whether advances in aircraft engines would benefit Ford and General Motors and the rest at all), but finally Susan asked pointedly, "Is something bothering you?"

"Me?" he said, astonished. "No. Not at all. Why, should something be?"

She hung up, and he went to bed. He dreamed of tiny figures, screaming and burning, falling from the dirigible over Lakehurst, New Jersey, and splashing somehow into the frigid waters off Newfoundland.

NINE

ANTONY STRETCHED IN the summer sun and said thoughtfully, "When this war is over, the only thing the same about airplanes will be the sky."

Grady said, "The same as what?" He was half asleep. They were lying in the Catskills, near the Dwarfworks, waiting for one of Antony's customers. Grady had agreed to come along in case he was needed, though Antony was getting much better at modern metalwork.

Just now, Antony was staring off over the hills, not looking at anything but the clouds and the birds wheeling under them. "Oh, you know. The new planes aren't the same as the Neuports and Spads and Sopwith Camels and Fokker Triplanes—Sacred Sun, but I loved seeing those, bigger than anything I was ever going to fly, and still they had more lift than anything I was ever going to take up. And before that, the Bleriot monoplanes, lighter than a dragonfly, and we all laughed at the idea that a plane could fly with just one wing."

He shook his head. "And they were made out of cloth and glue and wire and bamboo, and here we are with you trying to find new alloys that can fly, like new lamps for old. Kiddo, the other thing wars do besides change

borders and kill people is that they teach skills at an
amazing rate. And you look at the fighter planes out
there, and the Flying Fortresses and the German Junkers
88s, and you wonder: What's going to come of all this
learning? Are we going to fly the Pacific commercially
without seaplanes? Are we going to fly higher than anybody ever did, or faster, or farther? Is there anything in
the world that can hold us back?"

Grady read science fiction regularly. He thought about
people going to the moon and back on a regular basis.
He had never considered anything between the present
and spaceships.

Finally he said awkwardly, "I'm busy with the war. I
don't have time to think about where all these things
will go."

"You don't," Antony agreed. "Not to harp on it, but
that's always the argument, isn't it?"

This annoyed Grady no end. Antony's people each
had several centuries more time than the average human.
He said sharply, "We all do what we can. Sometimes
that means we underestimate the long-term risk of what
we're doing, even while we worry about it." He finished,
"So, do you figure you know more than *Popular Science*
about how all these plans will change history in the next
sixty years?"

Antony laughed and shook his head. "Kid, I've told
you what it was like to be in an airfield when it was
bombed—one of the first wartime bombings from an
airplane by anybody on earth. What I didn't tell you was
that when we talked it over afterward we weren't sure
what it meant from there. Were we still going to do
mostly reconnaissance? Were we just going up to shoot
down other planes, or was there a way to fight against
ground troops from the air? A lot of guys had ideas, but
most of us thought it wouldn't change the Great War
one way or another, and it wouldn't be more than a
novelty.

"But there was a flier, a tall, skinny guy named Sigurdsen from Taopi, Minnesota. Sig—hell, I never learned his real first name—spent half his time staring at things. Sometimes he'd stare at a motor, sometimes at landing gear, sometimes a propeller. Lots of times he'd look around the field and sit on a barrel and stare into the sky, mouth half open and his big buck teeth showing." Antony sighed. "I bet if he'd looked smarter we wouldn't have laughed so much at the stuff he said."

Grady nodded. Learning to listen was a big part of sales and, he suspected, a big part of everything else. "What did he say?"

"Crazy stuff about things he bet we could do if we wanted. Landing planes on boats. Planes with special doors in the bottom, for dropping bombs. Machine guns mounted inside airplane wings, so you could dive down and shoot at the ground. We laughed like idiots." Antony shook his head. "Of course, within twenty years they quit laughing at that one in Poland."

"And a few other places. What else did he say?"

Antony chuckled. "One night near the end of the war he got together with us at a sidewalk café. We had some wine, but he didn't drink. He just stood there dancing from foot to foot, too excited to sit down. He said, 'Ya know, Dutch, I want you and Curly to sign onto a project of mine.'

"We asked, 'What project?' and it hit the fan. He was waving his arms, talking a mile a minute. He stood in front of us looking like a scarecrow who'd enlisted, spilling all these crummy-looking sheets of paper out of his pocket like it was his stuffing, and unfolding them while he talked. Seems he'd been writing somebody back in the States—he talked about that, too, and how mail would be carried by air overseas someday—"

"He sounds pretty smart."

Antony snorted. "You say that now, but you didn't watch him moving like bad burlesque, leaping from idea to idea like Tarzan. Anyway, he was trying to grab every pilot he could, figuring that the ones who were alive after the war would be good investments. And he made us read a couple of the letters back from his investor, and it could make you sick how eager he was to believe this guy. His letters sounded just as crazy as Sig did.

"So finally Curly puts a hand on his shoulder and says, 'Sig, it's not you. It's just that we don't see any kind of future for this Mr. Hughes and his aircraft company.' "

Grady's mouth dropped wide open. "Hughes Aircraft?" Antony nodded. "So how much money do you figure you threw away?"

"No idea. More than I made working for Pieter, or Curly made working for Uncle Sam, that's sure." Antony was smiling. "I'll bet you don't get what I learned from that."

"Never to pass up an opportunity?"

"Nope. Never to be sure something isn't an opportunity. Listen carefully to people with crazy ideas." He sighed. "The other thing I learned is the reason I like magic. It's so much safer than science and technology.' "

Grady thought of the things he'd seen and some of the living things he'd fought. "Safer?"

"Safer. Science is unpredictable, because we just keep learning it. Magic mostly stays the same."

He stood up, brushing himself off. "Enough guest lectures. Kid, we've got another customer to meet. You'll like these guys; they're in the war. On our side." Antony sounded oddly depressed about that. He turned and walked back into the Dwarfworks.

Grady, his mind full of the new ideas Antony had just given him, followed slowly. "Are they driving in?"

"Oh, no." Antony looked up at the sky, ducking as though there had recently been lightning. "They always come in by air."

From the field ahead they heard a roar and a screech,

followed by a rumbling as loud as any locomotive. Grady, with visions of a crash, said, "Oh, Jesus," and thumped his cane against the rocks and moss, dropping down the hill at double time.

Antony said softly to himself, "When you've seen enough bad landings . . ." He walked down easily.

The plane was smoking but still in one piece. Something about the design looked odd to Grady, as though it were a plane constructed for a Bugs Bunny cartoon. The motor roared unceasingly.

The plane had come to a stop near a sagging barn with sliding double doors at the front. As the visitors climbed from the plane, Antony smiled and casually moved between them and the barn doors.

The visitors were dressed in khaki with no insignia on it. They wore leather flight jackets that had every conceivable burn, scrape, slash, and stain worked into them. Under the jacket they each wore a Sam Browne belt, but the holster had a wrench in it.

They were twenty inches high if you ignored their ears. It was impossible to ignore their ears, which stuck up like a rabbit's but ended in tufted points. Their hands ended in long, nimble fingers that were stained with at least three kinds of grease and oil. In other respects they looked like humans.

There was a single-engine plane, or something like one, lurking in the smoke of machine oil behind them.

One of the little figures strode forward and shouted, "You're from the Dwarfworks, aren't you?" The voice was startlingly high to Grady; he hadn't expected a woman. She wiped her hand on her greasy trousers. "I'm Fifinella."

"And I'm Dingbelle," called the other one. She looked up curiously, ignoring the smoking landing gear she had been tinkering with. "Anyway, you're from the Dwarfworks?"

"Grady Cavanaugh." He saw their confusion and added awkwardly, "From Rhode Island, but I'm in a partnership with the Dwarfworks." He gestured. "This is their representative, Antony van der Woeden."

"Nice engine," Antony roared, his voice sounding deafening as the engine coughed and died abruptly.

"Thanks." Dingbelle smacked it with a wrench and it thundered to life again. This time she leaped up to the cockpit and shut it down the normal way. "Rolls-Royce makes them."

"And this plane got you here in one piece?"

"Not always," Dingbelle said vaguely, then: "Oh, you mean did we stay in one piece, don't you? Of course we did."

"So, what do you need?"

Fifinella dashed back into the plane and hopped out, grunting under the weight of a box. "Can you help us?"

Grady stared down into the box. It was nothing but mangled metal, scored with gashes and dimpled with the dents of crashes and abuse.

Antony, peering in on tiptoe, said noncommittally, "It would be good if you could tell us what each of these pieces used to be."

Fifinella's ears drooped. "I'm not sure I can." The tufts perked up as she said hopefully, "How about if I gave you a list of the pieces we're missing and you matched them up?"

"We'll do our best." Antony looked over the plane, trying not to blanch at the combat marks and the obvious mismatchings of panels and parts. "Hell of a machine," he said flatly. "Looks like it would have a lot of drag."

"Not a problem, with this motor." Fifinella patted it affectionately. "Rolls-Royce."

Antony nodded. "Sounds good. Supercharged?"

"Of course. It gives it a greater service ceiling." Dingbelle twitched an ear. "Though we don't push it. One high-altitude stall is enough, even for us."

Antony was silently impressed. Anything that scared a gremlin scared the living hell out of him. "What about the rate of roll?"

Dingbelle nodded. "Good question. We cut down on maneuverability in favor of payload and range. She's a slow plane." She patted the plane's side. "Still, we can put her through her paces. You should see her do an Immelmann—"

"I'll be damned." Antony was genuinely delighted. "Like Max Immelmann, right? I saw him once, during the Great War. He made everything I was trying to do look easy. So, you do dogfight maneuvers?"

"Once in a while," Fifinella said noncommittally. "To be honest, that's why the parts box we gave you is so full."

"Right, sure." Antony frowned, looking down at the box. At one glance he knew that metal fatigue was a problem. So was impact, and so was fire. "How about if you come back in four days and we give you repaired parts?"

Grady wanted desperately to ask Antony if that were possible. Clearly, a sales partnership had its awkward moments.

"Four days?" Dingbelle said dazedly, and then more firmly, "If that's what it takes, that's fine." She turned to Fifinella. "Any plans to fill the waiting time?"

"No idea," Fifinella said positively. She brightened and turned to Grady. "Do you want to go up?"

"Up?" Grady looked blank. Dingbelle and Fifinella looked pityingly at him, then at their airplane. He said hastily, "Oh. Up."

Antony said quickly, "You know, that's an offer any of us would love to take up—and believe me, I've flown and I know what it's like—but, you know, forges, molds, castings, wax models, irons in the fire . . ." he laughed in a way he hoped was polite and discouraging at the same time.

They sagged. Fifinella said formally but sadly, "We know."

"I don't," Grady said.

Dingbelle turned to him. "You don't what?"

"Know." Now they were both looking at him. "What it's like. To fly."

Antony nudged Grady. Grady nudged him back.

Fifinella, eyes wide, said earnestly, "You don't?"

"Nope."

Antony kicked Grady. Grady kicked him back.

Dingbelle looked hopeful. "Would you like to come up with us?"

Grady said, "Sure, I'll go."

To Antony he said, "Change is good for me, and I'm not afraid."

Antony hissed back, "These guys will never change, and you should be vomiting into your socks."

Grady climbed in, grateful that there was room for him. Actually, there were also a good three feet between the landing gear and the runway. He had to hook his cane on the door's edge, pull himself up with both hands, and leap up from his good leg. He landed kneeling on his other leg and used his cane to stand, staring at his surroundings.

They were worth staring at, he realized uneasily. The cockpit had four windows of varying sizes. The seats were three different heights, and the leather cushions didn't match. Now that he was inside, he could see that the floor listed to the left; the front landing gears were different heights. He squinted out the porthole on the right and the window on the left; the left wing was longer.

Dingbelle popped up beside him. "We call her Auger I," she said desperately. "Like her?"

"Of course." He swallowed. "Never seen one like her."

"Never will," Fifinella said firmly. "The tail is a Spit-fire—"

Dingbelle pointed this way and that. "The hydraulics are from a Mustang—"

"The gas tank and fuel lines are from a Flying For-tress—"

"The controls are from a PBY, plus a P-38 with the double fuselage and a couple of other strays we picked up along the way."

Grady searched desperately for something compli-mentary to say and finally said weakly, "You two never throw anything out, do you?"

Dingbelle looked suddenly depressed. "I wouldn't say that."

"We try our best," Fifinella said sadly. "Our bit for the war."

"But you can't keep everything when you fly."

Grady was feeling less and less happy. "Why not?"

"Things fall off," Dingbelle said vaguely and unreas-suringly. Before Grady could pursue the topic, she snatched one of a pair of enormous wrenches and threw it to Fifinella. "Drill!"

"Got it." Fifinella pulled the other wrench free and threw it to Dingbelle. "Glory time!"

"Let's go." The two of them dashed past Grady in the ramshackle fuselage, barely avoiding knee-capping him.

Dingbelle leaped to one wall and hung by the wrench, which was now clamped onto a hexagonal bolthead. "Wing strut support, A-7 hex."

"Check! Fuel line clamp for leaky place."

"Check! Wing nut for loose landing gear lock."

"Check! Spar nuts one through five."

"Check! Seven-inch threaded thingy that doesn't seem to do anything, but we're scared to throw it out or leave it loose."

"Check!"

The two of them scrambled up and down the plane

like Harpo and Chico Marx, tightening bolts apparently at random.

Grady watched, swallowing. "Say, ladies, do you have to do that every time you fly?"

"We don't have to," Fifinella said thoughtfully, slamming a side panel back in place.

"But it's so much better when we do," Dingbelle finished, grunting as she tugged on a truly huge nut that was squeezing a sagging strut against the ceiling.

Grady stood helplessly as the two gremlins scampered through the entire plane, calling numbers and shouting "Check!" apparently without listening to each other. Finally the two of them leaped back to the front of the plane, slapped the wrenches into their holders, shook hands, shouted, "Keep 'em flying!" and collapsed, panting, into their chairs.

Something was nagging at Grady. "Don't you do any kind of preflight check?"

Dingbelle looked astonished. "That was it." She pressed a button on the control panel, tugged on a hanging canvas strap hooked to a brass chain, and the propeller ahead of them circled around slowly before picking up speed.

Auger I rolled out on the runway, rumbling oddly. The tires actually left the runway periodically from the vibrations of the oversized engine.

Grady, startled by the level of vibration but determined not to look afraid, waved to Antony. As Grady pulled his arm back, he crossed himself surreptitiously.

Antony, worried desperately for Grady but also cravenly terrified of what Kirsten would do to him if she ever found out, waved back.

Auger I didn't so much lift off the grass as veer upward away from it. Antony stared helplessly after the plane.

•   •   •

Grady said a quick act of contrition, the words sticking in his throat for a second. He crossed himself again and looked out one of the square windows, fascinated. There were fields below him, and telephone poles, and houses, and suddenly the Hudson River like a twisting gray snake . . .

He had lived his entire life from the ground, and for the first time he felt as though he were seeing what God saw when He woke up in the morning.

A crosswind woke him to the present as it threw him across the plane. He looked to the rear, where there was a door intended for paratroopers, right down to the guide wire for automatic deployment of chutes. He realized uncomfortably that he didn't have a parachute, let alone know how to use one.

A sudden dive threw him back to the front of the plane. Once there, Grady clutched his seat and stray brackets on the interior of the fuselage. "So you've done this a lot before?" he shouted for reassurance.

"My specialty was bombsights," Fifinella bellowed proudly. "I sat with the bombardiers."

"On real bombing runs? In Europe?" Grady was impressed.

"Oh, yes." Dingbelle nodded earnestly. "I would have been eligible for the Distinguished Flying Cross."

"And the Victoria Cross," Fifinella reminded her.

Dingbelle nodded. "We only came back here at the express orders of Ike—of General Eisenhower."

"Wow." Grady felt guilty; he hadn't thought this job that important. "He sent you after the fall of Berlin, right?"

"Actually, before." The tips of Fifinella's ears drooped slightly. "I can't imagine why he'd do that. Other generals sent us into the action."

"There was Monty," Dingbelle volunteered. "Montgomery, remember? The RAF sent us to join him. He sent us to join Patton in Sicily."

Now Grady was hopelessly confused. It had been said that the British general didn't like Patton.

"And we stayed with Patton right into Scotland, and after that little problem with the airfields—"

"Problem with the airfields," Grady murmured with a sudden chill.

"That could have happened to anybody," Fifinella said firmly. "And the fire was out long before the Germans would have noticed. But then he sent us to Eisenhower—"

"Back in London." Dingbelle sighed loudly and happily. "Just like our days with the RAF."

"You two get around."

"That's not the half of it." Dingbelle waved an arm, grabbing for her chair as the plane reeled with the gesture. "We've done maintenance, fueling, field weather reports, reconnaissance—if the boys in the air need it, we've volunteered." She giggled. "I'm not even supposed to be flying."

Grady froze. "And why is that?"

"My initial assignment was as a sorter in a mail corps for Wids—a women's division, from Canada." She shrugged angrily. "But somebody who was a senior officer wrote letters to two boyfriends at once, and it's easy to sort these things backward, and somebody decided to transfer me."

"To something involving airplanes," Grady said in confusion.

"Of course. The British Commonwealth Air Training Plan. They sent me to join Her Majesty's aircrews." She brightened. "That's how I hooked up with Fifinella, who was already in the RAF."

Grady turned to her. "You said you helped the bombardiers. How, exactly?"

"I made sure their concentration didn't slip," she said proudly. "I nudged them just before they dropped the bombs if they were leaning over their bombsights too long."

Grady wondered, uncharitably, where he and Antony might send the gremlins next.

The engine changed pitch. Grady looked down and had the unnerving feeling he was looking at sky. "Where'd the earth go?"

"You mean the land." Dingbelle was grinning. "We're over the sea, headed north. Don't worry; there's not a plane on the coast that can catch up with us."

Grady tried to find this reassuring. "Where are we going?"

"You said you're from Rhode Island, right?" Dingbelle didn't wait for confirmation. "You have to see this."

She tilted the nose of the plane down. Grady stared down through the glass, not certain what all that blue-green was in the sky.

Then he recognized it, and his world spun around as he reoriented himself. "That's the Atlantic," he said uncertainly.

"Of course not," Fifinella sniffed. "That's Narragansett Bay, in Rhode Island."

"You're kidding." He stared eagerly forward, seeing what looked like emerald waters set with forested islands and rings of stones. "My God, it's beautiful. That's the bay?" He could see the green of trees on the islands, and now he could see brown rings of sand and rocks at the edges of the islands. It was low tide.

For one frozen moment he saw everything he had taken for granted and driven around his whole life: every rock, every inlet, every beach. It was all one, a single necklace of the jewels that made up Narragansett Bay.

Fifinella pointed. "That's Prudence Island. That's Patience Island." Fifinella added quickly as the engine groaned, "And those little ones are the Dumplings—

Jesus. The Dumplings? Grady clutched his seat and stared straight down at a group of rocks, none of them

larger than a good-sized front lawn. He watched them
grow until he was afraid he could see every boulder that
would smash through his flesh, every stick of driftwood
that would impale him, every mussel and barnacle that
would slash him, and he practically screeched, "Pull up.
Pull back on the stick and pull up. Pull up."

Spray reached toward the cockpit, and Grady swore
he could smell salt. "Pull *up*."

He slammed into his seat as the airplane arced westward suddenly. Metal screamed somewhere in the belly
of the plane, and Grady felt a shudder tug at the entire
plane. He had a brief and dizzying view of the amusement park at Rocky Point, T. F. Green Airport, and a
mass of trees that grew into rolling hills and, terribly
quickly, the Appalachian Mountains. It would have been
easier to assess the oncoming green terrain if he hadn't
been sure that at any minute he would spiral effortlessly
into the rippling landscape below.

"There you are." Dingbelle beamed at him. "Nearly
back to New York already." She thumped the control
panel, and a couple of dials fell out, dangling by red and
green wires. She thumped them back into place hastily.
"You'll never have a ride like this again."

"Never," Grady said fervently. "Are we back at the
Dwarfworks already?" Metal screamed again—and this
time he knew it was in the neighborhood of the wings.

"Too soon," Fifinella said sadly.

Dingbelle said through clenched teeth, "Way too
soon. Hang on." Rivets popped out of the fuselage, and
the plane dropped like a suicidal stone.

Grady said his second act of contrition in an hour as
the plane turned its landing gear toward the sun. Light
seemed to blaze through every window at once, shining
off all the exposed copper and steel; Grady, briefly and
incongruously, thought of Icarus and Daedalus.

The ground leaped at them and then lurched back, as

though this flight had nothing to do with the real paths
of airplanes. Dingbelle said in warning, "Not my best
landing—"

Fifinella said sharply, "Not your worst, right?"

Dingbelle was genuinely hurt. "No flames, no screaming, no dead. What do you think?"

Grady reflected that he couldn't scream if he were
dead. He hung on tightly.

The plane did a final barrel roll, rose, stalled, dove,
and, with heartbreaking slowness, pulled out of the dive
to lift a scant ten feet above the meadow and stop dead
in the air, its forward momentum miraculously spent.
Then it dropped in a bone-jarring pancake landing that
left both wings sagging and sprayed glass in all directions from the cockpit.

Fifinella hopped from the shattered cockpit and said
happily, "You see? No matter how high you fly, you
know you'll always come down."

Dingbelle followed her. "Beats a belly landing. How
did we do it?"

Fifinella frowned. "Ground effect partly. Extra lift
when we got close. The question is . . ." She stopped,
completely stumped. Despite the gremlins' vast experience at crashing planes, apparently she didn't know what
the question was.

Grady crawled out of the plane, hesitating but decid-
ing not to kiss the ground. He looked back resentfully
at *Auger I* and asked, panting, "Why did we slow
down?"

Fifinella shrugged. Dingbelle scratched her head.
"Beats me," she said frankly. She walked down the bat-
tered side of the plane like a fly and poked at the wings.
"Bingo," she said happily. "Aileron flaps froze down.
Malfunction. Same thing happened to us in a B-17 over
the Rhône."

"Don't smile." Fifinella rocked a barely attached flap
to and fro. "I thought we had this licked. We checked

the pins, the airstream, the potential metal fatigue . . ."

Their eyes lit up, disturbingly like the glow in the gnomes' eyes, and they shouted in unison, "The hydraulics!"

Dingbelle shook Grady's hand fervently. "Thanks so for the solving the problem with us. Wait till you see what this plane does next time. It could win the war in the Pacific all by itself."

Their good-byes were brief. The gremlins were eager to go win the war.

Grady, thinking suddenly of his father, said, "Did you stop by Lockheed yet?"

Dingbelle said in confusion, "Lockheed?"

"Sure, Lockheed." He took a deep breath and brought to bear everything he knew about sales. "Think of all the flying time you've put in, all the experience they could benefit from. You know how to do a redesign of your plane. They designed the P-38 and God knows how many other planes." He spread his hands. "Can you really deny them your expertise and say you hope to bring a quick end to the war? You should go into some kind of project management instead of field flying."

There was a brief pause before Fifinella leaped up and hugged him, nearly breaking his collarbone. "Thank you! Thank you! You're absolutely right!"

Dingbelle added firmly, "Lockheed needs us." She hugged Grady herself, then straightened up. "Ship us our repaired parts. It's time for us to go create a plane and win the war."

After fifteen minutes of repairs, they leaped into *Auger I* and started the motor. Miraculously, the wings stayed on. The plane taxied across the grass, holding together over every bump even though the wings flapped visibly.

Grady and Antony waved as *Auger I* left the ground— grudgingly—and wobbled westward.

Antony said dubiously, "Kid, someday you may regret

suggesting they become project managers."

Grady shook his head. "Gremlins. Can you imagine thinking one piece of technology could win the war?"

He stopped. Antony was looking at him strangely. "I don't think you were listening today," Antony said slowly.

"Which time?"

"When I talked about magic and science. Science does things you can't expect." He waved his arms. "It's new. It changes things. That makes it a lot crazier than magic is."

"I don't think you believe that," Grady said slowly. "For instance, you know a lot about airplane technology."

Antony shrugged. "Back when I flew, you tried to know everything you could."

Grady said it like an accusation: "You know a lot about current technology."

Antony said neutrally, "It's an area where I've tried to keep up."

"Sure." He struggled with the question. "But once you know what's going on, what do you do with the knowledge? It's not like you used it to modernize the Dwarfworks."

Antony said easily, "Oh, I don't know. I brought you in, didn't I?"

Grady gave up. He wasn't the sort of person who kept secrets from anyone, but the war and a few other things had taught him that, sometimes, you had to accept that friends had secrets.

He had a nice dinner at the Dwarfworks and stayed long enough afterward to be part of a singing game with the children. He hugged Katrina, kissed Kirsten, shook hands with Sonny LeTour and Pieter, winked at Antony, and left. Antony walked him to his car. Watching Grady's taillights disappear, Antony felt suddenly, deeply guilty for the things he had hidden and the questions he had avoided answering fully.

For now he looked up at the stars. They didn't accuse him, and they didn't make anything clear. Long ago, during the Great War, Antony had known a Gypsy who truly could read the stars and tell the future. He wished the Gypsy were here now.

But the stars were silent or indifferent. Antony went to bed worried, confused, and ashamed of his silence to a good friend.

TEN

I T WAS ANOTHER warm summer day and another vig-
orous fencing lesson with Susan before work.

Grady could barely get her to slow down and practice
footwork. She was a quick learner, and passionate in
learning fencing as she was in all things—Grady assumed, at least, in all things—but he couldn't always be
sure that she was paying enough attention to form. He
would walk her up and down the parking lot, palms
touching, while he used his cane to make up for his lack
of balance and still tried to push her beyond her capacity
to move forward and suddenly shift backward, or to double advance and suddenly lunge.

She tossed her head when she felt she had done badly,
and smiled with all her teeth showing when she felt she
was closing in for the kill. Grady said in a helpless litany
every morning, "Remember that control is more important than anger."

"I'm not angry," she snarled, and lunged at him, her
upper torso forward and off-balance.

Grady sighed and parried, barely tapping his foil into
her exposed rib cage. He stumbled to one side, catching
himself on his cane. "Honest, I don't do it to make you

look dumb. You're not interested in winning, or in keeping balance so that you can plan three or four moves ahead. You just want to kill someone, don't you?"

"Thanks, Dr. Freud," she said brightly. "Now I feel much better. I bet I'll quit staring at smokestacks and naval guns."

"Okay," he said flatly. "Let's quit for the morning."

She looked suddenly contrite, and hesitated. In the end, though, she said nothing and left. Grady watched her go, wondering how he could love someone so unyielding and angry so very much. It was like falling in love with someone involved in a medieval Italian vendetta.

Actually, so was coming to work at Plimstubb. Grady had always thought that modernizing would never look so medieval. Instead, it seemed to involve watching ogres and golems, and it seemed that the plant was full of imps and poltergeists.

He had seen the future in illustrations on magazine covers, and in black-and-white on the title pages inside. Sleek, rounded towers reached out of the earth, looking in illustrations remarkably like the Calart Flowers Building on Reservoir Avenue, all concrete and streamlined. Above the buildings, needle-shaped spaceships dashed to far corners of the galaxy and easily solved inconceivable problems. In between, the captains—almost never the crew members—fell in love.

The problems involved aliens, attacks, and outside threats—things that Grady, reading about the war in the Pacific, could readily translate into modern terms. The solutions involved science, intuitive leaps, and frantic execution to create weapons, ships, or energy drives. Grady, looking at the piles of industrial proposals on his desk, fervently wished for instant, leap-of-intellect, modern solutions.

Instead he spent his time typing to Curtiss-Wright,

Thomson, Hughes, and Pratt & Whitney. No one seemed to know, or was willing to say, exactly what parts they wanted heated. No one seemed to understand that delivery times were dependent, in Rhode Island, on the movements of troop trains on the East Coast. Everyone remembered that the highest priority rating meant that their equipment was built and delivered first. The projects all lay half assembled for all but the last five days, and the projects always looked like scrap.

The notion of priorities always inspired him to check on Drake Stode's furnace. Stode had been unwilling to discuss his first contract with Plimstubb—unwilling, in fact, to discuss anything about the ultimate use of the furnace—but the War Department had agreed to divert all troop trains on the East Coast on the day that Stode's first project from Plimstubb had been ready for delivery. That said a lot more than enough.

He checked out on the floor and was pleased. The sheet metal shell of the heating chamber was ready. The stainless steel, jacketed cooling sections were ready, right down to the incoming pipelines for water and the outgoing, cup-shaped open sight drain for exiting warm water. The transformers lay near the project, and the curlicued ribbon heating elements, lying on their sides on Benny Behind's workbench, were all ready and had connection terminals welded onto their ends. He glanced around with satisfaction, pleased at how close the project was to completion. You could tell from the noise level: Most of the work was happening at the other end of the shop, where there was still welding and grinding. The only noise at this end was an occasional chirp from cooling metal at a workbench left deserted.

It was four-thirty; 90 percent of the shop had gone home. He turned and walked down the center aisle of the shop, where forklifts rolled back and forth on mostly unnameable errands, their front tines extended at the front of the head like walrus fangs.

There was another chirp from the near corner of the shop.

Grady had been listening for it this time, trying desperately to pinpoint the sound.

He thumped forward with his cane, for once unembarrassed by the sound it made and trying to use it to get a sense of the echoes of the place.

Something skittered away from the base of the cane. (Demons? Mechanical rats?)

It was still near the longest day of the year, and anyway, Grady was far from afraid of the dark. He put his cane forward again and started walking, confident in the other people in the shop and in the notion that people, no matter how frightened, just didn't die this way.

He walked slowly and steadily past a control panel in assembly. The multicolored wires hung free in the afternoon light. Below them lay the power wiring, and Grady heard a slow, heavy slither near the base of his cane. (Electric snakes?) The slithering moved in parallel to him.

From below one of the furnaces came a ratcheting, clicking noise. Grady stopped and swung his cane toward it, looking around the plant. Flash, welding mask over his face, was bent over a workbench at the far end of the plant, facing away from him. Betty was looking his way but was preoccupied with carefully feeding metal plates into the brake shear. Hammer Houlihan was waving his arms, bragging to someone else in the shop. From the gestures involved, he might have been describing a salami but probably wasn't.

If he screamed now, they might all look. If one of them understood, something might happen in time.

Grady took a deep, shuddering breath and stepped forward. Something nudged his cane firmly, trying to dislodge it from the floor. He used his thumb and index finger to twist the cane sideways, thwacking the source of the nudge. There was a rustling sound and, Grady thought, the ghost of a hiss.

A trio of clicking sounds came from under the furnace to his left. Grady spun his cane over and brandished it like a sword, limping forward and ignoring the pain in his bad leg. A skittering sound came from in front of him; Grady thought he saw a shadow. He spun his cane in a tight semicircle and smashed it down at the source of the noise.

There was an offended metallic squeal, and the floor in front of Grady was suddenly clear. He set his cane down and strode forward carefully. No one in the shop had noticed anything. He was two-thirds of the way back to his office.

The next five minutes were an agony of quiet shuffling, cane at the ready. He had no other weapon, but so far at least it was enough. Finally he made it to the hallway that led through the men's room to his office and some of the other front offices. Once he moved into it, he was completely alone. Grady, completely unnerved, set down and picked up his cane as quickly as possible, dashing toward the men's room door and his office on the other side of the rest room.

Behind him he heard the staccato snap of mousetraps, the legacy of diligent maintenance in the face of open garage doors. A number of the traps dropped off the wall on which they had been placed.

He stood, panting, in the bathroom and stared into the mirror over the sink. He had no idea that his eyes could look that big. His dress shirt was drenched.

Afterward, he took a deep breath and opened the doorway to the hall. There were more than a dozen mousetraps on the floor between the shop door and the men's room. All of the traps had been snapped, and they were all empty.

●　　●　　●

When he was calmer, Grady emerged from the rest room and walked out front. As he entered the lobby, Talia rapped on the reception-area glass and hissed in a whisper louder than any that Grady could remember, "THERE ARE MEN WAITING FOR YOU."

They were in overly ironed new suits. One of them was nearly smiling. The other was not quite frowning.

He winked at them and whispered back as loudly as he could, "WHAT DO YOU THINK THEY WANT?"

She hissed fearfully back with all the volume of a steam locomotive, "I DON'T KNOW."

Grady shrugged and went to the lobby.

After the usual handshakes but, Grady noted uneasily, before the traditional exchange of names, one of the men in suits said, "We'd like to talk to you about a story you wrote."

He said hopefully, "You're from *Amazing*, and you're going to buy it?"

He shook his head. "We're not publishers."

They pulled chairs into Grady's office and sat down backward, arms resting on the chair backs. They were between Grady and the door.

The one who had nearly smiled said, "We'd like to know where you get your ideas."

In spite of being nervous, Grady was flattered. "I read a lot—not just science fiction, other things, too." He added, "And listen when people have ideas."

"When who has ideas?"

"People I work with." For a moment he was proud of himself, feeling like a real writer being interviewed by *Time* or *Life*. "For instance, this story I got from—a woman who studied in the sciences. Physics, mostly. She studied with some guy at Columbia and later at the University of Chicago."

The nearly frowning man was actually frowning now. "Did she mention any names? When was this?"

"A couple of years back." Grady thought hard. "And

the guy's name was Italian, something like Firmo. Fermi, right. He studied with a lot of people." His heart went cold for a moment. "Did someone else write this story first?"

The one nearly smiling finally smiled for real. "Kid, you have no idea how many people have already written this story."

That did it. "Listen, I never meant to steal an idea. Susan never said it was anyone else's idea, and she doesn't know about the story. I don't think she'd have let me write the story if it was. Were."

Even the frowning man was starting to smile at the edges. "I'll bet she wouldn't. Listen, kid"—he was maybe ten years older than Grady—"do yourself a favor and pull that story in for the rest of the war." He grinned finally. "You scared hell out of an editor. He thought you were writing a real war story."

Grady gaped at him. "You mean, like something from news? That's ridiculous." He gestured at the manuscript. "I mean, who would believe that?"

"Exactly." The frowning man sighed. "I wish we didn't have to waste time on stuff like this. There's a war on."

"You're telling me." Grady gestured over his shoulder toward the shop floor, even though there was a wall in the way. "We've got a furnace there, scheduled to ship—"

But he shut up, knowing that he shouldn't tell even other government workers about Stode's project—and for a fraction of a second, while he looked at his writings and thought of Susan's lecture and Stode's furnace, he nearly understood what was going on.

But he shut up, because it was unimaginable.

The frowning man handed him a slip of paper. "This is the response from the editor. I said I'd pass it along." He added quietly, "Sorry."

The slip said, "We regret that the story you submitted

to us is not suitable for our needs. Please feel free to
send us other submissions." To Grady's delight, it said
in a title block across the top, identical to the magazine,
Amazing. "That's okay," he said simply. "I'm in sales;
people say 'no' to me a lot."

At the front door to the plant, they said good-bye and
shook hands. "No hard feelings, right?" the smiling one
actually said.

"Of course not." Grady shook their hands enthusiastically. "Do you read a lot of science fiction?"

"I do now," the smiling man said, and his smile wavered.

"I always did," the frowning man said unexpectedly.
"Jules Verne, and H. G. Wells, and Edgar Rice Bur-
roughs' John Carter stories." He added, "Kid, it isn't a
bad first story, but you're gonna have to work harder
than that to get published."

"Do you really think I could get published?" Grady
asked, and finished quickly, "I know, after the war. Listen, can I keep your cards in case I find out something
you need to know about?"

They gave him the cards, but from their amused at-
titudes it was clear that they didn't expect anything ex-
traordinary to come out of Grady or Plimstubb.

After they left, he told Susan the story of their visit,
excitedly building up how important the men were.
"They were G-men. Look at the way they were
dressed—"

Susan said, "They weren't G-men. I'll bet on it."

"How do you figure?" But he pulled out their cards
and looked at the top one. After a moment he passed the
top card to Susan.

The two of them looked at the card: JAMES STEVEN
UNDERHILL.

And, in modest black letters to the lower right: War
Department.

Susan frowned at the card. "You know what? I'd like to read your story."

"You would?" He was dazzled. He'd been afraid to show it to her. "I didn't think you read science fiction."

"I'd like to read it anyway."

He brought it for her. Predictably, she had a cigarette lit already. He hovered, watching her reaction as she read. She scanned down the pages, troubled, and handed it back in silence.

"Well?"

"Well what?"

"What did you think?" He was nearly unable to stand still.

"The science was pretty good," she said slowly. "You got most of what I told you right, and you put it down so it made sense. I guess you learned that from writing sales proposals." She was far away in her own mind, thinking.

Grady, nearly beside himself, said, "And the characters?"

"I didn't recognize anybody." That seemed to make her happy. "The scenes on the squash court were made up, and all that talk about a weapon never happened. I never heard any talk about a weapon," she corrected herself, and she wasn't happy anymore.

He burst out in agony, "But did you like it?"

"What?" She looked at him as though surprised to see him still there. "Well, parts of it were good. The romance was sweet. Sure, I liked it." She smiled at him and handed it back. "You're a good writer."

Grady knew that he was a good writer—for proposals. He had the distinct feeling that she had just lied to him.

He had the disturbing but nebulous feeling that it wasn't because she didn't want to break his heart by saying the story was a stinker. She was too concerned for that.

ELEVEN

ONE MUGGY FRIDAY morning in late June, when Antony arrived at work, the new backing board of his workbench was twice its usual height. The hooks and pegs for tools were at the top; Antony would have to stand on the bench to reach them.

Or not. In front of the bench was a baby's high chair, painted a garish pink. The tray had badly stenciled images of bear cubs, bows around their necks, with inanely happy expressions.

Roy, his armpits already dark on his work shirt, came by and did an elaborately false double take. "Now, who the hell did that to you? I can't control these sons of bitches for shit, and that's a fact." He hitched up his pants, stared at the roof, and said philosophically, "Sad part is, when a shop starts these tricks, everybody tries to play but somebody always comes up short."

Antony said lazily, "But at least you never do things like this, right?"

Roy was at least sharp enough to recognize what Antony's tone meant. "You got no right to say I did this till you got evidence. You got evidence?"

"If I did, you'd know." Antony looked around; no one

else from Plimstubb was within earshot. "But there are
a lot of people who might play tricks here. If I were
you, I'd watch myself."

Roy narrowed his already puffy, slitted eyes. "You
saying you're gonna make trouble?"

"Did I say that?" Antony, all innocent, raised his
palms toward Roy. "I just know that if people start these
kinds of tricks, it's tough to keep it from snowballing.
If I were you, I'd watch my back." And with that, Antony—rather insultingly, considering his last words—
turned his back on Roy and shuffled through the drawings for the parts he was cutting and grinding today.

Roy scowled and turned toward the open doors. He
shouted, "Get outta here, you dirty bum!" and charged
outside, bent on driving away a panhandler who had
been appearing on Promenade Street with monotonous
frequency. Afterward he strode in, brushing off his
hands with satisfaction, and disappeared into his office.

Fifteen minutes later, Hammer Houlihan came by with
a battered wooden stepstool. "This was in the stockroom,
back in obsolete inventory."

"Thanks." Antony lifted the high chair away from his
workbench with distaste. "You wanna put this there?"

"I woulda done it sooner," Houlihan said apologetically, "but I was waiting for Roy to start snoring. Once
he's asleep, he can't hear a goddamn thing. He does it
every morning about this time."

"Does he?" Antony said with interest.

"He comes in and bitches out anybody who's late.
Then he bitches out anybody who hasn't started working. Then he bitches out some poor bastard just for being
alive and dumb enough to work for him. Then he falls
asleep." He shrugged. "After that, he calms down and
it's a pretty nice place to work."

"You might say that," Antony said, but his mind was
elsewhere. "Every morning, you say . . ."

Hammer Houlihan looked at him sharply and gave a low, gravelly chuckle. "Count me in."

"On what?" he said innocently. "Listen, is there a conveyor belt in obsolete inventory?"

"A beat-up used Ashworth wire mesh belt, fifty-three feet long. Way too warped to give a customer, unless that son of a bitch Hastings finds out about it. Still, it'd run okay for emergencies, and Old Man Plimstubb's too thrifty to throw it out."

Antony noted the admiration in Houlihan's voice and that he hadn't said "cheap." "And Tom Garneaux never figured out a use for it in his house or yard."

"It's only a matter of time."

Antony considered and decided. "I'm not saying anything's gonna happen, but when you get a chance I'd like a list of everything in obsolete. How's that sound?"

"Like I'd better not ask too many questions yet."

"Good idea."

Hammer walked away but spun around. "But you'd better tell Tom Garneaux, or I will. It'd break his heart if he wasn't helping."

Antony grinned. "He's helped with other things already. Maybe it's time I learned about engineering from a pro."

"A pro? Christ, he's lucky he ain't a con." Hammer left, and Antony, whistling to himself, hopped onto the wooden stool and began work.

Grady came by. He noted with approval that at least the extra-long legs had been taken off Antony's bench. It was good to see Antony having an easier time of it. "Hey, Antony. How's it going?"

"Oh, it's going just fine."

Grady wasn't fooled. "So what did Roy do this morning?"

"The usual dumb pranks. Plus he cracked wise, looked important, and chased away a panhandler."

"That guy who's been hanging around?" Grady said

with interest. "He'd be better off around a restaurant."

"Go tell him that," Antony grunted.

Grady's eyebrows furrowed. "He never comes in the plant, does he? We can't have a stranger looking over our projects; there's still a war on."

"You never quit, do you?" Antony said, amused. "First you thought I was a spy. Then you thought Stode was a spy."

"All right." Grady said with mock suspicion, "But I still don't get why you wrote a letter here, of all places, before Stode notified us that he needed exactly what you could make for him."

Antony raised an eyebrow. "You think it was the only letter I wrote?" He left it at that and was happy when Grady did also. "How was fencing?"

"Great. Not for nothing, she learns fast. Plus she has a good sense of balance, and if she stops fighting angry and starts fencing with control, she'll be excellent." He finished with studied nonchalance, "It's good to be teaching a good pupil."

This time it was Antony who wasn't fooled. "I'll bet that's it. Now that the lesson's over, what's she wearing?"

His hands moved, not shaping a body but describing a flow. "This light blue dress with flowers on it, and when she walks, it . . ." He stopped abruptly and said, not too convincingly, "Looks pretty good for a work-day."

Antony laughed; he couldn't help it. "Kid, she's fun to fence with and fun to fight with, and as for the rest, don't bother trying to hide it. Everybody knows."

"There's nothing to know," he said heatedly, but surrendered before Antony's raised eyebrow. "I wish there was more to know."

"Me, too," Antony said with feeling.

Grady raised an eyebrow. "Are you thinking about me, or about you and Kirsten?"

"Keep it down," Antony said. "I'm getting kidded enough here, and you never know who's listening."

But there were no other workers nearby, just one of the gnome controllers. It was rolling, slowly and gracefully, over a heating chamber. A tape descended from its belly and, ignoring Grady and Antony, checked dimensions.

Antony jerked his head toward it. "You feel okay about them?"

"Sure," Grady lied, more to comfort himself than anything else. "They can do shop jobs, but they'll never replace me. Hey, according to my boss, not even I can do my job right. How are they going to?" But he was thinking about *Frankenstein*, and about *R.U.R.*, and about some of the scarier robot stories he'd read.

Antony shook his head. "I wish I felt as good about them. I've known the gnomes, even Klaus himself, longer than you have."

Grady sighed. "The truth? I'm in sales. And I know that if a bastard like Klaus sells you a grenade and it looks like a bargain, you can bet your life he didn't sell you the pin." He looked unhappily at the controller as it finished its work on the heating chamber and headed to the next piece of equipment. "And unfortunately, in this case it's Warren who's betting our lives."

Antony made a decision. He said, with a seriousness that seemed incongruous next to the question, "Kid, where is the grass longest around here?"

"Huh?" Grady thought. "The back of the shop and the edge of the company victory garden. Don't laugh at the garden; we've been busy." All through the war, Plimstubb Furnaces had kept and weeded a vegetable garden, donating produce to the local hospital. Lately everyone had been neglecting it, stubbornly telling themselves that the war was nearly over.

Antony slipped outside. A few minutes later he returned and knelt by his workbench, braiding clumps of grass.

"Taking up basket weaving?" Grady offered, but he knew that something odd was going on. Antony was humming.

Antony barely winked at him in reply and returned to his work. The humming sounded disturbingly like church Latin, but Grady didn't recognize a word. He heard, clearly, the word "Thanatos" as the roses outside the kitchen window began waving back and forth to the rhythm of Antony's speech. He also heard "met" and "emet."

Soon the braided object, a manlike figure, was waving its arms and legs to the same rhythm.

Antony shouted a single syllable and the rose bush collapsed and fell still. The doll did the same. Antony stood and said to Grady, "If you want to be sure what kind of magic is working in a place, lay this down where you want to know."

"And if I do that, what will happen?"

Antony paused before speaking. "Different things," he said finally. "The grass may burn—that would be bad. It may wither right away, which isn't that good. The doll's pose may change. And lastly"—he grinned— "nothing may happen, and you'll be sorry you listened to an idiot."

"I won't be sorry I listened," Grady promised, watching Antony stuff the grass doll in the bottom drawer of his workbench. It occurred to Grady that he also wouldn't be sorry, if a time came to use the doll, if nothing happened.

That night after dinner, the Providence Choral Society held a concert, an evening of Gershwin. Grady drove Susan and her mother to it, sorry Antony hadn't been able to delay—or hadn't wanted to delay—returning to the Dwarfworks for the weekend. He was sorrier still

that Mary hadn't found a baby-sitter and had to stay
home.

Julie's beloved Rosie Rocci wouldn't baby-sit tonight;
during the middle part of the program, Susan would be
singing a solo.

The Choral Society had reserved the Loew's theater
downtown. The manager, a music lover, lowered the rent
and reserved himself a front-row seat.

Just before the curtain opened, Maestro Mandeville
eyed the choir coldly. "Sopranos, don't warble out of
control on the high notes. Altos, don't disappear on the
low notes. Basses, dropping your jaws instead of singing
through your noses would work wonders. And tenors?"
He looked as though he might give up. "Sing loudly
except on 'I've Got Rhythm,' where it's clear that you
don't."

He strode off, giving a quick nod to the stagehand.
The red stage curtain was no more than halfway open
when he appeared in the orchestra pit, acknowledging
applause and giving the downbeat to the orchestra at the
same time for a jazzy, trumpet-and-woodwind fanfare.
The fanfare ended and he gestured to the stage. "Love
is sweeping the country," the choir warbled slyly.
"Waves are hugging the shore. . . ."

Grady sang loudly and happily, trying his best to obey
as Maestro Mandeville pointed a frantic finger to the
auditorium roof in an effort to get the men in tune and
up to pitch.

Grady fared better, or thought he did, on "I've Got
Rhythm." At least Maestro Mandeville wasn't looking
his way. He glanced briefly toward the sopranos and felt
that there was a certain irony in concluding, "Who could
ask for anything more?"

He moved up the left-side aisle quietly, glad that he
muffled his canetip for concerts, and sat near the front
for the soloists' portion of the program.

The soloists were all from the choir—a measure to

save money, but also a measure of Maestro Mandeville's pride in the group, despite his occasional forays from self-pity to open hostility during rehearsal.

Michael, a tenor who stood near Grady at rehearsals, sang "Stairway to Paradise" and, apparently unable to contain himself, broke into a softshoe on the last verse. The audience applauded, and Michael bowed to them, bowed to his accompanist, and bowed contritely to Maestro Mandeville.

Grady had been impressed with Michael's nerve, but noticed that the maestro winked; the "spontaneous outburst" had been planned.

The next singer, a wicked bass/baritone with a mischievous grin, sang "It Ain't Necessarily So" from *Porgy and Bess*. A hand-picked octet, including Susan, sang the scat syllables and the chorus verse behind him.

In the front row, an elegantly dressed middle-aged woman whom Grady had seen at other concerts clearly took umbrage at the lyrics. She stood, straightening to her full height, and moved to the aisle to leave.

The singer, in perfect character for Gershwin's Sportin' Life, leaped off the stage, took her hand, kissed it, and sang the next cynical lyric into her face. He walked her up the aisle and out of the theater as the chorus sang the final chorus, running back to take a bow as they finished.

Maestro Mandeville, covertly conducting the octet, nodded impassively to the returning singer. The woman had come backstage to speak to him before the performance. Grady wondered to himself whether anything in concerts wasn't preplanned, and resolved to be less affected by performances, which, after all, were almost cynically aimed at the audience.

An alto dressed in black stood with downcast eyes, waiting for the moment to start. She looked up as the music began, and her eyes were still sad. But she sang lightly and with half a smile about little things, the way

you hold your tea and your knife and the way we talked
till three, and finished defiantly, "No, no, they can't take
that away from me."

An older woman a few chairs away was wiping her
eyes quietly. The audience was dead silent. The song
was supposed to be about love, but too many of the
audience had discovered, during the war, just how many
little things "they" could take away. Grady thought, suddenly and irrelevantly, about playing cutthroat high-low-
jack with his father and Kevin, and how seriously they
all took the score at a quarter a game, a nickel a shoot.

At the end of the final verse, there was complete silence. Grady looked over at Maestro Mandeville and
saw the maestro wiping his eyes. The aim of the performance may have been calculated, but it was anything
but cynical.

The applause for the alto built slowly until it filled
the auditorium. Grady pounded his hands together, then
leaned forward in anticipation. It was Susan's turn to
sing. He glanced down at the program, not remembering
what she had said she was going to sing. He read the
title and froze. The piano rippled easily through the
opening chords and he looked up.

Susan stared into Grady's eyes, her own eyes deep
and luminous. "Oh, do it again," she sang shyly and
eagerly, and he turned bright red. "I may say, no, no,
no, no, but do it again. . . ."

"Couldn't you just," a man of sixty if he was a day
murmured to the right of Grady.

The woman next to the old man slapped his arm.
"You couldn't," she said, and kissed his cheek for no
apparent reason.

After a moment, Grady relaxed again. He was kidding
himself. He was in the lower center four rows back, and
of course it seemed as though she were singing to him.
He was silently glad that it was an illusion.

A scrawny and frankly envious high school student in

the front row turned to stare at him, and Grady realized
it was no illusion. A moment later, a woman his age
smiled and pointed him out to her friends; his ears were
turning red.

Susan wound up earnestly and hesitantly with "Mama
will scold me, 'cause she told me it was naughty but
then," and exploded into a dazzling, excited smile, "do
it again, please do it again."

She finished to a great deal of applause. The old man
next to Grady nudged him and he began clapping. The
man chuckled and nudged him again when it was time
to stop.

Grady returned to the stage with the rest of the choir
and sang "Of Thee I Sing, Baby," with fervor and occasional accuracy.

After the concert, Grady wandered around the basement
reception shaking hands and politely accepting compli-
ments for the music on behalf of the choir. It occurred
to him that, with a little planning, an event like this
could bring in a lot of money for a musical group. He
caught himself and grinned; he was beginning to think
like a salesman all the time.

He shook Maestro Mandeville's hand as well. "Say,
what a concert! Thanks for conducting."

"My pleasure." He opened his mouth to say something, changed his mind, and said, "Nice job tonight,
Grady. How did you like the soloists?"

"They were terrific." He added, half defensively, "All
of them."

Maestro Mandeville looked at him appraisingly and
said, "Never forget. Sopranos are passionate, altos are
sensual."

"I don't get you," Grady said finally.

Maestro Mandeville said flatly, "Marry an alto and
never look back." He moved away.

Grady said plaintively to his back, "But—" He cut

himself off before saying aloud that Susan was a mezzo-soprano. What the hell did that mean?

He went up the basement stairs and stepped outside for a cigarette. Maestro Mandeville had an irrational dislike of smokers. Susan, panting, caught up with him. "Did I sound okay?"

"I'll say." He passed her a cigarette and lit it, cupping his hands around the match. "You sounded like a million bucks."

"Thanks." She added contritely, "I'm sorry if I startled you by looking you in the eye. It helped me to focus."

He shook his head, grinning. "It sure made me focus."

"The maestro said that if I did that it would help me find"—she paused, trying to find his exact words—"a more dramatic expression of awakened passion."

He shifted back and forth, leaning on his cane, and said carefully, "Did it?"

"I think so." She smoked in silence for a moment. "Anyway, that's what the song's about."

"It sure was when you were singing. If Glenn Miller were still alive, he'd want you to cut a record with him."

"Or do a duet with Sinatra. Don't kid me." But she was pleased, and Grady was sorry, a cigarette each later, that her mother showed up and said firmly that she was ready to go home.

They chatted about the music on the way home. Rose said with emphasis that George Gershwin was good but that nobody would ever be as good as Verdi or Victor Herbert. "Your own grandfather, Susie, he was musical like you and took a job in Milan to try to audition for La Scala. He didn't make it," she admitted grudgingly, "but he sang real nice, and when Verdi died—this was before I was born—he stood on the road all night waiting for the coffin to pass and he started the crowd singing 'Va Pensiero,' how pretty, and he said afterward that he always remembered that when he came to America and he felt like the Jews by the waters of Babylon even though we were good Americans by then. . . ."

Eventually Grady noticed that she was the only one talking. He and Susan, side by side on the front seat, were sitting rigidly, and he would have bet the contents of his savings account that Susan was as aware of his body as he was of hers.

They parked at the Rocci house and, to Grady's immense disappointment, Susan opened her car door and got out a second after Rose Rocci stepped out of hers. At the front step, Rose said with studied formality, "I know that you two will want to say good night. I'll be right inside, honey," she said to Susan, and added, studiously not looking at Grady, "Actually, I'm gonna go to the kitchen, put up your lunch for tomorrow. Chicken salad on Italian bread, we'll add some lettuce tomorrow. . . ." And she was gone, still soliloquizing about tomatoes and mayonnaise.

Susan looked inside exasperatedly but with some fondness. "Ma can talk more about lunch than Roosevelt did about the New Deal."

"At least she makes your lunches."

"I think she's afraid to stop making lunches," Susan said seriously. "She used to do it for my dad."

Grady could have kicked himself. "Do you think tonight bothered her? There were an awful lot of love songs."

"I think she liked it. Anyway, it beat sitting at home alone." Susan glanced inside but clearly didn't want to go in just yet. "Funny . . . when Gloria was singing 'They Can't Take That Away from Me,' I thought of my dad."

"Makes sense." He saw Susan getting ready to say good night and steeled himself. "Susan? You haven't forgotten that I love you."

She smiled at him, suddenly shy but this time pleased. "I haven't. I'll see you at fencing on Monday." She kissed her index finger, laid it on his cheek, and ran into the house.

Grady took the amethyst pendant Kirsten had given him and pointed it at her. The pendant was definitely glowing, though it flickered as Grady heard Rose Rocci say accusingly, "Honey, is this pack of Pall Malls yours?"

Grady had more sense than to turn the pendant toward himself; people would think a signal flare had gone off. He walked back to the car, swung his cane jauntily, and tossed it in the backseat, and drove home singing "Oh, Do It Again" with more feeling than artistry.

TWELVE

WHEN THE PHONE rang, it was still dark. Grady blinked at it sleepily and then leaped at it.

"Cavanaugh?" Stode said. "Stode. Subject: Equipment repairs." He stressed "equipment" slightly. "What time does your plant normally open?"

"Eight. Seven, in the shop."

"Be there in an hour."

"Why? Where are you?"

There was a moment's hesitation and Stode said, "I'm at a telephone, near the Connecticut border. Can you open the shop?"

"Not alone."

"Call whoever you have to. Open it up. I want to be in and out before seven."

"Will do." Grady was wide awake, his adrenaline pumping from that first ring. He added conversationally, "You know, when the phone rang at this hour, I thought it would be something about my father or my brother."

"I thought you might," Stode said, and hung up without apology.

Grady glared at the handset futilely before tapping the cradle and getting an operator. Moments later, a

mumbling Roy Burgess slurred into the phone,
"Mmmmph?"

"Hi, Roy," Grady said brightly. "Remember how
much you like it when somebody owes you a favor?"

Grady was at the gate half an hour later. Roy was nowhere to be seen.

Down the street, a covered truck that looked remarkably like the ones bootleggers used to drive rolled down
the street. It had no company label, and its Connecticut
plates looked suspiciously new. If this had been twenty
years ago, Grady would have assumed the truck be-
longed to a bootlegger.

Grady looked up and down the street in agony and
saw Roy's decrepit Nash crawling indifferently toward
the gate. It barely beat the truck. Roy emerged, also
crawling indifferently and obviously hung over. He
snuffled resentfully at Grady and tried with shaking fingers to fit the key into the padlock. The lock clanged
against the fence, and Roy whimpered.

"Do you want help with that?" Grady said desperately.

"You," Roy snapped, suddenly coherent, "are hanging
by a thread." Grady shut up.

At the last possible second the lock swung open, the
hasp reflecting the headlights of the turning truck. Grady
hooked his cane onto the gate and pulled, riding it forward as his side of the gate opened. Roy sullenly opened
his side, and the truck rolled in.

Stode's head was framed in the passenger window
like a cubist portrait. "Open the garage door now."

Roy opened his mouth to speak, saw Stode's expression, and scurried to the door. Grady wondered where
they had driven from; Stode looked exhausted.

The door next to the steel rack slid up with a rumble.
Grady stepped inside before the truck could back in. The
driver, clearly experienced at maneuvering, rolled un-

hesitatingly past the shelves for steel and slowed as he neared the chain hanging from the ceiling crane. He stopped without bumping the chain, but within inches of it—no mean feat, since he wouldn't have been able to see the chain for the last eight feet.

Grady pulled the tailgate down and looked inside. There was nothing but a single wooden crate, up on four blocks of wood. From the bent nails and the hammer indentations, he inferred that it had been packed hastily. Between two of the boards he could see a dull metal surface, like a lining.

He hooked his cane on the side of the truck and pushed up on his hands to get in. Stode, for all his exhaustion, climbed past Grady—he seemed almost to stride in, one long skinny leg clearing the edge of the tailgate and straightening as he brought up his other leg. "Stay down, Cavanaugh."

Grady eased back down, offended but saying nothing. Roy looked blearily into the back of the truck and croaked, "You wan' help wi' that?"

"I have the help I need. Driver!"

The truck driver, who was walking to the back, sprinted and climbed up. Together he and Stode slid the end of the chain under the crate lengthwise, crossed it on top, and slid it sideways under the crate, then hooked it onto itself. The chain quartered itself like a ribbon on a Christmas present.

Stode gestured to Grady, who moved rapidly to the control buttons of the crane and pressed the green button. The slack of the chain moved over the ceiling pulleys, link by link, until the chain was taut. Grady pressed the red STOP button and the GO button alternately, raising the chain a link at a time until the crate swung slowly off the wooden blocks and moved out of the truck.

Stode steadied the crate, but Grady noticed that he

didn't want to touch it. "Send it to the other end of the floor. Do you have an open space?"

But he said it as though the question were rhetorical, and Grady wondered suddenly how much he had known about the plant before he had walked in.

Roy Burgess glared as best he could and snapped, "Hey, who the hell do you think you are? This is my shop. Mine, you son of a bitch. If you want to paint the castle, I get to choose the color."

Stode looked Roy squarely in the eye. Roy shivered all over like a wet dog and wandered off to go to sleep at his desk. For once, instead of waiting for seven-thirty, he would be asleep at it before anyone from the shop reported to work.

Grady said, "We have room near the loading dock at the far end. I guess you knew that. We'll need the loading dock again in a couple of days, but I'm betting that if you came in here this fast, you want to leave fast, too."

Stode ran a bony hand over his hair. "I wish you were in charge of this place."

Grady looked after the slouching Roy and made a fast decision. "Pretend I'm in charge of the shop. I'll straighten it out later, when Roy wakes up. What do you need?"

"Blueprints and repairs. People who have rebuilt Plimstubb equipment. Also"—he gestured at the dangling crate—"something to hide this from everybody else. Everybody."

"Welding screens," he said immediately. "I can tug some screens over if one of you can run the crane. . . ."

Stode nodded curtly to the truck driver. "Help him. And bring two tarps from the truck."

"Yes, si—sure." The driver actually ran ahead of Grady, stopping and waiting for Grady and his cane to catch up. Together they mustered up a tarp and four screens before the crane, proceeding with the slow grace of a Marian pageant from St. Ann's Church, could lay the crate reverently in a bare spot near the loading dock.

Grady snatched a crowbar from Hammer Houlihan's bench and pulled out nails from the lid. They came free with protesting creaks, one by one.

Stode said, "Save those aside and we'll drop them inside the box." He had spread the tarp on the floor.

"Won't they fall out between the boards?" Grady pulled the last nail and tried to lift the lid himself.

It didn't budge. He quit trying and looked more closely at it; the crate, lid and all, had been lined with lead. The truck driver fastened the crane chains to it and lifted it aside, then, with a strange delicacy, tied rags around the edges of the metal object inside and hooked it to the crane. Grady glanced into the box and recognized the cage from the Plimstubb equipment he had sold Stode. He cocked his head; even in the shadows of the box, it didn't look right.

The heating chamber cage, twisted and deformed, rose into the air and dropped onto the shop floor, a blackened, distorted, unclean thing. Once it lay on the tarp, the truck driver removed the chain, untying the rags with the tips of his fingers and dropping the rags into the crate.

Grady picked up the nails and dropped them in as well. "What the hell happened here?"

"An accident," Stode said heavily. "Be certain that no one works on it for more than thirty minutes at a time. Rotate staff. Keep ventilation or fans going at all times, and be certain that everyone washes his hands before eating after working on this project."

Grady was annoyed. "People here aren't pigs—"

"Enforce it."

Grady took another glance at the cage and resolved to cut the work shifts to twenty minutes.

A new voice said, "What are you doing?"

It was Susan, dressed in slacks and flats, and she was

holding a foil and a mask. She had come early for her fencing lesson.

Stode said, "Leave now."

"Of course not." She walked past the driver, stopped, and looked into his face. "Are you going to talk, or haven't you had enough coffee this morning?"

The driver didn't say a word, looking to Stode.

Stode said, "He's just a civilian driver."

"Of course he is." Susan shrugged, walked away, moved behind the driver, and bellowed in as close to a baritone as she could come, "Ten-HUT!"

The driver was ramrod-straight before he could catch himself. Susan smiled at Stode. "What a nice civilian. And well mannered, too."

She stepped around the welding screens, walked directly to the heating cage, and put her hand out to lay a palm against it.

Stode said sharply, "No!"

She spun around, her hair rippling with the motion. "Why shouldn't I?"

"I'm telling you not to." Stode licked his lips, and Grady had the odd impression that Stode was afraid. "Move away. Now."

Susan looked at it speculatively. "If I taped an undeveloped X-ray plate to this thing, would the plate fog up?"

Stode smiled, and his mouth actually curved, a single arc in a face that was all straight lines and sharp angles. "Try not to do that or ask questions like that, Miss Rocci. I prefer to have you working for the war, rather than spending the rest of it somewhere else."

For Stode, it was a remarkably gentle threat. He never said "Kentucky" or "Leavenworth."

To Grady's great surprise, it was enough. Susan shut up.

Stode's ramrod-straight spine relaxed slightly. "So. How long will it take you to repair this?"

"Given the conditions you've suggested—okay, laid down?" Grady considered. He knew his lips were moving while he calculated in front of a customer, but he didn't care. "A couple days, minimum. There's wire to weave into the cage and brackets to replace—look, I know the distortion looks extreme, but this cage is only designed to hold the insulation in place. This was never built to take a lot of heat." He added curiously, "And it took one hell of a lot. From the look of the metal, the temperature went up more than a thousand degrees, faster than hell, while it was already under heat. The heating elements can't do that. What can do that?"

Stode regarded him unwaveringly, not saying a word.

Susan looked at him pityingly, but when he looked in her eyes she blinked and turned away. That worried Grady more than anything.

Stode said, "I need it back in a day. Can you find a way to do that?" His voice still sounded imperative, but there was a new, disturbing note that sounded pleading.

Grady frowned, thinking. Susan tapped his shoulder and pointed. "What about that?"

"That" was the furnace for Stanislaw, for making cloaks of invisibility. It stood against the far wall, gathering dust. The insulation and heating elements were for a low-temperature furnace.

The cage to which they were fastened was meant to be lined with insulation for high-temperature processing.

Susan tapped Grady's shoulder again and said, "I'll need a tape measure."

They found one on Benny Blaws' workbench. The case had engraved on it, in block letters, I CARNALLY LOVE BENNY BLAWS. Benny had once told Grady that it was the only way he could be sure no one would "borrow" it and never return it. Susan turned it over with distaste. "I'll use it, but don't ever tell anyone."

They stretched the tape the length of the damaged cage. In spite of her defensiveness in front of Stode,

Susan whispered to Grady without moving her lips, "Be careful not to touch the cage."

"Why not?" he asked, but he stretched the tape and snapped it carefully tight an inch from the cage.

When they had taken the dimensions they needed, Susan said with relief, "Let's check the other furnace." She moved quickly away from the cage. Stode quietly shifted the welding screens in place behind them.

The cage on Stanislaw's furnace, in spite of its previous heat distortion, was within an inch of the dimensions on Stode's furnace cage. Susan strode to Benny Behind's workbench and sketched quickly on a scrap of paper. "You can use it. Weld tabs on it at each of the upper corners, and weld matching tabs inside the furnace heating chamber. Get somebody who knows high-temperature welding specifications—anybody from the aircraft industry will do. The tabs will give you enough play to hang the cage. Since the inside of the cage is insulated to hold the heat, you don't need to worry about the empty space outside it."

Stode nodded, but pointed glumly to the insulation wired to Stanislaw's furnace cage. "That's not the same as what we had. Where do we get new insulation?"

"We can . . ." Grady bit his lip, stumped. That stuff was expensive; they didn't just leave it sitting around.

Susan voiced his thought. "We'd have to order it."

"How long will it take to arrive?"

"If the government helps us give it a priority rating?" Stode shook his head. She shrugged helplessly. "A week, maybe two."

"Completely unsatisfactory."

She said defensively, "That's what you get for not buying extra insulation to begin with. I know you didn't want anyone to guess what you were doing—no, don't get shirty; you know that's why you didn't attract attention with a big order—but now it's come back to bite you, and what are you gonna do? It's not like this stuff is just lying around."

"Just lying around"—Grady had a sudden vision of Tom Garneaux's house. The furnace thermostat was a Wheelco controller for high-temperature industrial equipment. The flagpole up front was a fourteen-foot tube of expensive high-temperature alloy steel. Garneaux's birdbath had been a stainless steel bowl, but someone who realized its worth had stolen it. "Let's talk to Tom Garneaux."

Susan's eyes widened, and she smiled. Grady was often appalled with how quickly she understood ideas and their implications. She turned back to Stode and said sweetly, "Would you be upset by working with a bootlegger?"

Stode folded his skeletal arms forbiddingly. "If you mean Mr. Houlihan, he doesn't have the background to help me. If you mean Tom Garneaux, I have no objection whatsoever. He still gambles illegally, and he does several other things, but he was born, and will die, a patriot."

He let the implications of that sink in. Grady said slowly, "How do you know so much about Tom Garneaux?"

Stode looked at him without answering.

Susan said nervously, "How much do you know about us?"

Stode said, "Do you wish me to answer that in present company?"

"No!" She caught herself and added quietly, "Whatever you know, you're still willing to work with us."

"For now." He glanced around the shop. "After the war, security may be even tighter."

Susan shook her head. "I can't even think about after the war."

Stode nodded. For a fraction of a second, Grady saw what looked like sympathy on his face.

Then it was gone. Susan stared at him and shut up. Grady swallowed and said, "As long as you understand that Tom's sources for materials may be, uh, informal. If I ask him to find the materials inside of three days, he'll call in some debts—and believe me, he'll get them."

"Today."

"All right. I'll pull him off whatever he's doing. I can never tell anyway. If you tell him it's for the war, he'll do it."

Susan said diffidently, "I can convince him. Grady, can you give me a moment alone with Tom?"

He glanced at Stode, who inclined his head slightly. "Well, sure."

"Good." Susan looked at the blackened cage again. "What about the molybdenum hearth? Did you take it out before traveling?"

He sighed loudly, and for once looked tired. "No, we didn't. It's—gone."

Susan nodded thoughtfully. "Somehow, you cracked this furnace open to air while it was at high temperature. Maybe something exploded, or maybe the over-temperature control failed, or maybe there was an en-dothermic reaction and the temperature shot up. I won't ask how."

"Oh, you can ask all you want," Stode said dryly.

"And the air hit the moly hearth, and the moly turned to a little puff of expensive, poisonous white smoke, and that was that." She nodded as though he had confessed. "If we have a source for a new one—and I'm not saying we do—will you take it on faith?"

"I take nothing on faith."

Grady said quickly, "All right; we might have put that badly." Susan was glaring at him, but that couldn't be helped. "We can send the hearth for the new furnace down immediately. If we have a source for a moly hearth that can get it to you very fast, will you not fight the fact that we won't tell you who it is?"

If possible, Stode was more rigid than he had been. "I set the rules for procurement."

"Not this time," Grady said levelly. "You accept our secrecy or you don't get the part."

There was a long silence. Grady could hear seagulls crying in the parking lot, which meant either that there was a west wind or that the trash had been put out.

Finally Stode said, "Agreed. Tell no one."

"You've got it," Grady said, unsure of whether he was to keep secret the supply source or that he had won a concession from Stode.

"Done, then. Meet me in Engineering in ten minutes, no more. I'll go talk to Garneaux after I've walked my"—he glared coldly—"*civilian* driver back to the truck and discussed a few things."

The driver cringed. Grady couldn't blame him.

Susan said thoughtfully as they left, "He went to a lot of trouble to find out about us."

"I wonder if he dug up any dirt." Grady was casting his mind uneasily back to his college days, wondering if Benny Parrish or any of his former roommates remembered some of their wilder nights.

"Let's hope not," Susan said vaguely. "Listen, I'm going to give him two copies of all the drawings for the cage."

"That's nice of—whoa. Construction prints? Susan, that's crazy. They're proprietary."

She gestured over her shoulder. "Do you want him to drive back here again?"

He glanced at the garage door and said, "In a minute, I'll come help you run the drawings."

After Susan left, Grady walked quietly to Antony's workbench. He opened the lowest drawer and removed the grass mannequin, returning to the damaged heating chamber cage.

He knelt and bound Antony's grass doll to the side

of the cage, the doll's arms splayed against the metal like a crucifix. No one saw him, and if Hammer Houlihan and the others who were filing in for work now had seen him, they might not even think his behavior was odd. Plimstubb was an odd place to work anyway.

Grady stood, dusting his trousers off very carefully, and went to arrange for fans and a work crew.

Late that afternoon, Grady returned to check the cage. By now nearly everyone who had any welding experience at all had worked on it, following the drawing that Susan had marked up. Once Roy had woken up, he watched from a distance through narrowed eyes, clearly hoping Grady failed somehow.

Just now, Flash was kneeling at the edge of tarp, his knees on a battered pad. For once he had his welding mask pulled all the way down. Smoke was coming both from the blinding arc at the end of the rod and from underneath the mask.

"Flash?" Grady said loudly and curiously. The welder cut power to the rod and sat back, lifting his mask.

A puff of greenish-brown smoke drifted up from a cigar that Flash had clipped to fit under the mask. The end glowed a dull red, burning badly in the fetid smoke.

Grady nearly gagged. "How close are you to done?"

"Damn close." He pointed with a gloved finger to the bottom corner of the cage. "I quit my twenty in a minute and pass this torch to Betty. She welds pretty good now," he added grudgingly, "for a woman. When she's done, we're done. Say, how did you get a set of clangers big enough to tell Roy how to run a project in his own shop?"

"It was for a customer," Grady said simply, "and the customer said it was for the war." He hoped suddenly and penitently that Roy wouldn't take it out on any of

Grady's friends—most obviously and notably on Antony.

"It was still a pretty ballsy thing to do." But he said it admiringly. "You'd make an okay good manager."

"Or I'll get fired for trying." He checked his watch. "Finish up. And wash your hands really well."

He walked to the other side of the cage, knelt to check the doll, and sucked in his breath sharply.

There was no physical change to the grass, but there was a locust thorn pushed through its chest.

He stood and looked around. No one was nearby, though any number of people could have done it during the day. Grady glanced nervously at the door to Shipping. The gnome controller that could spit nails, pipe turned toward him, looked back. Grady shivered, pulled the doll free of its bindings, and walked quickly away from the cage.

He disposed of the grass doll in a trash barrel outside the plant and put it all out of his mind. A half hour later, Stode and his driver returned and picked up the cage and its crate. They had been at Garneaux's house. Between his garden pathways and the gardens of some of his close friends, they had been able to retrieve enough high-quality insulation. Some of it was chipped at the edges and had been in obsolete inventory, but most of it was in good shape.

Grady gave Stode the roll of furnace drawings. Stode tucked it under his arm and nodded to Grady. "Very satisfactory."

It was the highest praise Grady could have expected. On the way out of the plant, Stode looked sharply to the right and left at the parking lot and the street beyond.

As Grady himself exited Plimstubb that evening, he remembered Stode's cautious attitude and walked the perimeter of the building. To his relief, no one was in sight. Even the panhandler who had been regularly hang-

ing around at the start and end of workdays had disappeared.

But it was several days before Grady felt comfortable
standing in the place on the shop floor where the damaged cage had been.

THIRTEEN

I T HAD SEEMED like a great way to celebrate the Fourth of July: Get Susan and her mother out of the house, take Mary and Julie as well, and go to Roger Williams Park for a picnic, concert, and fireworks. And it should have been a good idea, Grady told himself defensively.

It had started well enough, picking up Mary and being just bowled over by Julie in a red, white, and blue dress. Julie tottered forward at a good clip. Grady ran forward as best he could and caught her. He swept her up in a tight hug and a kiss on the cheek. . . .

And Julie hugged him and called him "Daddy."

It wasn't loud, and it wasn't terribly distinct. But it was clear enough that Mary, behind them, started crying.

Grady said quickly, "No, honey, I'm Uncle Grady." He kissed her again and set her down, turning to Mary. "She's just confused."

Mary was shaking her head back and forth, crying. "I show her Kevin's picture every night. Not one of the ones in uniform, the one in a suit from just before our wedding." Her fingers made quick, futile swipes at the tears on her cheeks. "I tried every day to say 'Daddy' so she'll say it when Kevin gets home." Mary sat on the sidewalk, wailing, "I did it wrong! I did it wrong!"

Grady, who had been happy to see them both, felt like a war criminal. "She'll get it straight."

"I know she will." Mary blew her nose and tried to smile. "I'm okay now."

Julie, looking up at her mother, plunked her bottom down on the sidewalk, threw her head back, and wailed.

When they arrived at Susan's house, Susan was struggling down the front steps with a wicker basket, lugging it with both hands and glaring balefully at her mother.

Grady went hastily up the walk to take it from her, but she turned away. "You only have one free hand."

He barely glanced at his cane. "I could carry it."

"No, you couldn't." She lurched down the sidewalk, the basket bouncing against one leg as she tried to offer it extra support. Grady backed away as she advanced. " 'Cause Ma packed enough food for us, Mary and Julie, and the Sunday choir of Our Lady of Fatima."

"You got to eat something," Mrs. Rocci said automatically. "You looked so nice and healthy this winter, now you look something awful." She turned in appeal to Grady. "I'll be very honest with you. She looks terrible, doesn't she?"

Grady had learned a little this spring about awkward situations like these. "She looks terrific, but she should eat anyway." He held the car door open. Susan's mother stepped in, shaking her head at Grady's crucial lack of honesty.

Susan thunked the basket into Grady's hands and slid in beside her mother, taking the basket back immediately. Grady had just enough time to realize how heavy it was and feel a little hopeful that dinner would rescue their moods.

Their spirits rose on the way to the park. Susan took it on herself to lean forward from the backseat and tickle Julie into a good mood, poking the little girl's belly repeatedly and saying "Whee!" About the time that Grady thought it was the most annoying sound on earth, Julie laughed with delight. Mary passed her over the seat to Susan, and the ride became pleasant. Grady didn't understand why the pleasure of one baby should raise the spirits of three adults who each felt miserable for their own reasons, but he was willing to accept it.

At the park, though, Susan's spirits dropped again. Grady couldn't figure out why until he saw her reach furtively into her handbag and pull back, scowling at her mother.

Mrs. Rocci was peacefully unaware, pointing out the park plantings to Mary. "Look how pretty, the roses. Susan, honey, you gotta keep up with the basket; I don't want you walking around the park alone."

"It's not even dark," Susan said with an edge in her voice.

Her mother said back with still more edge in her voice than Grady had ever heard from her, "Wait, then, it's gonna get dark."

Susan's nostrils flared like a charging bull's.

Before she could speak, Grady said cheerfully, "You're absolutely right. I'm nervous around here alone myself. Susan, would you go with me to buy some lemonade? I can't carry it back by myself."

"Oh, no," Mrs. Rocci said quickly. "I got a jug of water—"

"That's great." He could hear how funny he sounded. "But I'd like some lemonade, and I'll bet Susan would, too." He pointed to the green slopes below them, downhill from the road. "You find a place for the blanket. We'll be right back."

Thirty feet into the crowd of other picnickers he lit up a Lucky and passed it to Susan. She muttered around it, "I could kiss you."

You could, he thought happily, and I could kiss you

back. And someday you will. He lit up a cigarette for himself.

Aloud he said, "Did your mother pack any knives? I don't want to get between you if she did."

"You couldn't," Susan said bitterly. "She never lets me that far away, except to go to work. And she calls me four times a day, and she makes excuses to keep me home at night or she goes with me—my God, it's like doing time."

"Why don't you just go out?"

Susan put her hand out, fingers parted, for another cigarette. She had sucked the first one down to a column of ash.

She lit it off the butt of the first one and sighed. "Because then she just looks at me and cries and says, 'I can't help, it honey. Now you're all I got.' " She stared at the lemonade stand, brooding. "I'd kill her, but now she's all *I've* got."

On the way back, Grady said, "You know, my dad tried to keep Kevin from enlisting."

"You're kidding." To Susan that seemed like treason.

"No fooling. I told him he was crazy, and he said he was glad I'd hurt my foot so that no branch of the armed forces would take me." Grady's jaw tightened at the memory. "For the first and only time in my life, I wanted to deck him."

"But Kevin enlisted."

"He begged me to help him, and we wore my dad down. And we threw Kevin the best damn party of his life, and he left for training." He paused. It still hurt to remember. "That night I dreamed of my mother, scolding me because my little brother was lost and she'd told me to watch him."

He passed a final cigarette to Susan, who was trying to pack an entire night of nicotine into ten minutes. She lit it off the butt of the second one, puffing thoughtfully.

"So when will my mother and I stop watching each other?"

Grady hesitated, not wanting to lie but not wanting to scare her. "You don't stop. Ever. Not completely. You get used to being with each other, that's all. You'll learn when to watch and when not to." He added, knowing what her reaction would be, "And you'll get closer to each other."

Susan shuddered. "At least you don't have nightmares about Kevin anymore."

Grady nodded, not saying that now he dreamed his mother scolded him about his father the night that his father left for the Pacific.

As they approached the blanket, Susan passed the half-finished cigarette back to Grady. "Thanks."

He stuck it in the corner of his mouth and said, muttering around it like Bogart, "Anytime, kid."

He said to Mrs. Rocci, "Nice spot." He sat down awkwardly on the blanket, one leg stuck out straight. "I'm starved—"

He stopped. Susan was staring with pitying amusement at him. Rose Rocci was glaring, and Mary was laughing. They were all watching the cigarette.

He pulled it out of his mouth and looked down at the Lucky with its coral-red lipstick stain on the butt.

"Guess I should get rid of this before we eat," he said lamely, and stubbed it out on the grass.

Susan said warningly, "Let's just eat, okay? We have nice food, you picked a nice spot for the blanket..." She looked around for the first time and said disappointedly, "Oh, *Ma.*"

Her mother said defensively, "There's trees, and those nice arched bridges, and that cute little stone lantern..." She trailed off, looking unhappily at Susan's set jaw and furious eyes.

Grady looked at the unobstructed view of the Japanese

garden. He really hadn't thought about it as they sat down.

"You liked it before the war," Susan's mother said.

Susan said icily, "Before the war, Providence had a Mussolini Street. Maybe you'd like to finish off tonight by going back to Federal Hill and putting the street sign back up."

That was the last thing she said through dinner. Grady munched glumly on a meatball sandwich, wishing somebody would start some conversation while they ate.

After dinner he said flatly, "Let's pack up the leftovers and see if we can get closer to the band for the concert."

He stood, but Susan moved even faster, whisking food and drinks back into the basket. She tugged the basket off the blanket so they could shake the crumbs.

Grady picked up the basket. It wasn't appreciably lighter. Susan took it away from him.

Her mother said placatingly to her, "You can take some of that for lunch tomorrow, honey."

"Good idea," Susan said neutrally, but at least she spoke.

Grady tucked the blanket under his free arm. They all walked back to the roadway and toward the Temple to Music. It looked like something from ancient Rome: huge fluted marble columns rose to a nearly flat roof maybe thirty feet off the ground. A small stage and amphitheater extended from its front steps. A concert band was setting up on the stage and steps.

It seemed as though all of the people in the park had the same idea. Grady moved across the road to the field in front of the temple as quickly as he could, leaving the others behind. He threw the blanket out hastily. A family of six right behind him moved disappointedly on, searching for a spot as good. Grady sat awkwardly again, but happy to have maneuvered Susan away from the Japanese garden.

She sat next to him, adjusting her skirt as she dropped,

and whispered, "Would it help if you could lean on the picnic basket?"

"It's a little short, but thanks."

"I'd let you lean on me," she said, "but Ma would go through the roof."

Grady took a quick glance at Mary, who was holding one of Julie's hands as Julie danced on the blanket. Rose Rocci, who baby-sat Julie a lot, was watching Julie wistfully; Julie adored her. After a shaky start, the night was calming down, fights and tears forgotten.

"There's no roof for her to go through," Grady said, grinning, and he lay down on the blanket, his head in her lap.

She ruffled his hair. "If she cuts up rough, you have to get up."

But Rose was watching her beloved Julie and studiously never looked their way. After a few minutes Grady realized that Rose had decided not to see them.

Mary, however, glanced their way from time to time. Once, while Susan was watching the field fill up with other picnickers, Mary furtively winked at Grady.

Not feeling half as confident as he looked, Grady winked back.

The shadows were deepening, and the field was nearly edge-to-edge with blankets. The concert was ready to start.

Susan looked up as the conductor came out and actually squeaked, "It's Maestro Mandeville!"

Her voice carried in the evening air. The maestro, looking profoundly uncomfortable in a dazzling white jacket with metallic gold braided epaulets, saluted her awkwardly with his baton. The crowd laughed, a warm ripple. He bowed curtly, turned his back on the audience, and raised his baton.

The music was patriotic and all familiar. First was a thundering arrangement of "Battle Hymn of the Republic." Next came a medley: "Yankee Doodle," "When

Johnny Comes Marching home," and "Just Before the Battle, Mother."

Next an enthusiastic cadre of veterans from World War I marched out in now tightly fitting uniforms and sang "Over There," "It's a Long Way to Tipperary," and, in an incongruous finale, "Johnny Doughboy Found a Rose in Ireland." They saluted and marched off, and the applause was probably greater for the uniforms than it was for the musicianship.

Grady tried to sink into the blanket. He had a momentary vision that he had missed weeks of rehearsal and that Maestro Mandeville was about to say so.

Maestro Mandeville turned to the audience and smiled faintly. "I'd like to hear another round of applause for the men who were just out here and who fought so valiantly," he said.

Whether he meant their military service or their present musicianship, the audience applauded passionately. He nodded in appreciation and said, "And now our tribute to you. Thank you for coming tonight." He turned around and raised his baton.

"The Stars and Stripes Forever" echoed over the park. As the band slowed into the middle part, a blinding light hung over the crowd. The fireworks display from Cranston Stadium had begun.

Grady stared up, transfixed. The echo of the aerial bomb seemed to shake in his chest. It had been three years since he had seen fireworks at night.

Another aerial bomb flashed and banged and another. A blue flower the height of the sky spread before banging and crackling, and Susan clapped her hands. Grady lay back and stared, too full of the night to think of another thing. Finally life was back to normal, back to his dreams of it before the war.

A man in his midtwenties, trembling, stumbled among the blankets. A woman who might have been his mother or his aunt held his elbow. He wore khaki pants that a belt could barely keep up; his shirt flapped. His tanned, weather-beaten face was moist in the light from the fireworks; his eyes were watering.

Grady and Susan pulled in the edge of the blanket, leaving a narrow path of grass. "Thank you very much," the woman said. The man never said a word. She added in a confidential voice, "Malaria."

"Sure," Grady said, and maybe it was. Another aerial bomb went off; the man twitched violently and looked desperately toward the cars. The older woman looked embarrassedly at them and shoved on the young man's elbow, hard, and they were gone.

Susan said suspiciously, "His tan says he served in the Pacific. The shaking could have been malaria, but not the flinching and the watery eyes."

Her mother said suddenly, sharply, "Honey, when a mother says what's wrong with her child you don't ever question her. God knows I've made enough excuses for you."

The fireworks ended, and they packed up quickly without speaking.

They drove home in silence—even Julie, cuddled against her beloved Auntie Rosie. She woke up enough to cry when Mary pried her loose to go to bed.

At Susan's house, Rose opened her car door and strode away before Grady could walk around to open the passenger side. As Susan got out, he looked at her helplessly and shrugged.

Susan hugged him. He held her close, not admitting how much he needed a little comfort. She said suddenly, "Your father's going to be all right."

"Thanks." He needed to hear it, even if it wasn't necessarily true. "You're kind."

"Not usually." She gave him a quick peck on the cheek. "My God, what a night. Happy Fourth of July." And she was gone, striding determinedly up the walk and slamming the front door.

Grady drove home and went tiredly to bed. He dreamed of a marching band strutting forward unheard, under fireworks that split the night with dazzling flashes followed by ear-splitting thunder. One of the marchers dropped his cymbals and put his hands over his head, twitching. Grady ran forward—in his dreams, he could run—and put the cloak of invisibility around the man, but it didn't help at all.

The man twitched and shook until his fear seemed to be Grady's own. Grady held him until he himself was shaking uncontrollably. He woke hugging his pillow tight, his arms sore from clutching it.

FOURTEEN

ONCE EVERY TWO weeks, Grady went back to the Dwarfworks and conferred with both Pieter and Antony about the contracts that Plimstubb was being offered in the Dwarfworks' area of expertise. He did this for two reasons: to gain insight into the contracts and to reassure Pieter that Grady would never take business out from under the Dwarfworks.

During his early July visit, Grady took extra time to have dinner in the Dwarfworks. After dinner, Katrina sang a children's song for him and then, to his delight, sang "St. Louis Blues." Sonny beamed proudly. "I taught her that."

Grady was thoroughly charmed. "Good job." He stood. "Thanks for everything. I'm going to take a quick walk around and then leave."

Kirsten said, "You may want to wait for an hour. Someone wants to see you."

Antony scowled. "Get going if you have to," he said shortly.

Grady didn't know what was causing friction between them and decided not to get involved. He turned away from the table and walked through the forge area, watching as the metal grates strolled to and fro. One of them, its top bent into a semicircle and its four legs tucked together, was sleeping beside a banked fire like a cat. He stooped and patted it, but carefully until he discovered that it was cool enough to touch.

Then he moved on and walked to the far wall, by the tunnel to the Gnomengesellschaft. He walked by it, peering in at the torches that lit the corridor and remembering his first encounter with the gnomes, which was in this very tunnel.

It happened too quickly for Grady to shout or defend himself. Large hands reached from the shadows of the tunnel, pulling him in. He was dragged several feet before all motion abruptly stopped and the hands let go of him.

He caught his balance, thankful that he had held on to his cane, and spun around. He was near a torch in one of the wall sconces. He took the torch in his left hand and swung it back and forth, feeling vaguely like someone from one of the *Frankenstein* movies. The shadows receded and grew as he moved. There was no one in sight.

Still . . . Grady glanced forward and back and called, "You're sticklers for contracts, aren't you? You didn't come in to the Dwarfworks, and you didn't drag me into the Gnomengesellschaft."

Klaus appeared around the corner of the entrance to the gnomes' factory. He had extended his legs until he nearly had to stoop in the tunnel, and his arms were fully seven feet long. His glare was as angry as the scar that still creased his face. "You're clever. Not so clever as your pretty blond friend, and not so experienced as your little allies"—he stressed "little"—"but clever enough. What else have you deduced?"

Grady thought but did not say "That you're trying to frighten me." The gnome had taken Grady away from his allies, mocked their size while increasing his own, and assumed an aspect for battle. Aloud Grady answered, "That you want to ask me something, here on fairly neutral ground."

Klaus moved forward slowly, letting one set of clawed fingers scrape on the rock as he came. "I do not want to *ask*," he said with a growl. "I am compelled merely to ask. It would be a great pleasure to do more." He gestured behind him. A second gnome appeared, a huge pair of dark calipers in his right hand. In his left he carried a ledger and pen. "You may remember Wilmer."

Wilmer's present face meant nothing to Grady, but that was hardly surprising when he was dealing with a race of shape-changers. "I think we've met," Grady said steadily, refusing to let either of them know how afraid he was.

Wilmer nodded without speaking and came forward, opening the calipers with a flick of one finger as he moved them toward Grady's head. Grady raised his cane to parry them, thought better of it, and held still.

"Clever," Klaus said with grudging respect. "I cannot hurt you unless you've broken a contract. Striking Wilmer by mistake, even if you thought it was self-defense, would have broken the contract." He finished with regret, "I truly did not believe you'd think fast enough."

"Show some faith." The points of Wilmer's calipers touched him on either side of his skull, as lightly as the wind might move his hair. "What are you doing?"

Wilmer grunted, "Just taking some measurements. Hold still, can't you? I can't make them accurate if you twitch like that."

"On the other hand," Klaus commented, "if you do move, it could subsequently hurt you very much, and it won't be our fault. So suit yourself. What is your superior, Warren Hastings, doing with the controllers that I sold to him?"

"God knows," Grady said frankly. "He's put one of

them on the lathe in the shop, another on a drill press, and one as some kind of voltage regulator on a welder. One is operating the brake shear—you know what that is, don't you?"

Klaus looked bored. "A mechanism for mundane production. Go on."

Grady considered and said, "I don't know where he put the rest."

Klaus said sharply, "Someone in your plant must know."

"I doubt it. He does the installing himself, including the wiring." Grady added, sounding as grudging as Klaus had earlier, "He's not stupid."

"No. And that bothers me." Klaus ran a hand over his forehead, affecting not to notice as his own claws gouged furrows in his own scalp. "May I confide in you?"

Grady waited until Wilmer's calipers were removed and nodded, not trusting himself to answer without sarcasm. Wilmer wrote hastily in the ledger, muttering, and narrowed the calipers quickly, applying them to one of Grady's shoulders.

Finally Grady said, "Tell me what you want."

"I'm concerned about Mr. Hastings' dealings," the gnome said. "I would hate to think that he had violated a contract."

"Don't lie till you're good at it," Grady retorted. "You'd hate to think he had cheated on a contract unless you knew he had and could prove it."

Klaus chuckled involuntarily. At the sound a bat dropped from the roof, flapping away.

Klaus stretched an arm out quickly and caught it with tendril-like fingers. He tucked it into his mouth, which had grown huge fangs, and smiled at Grady.

Grady, sickened but refusing to show it, listened to the panic-stricken chittering and flapping of the bat behind those teeth. All he said was, "Warren hasn't done anything in violation of your contract that I know of. I'm hoping he doesn't."

Klaus raised a long finger, waiting obscenely long, until he had crunched and swallowed the bat. "Oddly, you don't seem to be lying. Remember, it is to your benefit to help me discover wrongdoing by him."

"If it were to my benefit," Grady said evenly, "you wouldn't want it to happen, and you surely wouldn't tell me. You hate me."

Klaus's eyes glowed. "Let me clarify myself. It may be to your benefit to help me. It would definitely be dangerously to your disadvantage if you worked against me. For now, I'm more interested in following the dealings of your Mr. Hastings."

Grady shrugged. "Sorry. Can't help you."

Wilmer said peevishly, "Hold still." He added, almost apologetically for a gnome, "Are your legs asymmetrical?"

"Around the feet and ankles, yes. Not by much."

"I'd best measure them both." He checked them swiftly and stood up, dusting off his knees with an absurdly fussy motion.

Grady said, "By the way, have you kept all articles of your contract with Warren? For that matter, have you kept all of the articles in your contract with the Dwarfworks?"

Klaus tapped a long finger on his own chin, considering. "The implication is insulting enough that I decline to answer. I should also add, although the general tone of this meeting has been cordial, that there is no God in heaven or devil in hell who can help you if I see you over here again."

Wilmer had grown a large pointed ear and tucked the calipers behind it as he pored over the ledger, muttering to himself. "Are you finished?" Klaus said irritably, but he seemed satisfied with how things had gone.

Wilmer checked his ledger. "One more . . ." He came

forward and with surprising gentleness took Grady by
the jaw. His fingers felt cold. He spun the calipers open
and slid them expertly on either side of Grady's jaw-
bone. "Marvelous," he said with real pleasure. "A truly
marvelous mandibular span."

Grady said, "What was Garner Stanley Irving's jaw-
span?" Garner Stanley Irving had been imprisoned by
the gnomes and turned into a human furnace—loaded
with metals and heated repeatedly to high temperatures.

Klaus nodded. "Perceptive of you. I'm not saying that
is the sort of project my cohort is working on, unless
you do hinder me. . . ." He shrugged, letting his shoulders ripple up and down like a wave.

Wilmer said reproachfully, "However, if that were
what I were working on, you should know that accurate
concern for clearances and joint motion saves discomfort."

"For you, or for me?"

"For you, of course."

"Then I can't imagine why you do it."

Klaus shook his head pityingly, smiling. "You mis-
understand me. It saves discomfort for later."

He turned and left. Wilmer followed, murmuring,
"That mandibular span. Promising, promising."

Turning his back on them and on the Gnomengesellschaft was the hardest thing Grady had done in a long
time.

Grady stumbled back into the Dwarfworks, catching
himself on his cane. He moved shakily past the cabinet
where the cloak of invisibility was hidden, unable now
to hide how much he was trembling.

Kirsten and Antony appeared beside him. Kirsten put
out a single strong arm and steadied him with a touch
that seemed gentle even while it was strong enough to
still him. "Where have you been?"

He told them. Kirsten stood, her right fist opening and

closing with anger. "If he ever reaches those arms in here while I'm in sight—"

"Don't worry," Antony said grimly, "he won't."

Kirsten said, "So who do you think is losing on the deal, Warren or Klaus?"

He considered. In spite of his trying to be brave in front of Klaus, he was having a hard time thinking. "It's hard to tell. They're both being watchful, and they're both hiding their business from their own plants, and they're both acting angry but feeling smug."

Kirsten said feelingly, "That makes me twice as nervous."

Grady thought of Susan and said, "Maybe in their own ways, they're each winning. It's like Einstein said about frames of reference. The deal looks different from where they're each watching."

That made no sense at all to Antony and didn't reassure him. "Do you think Hastings would cheat on a contract?"

"In a heartbeat, if he thought he could get away with it. Do you think Klaus would know that, and write a contract designed to tempt Warren into being stupid?"

"In a heartbeat, if he has a heart. We'd better keep watching them then, kid. You tell me how it looks to you, and I'll say how it looks to me."

"You've got it," Grady said feelingly. "I just wish I could go over to the gnomes' side and see what Klaus is up to."

It was now slightly past sunset.

The knock at the stone door of the Dwarfworks was forceful but controlled. Grady moved to open it, but suddenly Kirsten was ahead of him, nudging him aside as easily as if he had been little Katrina. She stared into the twilight, letting her eyes adjust, then said politely, "You may enter for business."

A voice from the gathering darkness said cheerfully

with an Eastern European accent, "Well, I have come for business."

Antony said quietly, "Kiddo, I did say you could go home early."

Kirsten moved aside. A young man in khaki pants, an immaculate white shirt, and dark suspenders entered. In his hands he held a flat, billed cap. His complexion was nearly as white as his shirt. He walked easily and casually but gave the impression of great strength. His dark eyes looked everywhere quickly. When they turned to Grady, they seemed to light up. Perhaps they did. "Grady."

Grady felt a rustle at his neck as Kirsten, on tiptoe, fastened a garlic necklace on him. "Hello, Zoltán. How have you been?"

"I have been well, very well. How am I always?" He put his hands in front of his mouth as though trying to hold the laughter in. "Little joke. But it is true," he said, suddenly earnest, "I am fine. I was sorry to not see you here, this last time when I came. That is why I asked these kind people to tell me when I might find you, and they have told me which days you come here." He reached into his right trouser pocket. "Look."

Grady took the offered photograph curiously. It was already crumpled. Zoltán continued, "Your friends send me two copies, so one I send—I have sent—to my mother and this one I keep. I kept," he corrected.

The photograph was of Grady, his hair too long from saving money on haircuts, with his arm around what appeared to be a double exposure. Behind the smiling Zoltán, Grady could clearly make out the rocks and, alone on the wall, Grady's shadow.

He handed it back. "That's great."

Zoltán nodded vigorously. "It is. And I have shown it to a real New York City photographer, who says he will find a way with light and film to make a picture of me even better."

"It's good that you found a photographer who works nights."

Zoltán chuckled, and his fangs showed slightly. "Well, he does now."

Grady wasn't sure how to respond to that. "How is your project going for your mother?"

"I have come to pick up the last of the handles." From his pocket he pulled a lovingly wrapped bundle, tied with a satin ribbon. He undid the ribbon. "This was the first one. I said, I want changes and will pay, and they have now done changes for a set of eight."

"I would have thought six," Grady said.

Zoltán shook his head firmly. "No, my American friend. A truly splendid coffin has eight. And a black lid with a silver—in our case, better to be pewter; so smart you were, Grady, to think of that—engraved plate." He held a scrap of paper out to Antony. "That will be the text. I will return for the plate soon."

"Oh, good," Antony said without enthusiasm, and left to retrieve the coffin handles.

Grady covered for his rudeness by asking, "Have you told your mother about it, or are you going to surprise her?"

"I have written her," he said too casually, "several times. Always I have received no answer." He paused, looking at each of them in turn.

Kirsten said uncomfortably, "Well, with the end of the war and so many displaced persons in Europe, I imagine mail is fairly disrupted."

"Even our letters?" Zoltán asked pointedly.

"I'm no expert on your postal system, but yes. A lot has happened in Europe." Her mouth set in a thin line. "A lot always seems to."

"Well." He shifted from foot to foot soundlessly as Antony returned with a small bag. "Thank you," Zoltán said, handing over a small roll of bills. "I will take these handles and go. Perhaps some night I will return here and say hello, yes? Thank you for your help and for your kind words." He shook hands all around. "And Grady, you stay out of danger. I hope to have you with my mother to dinner in New York City yet. I still promise that I will not harm you."

And he left. As Grady had noted before, Zoltán had still not promised that his mother would not harm Grady.

They watched him walk into the night and vanish. Kirsten closed the stone doors before saying to the others, "What do you think?"

Antony said unhappily, "I think he's beginning to worry about his mother, and I think he ought to."

That bothered Grady. "Is there anything we can do for him?"

"Grady," Kirsten said exasperatedly, "I'm sure he's very nice, but he's dead, and he drinks the blood of the living. It's good of you to want to help him, but please don't. Every time that he comes here, every time that he meets you, you are in some danger."

"I've kept out of trouble so far," Grady said. Antony rolled his eyes.

"Don't get cocky," Kirsten said. "Antony didn't even want to tell him when you'd be here, but it seemed so important to him." She added, "And I would hate to have been the one to put you in danger."

Grady looked at the great front door, then back at the tunnel to the Gnomengesellschaft. "We always seem to put each other in danger."

Before leaving the Dwarfworks, Grady went back to the locker where the cloak of invisibility was stored and checked it. The cloak was still there, simple and shiny with threaded gold and, so far at least, commercially useless. On impulse he tried it on quickly, checking the floor for his shadow. There was no shadow at all under the electric lights.

Grady walked to the tunnel of the Gnomengesellschaft, looking carefully as he walked and hiding his cane beneath the cloak. He stepped into the tunnel. He had no shadow under the torchlight.

From the bend directly in front of him a long, crooked shadow projected on the floor. The head of the shadow turned, cocking an ear.

Grady walked back into the Dwarfworks as quickly and as quietly as possible. He was on the road to Rhode Island in two minutes, his headlights on and, though he felt foolish, the dome light of the car.

FIFTEEN

O N A LATE July morning, Grady dreamed that he was
fourteen again and that his younger brother Kevin
was wrestling with him. He was happy to wrestle Kevin,
happy also because, in the double vision that dreams can
have, Grady was rejoicing in having two sound legs and
finding his brother young and not off at the war. He
wrestled back vigorously until Kevin said in Antony's
amused voice, "Two falls out of three?"

Grady opened one eye and saw that it was still dark.
He was instantly resentful of a houseguest who, having
practically become family, was perfectly comfortable
waking Grady up too early. Grady rolled his head under
his pillow as though hiding and said firmly between
clenched teeth, "Go away."

Antony continued shaking Grady's shoulder. "Up and
at 'em."

Grady blinked at Antony. "It's six-thirty already?"

"It is somewhere."

Grady could vaguely see that Antony was winking.
Grady's hand groped over to his alarm clock and turned
it to his face. He was shocked fully awake by the injus-
tice of it all. "Dammit, Antony, it's five in the morning.

You're not even supposed to be here this week."

"You asked me not to let you miss anything." Antony tugged at Grady, effortlessly pulling him half out of bed.

Grady sat up under his own power, suddenly alert. When Antony thought something was worth seeing, it probably was. "What's up?"

"You wanted me to learn about engineering?" Antony was grinning, happy that this day had finally come. "I did. I took a course in it, based on a project I wanted to do."

"Who taught the course?" Grady said nervously.

"Tom Garneaux."

That settled it. Anything Tom Garneaux and Antony worked on together was likely to be pretty good. Grady grabbed for his pants and found them on the third try.

For once, Grady took his car into work, not worrying about gas rationing at all. From his office he called Mary and apologized for his and Antony's not showing up for breakfast. He glanced around the empty front office, moved hastily out to the shop, and arrived in time to see Antony shake hands with Tom Garneaux. "Thanks for coming."

"I wouldn't miss it." He was grinning ear to ear, not at all put out by being up early. He nodded to the small crowd in the shop: Hammer Houlihan, Joe Cataldo, Flash, and Betty. Hammer Houlihan made a quick nod back. Grady could tell that Hammer and Tom had served together, though it probably wasn't in the navy. Garneaux said, "Tell everybody to be ready." He waved the folder in his right hand. "We've got plenty to do." He passed the folder to Antony.

Wasting no time at all, Antony sorted through the sketches. Grady, bemused, looked at them over the top of Antony's head. By the third sketch Grady was beginning to laugh.

"Flash, you and Betty and Hammer start early. I'll

keep watch." He handed them a parts list and sketch from the folder. "By the way: When we're all done, burn these."

Hammer looked hurt. "You think I'm some kid from East Capeesh? Of course I will." He smacked Tom Garneaux with the rolled-up sketch on his way past. "Like the old days, Tommy—no evidence."

"No coast guard, either," Garneaux said.

Each of them read the sheets in silence—at first confused, then intrigued, finally grinning. The last to grin was Joey Cataldo, who rolled his sheet up and smacked Antony enthusiastically on top of his head. "If you don't take the cake you jump out of!"

Antony grinned back, unoffended. "Thanks for helping me."

"Thank God old man Plimstubb isn't here," Grady said fervently.

Garneaux shook his head. "He has a better sense of humor than—that's right; you started here sometime after Pearl, didn't you? You wouldn't know."

"Know what?" Antony said suspiciously.

Garneaux looked contrite. For someone with no shame, he did it surprisingly well. "I couldn't resist adding a little something to the plans today."

Antony and Grady both looked nervous.

At seven o'clock precisely, Roy Burgess came into the plant. He glared down the shop floor, looking to see if anyone had arrived later than he had. Nobody had. They all were bent over lathes and presses and drills, studiously ignoring Roy. He scratched his head and walked up and down the plant, looking for someone to chew out. Grady kept well out of sight.

At a quarter after seven, Susan came by in her slacks and flats for fencing. She looked at row on row of innocent faces bent over their workbenches and grinders and asked Antony, "What's going on?"

Antony pointed at Grady, who pulled her into the corner where he was hiding. "Keep watching. I think this is gonna be good."

Precisely at seven-thirty, Roy sat at his desk, pulling the *Providence Journal* from his back pocket. Five minutes later, predictably, he was leaning back asleep, and the first snore reached the shop.

Antony leaped on top of his workbench and pumped his upraised fist three times vigorously.

Joey Cataldo shut down the lathe and came running. Flash followed more hesitantly, one hand extended in front of him to ward off unseen obstacles. Betty Quist grabbed his elbow to guide him. Hammer Houlihan strode determinedly from Shipping, a canvas bag of tools slung by a strap over his shoulder.

In short order, Joey and Hammer had tiptoed past the sleeping Roy and moved his desk outside. Flash, Betty, and Antony carried four twenty-foot pieces of pipe with flat rectangles welded on one end. Hammer tipped the desk on its side, drawers up. Betty and Flash had already welded four threaded pipe unions to the desk, one around each leg.

Antony dropped to the ground and slid the open end of the pipes up over the legs. He and Flash rapidly screwed the pipes to the desk, barely tightening the last leg before they slid the desk upright. Betty and Tom Garneaux returned with a second set of four pipes with rectangular bottom plates. Hammer and Flash treated a chair as they had the desk, then tilted the whole cartoonish office set back upright, a desk and chair silhouetted against the sky.

Joey Cataldo leaned out the window of Roy's office. "Ready." He gave a thumbs-up and, for some unknown reason, kissed his fist.

The frame of Roy's window dropped silently out of the office wall, caught by multiple hands. Garneaux strode over and gave instructions in a hoarse whisper. A short conveyor, mounted on inclined trestles, seemed to assemble itself outside the window of Roy's office.

It had taken five minutes to assemble the sky-high chair and desk. In five minutes more, the conveyor was complete. In five more Roy's desk and a chair were outside. By ten minutes to eight, Garneaux waved an arm from the wiring department; the conveyor had power to it. He squinted upward and said with quiet satisfaction, "Looks like rain."

"Come on," Antony said to Grady. "Either we all get fired, or this oughta be good."

Grady followed him into Roy's office. There were a number of Ridgid Tool & Die calendars featuring women in swimsuits; Roy had kept the calendars from 1941 on. Antony glanced at a swimsuit-clad woman caressing a threading device and muttered, "You know, if I were doing that kind of work, I'd want more protective clothing."

"Just work on getting him out the window," Grady said.

Antony grinned at him, throwing a mock salute. "Yes, sir." He and Grady tilted Roy's chair down as gently as possible and slid him onto the conveyor. On stepladders to either side of the sky chair, Hammer and Flash waited to receive Roy.

At eight o'clock precisely, a phone woke Roy. He reached for his desk and froze, staring down.

His desk and the chair he was perched on were outside the plant and, unbelievably, twenty feet above the ground. Telescoping legs made of nested sizes of pipe held them there; the legs were fastened to the furniture. A spliced telephone line ran from his telephone to the window of his office, ten feet behind him.

A conveyor belt, still slowly retracting through the window, told him how he had arrived here.

The phone was still ringing.

Roy leaned forward, waving one hand for balance, and picked up the handset. In two tries he picked up the phone. "Burgess here."

The voice at the other end of the line said, "Roy?"

"Yes?"

"Hiram Plimstubb here. I'm just checking in. I really ought to more often. Is everything all right in the plant?"

"Yes, sir." Roy blinked, looking first up at the cloudy sky and then down into the trash bin impossibly far below him. It was full of papers and old lunch wrappings. It looked soft but hardly inviting, and it was his only option for a soft landing. "Everything's just swell, Mr. Plimstubb. It sure was lucky you caught me at my desk. I was just catching up on some paperwork—"

"Roy?" Standing beside Antony and the others, Hiram Plimstubb said gently, "I'm calling from the phone in the shop."

"Ah." For the moment, Roy had nothing else to say.

"I stopped here to grab my mail before I caught the train to Washington, and I saw you rolling out of your office on a conveyor. Were you asleep?"

"Ah—um . . ." The speaker in the shop carried every word, echoing out the windows to where Roy could hear it. He said nothing.

"I like your new office. It has a lot of style. Frank Lloyd Wright would say it keeps more in touch with its surroundings than the old office. Did you plan it this way?"

"Yes. No." He rubbed his forehead, clearly trying to press a headache out of it. "Actually," he said as though he were admitting a change of mind, "Now that I'm up here, I'd rather be back down." He added plaintively, "Can you help me out?"

Antony and Grady looked at Mr. Plimstubb with interest. He looked around the shop, suddenly smiled, and said into the handset, "I've got to get back to Washington. Do your best. Meanwhile, it's good to see that the shop is in such good hands until you can come down and manage for yourself. Keep these guys around, won't you?"

Roy said over the speaker in a strangled voice, "Sure, but what about getting me out of this?"

"Oh, you're a good manager. You'll find a way out." Antony chuckled appreciatively as Hiram Plimstubb added with concern, "But you'd better hurry. It looks like rain."

The phone went dead. Grady watched through the window as Roy Burgess shouted into the telephone, slammed the handset into the cradle, and windmilled his arms frantically to keep his chair from falling over in reaction. On cue, it began to rain. The drops ran down the plant windows, then coated them. Outside, Roy Burgess, arms folded over his chest and body hunched over, contemplated the dive into the trash bin.

Hiram Plimstubb shook hands with everyone. "Just remember to get him back down alive. After all, he is my foreman."

"You bet, sir," Antony said.

"A pleasure to finally meet you, Grady." He shook hands again. "People tell me you're doing wonders for the war effort. I hope it's not wearing you out."

"I'm fine, sir." Suddenly the work seemed more worthwhile.

The old man turned to Susan. "And you're Vince Rocci's daughter, aren't you?" I'll miss Vince; he was lively and intelligent. Thank you for taking his place."

"Thank you," Susan said, looking radiant.

Tom Garneaux coughed to get his attention. "There's a paper bag on the passenger seat of the car, Mr. Plimstubb. From Hammer and me, for old times' sake."

"Ah." He looked happy. "I hope it's as good as the old stuff, then." He reached into his back pocket. "How much do I—"

Garneaux waved him off. "For old times' sake."

Harold Plimstubb nodded. "In that case, thank you." He glanced around a final time. "And see that everything from this morning is disassembled and put back so we can use it, won't you? For old times' sake."

And he was gone. Grady was wistful watching him go; working directly for Mr. Plimstubb would clearly be nothing like working for Warren Hastings.

Antony voiced the same thought: "Wouldn't you love it if he were handling things in this plant instead of Hastings?"

Somewhere under a workbench, a thing that might have been a rat squeaked in what sounded like a giggle. Antony and Grady looked at each other, but neither made a move to investigate.

Grady said, "Wouldn't you love to know what Klaus is doing at his end as his part of the contract with Warren?"

"We don't have any way to know, Grady—Sacred Sun, kid, don't do it."

"I've got to," he said bleakly. "Look at the things that are happening at Plimstubb." He gestured toward the squeaking thing under the bench. "If it's the gnome controllers that are doing it, I need to know that. If it's not, if it's something else that Warren Hastings has done to the place, I need to know that, too. All that I'm asking is a quick tour on the wrong side of the wall, over where the gnomes work."

Antony considered. He wanted very badly to say "yes" to Grady, to pretend that Grady could make everything all right, to believe in his heart that one contract as badly written as Warren had implied could do as much damage to the gnomes as their last contract with Plimstubb had.

He gave up. "Kid, there's too much at stake. There's not a chance in hell that you can sneak into the Dwarfworks and find out anything that matters." He added, frankly, "Even if there were one chance in a hundred, I wouldn't dare let you. The risks are too high."

Grady swallowed. "But you would have taken those kinds of odds when you were risking your life in the First World War."

Antony nodded. "You don't know all the steps I took to make sure that no one could find the Dwarfworks simply because I enlisted. As near as anyone could tell, I was a teenager from Chickasaw Center, Iowa. If I had died in the war, there would be a silly little monument to me out there even now, somewhere in a prairie cemetery."

Grady, apparently deflated, said, "I guess you're saying you want to handle Klaus yourself?"

Antony had a brief vision of Klaus turning a portion of the gnome's body into a blade. "I'm not sure I can handle him. I'm sure that it's wrong to make you handle him."

"All right," Grady said after struggling with himself. "You work everything out with him yourself. I'm sure you don't want me to try," he said bitterly. "You do what you have to."

"Thanks." Antony meant it.

"You're welcome. When are you heading back to the Dwarfworks?"

Antony shrugged regretfully. "Kid, I'm leaving now. I only came in for the joke on Roy. I've got orders to fill back home. A bracelet of silence—you've never seen one of those; mostly they're gifts—and an ax unfailing for a Scandinavian buyer, and a necklace that allows the wearer to dance all night." He winked at Grady. "Want me to get a copy of that for you?"

Grady smiled ruefully. "I've done my dancing for this year." He treasured the memory, despite his having used a valuable wishing ring up for the frivolous pleasure of dancing with Susan.

"You cut quite a rug," Antony said, remembering. "Okay, I'd better go. You take care."

"I always do," Grady said.

• • •

And he did. Grady waited until Antony had been on the
road for ten minutes before hopping into his car and
rolling south and westward through Connecticut toward
the Hudson and the Dwarfworks. Grady hung his cigarette sideways out of his mouth like a racing teenager,
letting the smoke stream out the driver's side window.
He felt a little as though he were racing, with the
dwarves trying to cut him off in one lane and Warren
blocking him in another, and the gnomes . . .

Grady had a brief, unpleasant vision of a gnome that
looked like Wilmer flipping Grady's car end-for-end, the
wheels spinning off as the roof collapsed to the height
of the seat backs, while Klaus sped across the finish line
and a stadium of gnomes clapped politely as though they
were at the Ascot horse races in England. Grady took a
last drag and threw the cigarette out the diver's side
window. It was an extravagant gesture, but he was no
longer enjoying it.

SIXTEEN

ONCE HE HAD pulled into the field below the Dwarf-works, the hardest part for Grady was sneaking in. He knew that the floor would be busy, but knew also that Kirsten would be watching the doors.

Accordingly, he went to the culvert that Antony had inadvertently shown him so long ago and crawled in on his hands and knees, hoping that the raccoon (Antony had subsequently told him that she was named Becca, for Calvin Coolidge's raccoon) would be out at the moment.

The culvert was empty. He pushed on the iron grating and dropped into the Dwarfworks as it swung open. Grady dropped silently into the Dwarfworks, much as he had on his very first visit.

The production floor was busy. Antony and Sonny were examining the wiring for the electric lights and for the electric furnace. The forges were running full blast, with Gretchen and others scurrying from station to station, striving to keep up with the work. In spite of his own concerns, Grady was pleased; he had helped bring business in, and the plant was thriving.

He edged into the stalactites at the edge of the plant,

easy hiding places for the dwarves in a crisis and adequate concealment for him. When at last he was at the
opposite wall, he strode quickly to the wall cabinet,
threw it open, and swung the cloak of invisibility over
his shoulders in a single motion.

He closed the cabinet door and glanced around. No
one was looking his way. To his immense relief, Kirsten
was bent over her desk, completely occupied with
record-keeping. He straightened his shoulders, careful to
keep his cane under the cloak, and walked silently to
the tunnel labeled GNOMENGESELLSCHAFT.

Once inside, he checked a final time for his shadow
under the torches; there was no trace of it. A bat
squeaked as he passed, but that was all. He paused a
moment, trying to relax his breathing so it made less
noise.

He tiptoed past dark burn scars on the cavern floor, the
only visible sign of the previous battle between the
Dwarfworks and the Gnomengesellschaft. The scars
were from electrical discharges.

Grady glanced at the cavern ceiling again. The horrible dangling hook, sharp and menacing, still swung
from a ceiling chain. To either side of it, new electric
lightbulbs glowed in severe, protective wire cages. The
gnomes had learned a great deal about electricity, and
they would not be daunted by it again.

He slid as quietly as possible past working gnomes at
their toolbenches. Unlike the polished steel benches in
the Plimstubb shop, these were dark and forbidding tables and cabinets of black iron. Grady wondered why
cold iron didn't hurt the gnomes, then gave up wondering. Perhaps it did hurt; the gnomes' business was
founded in pain.

The shop was alive with the hammering and grinding
sounds of work. Unfortunately, there were also screams
and groans; some of the work itself here was alive.

The tools on the racks were in keeping with that thought. The racks held appropriate amounts of the usual hammers, pliers, tin shears, and screwdrivers, but they also held far too many rasps and files. Some of the files had hooks projecting from them. All of the hooks were barbed. Grady was reminded, unhappily, of a conversation in the Plimstubb Furnaces shop during which Hammer Houlihan described the different files on his bench. "Kid, that's a rat tail, this is a flat bastard, and I'm a mean bastard."

On the other hand, Grady noted that the metals processing equipment was both familiar and reassuringly primitive. Heat-stained anvils stood next to forges with leather—he hoped fervently that they were leather—bellows and brick forges. Hammers for metal beating rested against the anvils, and buckets for quenching—Grady hoped that they were filled with water, though the liquid looked too dark—stood beside them.

Some of the smells were comfortingly familiar from metal treating plants—warm air, spilled machine oil, and that unnatural but unmistakable smell of heated or ground steel. Underneath it were other smells: burned hair, charred meat, and a salty smell that reminded Grady of the taste in his mouth after he had bitten his lip.

("What do we make?" he remembered Klaus saying silkily during a terrifying plant tour. "I like to think that we make unhappiness.")

He thought of the furnace he had sold and set up next door at the Dwarfworks. It had a conveyor belt that moved work into a high-temperature electric heating chamber and on to two water-jacketed cooling sections before dropping it off, at nearly room temperature, into a box at the other end. The gnomes could process dark projects on their dark forges, but they couldn't approach the volume of work that the dwarves now could.

Maybe that meant that, someday, the world would be more good than evil.

He moved quietly and, he hoped, unseen past four pairs of rust-stained bolt holes in the cavern floor. They were all that was left of the underpinnings for restraining Garner Stanley Irving (1803–1945), who had once attempted to cheat the gnomes and had spent nearly a century as a human furnace, swollen to grotesque size and heated to high temperatures to process metal parts that had been unceremoniously loaded into his mouth.

Grady looked at the holes with relief and a sense of triumph. He and the others had fought with gnomes for Irving's freedom and had won it. Maybe it was possible to win against the gnomes—against any evil force—after all.

He stepped around a corner and nearly bumped into a trousered leg, clamped and bolted to the cavern floor.

He tiptoed around the body, which lay sprawled like something left over on the sidewalk from a twenties bootlegger's war. It still had an overcoat on, which looked intolerable in the heat of the cavern as well as the heat of the summer outside. Grady peered into the face.

It stared emptily, not seeing him. The stubble on the chin had quit growing, or had been seared off. The man was the panhandler who had recently disappeared from in front of Plimstubb.

Grady moved quickly and stealthily to the workbench next to the immobilized man. The surface of the bench was stacked with construction drawings, and Grady was sickened to recognize the format if not the style.

For now he only glanced at the layout drawing, a penciled sketch of a prone figure invaded by pipes, wires, and a loading table clipped to an impossibly stretched mouth. The bill of materials was printed in runes except for the numerical print references and the part catalog numbers. The title block of the drawing said simply,

GENERAL LAYOUT. In the designer's block were the initials "WH."

In the approval block was a spidery K, its arms the claws of a scorpion—Klaus's monogram.

In spite of the Plimstubb look and feel to the drawing, Grady was betting that it was an EGAD drawing: Elf-Gnome Assisted Design. He looked from side to side; the nearest gnome was, he hoped, out of earshot. He slammed his fist down in the center of the layout drawing and whispered firmly, "RAUS!" He waited for tiny figures of workmen to stand up on the print, as they had on prints in the Dwarfworks.

Instead, dark, misshapen heads appeared at the four corners of the print and pulled themselves out on— Grady looked away, then back. He had to be wrong; they were arms of some sort. The figures slid to the bill of materials in the upper right-hand corner of the print, silent except for an occasional snarl or snap of fangs when one figure jostled another. Where there were materials listed and catalog numbers for parts, they pulled the real parts. They ran back to the center, chattering menacingly to each other, and pulled the drawing of the panhandler upright into a three-dimensional, terrified figure.

While the tiny panhandler screamed, they inserted pipes, attached wiring from his body to a transformer, forced a steel door into his jaws, and set up a loading table in front of his terrified eyes. Last, they opened the piping valves and turned on the current.

The design had clearly been tested before; it worked perfectly. The panhandler gradually heated to a glowing red, and flame shot out of the vent pipe stabbed through his back into his lungs.

The loading mechanism was relentlessly automatic. Grady hastily deactivated the print.

Clipped to the drawings was a note from Klaus, dated July 10:

The consignment and the drawings accompanying him have been received and are under review. At our present level of electrical power we will be able to supply him with electrical resistance elements and operate him under a reducing atmosphere (nitrogen and hydrogen) at 1,800 degrees Fahrenheit (982 Centigrade) with no processing drawbacks other than his own extreme discomfort. Output should be satisfactory if he is fitted for now as a batch furnace rather than a conveyor.

Once this portion of the project is signed off on, the contractor is willing to proceed. The remaining drawings and the remaining consignments to be supplied with them are on schedule and await delivery.

The remaining consignments . . .

Grady considered and moved close to the panhandler. "You can't see me. Can you hear me? Blink once for 'yes.' "

There was a long pause before the man's eyelids moved down with agonizing slowness.

"I'm from Plimstubb Furnaces in Rhode Island. I think my boss is part of the reason you're stuck here. I'm betting I can get you out of here—not right away, but soon. Be brave." He added, from his heart, "Jesus, I'm sorry this happened."

The eyes blinked "yes" again. There was nothing to say to that. Grady left quickly and quietly.

He moved into the Dwarfworks with relief, happy to be safe again and happier still that he hadn't put any of the dwarves at risk. The dwarves were deeply in debt to the gnomes, and it was wrong to give the gnomes a lever of any kind by which they might exploit the vulnerability of the indebtedness.

He looked around the dwarves' cavern before removing the cloak of invisibility. Antony was working at the

Plimstubb furnace; Pieter was chatting with Gretchen about something. Sonny LeTour, frowning with concentration, was working at the wiring for the lights and the furnace; Katrina was sitting on Sonny's shoulder like a tiny guardian angel.

While no one was looking, he took the cloak off and put it in the cabinet in the wall. He closed the door carefully, watching as the crack of the door line disappeared into the cavern wall. The cloak was safe and hidden, and he had not endangered the Dwarfworks.

Grady heard a scraping sound and spun quickly. The shadows of the rough cavern wall made it difficult to be sure, but he saw, or thought he saw, a single dark clawed hand retracting around the edge of the tunnel to the Gnomengesellschaft.

Grady looked back at the cabinet with the cloak of invisibility in it and felt terribly cold, with a sudden prickly sweat on his arms nonetheless.

Aloud he said, "Antony?"

Antony turned to look, astonished that he hadn't seen Grady come in. "What are you doing here?"

Grady looked at him expressionlessly and jerked a thumb toward the tunnel to the Gnomengesellschaft, and suddenly Antony was afraid.

Kirsten joined them before Grady could say a word. He explained what he had seen and finished, "I have to go back to Providence."

Antony said apologetically, "I've gotta go with him. I have friends there now."

Kirsten frowned. "I have to stay here until I've made the Dwarfworks secure." She glanced anxiously but fondly at Pieter in his office. The older dwarf was writing processing records with a steel-nibbed pen, his head bowed. Grady, remembering the recent months guiltily, was glad that this time he and the Dwarfworks had been kept out of danger. He hoped to keep it so, but he wasn't sure how to.

Aloud Grady said, "Antony and I will try to find out what else Warren has planned."

Kirsten chewed her lip and said with finality, "I must make this place secure. It's my job and my duty." But she added, "After that, I'll try to follow."

"Best we could hope for," Antony muttered.

Kirsten looked at him and smiled crookedly, shaking her head. "Enlisting in other people's wars again?"

Antony was feeling as guilty about Grady's danger as Grady now did about endangering Antony. "This was originally the gnomes' fight with us, if you'll think back to when we first met Grady."

She nodded. "This time, at least, you have a duty." She looked proud of him.

Grady watched them bemusedly, wondering if finally Antony's love for Kirsten was getting somewhere. There was a sudden knock at the stone Dwarfworks door: a staccato rap of energy, enthusiasm, or anger. Grady called automatically and absently, "Come in."

He saw Kirsten's face; she was looking at him in horror. Grady quickly checked his watch. How the hell had it gotten so late? It was past sunset . . .

A slender, manlike figure burst straight through the door of the Dwarfworks, and it seemed that some ghostly part of the stone exploded soundlessly out of the door with him, leaving only dead matter behind.

Grady brandished his cane in front of him, not recognizing the figure before him. Then it landed, sliding gracefully on spread legs like a figure skater, and Grady knew who he had just invited to enter, freely and of his own will. He touched his own neck, realizing that there was no garlic there. "Zoltán, what's wrong?"

The young man—he still seemed young, though he had probably been dead longer than Grady had been alive—seized Grady by the rib cage and lifted him off the ground, nearly crushing Grady. Zoltán cried in a voice distorted with grief, "They are gone!"

Behind Grady, Antony and Kirsten scrambled for weapons, but it was clearly too late. Zoltán, normally friendly but shy, stood panting, his fangs inches from Grady's throat. "Who?" Grady asked, gasping.

Zoltán glared, his eyes glowing like embers for a moment. "Who, you say, just like the names are who they were, are all they were. Why not? It is all they are now." The fire went out of his eyes before he closed them. "You want to know, I'll say the names. My Uncle Einar, who laughed every sunset when he rose and knew every joke told for two hundred years. My Aunt Magda, who would tickle me when I was a child, and even after she was dead she would do it and make me laugh until I had no breath. Beautiful Sofi, with the red hair and green eyes, first they put a bayonet through her pretty chest and when that was not enough for them, they took garlic and asafetida and a cedar stake . . ." The sound stopped coming out of his open, fanged mouth, and two red tears coursed from his eyes. They flowed down his cheeks, not clotting.

Grady said, "I'm afraid for my family every day of my life."

Zoltán didn't hear. He held Grady tighter and wailed with guilt and anger, "They took the Rom—the Gypsies—and we did not cry; who cries for the Rom? And then they took Jews and the homosexuals, and the mad, and the Fey and the kobolds and the people of the wolves, and still we did not cry. And by the time they came for my people, our tears were red and all alone." His eyes locked with Grady's, and it seemed to Grady that he had never seen such hatred in the eyes of the living. Zoltán said with a snarl, "You did this. Your people. To your own kind and to the rest of us."

Grady twisted his feet downward, but the floor was far below. Zoltán's iron-hard fingers dug into his ribs, crushing the breath from him.

With an effort he reached down and grasped Zoltán's

shoulder with all the strength of a man who has used a cane for years. Zoltán looked up, startled, as with every last bit of his strength Grady pushed his cane into the chest of the vampire.

Grady fell to the ground, scrambling as he hit and pulling his prone body along with his cane. In seconds he was at the wall cabinet, throwing open the door. Before Zoltán could reach him, Grady grabbed the cloak of invisibility and swung it over his shoulders.

Zoltán stood gaping and pointing, swinging his head from side to side so quickly that his dark hair waved above his forehead. A moment later, beside him, Grady took a deep, shuddering breath, noticing how sweet the air seemed. "Is your mother all right?"

Zoltán, frightened, slashed sideways with clawlike nails. A moment later the vampire said contritely, "Grady my friend, was that you? I am sorry. I hope I have not hurt you, and am glad that I smell no blood." His pale nostrils flared. "My mother lives. Well, no, not lives, but she goes on. But now the Allies control Europe and all the borders are guarded. They look for fleeing Nazis and collaborators and sympathizers, and this is why I come to ask you: How am I to get my mother to America?" He repeated, "I am sorry. Understand that I am sad for my family, afraid for my mother. How will I get her here safely, with the ports being watched for escaped Nazis and collaborators?"

Grady shed the cloak, tactfully out of Zoltán's reach. "It works good, doesn't it? Here." He held it out. "Try it on."

Zoltán took it gingerly, wrapped himself in it, and disappeared.

Antony said unhappily, "Oh, real smart, kid." Kirsten whirled this way and that, her sword flashing unceasingly. Her eyes were the size of quarters.

Zoltán stood beside the cloak, which had dropped on

the floor. "I can hide her." He was happy, but suddenly frowned. "Yet how will get I it to her?"

Grady turned to Antony. "Show him a bill of lading. You know which one."

Antony ran to the files, returning with a scrap of paper. "He'll get you across the Atlantic—if you want it that badly," he said, suddenly feeling awkward. He handed it to Zoltán, who read it and froze in place.

For a moment, the entire cavern of the Dwarfworks seemed dark, and Zoltán seemed to turn even paler. "The Dutchman," he whispered, clutching the cloak of invisibility as a frightened child would a blanket. "Passage on the Cold Ship to Europe . . ."

He stiffened, and held the cloak with the same poise a matador would a cape. "Then I will, if I must. For my mother I will face the Cold One and his nightmare death-in-life."

Grady, intrigued at Zoltán's fear, opened his mouth and shut it immediately. There were some things you didn't bother asking someone who was being this brave.

"But how do I avoid the crew?" Zoltán said anxiously. "I am one, and they are many. By day I am more helpless than any child. How can I be sure I will even reach my mother?"

Wordlessly, Grady reached for the cloak of invisibility and wrapped it around Zoltán again.

Zoltán took it off, his face fearful and questioning. Grady said, "Since you can't use a mirror and check, you'll have to take my word for it. We couldn't see you."

Zoltán, for a moment his old self, thumped the side of his head. "What does Bugs Bunny say about people like me? 'What a maroon!' So funny, the rabbit. I knew you or the dwarves would solve my problem if I came here. I will wear the cloak over the Atlantic, and up the Danube, and as I go to her. By night it will wrap around us both."

Once again he lifted Grady off the floor. "Thank you, American friend. I cannot pay you for this. . . ."

"Take it." Grady avoided looking at Kirsten or Antony.

Zoltán set Grady down. "I will give it back." He turned to Antony. "How soon, when is the time that the Dutchman will . . ."

Antony sighed. "Next full moon. Do you need directions to find him?"

"I know where he lands." He shivered. "Even in New York, we can feel when the Cold Ship touches the coast." Zoltán knelt and offered his hand. "Thank you for the help you give."

"Hey, don't thank me, kid." But Antony took the cold, strong hand, afraid to touch it but moved by the affection in the grip.

Kirsten took it as well. "Use the cloak well. It was meant for service in battle," she said in a voice trembling with anger.

"Then I will give it back, little warrior." He stood. "Grady, my friend, when we return from Europe I will give you a good meal. And I swear I will not harm you, nor will anyone with me, and you will be our guest. I owe you that."

"And I'll come. If you want, I won't even wear garlic." He added, curious in spite of himself, "Maybe I've eaten too much Italian food, but how do you cook without garlic?"

Zoltán laughed, hugging him so tightly that even the ribs that were numb were sore again. "Have you never had paprika? I will make pork paprikash. It is an old recipe, with sour cream, and bay leaf, and the paprika—I will bring paprika back, along with my mother. The best, reddest spice, you cannot know—and the wine will be Egri Bikaver, bull's blood. . . ."

He saw Grady's face and laughed louder. "It is just a name, my friend. It is the blood of the grape only."

"I'll bring something."

"No," Zoltán said firmly. "You have done much for my mother. This night you will be a safe guest, and a guest alone."

He leaned forward, kissing Grady on the cheek with dry, tightly closed lips, and leaped through the stone door to the Dwarfworks.

Antony waited until he was gone, then sagged onto a bench.

"Congratulations, kid. You brought another vampire safely to America. Oh, I'm real impressed." He finished bitterly, "And you gave them a cloak of invisibility. What a swell idea."

"He promised to give it back," Grady said defensively.

"Is there any oath that can bind him or his kind?"

"Promises don't bind anyone who doesn't want to be bound."

Kirsten said tiredly, shaking her head, "Once you used up a wishing ring to dance with Susan. Now you give away . . ." She shook her head. "How can I help you? How am I to train you?"

"First," Grady said sharply, "don't underestimate me." He went back to his car. Antony looked after him curiously before following him out the front door.

It was a long, dark ride back to Providence for Antony and Grady. They talked intermittently about metal, sales, and the coming end of the war, but Grady refused to offer any explanation of why he had given up the cloak of invisibility.

SEVENTEEN

At PLIMSTUBB THE next morning there was no fencing lesson; Susan was waiting for them in Engineering. The first thing she asked was, "Antony, what are you doing back here already?" and before he could answer, "Grady, what did you learn?"

Grady told her. Antony ruefully told her about having fed the panhandler.

Susan chewed her lip and said, "Tom?"

Tom Garneaux laid a newspaper casually across his desk. "You have my full attention, sweetheart."

She either didn't mind or ignored him. "Remember the time I borrowed some lock picks from you?"

"You broke into someone else's office, too," he said with disapproval. "I wouldn't be surprised if he figured it out, too."

She said solemnly, "I think he did."

"What are you going to do about that?"

"Borrow the picks again and see if he's doing anything about me."

Garneaux beamed. "Atta girl. I oughta get you your own set."

A minute later they were at Warren's door, with An-

tony and Grady standing watch. They had considered
calling Talia and asking her to warn them when Warren
came in the front door. Instead, Tom Garneaux saved
them the trouble. "Talia's not much of a Home Guard.
I think I'll go help." He ambled out front as Susan
started on the lock.

It was a simple tumbler lock. Susan had two picks
inside the keyhole and was manipulating them carefully
when Antony said, "I just had a thought."

She sighed loudly. Of course you did. And I'll bet it's
worrying you all to hell."

"We're not sure he put all the gnome controllers in
the plant, right? What if he's got one in his office, keeping watch on it for him?"

That nearly stopped her. She rocked back on her
heels, considering.

Grady said thoughtfully, "He wouldn't dare. The last
thing he'd want is a spy for Klaus inside his office."

Susan nodded. "That makes sense."

"Enough so you'll risk it?" Antony said.

"We have to anyway." She bent down again, working
the picks, and the door clicked open.

Grady strode past her before she could stand up. Antony caught her expression and bowed sarcastically. "After you." But he followed her closely, his sharp eyes
checking every corner.

"Close the door," Grady said to Antony.

"Why?" But he did it. "It won't stop Warren."

"I'm not worried about Warren." He added, half defensively and half apologetically, "I'm jumpy. There's
too many things crawling around this plant."

Antony nodded and locked the door.

Susan was already after the files. She picked open the
locked drawer and said disappointedly, "There are no
gnome file folders in here."

"Nobody's that stupid twice," Grady said. "Talking
files can talk too much." He picked over the files care-

fully. Most of them seemed to be routine quotations for furnaces, though some of them were for overseas companies. Grady recognized the folder for the Seraphim and looked inside. It was empty except for an outrageously inflated quotation and a brief, brilliantly written response in gold ink, rebuking Warren for greed and warning him to look to his soul.

He shut the file and looked at the rest of the drawer glumly. "There must be fifty of these in here. I wish I knew the poor bastard's name."

"Look under Eddy," Antony said. "That's what he told me his name was."

"There won't be a name on it," Susan said suddenly. "Would Warren bother learning the man's name? He only knows our names so he can threaten to fire us." She added with sudden contrition, "Grady and I didn't even ask his name."

"She's right. Let's look for a folder with no name on it, or with some general label. Split them up three ways," Antony said. He added with pride, "Susan and I are both used to reading them by now."

Grady grinned at him, just as proudly. "That's right." He split them up and they flipped through them, one by one.

Antony said, "Here we go." He scanned the folder in disgust, shut it, and passed it to Grady.

Grady looked at the label, "Vagrants." The first sheet inside was a handwritten memo of understanding from Klaus, describing the delivery of "tramps, immigrants, displaced persons, and those whose absence will not be noticed" to the Gnomengesellschaft. The second sheet detailed Plimstubb's designs for addition of heating elements, controllers, atmosphere pipes, and loading systems for metals to the immobilized humans. The process involved a confusing and odd, chilling phrase from the gnomes: "retrofitting and reengineering."

The third sheet described subsequent plans to "reengineer" Grady, Susan, and possibly Antony if it could be done without violating any prior contracts with the Dwarfworks.

The final eight sheets were sketches and bills of materials for the transformation of humans and dwarves into heat-treating furnaces. The first three were generic overhead, side, and cross-section drawings of biped figures, showing how to insert pipes and wiring.

The next three were detailed portraits of Antony, Grady, and Susan in place on the Gnomengesellschaft floor. The drawing of Susan showed a blush of heat on her cheeks. Her mouth had been stretched with an iron frame to accommodate a metal basket, lovingly detailed, with upright metal bolts wired and fixtured through it for heat treating.

Grady crumpled it in his fist. Antony saw the look on Grady's face and hastily put it back and passed him another folder. "Read this."

It was the contract with Klaus. The language was legal, but arcane and circuitous. As far as Grady could determine, it was an agreement to purchase ten controllers. The exchange was not for money but for "equipment to be provided through the purchaser in barter." Another paragraph stated explicitly that the controllers were only to be used in-plant. Penalties were described only as "immediate and extreme." There was no explanation of how Klaus would know if the controllers were sold out-of-plant to Plimstubb customers.

The final paragraph, stating that the gnomes were not responsible for damages incurred through malice, was familiar to Grady but no less worrisome for that. Grady put it back in the folder and handed it back to Antony.

Antony stuffed folders back into the file drawer. "Time to go. Susan, give me your stack."

She did nothing. He turned toward her. "We're done, kiddo. We've found everything—"

Susan was rocking back and forth, holding two

grease-stained folders. The corners were dog-eared and dirty. Grady thought disapprovingly that no sales folder should look like that.

They weren't. They were shop folders, identical to office folders except for the stains, and they held battered construction drawings.

She laid the first one on Warren's desk. It was a wiring schematic, detailing each numbered wire from a control panel into a temperature control instrument. The instrument was neither Brown, nor Honeywell, nor Wheelco, nor any other type with which Grady was familiar. The drawing was labeled, FAHDI AND FAROUKH.

"Wow," Grady said softly. He wasn't sure what powers Mr. Fahdi and Mr. Faroukh had, and he was afraid to ask Talia. "He cheated Klaus, and he cheated . . ." He shook his head, trying to imagine the consequences for Plimstubb Furnaces if Warren got caught.

"That's not important."

Grady and Antony turned to Susan, astonished. She laid the second folder on the table, and her hands were trembling as she spread out the drawing.

It was remarkably similar to the drawing in the other folder, except that the numbers for the wire connections were different. The connection references were on the prints for Stode's furnace.

Grady whistled. "I was worried enough when Stode bought material from the Dwarfworks."

Antony did a double take. "Stode's furnace got a gnome controller? Sacred Sun. You can bet he doesn't know about that."

"Do you want to tell him?" Grady said.

But Susan's reaction was beyond either of theirs. "This can't be allowed to happen."

Antony was confused. "Susan, it already has. It's shipped."

"That doesn't matter."

Grady half expected her to say something strange about time and space, but she merely said, "We need to talk to Warren."

On cue, the phone rang.

On the second ring, Grady picked it up. "Cavanaugh, Sales."

"And what would you say if I'd been Warren, calling in?" Tom Garneaux asked.

"That I'd gotten Talia to give his calls to me. He'd have chewed me out, but not as much as for a break-in. Is he coming?"

"Fast."

Grady gestured to the others and slammed the receiver down. Seconds later they were out of the office. The lock clicked behind them.

Grady sighed with relief but heard Antony inhale sharply. He turned and saw that Susan had picked the folders back up and taken the wiring drawings with her.

"Susan, are you out of your mind?"

Susan said, "I'll do this alone."

Antony said with surprising abruptness, "Kid, don't be an idiot. Why risk it?"

Grady could have told him that was the wrong tack to take. Susan furrowed her nicely plucked eyebrows and said, "Because I don't need you."

Warren passed by the three of them with no more than a sidelong contemptuous glance and unlocked his office. Susan leaned into Warren's office. "Warren, would you mind coming to the shop for a moment?"

She left. Warren, with a sudden suspicious frown at Grady and Antony, followed her.

Antony sighed. "Now, that's stubborn." He glanced at Grady and ran after him. "Where are you going?"

"Just follow."

Grady led Antony through the men's room, into the back of the stockroom, and behind some stored welding screens. The last one was near the door to the front office. Grady and Antony moved quietly to the screen. The oil-soaked canvas was taut on its pipe framework. The canvas was pocked with holes from welding sparks. Grady alternately put an ear and an eye to one of the holes. Antony, fervently hoping that Warren wouldn't notice their feet in the narrow gap under the pipe frame-work, did the same.

Warren held his hand out to Susan. "Give me those folders."

She put them behind her back. "Not until we've talked."

The move emphasized her figure. In spite of his anger, Warren looked her up and down and licked his lips lightly and quickly. "All right. Talk."

She was shaking. "You cut a rotten deal with Klaus for the controllers."

"It didn't cost much at all."

"It was wrong!" she said angrily. "It was slavery, not to mention torture. And it could have cost Plimstubb a lot. You brought Klaus here to take away that poor bum—"

Warren laughed out loud, and in spite of the noise from the rest of the floor, the sound echoed. Grady thought, or imagined, that some of the scurrying paused and resumed in their direction.

Warren went on, "Do you think I'm crazy? Do you know what Klaus would do if he found fewer . . ." He stopped.

"Fewer controllers than he sold you? So you did cheat Klaus."

"Just a little." But he was practically purring. "That contract was an engraved invitation to make an idiot out of him. It was unenforceable. How would he find out? Who could resist taking him for a sucker?"

Behind the screen, Grady closed his eyes.

Susan said in confusion, "But if Klaus didn't come

down here and kidnap the panhandler—oh, my God, no.
Not even you."

"Don't underestimate me," Warren said. "All it took
was a bottle of cheap whiskey and a twenty-dollar bill.
After a few gulps, he slept like a baby all the way to
the Catskills."

His voice turned wheedling and, Grady recognized
with disgust, something else. "Of course, you realize it's
in your best interest to keep this quiet, now that I've let
you in on it."

"Let me in?" Susan was outraged. "I figured it out."

"Halfway. But I never felt like hiding it from you."

Antony thought there was enough oil in Warren's
voice to fry fish and chips. He heard a low growl from
Grady and grabbed his arm.

"What do you think you're letting me in on?" Susan
said suspiciously.

"On everything." He had moved toward her. "Why
not? You're fairly bright. If I can keep stringing Klaus,
I'll need help designing wiring and piping, other things
as we get busier." Warren's voice was oozing something
he probably thought was charm. "And you know, I could
teach you things you never dreamed."

In spite of the tension of the moment, Susan snickered.

"What?" Warren said, genuinely startled. Apparently
he hadn't considered the possibility that she would re-
fuse him.

"I'm sorry. I was just thinking about your knowing
anything I could possibly want to learn."

For a fraction of a second, Warren's face relaxed, and
Grady could see behind it a man who had learned that
he was not worth loving, not worth respecting—a man
who strived for achievement on any terms because he
knew, without question, that nothing else would ever
make him worthwhile.

Then Warren recovered, and he was dangerously, solicitously smooth. "Is this about Cavanaugh? Susan, I couldn't let him take advantage of your pity for him. What benefit is a cripple going to be for you and your mother?" He clucked in imitation sympathy. " I've tolerated him, but for your sake I can see it's time to fire him."

"No!"

"Ah." The triumph in Warren's voice was unmistakable. "But he's a drain on Plimstubb. Still, I might keep him on if you convinced me to."

"How would I do that?" Susan said helplessly, genuinely confused. She followed a moment later with, "Wait. Stop!"

Warren was still chuckling and fumbling at her blouse when Grady hooked the top of the welding screen canvas with his cane and ripped it off the frame with one smooth motion. As he stepped through, Susan's windmilling arms were taking most of Warren's attention, but he glanced over her shoulders and said with a snarl, "Cavanaugh, get the hell out of here if you want to keep your job."

Susan's right heel came down hard on Warren's instep. He grunted and let go of her. She drew her arm back for a punch to the jaw.

Grady said to Susan, "Do you mind?"

"I'll do this my . . ." She stopped, looking at his expression and at the veins standing out on his forehead. "Be my guest." Grady moved toward Warren.

Grady had been walking with a cane for several years. At close quarters, he often used his arms on tables, chairs, and counters, holding himself up with every other step. Also, he had worked in the Dwarfworks, trying to match the considerable strength of the dwarves.

Warren, sidestepping to get out of Grady's reach and to take advantage of his own height, confidently threw the first punch. It was to Grady's bad side; Warren wasn't above fighting dirty to be sure of a win.

   The sword-fighting practice of the past year paid off.
Grady ducked sideways, grabbing Warren's arm as it
shot by him. He pulled Warren on tiptoes and threw him
backward, spread-eagling Warren against the brick wall.

   Warren put up his arms in defense. Grady feinted with
his left; Warren fell for it and shifted his arms. Grady's
right arm flashed forward and his fist sank into Warren's
gut, and to Grady it seemed like a punch he'd pulled
back to deliver years ago, when he'd begun working for
Warren.

   Warren wheezed but stayed in place. Grady drew his
arm back again, not bothering to feint this time.

   Antony caught Grady's arm. "Kid, don't."

   Grady's blood was singing in his ears, and he felt
light-headed. "I owe him more than one."

   "Are you sure he can take more than one?" Antony
let go of Grady's arm as Warren slid down the wall.

   Grady looked at him indifferently, clenching and un-
clenching his fist but slowly relaxing his muscles.

   Warren rose shakily to his feet and said, gasping,
"You're fired. Get out."

   "I'll be safer fired," Grady said through clenched
teeth. "You goddamned idiot, did you seriously think
you were smart enough to cheat Klaus?"

   "I am, and I have," Warren retorted, his breath coming
back. "Who's going to stop me—you?"

   There was a scraping sound behind them. One of the
gnome controllers, the one that welded furnace tops, was
peering through the gap in the welding screen frame.
Two red lights in the front turned toward Warren, and
the controller cocked to one side, remarkably like the
head of the RCA Victor dog, listening at the phonograph
trumpet to his master's voice. The controller shook from
side to side in pantomimed disgust and turned majestically away, striding on pipe legs to the nearest metal
bench.

Grady watched it, reminded uneasily of the tripod robots in *War of the Worlds*. He turned back around and said bitterly, "Do you still think Klaus won't find out?"

But Warren was gone, and the front office door was swinging shut.

The controller banged rhythmically with one pipe arm on a metal bench: *Tap-tap. Tap-tap-tap slide tap. Tap-tap slide-slide tap.*

Antony put a hand to his ear. "It isn't Morse code, but I'll bet somebody's reading it."

"Some*thing*," Grady said tightly. There was a sudden hum of electrical power in the building, and the lights dimmed. "We've got to clear the shop. Susan, get the people in the front offices out of here."

She nodded without argument. "Be careful."

Seconds after she left, the nail-spitting controller from Shipping walked to the length of its compressed air hose. It was within reach of the rack for air hoses. With a sudden spit of air it pulled the hose connection free, jacked two new lengths of hose onto the old hose, jacked the end of the final hose into itself, and walked to the center of the shop floor. It paused there while the workers stared at it: Flash squinting watery-eyed with his welder's mask tilted up above his stubby cigar and backward baseball cap; Benny Behind working his folded hands as though straining to squeeze out a prayer; Betty glancing sidelong at the controller on the brake shear; Hammer Houlihan, cagiest of them all, edging quietly toward the exit with a crowbar in hand for a weapon.

The controller from Shipping reared up as far as its legs would allow and let go with an ear-splitting screech like a steam whistle.

In the silence that followed, Antony bellowed, "Everybody out, now!"

The automated equipment stepped away from its posts. A blowtorch waved evilly at Hammer Houlihan;

a discarded rotary saw blade at the end of a pipe arm hummed at Benny Behind.

They all headed for the doors like Thoroughbreds out of a starting gate.

EIGHTEEN

A MINUTE AND a half later, they were out. The garage doors of the plant had slammed down behind the last of the shop workers. July heat shimmers came off the parking lot, but no one seemed to care. Grady and Antony were moved through the lot, trying to account for people.

Benny Behind pointed a shaking finger at Hammer Houlihan. "This is because of your sinning."

Houlihan, still hanging on to his crowbar, admitted grudgingly, "In my twenties I'd have bought that in a heartbeat, but I've slowed down since then. Oh, sure, there might be an outstanding warrant or two, but what the hell." He jerked a thumb at the plant door, where smoke and steam were seeping out, accompanied by noises like steam engines fighting buzz saws. "Nothing real recent that I've done earned that."

Chester Traub muttered, "The machines are all dancing. It's like a scary Betty Boop cartoon. Or Disney gone bad."

Joey Cataldo had his hands on Talia Baghrati's shoulders. She was trembling but unharmed. Behind them, Betty Quist was staring at the building. The whites of her eyes were huge, like a frightened horse's.

"Are you all right?" Grady said to Tom Garneaux.

Garneaux looked up imperturbably from a newspaper containing names like FLEET FOREMOST and MICKEY'S MAIN CHANCE. "You know how I hate being kept from my work. You know what caused this?"

"We're pretty sure," Antony said.

"Think you can fix it?"

A woman's voice said, "Of course." They turned and saw Kirsten, a burlap bundle over her shoulder.

Antony was delighted. "How'd you get here this fast?"

She gestured behind them at the Dwarfworks truck. "I left as soon as I could. I knew you'd need me."

Garneaux said, "Do you need any help?"

"Oh, no," she said seriously. "We're outnumbered but not desperate."

There was a scream inside the factory, followed by the screech of metal on metal. Grady looked hastily around the parking lot at the others. "Where's Warren?"

Garneaux shrugged indifferently. "He ran out the front door like a bat out of hell, or like one was chasing him. Didn't warn any of us, either. Good thing Suzie followed."

"What about Flash?"

No one knew. There was another scream from inside the factory. Tom Garneaux set down his newspaper and moved toward the garage door.

"We have at most"—Grady tried to remember what the contract with gnomes had said—"ten opponents in there. Probably less, I'm afraid."

Kirsten looked at him sharply. "You're telling me that Warren—"

"We're telling you nothing," Susan broke in quickly. "Not in this crowd."

"Agreed." Kirsten said loudly but calmly, "All of you move back from the door except for Susan Rocci, Grady

Cavanaugh, and Antony van der Woeden."

They all moved, even Benny Behind and Hammer Houlihan. Grady concluded that it must be something in the voice.

She laid down the burlap package. It was an appropriate length for pool cues or for disassembled surf casting rods. She unrolled the package carefully, lifting the contents out one piece at a time. None of the weapons touched the other.

The first two were full-sized human rapiers, with sharpened blades and mirror-polished baskets above the hilts. The blade edge was silvery and hard to focus on; Grady assumed that was the heat. He lifted the weapon on his index finger at the forte, above the basket. The balance was perfect. He took it in his hand and straightened his arm to lunge, doing a tight circling disengage halfway through the motion. The blade followed the twitch of his thumb and index finger effortlessly.

Susan was doing the same with hers, testing it wonderingly. Grady noted with pride that she looked as though she knew what she was doing. Automatically they turned toward each other and went *en garde*.

Kirsten, her own short sword in hand, said hastily, "Don't touch the blades to each other."

Susan had already swung hers sideways, parrying Grady's lunge. Grady disengaged hastily, rolling the blade to one side. He brought it back upright in a salute and stared at the rapier edge. Even up close, it rippled strangely.

Antony held his own sword, a shorter, thicker blade in the fashion he was accustomed to. Kirsten, watching him, said, "I also brought a hammer for you."

It had a head fully the size of Grady's fist and must have weighed fifteen pounds. The hammer head was coated with silver and carved with runes. Antony tucked it in his belt gratefully.

Susan slashed her blade sideways energetically. Kirsten frowned. "Always lunge. A stab is sufficient with these weapons, and it keeps you at the greatest distance from the enemy. Susan, I assume you've had some fencing training."

Susan, startled, said, "A little."

"She's had the basics," Grady said. "It's not the same as being in battle."

"Of course not," Kirsten said patiently, "but she's also already been in battle. If you've taught her well, she'll do just fine putting the two together. Now, how do we get inside?"

Antony pointed with the rapier to the door with the sign that said Employees Only. "We could go in there."

"And get cut down one at a time as we go in? No. We duck through the garage door all at once. Grady, where is the closest wall to this door?"

"What?" He thought. "About three feet to the right of the door. It shields welding sparks from the employees' door."

She nodded approvingly. "We enter, step to the right, and we only need to guard the front and one side at first."

"Plus we can still retreat," Antony said hopefully. Maybe they could just find Flash and get back out.

"This is a fight about right and wrong. We don't retreat."

That meant that Kirsten never would. Antony sighed loudly and sang under his breath, "He has sounded forth the trumpet that shall never call retreat . . ." Kirsten looked his way, and he quit singing hastily.

They moved to just outside the loading door.

Kirsten said firmly, "I'm first."

Grady said, "Fine." He half bowed, though it wasn't his place to invite her in. "Just remember, all the wood in there is impregnated with oil. If a fire really starts, it'll spread faster than we can run." He didn't add, "Faster than I can run." He tested his bad ankle, feeling like the Scarecrow of Oz in the presence of a match.

Kirsten looked uncertainly at the smoke curling through the garage door. "It seems to me it's already started."

Grady waved an arm. "It hasn't caught any of the beams or interior walls yet, I guess. Believe me, we'd know." He added, "If there weren't people in here, I'd say the hell with it, let it burn."

She said in genuine shock, "But this is where you work!"

Antony said dryly, "You didn't get out much during the Depression, did you, kid?"

Susan shook her head and, to Grady's surprise, said glumly, "No, Kirsten's right. We owe the place to try and save it if we can."

Grady said out of the side of his mouth, "Great speech. Are you starting to like it here?"

Susan said back the same way, "My mother and I need this job."

Grady, startled, realized that he had forgotten for a moment all the jobs that would go up in smoke if the plant did. Until Warren had fired him today, one of those jobs had been keeping his household and his brother's household out of debt.

Kirsten pulled the garage door handle. The door didn't move. She turned and gestured toward the others in the parking lot. "You."

"Hammer Houlihan," Antony whispered, wishing she had pointed to someone else.

"Mr. Houlihan," she said calmly, "we hope to save your friend Flash. Can you get us in?"

"I can if he can't," Tom Garneaux said.

Houlihan glared at him. "The hell with you and the rest of Engineering." He stomped over to a pickup truck in the lot and returned with an eight-foot length of pipe.

Hammer Houlihan slid the crowbar teeth under the bottom of garage door so the bar stuck up at an angle.

He slid the pipe over the end of the crowbar and put a sawhorse halfway down the pipe to use as a fulcrum. He flexed his arms and grabbed the far end of the pipe, moving it into position for raising the door. He glared through his eyebrows at Susan. "You be careful in there. Vince would crunch my . . ." He started over. "Vince would give me hell for letting you go in there."

"He's not here," Susan said tightly.

Kirsten said briskly but with respect, "Mr. Houlihan, she truly is better equipped than you are to help me return the plant to normal. Believe me, if I had trained you, I'd want nothing better than to call on your assistance."

"All women want to," Hammer said, mollified, and leaned on the pipe. The prybar raised the door, grating in protest, three feet.

Kirsten said, "Now." The four of them, Grady and Susan and Antony and Kirsten, ducked under it.

Something hit the door with an ear-splitting CLANG. A wrench from someone's toolbench dropped to the floor. Outside, Hammer Houlihan swore and let go of the pipe. The door dropped down.

Grady shouted, "Duck!" They dropped to the floor. A steel rod, thrown like a javelin, stuck in the garage door just below the doorframe, making it impossible to raise the door.

Antony stood and dusted himself off. "I guess we're not backing out."

"We weren't anyway," Kirsten said. "Grady, act as rear guard. Susan, on my right, Antony, my left. Forward." She raised her sword.

She lowered it quickly, slashing at something dark that scuttled out from under a workbench and dove for her left leg. A metal rat rebounded off her sword and lay inert.

An electrical cable hissed with power and struck at

Grady. He slapped it down carefully on the insulation, expecting it to die.

Instead it arched back, the bare wire at the end hissing and sparking. Grady parried quickly, disengaging hastily as the bare end of the wire—he couldn't help thinking of it as the "fangs"—struck at him.

Susan stamped her foot down on the insulation and dropped her sword on the bare wires, losing contact with the hilt. There was a blinding spark, like something from the end of a welder's rod. When Grady could see again, he saw the wire lying still and Susan carefully picking up her sword.

She said to Kirsten, "Are the hilts of these swords insulated?"

Kirsten bit her lip but only said, "Something to think of for next time. For now, all of you remember Susan's tactics—but pick up your swords quickly afterward." She swatted another mechanical rat, stamped on a wire snake, and moved on.

Grady said out of the side of his mouth to Antony, "I thought gnomes didn't know much about electricity."

"They didn't," he said back the same way. "You taught them. They learn quickly."

Kirsten raised her sword again. "Step to the right. Check under your feet."

Antony's hammer clanged three times. Flat, scuttling things struggled briefly and died. The others moved toward him.

A moment later he said with relief, "We're here." A wire dropped over the door. He lifted the wire on his hammer and threw it into the smoke and gloom ahead. Grady strained, trying to see it land.

The entire shop floor was shrouded in black smoke and puffs of steam. Light came from the electric lamps, but also from random sparks, flames, and light from erratically moving cutting torches.

A figure shambled out of the smoke, dragging one leg.

It wore a welder's mask, and it reeked of cigar smoke.

Antony said uncertainly, "Flash? Are you okay?"

The scrawny figure tipped up the welder's mask and cackled horribly.

But it wasn't Flash. It was a mechanical controller mounted on a swivel fastened to a vertical pipe. On top of the controller was a backward baseball cap. The controller spun around once, the cigar below it growing red.

Before they could strike, the figure was gone.

Grady said, marveling, "What in the hell was that?"

Antony said, "You're the one who reads science fiction. That was a killer robot."

Susan said tightly, "That was Flash's baseball cap. There was blood on it."

Kirsten said, "That's why I'm here."

There was a gap in the smoke and they saw Flash, flailing helplessly against the wires that bound him to a metal cart, paraded past them. Behind it, the gnome controller for welding paraded proudly, holding up a welding rod so it sparked against objects near the cart. Flash thrashed in panic against the bonds with every spark. The controller was humming like a live wire, but to the tune of "When You Wish upon a Star."

The smoke rolled back. Grady shook his head, unsure of what he had just seen.

Kirsten, more certain, said "Follow me" and disappeared into the smoke. Susan, recovering first, followed.

In the distance now, from the corner near the brake shear, they heard Flash whimpering. Grady moved forward, only to find Antony's hand on his arm, holding him back.

Grady said, "I know the factory. You follow me; I'll go ahead—"

"Not this time." Antony lay down on top of a machinist's cart, his sword in his right hand. "Give me a push."

Grady opened and shut his mouth helplessly, looking

for an alternative, but Antony was right. Grady would never fit on the cart without overbalancing, and it was the fastest way. He bellowed over the clanking, "Okay, but watch your balance. The shop floor's pretty uneven."

He braced his body against the wall and, wincing, put the remainder of his weight on his bad leg. He tucked his other leg up against his chest, pulling the cart toward himself with the crook of his cane. The cart rolled easily and, he was relieved to see, smoothly. He looked ahead into the smoke, said awkwardly, "Good luck," and straightened his leg out suddenly.

Antony held on tight with his free hand. Grady watched as the cart rocketed into the smoke ahead and disappeared.

The smoke cleared in front of him. He saw a welding rod, sparking intermittently as it waved near a grounded metal surface, and heard a metallic voice singing emotionlessly, "Are the stars out tonight?/I don't know if it's cloudy or bright . . ."

Below the sparks lay Flash, bound and struggling helplessly as a gnome control instrument swung a welding rod toward his right eye.

Antony leaped up and slashed at the wires holding Flash immobile. The shipping controller, on the front of the cart, swiveled and spat nails at him.

Antony ducked and rolled Flash off the cart, shouting "Run!" Flash landed on his hands and knees, crawling away as fast as he could. Grady, thirty feet away and slashing carefully at electrical snakes, made his way toward Flash.

The controller tilted down toward Antony and took aim. Antony swung under the cart and up the other side. He swung his sword once, hard.

The compressed air hose on the rear of the nail pipe split off with a loud POP. The hose fell, thrashing impotently on the floor.

The controller swung to face Antony and hissed indignantly as the last of its air escaped. A nail, pointed at Antony's heart, dribbled out of the pipe and fell to the floor.

Antony climbed onto the cart and stood on it, facing the controller. His sword was poised over his head; he was ready to deliver the *coup de grâce*.

An insulated electrical wire swung around his neck, catching him by the throat and toppling him backward as it tightened.

Antony barely managed to slip his free hand inside the noose and keep his airway from being crushed. He twisted his sword around awkwardly, trying to cut the wire without cutting his own throat.

The controller from Wiring, perched on the back of the cart now, slipped a loop over his sword arm and lashed it to the nearest front cart leg. Antony kicked at the controller. It dodged nimbly and lassoed the leg, tying it down. In seconds, Antony was completely immobilized.

The cart rolled to the front of the brake shear and stopped, leaving Antony feet first in front of the shear entrance. The shear was slamming up and down, chewing the last of a steel plate into thin strips.

Both controllers, the one from Wiring and the one from Shipping, scuttled off. Antony raised his head and looked uneasily at the shear opening.

The controller for the shear rolled to the cart, gripping it between strong legs. Antony felt a pressure at his shoulders as the flat carttop slid with terrible slowness toward the slamming, snapping brake shear. He pulled his feet back until he thought the wires would cut his ankles off.

Grady returned from helping Flash to the door and looked around in confusion. Antony was nowhere to be seen. "Antony?"

He heard a yell between crashes from the brake shear.

He stood on one tiptoe, bracing the rest of his weight on his cane.

What he saw made him spin around and shout, "Kirsten!"

She looked his way, startled, and fought her way over, slicing down into the clumsy mechanical rats between them. She looked at him in confusion. "Are you all right?"

By way of reply he grabbed her around the waist, lifting her onto the cart he had used to send Antony into the shop. "Go save Antony."

She looked ahead alertly as Grady shoved the cart forward as hard as he could. Her eyes went wide as she saw Antony, and she leaped to her feet on the moving cart.

The cart rolled forward forty feet and smashed into a tool cabinet. Kirsten leaped to the top of the tool cabinet and kept leaping, moving unerringly from workbench to workbench until she reached a metal table just before the brake shear. She paused for balance. Antony, his feet inches from the slamming jaws of the brake shear, rolled his eyes at her helplessly.

Kirsten let out an inarticulate, furious cry and dove toward the cart on which Antony was bound.

Her first blow smashed through one arm of the controller feeding Antony into the brake shear. She rolled under the cart, somersaulting; her second blow smashed the other arm.

The feeding controller screamed at her in fury as her third sword stroke sliced through it from top to bottom, continuing through the top of the cart and its frame.

With her free hand she pulled the cart away from the brake shear. "Antony, are you hurt?"

She sliced through the wires on one side with a single sweeping stroke. Antony rolled to his other side, freeing his other arm and leg. "I'll have some bruises. Thanks for the help." The danger over, he was embarrassed at having been so helpless.

But Kirsten's blue eyes were wide. "You nearly died." Her eyes narrowed. "They tried to kill you."

Antony opened his mouth, but gave up and picked up his sword. She didn't look like someone to discuss with just now.

Susan backed toward them. In one hand she held her sword; in the other she held a coil of unconnected electrical wire. Something with five or six waving steel arms was moving stiffly toward her, its legs a sawhorse modified with two hinges.

She slashed an arm, but only that arm fell dead. She grunted, holding the coil of wire sideways, and heaved it over the top of the construct as though playing ring toss.

The remaining live arms struggled under the weight of the wire. She lunged forward, touching each of them in turn—then the legs—and finally put a foot against the sawhorse and shoved it, hard. It fell to earth with a clatter.

Grady, cane in one hand and sword in the other, arrived, panting. "Are you okay?" he said with a gasp to Antony before spinning and lunging in turn at three pursuing mechanical rats.

"He's fine," Kirsten said, and the edge in her voice made Grady turn half around toward her. "Raise your swords and follow me."

A tripod construct of the controllers, all swivel arms and circular saw blades, clanked toward her threateningly. With one swing of her sword, Kirsten severed three of its arms. With the next swing she sliced one of its legs off, leaving it to topple helplessly to the floor, its remaining saw blade striking sparks against steel scrap. She kicked it contemptuously, and it severed its own head and lay still. "Follow!" she snapped at the others. Then she moved forward through the smoke, hell's fury on her face.

Grady and Antony followed. Grady was suddenly, immediately confident that they would win.

The next ten minutes were largely mechanical, even on the part of Antony and Grady. Grady was astonished to find himself following the motions of fencing: parry in six, parry in four, riposte in seven—the attacks meant nothing against an antagonist who had limbs but no body. He kept the point of the sword in line with the controller, ignoring the wild, wide motions of the arms. When Kirsten shouted, "Now!" he thrust forward, the point of his sword between the red "eyes" of the control instrument. It thrashed, its legs sliding off the blade of the sword, and lay still.

Antony swung a pipe as though it were a bat smacking the last pitch in the bottom of the ninth. A gnome controller flew halfway across the shop, struck a pipe, and dropped lifelessly like a stone. Antony raised the pipe back up to the at-bat position, looking across the smoking shop.

The electrical snakes and mechanical rats stopped moving. The last of the pipes quit thrashing. Except for the crackle of dying fire, the shop floor was quiet.

Kirsten surveyed the ruins, muttering to herself and counting. Finally she said, "Eight controllers. That can't be all of them."

"Of course not," Grady said unhappily.

"Tell me now."

Susan said tightly, "The contract was for ten. That's what the fight was about; Warren sold at least two off the premises against the terms of the contract."

Kirsten looked horrified. "Then they'll know about this."

Grady said blankly, "The gnomes?"

"The remaining two controllers," she said flatly. "They'll know what happened here—don't ask me how;

I don't know—and they'll do the same thing, the same sabotage, wherever they are."

Antony blanched, looking around the damaged factory. "But who has the other two controllers?"

Susan said immediately, "I know one."

Grady said, "I know both." He kicked at one of the dead mechanical rats. "Antony, run and find Talia. Bring her here."

Antony glanced at Kirsten, who waved her sword. "Do as he says." He dashed away, happy to be out of the ruins.

They met her halfway to the Employees Only door. Antony was holding her elbow, walking her through the scrap metal and the now-dead electrical wires. Joey Cataldo solicitously held her other arm.

Grady didn't hesitate. "Talia, remember when Mr. Fahdi and Mr. Faroukh said you could call them if you needed them? That wasn't by phone, was it?"

Talia laughed, in spite of the serious surroundings. She reached into the bodice of her dress—there was room to store a softball—and held up an ornate ring on a chain. The writing on it was in Arabic. Joey, scratching his gray head, looked confused and jealous.

Despite the urgency of the occasion, Grady was intrigued. "I didn't see them give you that."

"It came to me later." Grady noticed that Talia, normally confused in her speech, adroitly sidestepped the issue of whether it came by mail, by messenger, or by some other means.

"Use it now and call them. Tell them—tell them to call me on the telephone."

Antony gestured at the disarray around them. "The phones may be out."

"Tell them that. Tell them to call on the phone anyway."

Talia looked around at the damage and, incredibly, said hesitantly, "Are you sure it's that important?"

Kirsten murmured for Grady's benefit, "She knows not to waste the power of a ring or of anything else."

Grady ignored Kirsten. He said to Talia, gently, "I'm afraid your friends may be in danger."

Talia immediately rubbed the ring and murmured into it. Grady hurried to his office.

He realized belatedly that, without Talia to run the switchboard, there was no one to connect a line to his phone. He was moving away from his desk, toward the door, when the phone rang.

The voice at the other end said, "You take a liberty, my friend." The static behind the voice rose and fell like the sound of a great wind.

"I had to, Mr. Fahdi." He explained about the controller.

He had almost finished when Mr. Fahdi broke in, "Please excuse me." He called out in a voice that rattled the telephone, the office, and Grady: *"Faroukh!"*

The rest was a rapid-fire stream of what sounded like Arabic, but perhaps wasn't; the telephone handset glowed blue, and Grady's hand tingled. He grit his teeth and held on, pulling the handset partway from his ear.

In a moment a second voice answered Mr. Fahdi, who sighed loudly with relief. "It is done. We were in no danger, so long as we knew . . . my friend, is Mrs. Baghrati well? Is she safe?"

"I promise you she is, and will be. Are you and—well, are those you care for safe?"

"God is good and they are. I thank you." Mr. Fahdi's voice was suddenly cold and hard. "I speak of you the man and friend, not you the company. A man in your business place did not lie to us, yet he deceived us nonetheless. It was not wise of him, for himself or for the rest of you."

The telephone line rose up, swaying back and forth like a cobra.

Grady thought of Warren's pass at Susan and said

fervently, "You have no idea how many people want to kill him just now."

"Do not kill him, if that is not your law," Mr. Fahdi said unwillingly. "See that he receives the justice of God." He finished, with an anger that seemed almost human, "All of it that he can bear, and more."

In the next second he sounded like the genteel businessman who had visited them. "In exchange, and in gratitude for your warning, we will not intervene. Thank you for your goodness in making this call. We shall not forget it, young friend. Please tell the lovely Mrs. Baghrati that she is in our prayers."

The line went dead—in both senses; it ceased to move, and there was no sound from the telephone. There was no way to call Drake Stode and warn him. Grady went back to the others.

"That could have been a bigger problem," Grady began and shut up as Warren Hastings made his way toward them across the metal carnage of the factory floor.

"Where the hell were you hiding during the fight?" Susan asked.

Warren, unabashed and ignoring the question, scanned the still-smoking shop and said irritably, "Do you realize the amount of damage you are liable for in this company?"

Antony's jaw dropped. Kirsten began, "Do you realize . . ." and shook her head. "No, of course you don't. You have no intention of understanding that this is partly your fault."

"Partly?" Susan said blankly.

"The rest of the guilt lies with Klaus." She gestured out the door. "Go to the company car. Antony, drive the truck. We're off to confront Klaus." She added curtly to Warren, "You're going to help us."

His lip curled. "Happy as I would be to get the better of Klaus, I don't think it will happen through you. Why should I help you?"

The muscles in Kirsten's right cheek were jumping in a way that made Antony step back involuntarily. "Because I told you to, and because if you don't . . ." She gestured to the others. "Turn your heads a moment."

They did so as Kirsten pulled Warren forward by his tie and whispered in his ear. Grady strained his ears but heard only a low murmur from Kirsten, followed by a sharp intake of breath from Warren.

When Grady, Antony, and Susan turned back around, Warren was already striding toward the plant door, straightening his tie as he went. Kirsten looked at them all, too furious to change her expression. "Back to the Dwarfworks. Now."

The others ran for the door. Grady moved first toward Warren's office. He dashed in, thanking God that it had been unlocked, and hurried out clutching a manila folder. He hadn't known that he could still move this quickly.

But the others were waiting when he got there. He felt Kirsten prod him impatiently, and he hurried to the company car.

NINETEEN

THE DRIVE TO the Dwarfworks always seemed longer to Grady when Warren went. No matter what topic anyone brought up, conversation degenerated into silence under his sullen glare and occasional snorts.

Susan drove the Plimstubb company car. It was the only vehicle that could carry four people, and Kirsten had no intention of letting Warren ride by himself with Susan and Grady. Antony was following alone in the Dwarfworks truck.

They pulled onto the side lane that was the hidden main entrance to the Dwarfworks. Kirsten parted the vines and threw it open, gesturing curtly to Warren. He walked in first, head held defiantly high.

But they all paused as the figures at the far wall spun to stare at them, and what had been an angry conversation stopped. The shadows from the figures were tall and narrow, shortening as the figures themselves seemed to melt and run before rising again to threatening heights.

The shadows of the dwarves facing the gnomes remained constant.

"Uh-oh," Antony said.

Kirsten said sharply, "Keep your weapons in evidence but not threatening. Advance spread out, slightly behind Warren." She gestured. "Warren, please move forward."

His lip curled. "I don't take orders from you."

"Of course not." Her sword barely moved toward him but looked infinitely more dangerous. "I assumed you would take orders from this."

He snorted with disgust, but he did walk forward.

As they approached, Grady looked carefully at Heinrich and Klaus. Pieter was standing close to them, hands on his hips, looking angry. Sonny LeTour, frowning and mistrustful, stood leaning on a six-foot prybar. Beside him, Gretchen stood with a forge hammer.

Kirsten called to them easily, "I'm sorry we're late. I had business elsewhere." She said to Heinrich, "You know I would never miss business with you if I could help it."

He bowed. "I was sorry to think you would miss our business, if it came to your specialty." He finished mockingly, "Welcome back, Dread One," but he watched her sword and every move she made, and his malleable body pulled slightly away from her.

"Welcome back," Pieter echoed, and sighed. "And thank you for bringing this—Hastings. Most of this is about him, as always."

Grady said, "Who else is this about?"

But Sonny looked worriedly at him, and Pieter only said gently, "We may not get to that, boy." And whenever Klaus wasn't glaring at Warren, he was shooting smug, angry glances at Grady. That was all Grady needed to know.

Something snapped into place for Grady, and he glanced searchingly around the Dwarfworks. Katrina and the other dwarf children had vanished, hiding in the cave. The Dwarfworks was already prepared for war.

All Grady said aloud was, "We've brought as much paperwork as we could find about Warren's recent dealings with"—he hesitated—"Gnomengesellschaft personnel. Could I summarize them for you as I understand them?"

Klaus's and Heinrich's chins nodded in unison, nearly touching the floor as their faces extended.

"All right. Warren—my boss—made a deal to buy gnome controllers from the Gnomengesellschaft. From Klaus, specifically. There was a clause banning the off-site sale of those controllers, and there was a warning disclaiming responsibility for the damage that might result if he did sell them to others."

Grady added, "That same day, Warren signed a note stating that no action of his would put Antony in danger while he was working at Plimstubb."

The gnomes leaned forward with interest. Klaus, in spite of himself, said, "You've been out being part of the war effort? You never change, do you?"

"I don't," Antony said bluntly. "Your kind shift, you twist, you can't be relied on at all." With a great effort he avoided looking at Kirsten as he said, "I'm constant."

"At any rate," Grady broke in quickly, "Warren broke his word twice. He sold your controllers to a number of customers, some of whom he'd first made contact with after getting their names from—"

"From conversations with the Gnomengesellschaft," Klaus said sharply.

"From one of the gnomes, yeah." Grady smiled at him, and for a second he was very sure of himself. "Maybe you'd like to suggest who that was?"

Klaus gestured irritably, his arm growing to underscore the gesture. "Never expect disclosure when you have no evidence."

Antony looked up sharply, realizing at least one path this conversation might take. Grady was careful not to look at him. "Anyway, Warren's actions resulted in danger to Antony, who worked at our plant. And they resulted in a lot of damage to the plant, where he was an officer. I think if we all put our evidence together against him, in the three plants, we'd have a case against him somewhere." He dropped his arm, sword in hand. "My question is, where would we have the case?"

Warren folded his arms and regarded them defiantly. Antony was fascinated and repelled by the man's refusal to acknowledge guilt and accept punishment while there was a single way out.

"He's ours," Susan said. "We'll throw him in the slammer." But she bit her lip as she said it, and Warren Hastings smiled thinly. Grady knew that, in most courts, the evidence against Warren Hastings would be thrown out.

Pieter shook his head. "He's ours. My Antony worked in his factory, and look how he was nearly destroyed."

Kirsten echoed with shaking anger, "*My* Antony." Antony looked at her speculatively.

Klaus said with a chillingly quiet, low growl, "He attempted to cheat me—my firm. He owes restitution. He is mine, and I have long-term plans for him."

Warren regarded them all indifferently. "I have nothing to say until you prove your prior claims against each other."

Grady looked at the assembly uncomfortably. Warren's denials might stand against each of the charges against him, if he could get each interested party to argue against the other. Only cumulatively, with each other's cooperation, was the chain of evidence against Warren Hastings complete and devastating.

The Dwarfworks cave had bats, stalactites, and scars on stone from a recent battle, but nothing in the cavern was as disturbing as Warren Hastings' self-confidence. He glanced from side to side, assessing the mood in the room, then said belligerently, "Why have I been denied a lawyer?"

"You shall have a lawyer," Pieter rumbled, "if the world of their law is the world for your defense."

"What do you mean?" The Warren of unworldly deals and magical negotiations had vanished, to be replaced by the Warren of cold facts and figures. "Do you have something to hide? I may need to see your books on projects related to your outrageous accusation." He coughed. "My God, I'm hoarse."

Pieter nodded to Antony, who reached into one of Kirsten's desk drawers, opened a bottle, and said indifferently, "Here, have a beer."

Warren nodded without thanking him and drank it down. "That was good. Now I am ready to discuss my future," he said. "I think . . ." He collapsed, snoring. Grady caught him, cued by a completely alien moment of universal generosity in Warren's eyes.

Grady said flatly, "How long will he sleep?"

Antony crouched over Warren's inert frame. "Twenty years. That takes him past most of your criminal-theft laws, doesn't it?"

Grady, dazed, considered. "I'll have to check the statute of limitations—"

"Don't kid me. He'll wake up home free. Old, maybe, but home free."

That was true. Grady hoped, fleetingly and uncharitably, that on waking Warren wouldn't think to insist on his pension from Plimstubb, which would probably be fairly substantial by then.

Klaus rasped, "He was to be mine."

Antony said blandly, "He still could be. Geez. Klaus, I've forgotten: Did your people ever put some kind of temporal limitation on betrayal and contracts?"

Klaus stiffened and moved close to Antony. Grady moved forward; Kirsten restrained him. Klaus said quietly, "Mr. van der Woeden refers, of course, to the established notion of limiting the term for punishment and recompense. Clauses like this are common to contracts in the Gnomengesellschaft. That term for my contract"— he hesitated, then went ahead—"was eighteen years." He glared balefully at Antony. "As I suspect Mr. van der Woeden knows."

Antony, despite feeling threatened, refused to move away. He was grateful in a number of ways when Heinrich moved toward Grady to speak.

Heinrich cleared his throat. Since his throat was at the present moment at least two feet long, this was a truly horrible sound. "Tell me—and I know I have no right to ask you this with any presupposition of camaraderie and good feeling—is there anything in the records Warren Hastings left behind that would imply malfeasance on a gnome's part?"

Grady was torn several ways.

If Warren had failed to entangle Klaus in his business dealings, Klaus would be free to go after Grady, Susan, and the Dwarfworks again. Given Warren's behavior toward Grady—and particularly toward Susan—his future absence from Plimstubb was not a bad thing, but it would have been nice to have him as the first target of Klaus's malice.

If Warren had implicated Klaus in a contract-violating project that the Gnomengesellschaft had openly condoned, then Pieter and the dwarves could possibly negotiate a deal that would free them from their debts to the gnomes. That would be something wished for, not just in normal commerce, but also in fairy tales. It was highly unlikely.

If Warren had implicated Klaus in a project that the Gnomengesellschaft had not condoned, then Klaus would be subject to extensive punishment—or to blackmail by Grady, if Grady felt he could do it. This was a serious temptation, since the notion of owning a "tame" gnome offered untold possibilities in future negotiations.

Grady had grown up reading constant revelations about shady public officials in Rhode Island who took advantage of contractors or of taxpayers; the notion of milking hush money out of a servile gnome was seriously attractive.

Clearly, it wasn't attractive to Klaus. "There is another matter of penalties and punishment, the one we were discussing before these others arrived." He pointed at Grady, lengthening his fingers to within inches of Grady's unblinking eyes. "He has broken prior arrangements."

Heinrich looked at Klaus with polite interest. Klaus tried again. "He trespassed in our factory."

"Recently?" Heinrich regarded him dubiously. "Given our present security, that seems unlikely." He gestured toward the Dwarfworks end of the well-lit tunnel to the Gnomengesellschaft.

Grady kept his face as blank as possible.

"Oh, he did it, all right," Klaus said eagerly. "He examined my—our—most recent project—"

"*Your* most recent project," Heinrich said casually. "I gave you my approval, but made it clear that your efforts to find manufacturing employment for the destitute—"

"As furnaces," Grady put in.

"—Were laudable, but were your own should there be a problem. Evidently there is a problem, and he discovered it through the paperwork."

"He discovered it through criminal trespass, and the problem is his!" Klaus pointed triumphantly at Grady. "He went through our factory near the very end of the day shift."

Heinrich shook his head slowly, letting his forehead grow with the gesture. "Klaus, this is a pathetic attempt to sidestep your own poor business practices. If he came to our factory, how is it that no one saw him?"

"He made himself invisible."

Heinrich looked pained. "Come now. He's a mediocre

fighter and an adequate engineer, and has so far proven an above-average salesman and contract writer. But a sorcerer? I doubt it."

"Then explain this." Klaus strode to the locker where the cloak of invisibility had been kept and threw it open.

After a moment he dropped to his knees and felt in the cupboard. "It was here."

Heinrich said dourly to Grady, "I don't suppose, in the absence of physical evidence, that you would like to confess?"

Grady replied, "Never expect disclosure when you have no evidence."

"Just so," Heinrich said. *"Touché."* To Klaus he said with quiet fury, "Is it your secret dream to teach these beings as much about our business practices as possible?"

Klaus whispered urgently, "I'm telling you what he did."

Heinrich hissed back, "He's telling you to prove it. You can't." He turned toward the humans and the dwarves. He was clearly unhappy. "I"—he stopped, struggling with the next word—"apologize for the childish attempts of my colleague to evade accusation."

At the word "apologize," Klaus seemed to shrivel. His arms drooped to the floor and retracted slowly.

Heinrich extended a hand—at the normal human extension, for once. "Please, may I see the documents?"

"Please" and "apologize"? Grady considered, then gave the manila folder from Warren's office to Heinrich, who snatched it greedily, looking at the purchase records, the shipping manifests, and the storage invoices for goods unimaginable to most people.

Klaus sagged, bones and all, as Heinrich said deliberately, "While I do not think that you would win a contract dispute even under your own legal system, I accept that the contract is an awkward enough document that we must open discussion—"

"We'll drop the contract dispute," Susan said. She swallowed visibly and continued, "In exchange for a favor."

There was a moment of stunned silence. The first sound to break it was Kirsten, half strangling. She said to Grady, ignoring Susan, "We may have the means to destroy Klaus."

"I know." On the way down from Rhode Island, Grady had read the contract between Klaus and Warren. Klaus had skirted the edge of violating the gnomes' contract with the Dwarfworks. One look at his face said that he knew it.

Grady said raggedly, "Excuse us." He took Susan aside. For once he was able to ignore being wildly in love with her as he dragged her by elbow to a quiet corner and said urgently, "Suzie, what the hell?"

"Take the deal," she said flatly. "We need to find that controller, and fast. Klaus doesn't know he's got us by the throat, but he does."

Grady looked at her dubiously, and she broke. "Please. I've figured it out. Grady, you know that the missing gnome controller went out on Stode's second furnace."

"I'll phone him."

"You can't. Not and be sure it's in time." She was pale and shaking. Everything about her warned Grady that he was missing something important about this whole situation. "And what would you say to him? That we put an evil magic component on government equipment? It's no good."

"I could try." He looked across at Klaus, who had lowered his brows until they overhung his eyes like the eaves of a house. "Are you sure it's that urgent to stop the controller?"

"Do you remember the telegram diverting troop

trains on the whole East Coast to ensure on-time shipment of the first furnace? Do you remember the men who came to check up on you, just because you'd written a science fiction story about atomic power?" Susan looked strained and unhappy and, Grady realized with unease, insecure. "I don't think that Manhattan is a small project. I can only guess how important those Stode contracts were, but it's a good guess. This could end the war, Grady. Please make a deal with Klaus." In desperation she added, "What do you want from me? What do I have to promise to do, that you'll accept this deal?"

That decided him. "Klaus," he called, "we're offering to drop the contract dispute as part of a new deal."

"A New Deal?" Heinrich said, amused. "How sentimental of you. You must truly miss President Roosevelt."

"We all do," Susan said, "and that's why we're not going to let him down. We'll drop all contract disputes on this contract," she added with emphasis, "in exchange for the device you use to track the controllers."

Klaus looked stunned. Heinrich said with a hiss, "What did you tell her?"

"Nothing. I said nothing," Klaus answered flatly "I don't know where she gets such an idea." He glared at her.

Kirsten, sword at the ready, moved beside Susan, who didn't blink. "It's the price of a settlement."

"She's bluffing or guessing." Klaus sounded desperate. "I swear, I told her nothing."

Heinrich regarded him balefully. "Your reputation does not inspire trust." He tapped his long fingers against each other; the claws at each end clicked. His face rippled with fury, veins pulsing and disappearing. "You know how we feel about allowing outsiders access to our technology."

Grady struggled to understand the implications of the

tracking device. "Then you knew that Warren was breaking the contract?"

Klaus looked suddenly uncomfortable.

"Oh," Susan said, "he was counting on it." They all swung to look at her. "Klaus wrote a contract offering Warren a way to make a lot of money and cheat Klaus at the same time. And it didn't look enforceable. To Warren it was irresistible; Klaus had no way to check on him, as far as he knew."

She was speaking to Heinrich, who answered coldly, "There's nothing wrong with writing a contract with an eye to enforcing penalties. It's sharp dealing, and it's an art in itself."

Klaus looked more sure of himself as Heinrich finished, "At the higher echelons of management we actually encourage it."

A thought struck Grady. "Even when it will only work if it makes your technology available to others?"

Heinrich could only stare. Grady continued, "Klaus knows where the other gnome-built controllers are. He let Warren sell them to Plimstubb customers."

"Now that," Heinrich said quietly to Klaus, "you cannot deny."

"I cannot," Klaus admitted. "But it was the only way that I could catch Hastings. It was worth it."

"To whom?" Heinrich thundered, his voice so loud it pounded against Grady's eardrums. "Will this, this complete charade earn us a stone's worth of profit? Did it not in fact cost us a great deal?"

Susan said urgently, "This is between you and Klaus. Give us the control finder, tell us how to use it, and we'll go."

The dwarves looked at each other in disbelief. Susan had brought Klaus to their mercy and was anxious to let him go?

Heinrich broke the silence, turning to Klaus. "You are

fortunate in your—business allies," he spat. "Get the tracer."

Klaus said bitterly, "Yes sir," and vanished into the tunnel. Heinrich, watching him go, sighed. "He had such promise." For a moment he seemed less like a monster and more like a frustrated human manager watching a protégé fall from grace.

He rubbed his eyes tiredly and turned to Susan. "We'll want it back, of course. We've let too much out already."

Grady broke in, "We'll give you the tracer back when we're done. We've also asked one of our customers to disable their controllers. They have—at least they say they have. And we've destroyed all of ours at our plant."

"Our thanks." That clearly cost Heinrich a great deal.

"There is a final price for return of the controller," Grady said. "Considering that in what we are trying to do, we are doing you a favor—"

"Yes, of course." Heinrich fixed his eyes on Grady, who felt a ghost of the chill he had when talking to Captain Vandervecken. "I accept that you are in the strongest bargaining position. I will accept your terms, but be careful what you ask for. I am evidently a much better bargainer than Klaus is, and I assure you I will be a worse enemy."

"I understand," Grady said slowly. "I want the following agreements—in writing." He said as carefully as possible, "The captured panhandler is to be freed and returned to the world unharmed."

"Done."

"The Nieuw Amsterdam Dwarfworks is to be compensated for the endangering of Antony—"

Heinrich bristled. "That was the fault of your principal, Mr. Hastings—"

Grady continued with emphasis, "Which was an implicit danger of the contract, and which your principal

Klaus failed to make clear to Plimstubb or to the Dwarfworks, who had an employee on the premises."

Kirsten, Antony, and Pieter watched with interest.

Heinrich subsided, glowering. "Done."

"Good." Grady smiled amiably, trying to look more
confident than he felt. "The compensation can take several forms. You could forgive a portion of any debt the
Dwarfworks has, or you can help them to acquire greater
production capability—presumably from us. All things
considered, that would be gracious of you."

Heinrich's teeth grated over one another like bull-
dozed rock as he said, "We will consider it. You are
fairly considerate to your business partner."

"As you say, they're a business partner." He grinned,
but nodded respectfully to Pieter. "Plus I worked for
them, and I haven't forgotten their kindness."

Antony and Kirsten blushed. Pieter smiled proudly.

Klaus returned with a small, ten-pointed star-shaped
object. It looked a little like a sea urchin. One point of
the star was glowing, pulsing intermittently.

Klaus spun it in his hands. The light shifted from
point to point, staying in the same direction. "Yesterday
there were still ten lights."

He handed it to Susan, who shifted it and watched the
light flicker from point to point and pulse slowly and
steadily. "That's the last one?"

"The last," Klaus said. He seemed to be waiting for
something.

Kirsten snatched the star out of Susan's hands. "I want
to hear both of you guarantee that the star will not hurt
us under any conditions."

Heinrich smiled faintly and nodded respectfully. "You
have a fine sense of business." He extended his arm and
took the star from Kirsten, passing it to Klaus without
looking. "Done."

Klaus, scowling but obedient, chanted softly over the
stone. A dark-red drop oozed from it and splashed, hiss-

ing, onto the cavern floor. Within a few seconds, the dark gobbet had disappeared into a smoking hole in the stone.

"Now it's harmless." He passed it back to Kirsten. "I would have liked to think of you carrying it as it was."

"One moment." They spun around. Klaus went on, "In exchange for this technology—"

Kirsten said sharply, "For the successful application of this technology—"

Klaus bowed his head in acceptance. "For the mutually accepted successful application of this technology, I will render a means to trace gnome-generated controls. And in good faith, I offer the tracing means immediately upon signing, recognizing that acceptance is dependent on a successful and efficacious trace."

Susan said, "And in exchange we will not pursue any damages or injuries incurred at Plimstubb by this agreement or Warren Hastings' actions in connection with it."

Kirsten and Pieter glared at her resentfully, Antony and Grady thoughtfully.

Grady said quietly for the humans, "Done."

Pieter echoed "Done," though it was a formality; the dwarves had a grievance but, with the twenty-year sleep they had tricked onto Warren, no really enforceable contract.

After examining the star suspiciously, Kirsten gave it to Susan, who turned it in her hand and watched the faint light as it blinked on and off with deliberate slowness. "This tells distance and direction, doesn't it? How far away is the controller?"

"Tell them," Heinrich said with a rasp.

Klaus bent forward, peering at the light, and his lips moved in slow waves as he thought. "Possibly two thousand miles," he said. "From the direction, either the American Southwest or Mexico. When you're used to it, you can tell by the intensity of the light and the frequency of the pulses."

"Then we can find where it is," Grady said. "Thank you for a good deal. Do we need to shake hands on it?"

Heinrich shook his head. "Our lives have already touched each other's more than I enjoy," he said dryly. He turned to Klaus. "Know that by the negotiations here you have evaded punishment."

Klaus bowed, his cheeks pulsing with anger, and he shot a baleful look at Grady.

"However," Heinrich continued, "your dealings have made it clear that you have no caution. Wilmer?" he called down the tunnel, and finished to Klaus, "Remember, when a worker refuses to adapt to business necessities, it is always possible to make the worker fit the job."

Klaus paled, from the feet up, until he looked carved from gypsum.

Wilmer, rasps and tools in hand, took him deferentially by the elbow and dragged an unhappy, hesitant Klaus back to the Gnomengesellschaft. Antony, watching, recalled how often the business vocabulary of the gnomes had a double meaning.

Heinrich turned to Susan and Grady, and all pretense of civil dealing was gone. "You have shown me the shortcomings of my own organization. I will never thank you for this, though I promise you I shall remember it."

He left without good-byes. Presently the dwarves and the humans heard a series of high-pitched shrieks that reached a fairly strong volume and did not fall below it again.

Pieter shook his head sadly and left for his office. Susan shuddered and turned away. Grady wanted to, but instead grabbed Antony's arm and said, "I don't know if you folks have a way to get us there."

In spite of Grady's urgency, Antony hesitated. This was a big secret.

Grady continued, "If you can't help us, I'll need to bargain with Klaus and Heinrich to see if they can help us travel fast."

"Sacred Sun. You wouldn't." Klaus's screams had not diminished at all.

"Not happily." Grady eyed him narrowly. Negotiating contracts had taught him a lot about reading people's faces. "And you think you have a way. If we need to bargain with you—"

"Never," Antony said, hurt. But it decided him. "Come on outside."

He led them to the field where the gremlins had landed. Beyond it was a barn, its roof sagging and its boards gray and warped with age and neglect.

Antony slid the door open and, abandoning his regret at disclosing a secret, gestured proudly inside. "Pretty good, huh?"

It was silver and aluminum where its ancestors had been brown and canvas. The two cockpits were covered over with glass canopies. The air intake for the engines was a scoop. The wings were hung end-to-end with fuel pods. Despite being a biplane, it had a lot of up-to-date technology on it.

On the other hand, the twin engines appeared to be silver, metal-forged dragons.

Grady looked it up and down, unbelieving. "This was a plane in World War I?"

"The Great War. Parts of it were. I've updated it." He stretched up to pat one of the silver engines affectionately. "Plus I made some additions of my own."

Grady was struggling to understand. "It's the plane you flew home from—the Great War, across the Atlantic? How long did it take?"

Antony hesitated and said, "Six hours. I don't know if it will go that fast with three of us on board—"

"Six hours." Grady tried to do the math in his head

and gave up; it made no sense. "You hid an airplane like this for twenty-five years?"

"Sure," Antony said easily. "You think that Uncle Sam is the only one who could hide a project? Plus, I couldn't show the brass hats in the military these engines; there's only one explanation for them." He glanced back over his shoulder at the hill that hid the Dwarfworks and the Gnomengesellschaft. "The gnomes are right to hide their technology. Maybe we all are." He slapped the side of a large barrel on legs connected to the plane by a hose. "It's fueling now. Ready to go?"

Grady was beginning to admit to himself that Uncle Sam might be able to hide a fairly important project. He turned to Susan. "Are you ready to go?"

"One moment." She turned to Kirsten. "Can you go with us?"

Kirsten shook her head sadly. "We're still concluding negotiations with the gnomes, thanks to you. I can't desert Pieter or the Dwarfworks."

"Dead right," Antony said. "Listen, can I speak to you alone?" They stepped aside. When they returned, he was calmer than he had been, and Kirsten was considerably more uneasy.

As Grady disconnected the fuel hose and Antony ran through a preflight check, Susan said nervously, "Is this going to be all right? I've never flown before."

Grady remembered his experiences with the gremlins but said, "Relax. You're gonna love it."

They rolled it out onto the grass. Susan climbed into the front cockpit with Antony. Grady settled in the passenger cockpit. The last person Grady heard before taking off was Kirsten saying anxiously, "Antony? I want to talk to you when you come back."

The last thing Antony said before taking off was to Susan, after the cockpit canopy was down and latched. "She says, 'when you come back.' I want to have the confidence she does." He sighed. "As Grady says, optimism and confidence."

Susan looked around at the fuel gauge, the altimeter, and the engine temperature gauges. "I'd rather have you tell me that change is good for you and you're not afraid."

"Of course," he said aloud easily, thinking, *After all, what's another two lies?*

They flew into the West.

TWENTY

T HE AIR WHISTLED by faster than it had even in *Auger I*, and the strange engines thundered. For all that, the ride was smooth.

Shortly after sunset they landed, smoothly and easily, in pastureland by a river in western Iowa. Antony saw a farmhouse on the other side of the river and brought the plane in by a line of willows tracing the winding route of the river.

As the plane rolled to a stop, the three of them dropped from the plane and, as though choreographed, dashed without looking at each other into patches of underbrush. Afterward, they practically strolled back to the plane, savoring the chance to stretch. The night was calm but not too cool, and the only sound was the chirping of crickets. Grady stared at the sky; the stars were coming out. He had never seen so big a sky or so many stars in his life.

He looked at the rows of fuel pods strapped to the wings. "What's the range of this thing?"

"I'll have to refuel sometime," Antony admitted. "But if we find the thing before we hit the Pacific Ocean, we're fine." It was too early to worry about flying back.

Grady pointed to one of the engines. "What are those?"

"Ah." Antony grinned, in spite of how tired he was already. "They're a little like Messerschmitt engines and a little like dragons. Don't put your finger too near the mouth—the exhaust."

Grady pulled his hand back hurriedly. Antony said, "Grady, you ride with me. Suzie, pass him the control tracer. How does it look?"

She held it up. The single point was still glowing. The pulses were closer together, though still slow, and the light was brighter. "Twice as bright, I think. We're half-way at least."

Grady took it gingerly. "Thanks. Antony, you look beat."

"I am. Maybe you can fly us while I catch forty winks."

"Fly the plane? But I never—I don't have any idea—"

"It's not hard," Susan said. "I did it, and you didn't notice." She added urgently, "Come *on*," and slammed the rear cockpit shut almost as she leaped in.

Antony and Grady looked at each other. Whatever Susan expected the gnome control to do terrified her.

Somewhere between western Nebraska and Colorado the clouds got closer together. After another half hour, Grady stared at an especially large one looming under the others and realized that it was touching the ground. He shook his head and looked again, but it was still there. They were nearing the Rocky Mountains.

Antony shook his head, yawning. "If you're gonna spell me, it had better be now." He shifted to one side.

Grady took hold of the wheel nervously. Antony, amused, said, "It's not a gremlin plane. Relax and grab the wheel. Pull back a little—not quite so much—fine. Now push it forward some—nice. No power dives, okay?"

"I promise." Grady tried to sound relaxed. "Let me try a turn. . . ."

The plane banked sharply to the left. Grady grabbed at the wheel and the plane climbed steeply, still turning.

Antony said, "If you're trying to do an Immelmann, you're doing fine. If you don't want to bank and roll, straighten the wheel out. SLOWLY."

A tense minute later, Grady exhaled. The altimeter said that the plane was a thousand feet higher. Grady brought it down slowly. Antony, careful not to let Grady notice, closed his eyes and exhaled. "Great job."

He closed his eyes. "I just need a nap. Wake me when we're close to the mountains." Antony leaned back, closing his eyes, certain that he wouldn't really sleep.

Grady stared into the night ahead, gradually getting a feel for the motion of the plane. He pulled the tracer from his shirt pocket and banked the plane to turn more southwest. The pulse of the light was marginally faster.

He flew on, gradually drifting into a daydream in which he was in the Pacific, flying rings around the Japanese and bombing a carrier. If he could have hung a cigarette from his lower lip, just like Bogart, the daydream would have been perfect.

Antony woke because he'd been kicked. "Sorry," Grady said loudly, over the wind. "I needed to wake you, but I need both hands here."

Antony jerked his head up and stared down as a bolt of lighting struck ahead. There were mountains all around them, and Grady was fighting a crosswind. To either side were thunderheads.

"You should have woken me earlier."

"I was doing all right. I had to go around these storms, though. Can you fly through them?"

Antony shuddered. "Nope. Can't go above them, either." He took the wheel, grateful that he was stronger than humans. The plane was bucking, fighting the controls.

He checked the map beside him. "We're near New Mexico. How close are we?"

In answer, Grady took out the tracer. It was very bright, and the pulses were faster than the turn signal of a car.

"Okay. Keep it out, and keep an eye on it." Antony banked westward. "This uses up fuel," he said unhappily to himself.

Grady, equally unhappy, said, "I heard that."

"Good thing Suzie didn't." And that was the last thing he said as a heavy crosswind hit and the plane slipped sideways.

The rest of the flight was a war between Antony and the winds. Grady listened to the plane, reassured that only the motors sounded labored. For the past half hour he had been remembering the shriek of complaining metal in the gremlins' plane.

"Look at the map!" Antony shouted. "Where are we?!"

Grady flipped the map over, reading by the light of the tracer. Finally he found the slowly moving plane symbol that seemed to crawl across the map. "We're over the Sangre de Cristo Mountains. Ahead of us are the Sierra Oscura Mountains, near the Rio Grande. I thought that was just on the border with Mexico."

Antony had studied the map ahead before sleeping. "Nope. Goes through New Mexico. Colorado, too. What else is down there?"

"A valley. It's marked like desert. There's a name here—'Jornado del Muerto.' Do you speak Spanish?"

"Enough, kid." He pulled out of a particularly nasty stall and continued heading for the Journey of Death.

They were under the clouds, and there were scattered lights below them. Antony, sighing with relief, throttled back and descended.

Grady guided them in from the south, watching the tracer. "North—a little west—too much—that's good."

At a couple hundred feet from the ground, they passed over a cluster of low-lying buildings. There seemed to be an awful lot of lights for the number of buildings.

Two pairs of lights broke away from the buildings. Below the plane, tracking its motion, were two pairs of headlights.

Grady squinted. "Jeeps, I think. The headlights are pretty close together."

Antony reached to his left. "This might help." He flipped a switch.

They were near a steel tower maybe a hundred feet high. The light from the tracer was bright and nearly steady. "That's it," Grady said.

Antony circled it once. The light in the tracer shifted from point to point, always toward the tower. Antony descended to fifty feet.

"Turn away from the tower," Grady said suddenly.

"Why?" Antony said, but banked obediently. "We have to land somewhere, and it's all flat—"

Grady pointed at the jeeps, visible in the plane lights. The jeeps were packed with soldiers, their rifles now tracking the plane. "I think if we get too close, they'll shoot us."

Antony obediently turned back toward the small group of buildings to the south.

Even at night, the landing was smooth. There were plenty of lights near the field, and they had an audience.

"Where are we?!" Grady shouted as the plane engine stopped.

Nobody answered. Several rifles were pointed at Grady. He said quickly, raising his hands but still holding the control tracer, "This isn't a weapon. Honest."

There were plenty of army men, about half of them MPs, around them. There also were a number of civilians, mostly men. None of the civilians had guns, but Antony, climbing slowly out of the cockpit, felt that there were more than enough guns pointed at him, "We came for a reason," he said. "We need to speak to the officer in charge."

A colonel came forward, ignoring the guns. "Dutch?"

Antony squinted. "Curly." He ran forward and pumped the colonel's hand. "What the hell happened? You got gray."

"You got fat." He bent forward, laughing. "You always were fat, I guess. Didn't get gray at all, did you?"

A stocky man in an army uniform ran forward. Grady counted the stars on the man's shoulder and flinched, though they were all in enough trouble already. The stocky man said to the colonel, "You know them?"

Curly said bluntly, "General Groves, I know Antony van der Woeden only. He's an army veteran. The other two could be anybody." He gestured to Susan, who was scowling at the guns and tapping her foot impatiently.

Grady looked at the colonel curiously and said, only half guessing, "Curly Larson?"

"Colonel Larson, to you." He eyed Grady narrowly. "Do I owe you money?"

"Nope." But a lot was becoming clear. "Antony spoke of you. I'm Grady."

"Nice to meet you, kid," Curly said lazily, and Grady understood where many of Antony's speech habits came from. Curly gestured toward Susan. "But I don't know her, and I don't know you."

Susan said, "Dr. Fermi knows me."

"I can vouch for the young lady," a cultured voice with an Italian accent said. "Suzie, how very delightful."

She looked delighted as well, but only added, "I knew you'd be here."

He chuckled. "Of course you did. When you left physics we lost a fine mind."

Grady looked at her with new respect. One look in Fermi's eyes and you could tell he was absolutely brilliant, though on closer inspection you could also see that he shared with Susan that look of someone who shouldn't be trusted alone with machinery.

"Terrific." But the look on Curly's face said it wasn't. "Who's gonna vouch for the kid Grady?"

Antony said, "Curly, I can. Doesn't that count?" No one bothered answering.

Grady looked around hopelessly. Nobody knew him. Drake Stode moved from behind General Groves. "I can."

"Can you really?" Groves said.

A man as impossibly slender as Stode moved out from behind the civilians. "Let me talk to them."

The colonel barked, "*Dr.* Oppenheimer, this is a job for the army. These three arrived here"—he shook his head—"not that I can figure out how they knew to come here—"

"Which is why it's a job for me. My group has been tracking the untrackable for years now." He turned to Stode. "Always start with what you know." He pointed a skinny arm toward Stode. "How do you know the young man?"

The general tried once more. "Oppie, he's the least of our worries."

"Then he's where I start." The slender man turned again to Grady, and Grady was disconcerted by the other man's eyes. They had a hungrily brilliant presence that made Grady feel as though he himself were only there as evidence, not as an intelligent mind at all. "What is your full name? Why does this man know you?"

"Grady Cavanaugh." For once, saying "sir" wouldn't be enough. There was no way to acknowledge a brain like this. "I supplied a furnace through Stode. I came here because I'm concerned about something we supplied to the project—"

The man called Oppie waved an arm. "We'll get to that." He spun, not terribly smoothly, to Stode. "And you knew this man, the least of our worries, I'm told.

Where did you know him, and who brought him here?"

To Grady's interest, Stode looked unsure. "I know him. Grady Cavanaugh, sales engineer at Plimstubb Furnaces. They built two high-temperature furnaces for us." He hesitated, then said, "Dr. Oppenheimer, I can vouch for his loyalty. If you told me to shoot everyone here who might betray the United States, I'd shoot half the people here before I'd even consider killing him."

The people around looked disconcerted, Oppenheimer half amused. "I'm not authorized to give that order, and I'm not sure whether you'd shoot me."

Stode didn't smile. Oppenheimer closed his eyes, collecting himself, and said, "Did you invite these people?"

"I hooked up with them, through Dutch." Everyone turned toward Curly Larson. He went on, "We were having trouble getting materials." He looked disgusted. "Highest goddamn priority job in the war, and we couldn't get suppliers."

He nodded toward Antony, "So I had a way to write Dutch—"

Stode said tightly, "All mail was monitored."

Curly said with injured dignity, "I didn't say I'd sent mail, I said I had a way to write him." He made an obscure fluttering gesture that Grady and Antony recognized immediately. "So I did, and when I get this letter from Dutch, singing the blues because his boss won't let him reenlist and because his business, with all its talents, can't be part of the war effort, I think: Why not send a little something his way, help us both out?"

Stode said even more stiffly than usual, "What did you tell him?"

Antony answered, "He helped me write an ad or two. Also, he gave me a list of suppliers, furnace companies—"

"Which he got from me," Stode said, disgusted. "So we both contacted the same supplier? You're lying."

Curly shrugged. "It solved your problem."

But Stode shook his head. "It's still too big a coincidence. Tell me what happened."

"I went looking through records to see if someone— one of the suppliers—was already involved with the project in any way." He stood very straight. "Security was important."

"How patriotic."

Curly ignored his tone. "And when Enrico here showed me a return address on an envelope from a letter he'd gotten—"

Fermi stiffened. "Suzie—"

"And she was at one of the furnace plants, I figured, I'd bet odds like that any day. So I wrote Dutch, and I told him to contact the Sales Department at her plant, and it worked." He shrugged as though a breach of security in the most secret project in world history were nothing at all.

"When something wants to be built," Fermi said softly, "it will get built."

Grady was reminded of Antony talking how gold wants to stay pure, molybdenum wants to be out of the air when it heats up.

Susan looked astonished. "Determinism? I thought you liked the Copenhagen Interpretation—"

"For quantum mechanics, yes. That is at the subatomic level." The amused look in his eyes was masked momentarily by anxiety. "This is somewhat larger."

General Groves said wearily, "It's like keeping a secret in an aquarium. Colonel, you had no right to do an end run around security—"

"Then shoot me, goddammit," Curly barked. "Shoot me and end the suspense. Shoot me and start the cleanup. Shoot me because it's easier than talking."

Stode said, "I'll shoot you."

Curly grunted, "I know you would. You're the only person in this whole goddamn war who's heartsick because nobody lets him shoot people. I'm talking to Mustache Pete here." He poked his superior officer, General Groves. "But later, you can explain why you shot the man who helped you win the war early."

He walked away, looking at no one. After a moment's silence, Antony said apologetically to General Groves, "What's the use, General? They're not impressed with anybody once they've crashed a plane or two."

Oppenheimer and Fermi chuckled. Groves shrugged irritably and turned to Antony unerringly. "You, soldier, haven't said why you came here."

Antony found himself saluting automatically. "Sir, we've come into possession of knowledge that there is a piece of equipment here that could be used for sabotage."

Grady stared at him. This was not the language he was used to from Antony. He looked around for other people's reactions.

No one was moving. No one was speaking. Nothing had been said at all after that last word, "sabotage."

Finally General Groves said to the newcomers, "Is it your fault that there was—sabotage?"

Grady cleared his throat. "In a way, sir." All heads spun to stare at him. "One of our managers sent a component on equipment your way without running it through channels."

The general stared down at him woodenly. "Yet the other materials you sent, and the furnace, were not a problem—even though they didn't come through the usual channels."

Everyone was looking at Grady. Some of them looked hungry. Grady realized that whatever the project was that concerned them so, it was vital to find a scapegoat in case it went badly.

He said flatly, "If that's a problem, blame me. In the meantime, whose fault is it if it affects an ongoing project?"

General Groves snapped, "Mine, but that's minor." He

glanced at the surrounding soldiers. "Let's go inside. Stode?"

He nodded and gestured to the others. The small group spun on their heels, moving the prisoners toward the buildings.

Oppenheimer, striding alongside and pausing when he pulled too far ahead of Grady, said quietly, "Your furnace isn't here. Why did you land here?"

He handed over the tracer. "This showed us where to go. Where would the furnace be?"

He pointed. "South of here." But he turned the tracer over and said, intrigued, "But if I understand this thing, it's pointing north—"

He stopped dead. Grady nearly bumped into him as Oppenheimer said loudly and urgently, "General Groves?"

The general turned. Oppenheimer went on, holding the tracer up and sighting down the line of his skinny arm. "This star points to where the point of potential sabotage is, am I right, Cavanaugh?"

Grady nodded. "It's the tower."

"The tower," Groves said, sounding shaky for the first time. "Oh, God."

Stode moved to stand beside Oppenheimer. The two of time looked like skeleton brothers, the angles of their jaws and cheeks sharp in the lights. "That's impossible," Stode said. "I supervised the installation of the second furnace; it's in the materials lab—" He looked sharply at Grady, Susan, and Antony, breaking off.

Oppenheimer nodded. "South of us. What are the odds that it's a coincidence that this points to the tower? How many people worked on installing equipment on that tower? What if one of them—"

"Come with us," Susan said urgently. She had grabbed Groves's arm. "Send somebody to watch us and shoot us, but get us to that tower."

Antony said, "Sir, please. She's right. Shoot us afterward anyway, if you want."

Groves stared at him and said finally, "If something goes wrong at that tower, we'll all hang—if we live." He gestured to one of the MPs, who had followed at a discreet distance. "You! Get a jeep, take these three, under guard, to ground zero. If they get too near the top of the tower, shoot them at your discretion. Move!"

He added, "Stode, go with them. You have no command, but you can advise those boys when to shoot these three."

Stode startled Grady by saluting. Stode's hand moved unobtrusively to his hip pocket, but Susan, her eyes wide, had obviously noted the movement.

A jeep roared in from nowhere. The others ran and leaped in. Grady followed as quickly as he could.

The tower was more than five miles away. Stode drove so the MP could watch Grady, Antony, and Susan. Flashes of lightning, now farther off, lit the sodden ground along the way. Grady fretted that the jeep would be mired down, but the MP didn't seem the least worried.

As they approached, the MP said with relief, "The storm's moving off."

But there were still flashes across the sky, and the clouds seemed low to Grady. He held the tracer and groaned. "We have to go up."

"Not far," Susan said. The lit point of the tracer was barely off the horizontal.

But as they watched, the light moved to the next higher point. "It's climbing," she said tensely and ran from the jeep. Grady and Antony followed.

"Y'all come back here." The MP pulled a flashlight from the jeep and followed her. At the tower base Susan pointed upward and he played the light on the bare metal rungs of the tower ladder. "Who are you fooling, miss? I don't see anyth—wait. What the hell?"

He played the flashlight on the ladder. A small metal box on crablike metal legs was at forty feet and climbing, headed slowly for the corrugated-metal shack at the top. It was chuckling softly and not nicely at all. It was definitely a Gnomeworks controller.

The MP aimed his rifle at it. Stode slapped the barrel aside. "Don't shoot toward the platform. It has a bomb on it."

Susan was white-faced, Antony suddenly afraid. Grady thought of the story he had submitted to *Amazing* as Stode said for emphasis, "A very big bomb."

The MP pointed the rifle down but complained, "It ain't like I can get above that thing and shoot down at it."

"You don't have to," Susan said. "We're going up."

"The hell—"

"It's what they came for," Stode said. "If we see them do something wrong, we kill them."

"Fine," Susan said. "Up we go." She turned. "Not you, Antony. There's only room for one of us on each rung, and your reach is smaller than Grady's."

Antony wanted to argue, but knew she was right. Grady was a fighter, and he had long arms. "All right, kiddo. Good luck." He reached out to shake Grady's hand—

Susan whirled and sprinted for the base of the ladder, climbing frantically.

Grady half ran after her, realizing belatedly that she'd planned all along to leave him behind.

By the time he reached the base, she was twenty feet above him. He hitched his cane to his belt and began climbing.

The strength that using the cane had given Grady was more than a compensation for his bad leg. He hauled himself up rapidly, closing the gap between him and

Susan. A rumble of thunder reminded him that this tower wasn't the safest place to be. "What do you think you're doing?" he called upward.

"I'm the only one who can do this," she said. "I can climb faster than you."

Grady thought irritably that she was finding ways to leave both him and Antony behind, but he saved his breath for climbing.

At fifty feet off the ground he was directly under Susan. "I've caught up with the controller," she announced in a strained voice. "It—oh!"

The controller had stopped climbing. It turned around on the ladder and reached at her. The pincers at the end of its metal legs glittered as they waved to and fro in front of her face. One was a wire cutter, one a tin snips, one an unidentifiable scissors made from two knives.

She ducked to one side, swinging one-handed on the ladder. A lock of blond hair drifted past Grady's face.

She was right, of course; if he'd been up there trying to do what she just did, he'd be blind or falling right now.

"Come back down," he said urgently. "Are you crazy?"

She swung back onto the ladder, dropped down a rung, but said stubbornly, "I have to kill it."

"With no sword." He thought bitterly that she could have at least snatched up a piece of scrap metal before she started climbing. Now it was too late. "It's not gonna let you touch the control box and shut it down. You'd lose your hand first."

Susan said suddenly, "Give me your cane."

Grady looked at her, confused. She insisted, "Do it!"

He passed it up to her, feeling suddenly vulnerable. In a lightning flash he looked down at the ground and hung on tighter to the girders.

As the controller moved closer, she lunged with the cane. The controller retreated onto one of the tower

crossbars, then moved forward again, one long leg circling, the pincer at the end open.

Susan still had the cane extended. The controller
leaped forward like a spider in a web. The near arm
snatched at the cane.

Grady shouted, "Disengage!"

Susan, startled, spun the cane under the controller leg.
The pincer, grabbing frantically, missed.

Susan lunged again; she missed, too. The controller
lunged at nearly the same time, parallel to the cane.

Grady said, "Beat attack."

She slapped at the long metal leg. The controller slid
sideways on the crossbar, grabbing with three legs for
support.

But it found its balance again. This time the leg
streaked in low, aiming for her hand on the cane handle.

"*Coupé* and lunge."

She spun the cane over the controller leg. Her lunge
fell barely short; the controller dodged to one side.

The controller snapped two sets of pincers in obvious
fury, hissing. It reared up on two legs, stretching them
straight forward as it made a lunge straight for her chest.

He shouted, "Parry and riposte!"

She pushed off the rung she was on with one leg,
soaring toward the controller, and for one moment as the
controller waved its pincers and lightning lit the tower,
he thought she looked less like Betty Grable and more
like Joan of Arc.

She caught the controller squarely with the end of the
cane. It squealed loudly, scrabbling at the steel beam as
it slid off. She ducked to one side as its legs flailed past
her.

Grady, wincing, stood on his bad leg and kicked out
with the other one, hard. The controller took a purchase
on the cuff of his trousers but couldn't hold it. It spun
free of the tower, spinning in the air and shrieking.

It landed on a rock beside the jeep. The MP turned

his rifle on it, but Stode, army .45 in hand, was faster with the first four shots.

The MP said, "What in the Sam Hill was that?" He was pale.

Stode, checking his watch, was paler. "We should get going."

Grady, confused, said, "What's wrong?" He gestured with his cane at the ruins of the controller. "It's over."

Stode leaned forward, pointing straight up the tower. "That thing's going to go off in a short while."

"Oh, right." But Grady barely felt worried. Compared to the events of the past hour, whatever they were testing on the tower seemed inconsequential.

Susan blurted shakily, "Jesus Christ Almighty," and hopped into the jeep.

Grady turned to stare at her, not sure he'd ever heard her say that. Her hands were shaking, and her shoulders were hunched. "Please, please, get in."

At two miles away, Grady relaxed. They might feel a concussion from the test, but nothing else.

He glanced sideways. Susan was still tense, Stode more so. Stode drove, bouncing the jeep through the desert night as though they were being pursued.

The first thing Grady did when they got to S-10000, which Stode said was the name of the control bunker, was bum a cigarette from the MP. He lit it and inhaled raggedly. "Thanks."

"For the butt, or for not shooting you?"

"Both. Not for nothing, what's going on here?"

The MP shook his head. "They don't tell us. If I knew I couldn't tell you." They walked along together, and Grady realized they were roughly the same age. "I'm taking you back to Groves."

Stode checked his watch. "It's too late to take them anywhere. Go with me to the control bunker and watch them." Stode added grudgingly, "That's a suggestion, not an order."

The MP grinned. "You sure give a lot of suggestions, sir. Okey-doke. Come on, you three."

At the control bunker, people regarded them curiously but said nothing. Everyone was staring at gauges and instruments, at photographic equipment, or in the direction of the tower.

"You three." Stode handed them each a pair of dark glasses. "Put these on."

Grady said, "At night?" but put them on. Susan put hers on uncomplainingly. Antony put his over his head. The strap was loose. He tied a knot in it and put it on, then tipped the lenses up to his forehead. He was too nervous to walk around half blind in the dark.

The MP, also in dark glasses, walked outside. Grady went with him, not sure where to go or what to do, and the others followed.

Fermi, his back to the tower, had scraps of paper ready to drop. "From measuring how these travel, I can know the size of the blast."

Susan nodded, looking impressed. Grady was dubious. He scratched his head. The goggles were too tight.

He looked to one side. Antony, by the side of a building, was hugging his knees and rocking back and forth, his eyes wide. Grady said, "Goggles," and Antony snatched them from the top of his head and pulled them against his eyes.

Grady turned to walk toward him, concerned. He took a stride and was startled at the sharpness of his silhouette on the rear wall of the bunker, caught in midstride.

For a fraction of a second the silhouette of the yucca outside was thrown on the wall beside him as sharply and clearly as a shadow at midday, but under an unnatural, sideways midday sun. Later he remembered the light as whiter than anything he had ever seen.

There was no noise, absolutely none. Either everything had fallen silent at the moment of the flash, or Grady's mind simply had no room for anything but that light.

Now, less than a quarter of a second later, the light was pushing the clouds aside, darkening and climbing on a tower of fire. Bright orange and purple flashes glowed in the explosion, which was fading to red and getting darker every second.

At ground level, a line was rolling across the desert toward them. It turned into an arc, then Grady could see that it was a circle of dust rolling out from ground zero and the flash—

The shock wave hit, nearly knocking Grady down. He felt his lips pulled tight against his face, as though he were in a terrible storm; he felt the grit hitting his teeth.

He was dimly aware of Fermi, leaning against the wind to stay upright, dropping his pieces of paper.

The cloud, rolling now above them, stayed visible what seemed like a very long time. Grady licked his teeth, tasting the grit on them. His mouth tasted like metal. He looked at the transformed desert around him, trying to understand that all of this was real.

From that moment on, the physicists, the soldiers, and the project workers—everybody except the MP assigned to watch them—completely ignored Susan, Grady, and Antony. Grady was unoffended. At the moment, the three of them and everything they had been through seemed small and unimportant.

Someone said to Oppenheimer, "Now we're all sons of bitches."

Oppenheimer muttered quietly, "Maybe I always was, but I did it. Someone had to." He added aloud, "It reminds me of a passage about Shiva, in the Bhagavad Gita. 'Now I am become Death, the destroyer of worlds.' "

He looked pleased with the transformation.

Then Susan, the anger fresh in her voice, said through gritted teeth, "Next stop, Tokyo."

Grady blinked. In the rumbling, numbing aftermath of the blast he had completely forgotten that the Manhattan Project was a weapon.

Men and women were crying. "That's it. We did it. The war's over."

Grady, thinking suddenly of his father in the Pacific waiting for a land invasion, felt as light as if he were floating. He talked to Susan some more, but had no idea what he said for the next hour.

They rode back from S-100000 to base camp with Fermi, because everyone else official had passengers. That meant they had to wait for him while he went over some calculations, the crudest of results from a test larger than anything anyone had seen here in his life. The MP assigned to watch them sat in the back.

Less than a third of a way from the base camp to Los Alamos, the physicist pulled over and looked at his hands in confusion, than turned apologetically to the others.

"I have never felt like this in my life. The road keeps jumping around; it is like I see only the changes and none of the straight parts."

The MP said apologetically, "Sorry, Doc. I have to keep tabs on these three." He gestured with his rifle.

Fermi nodded. "Suzie, would you please . . . ?"

She drove the rest of the way back. Enrico Fermi, a Nobel Prize winner suddenly vulnerable with his thoughts unknowable, stared at the sand and the dust. Grady tried to think of his father but felt distracted. Everything today was larger than any thought in his head.

The main base at Los Alamos was a small town composed entirely of barracks and multifamily cabins. Grady was struck by the illusion of permanence; he felt sure there was not a building older than three years.

Increasing ranks of counterintelligence officers questioned them, getting more and more sarcasm from Susan, more and more anxiety from Grady, and the same level of patience from Antony. Finally the three of them were escorted to a single building, a barracks. "You'll be locked in," the MP who had brought them there said stiffly. "I'll be watchin'. Don't try to break out."

Susan opened her mouth. Antony, in a rare display of authority, kicked her shin quickly. She grimaced, reached for her leg, and said nothing.

The MP grinned. Grady concluded that the MP might be a country boy, but he didn't miss much.

"So we sleep here?" Susan said, looking at the cots and window shades.

"When they tell us to," Antony said, moving away from the bunk. He had been in the room all of one minute, but his bunk was immaculately smooth, the pillow arranged carefully at the top.

Susan tucked her bed in a clumsy imitation. Antony shook his head pityingly and helped. "You've never been in the army, have you?"

Susan shook her head violently, her curls waving. "And they wouldn't like it."

Antony chuckled. "Sweetheart, they're bigger than you are. They're bigger than anything I've ever known. . . ."

He trailed off. They'd all seen something bigger even than the U.S. Army today.

Susan moved to the far end of the hall. There was a movable screen; she pulled it in front of her cot. "This is perfect. I can sleep behind it."

Grady nodded, his head sagging too far to pull up. He was tireder than he could imagine.

•   •   •

The MP brought in dinner, something vague involving processed meat, carrots, and mashed potatoes. "Sometimes we bag some antelope," he said apologetically, "but we've been kept pretty busy lately." He locked the door behind him when he left.

The three of them ate mechanically. Grady barely noticed anything about the food except that it was gone.

Late that night, when he slept, he dreamed of a huge light swelling toward him as he crawled to the safety of the darkness on his hands and knees. The light shone on him, hard enough to exert pressure on his body before he burst into flame and screamed, watching his body burn but unable to acknowledge or understand what was happening to him. He woke to find that the shade in front of his bed had rolled up; a yard light was shining in on the bed. The filament bulb looked tiny and ridiculous.

TWENTY-ONE

ANTONY, GRADY, AND Susan were detained at Los Alamos for three weeks. Antony spent much of the time reminiscing and catching up with Curly Larson; Susan spent it trying to learn about the new bomb. Fermi answered her openly until Stode caught her at it; after that she was frustrated but otherwise pleasant company for Grady, who alone had no interest in being there.

Once she said, "Dr. Fermi, now that the war's over—"

"It's not over yet," he said with amusement.

"Now that it's almost over," she said determinedly, "because of the new bomb there'll be more respect for physicists, won't there? And there'll be lots of jobs for them."

"Oh," he said sadly. "Oh, Suzie. There will be respect for physicists, but it will be a wartime respect, for warriors. And so all of the respect will go to men." He closed his eyes. "There will be many jobs, yes, but few for physicists. Most of them will be for bombmakers."

He patted her shoulder. "Go find another life. Find another science, if you want. You were always good at mathematics; go back to a university and become a professor. But don't join our little company of prisoners.

We surrendered our freedom to make a weapon. I do not think at war's end that anyone will wish to give it back."

He walked off. Susan, confused and hurt, watched him go. "He thinks I can't be a physicist?"

Grady put an arm around her. "He thinks you can, but he likes you. He wants something better for you."

She didn't shrug his arm off, but she didn't look happier.

Grady spent some of his nights playing poker with Curly Larson and Antony. One of the physicists, Isidore Rabi, sat in with them when he could. Grady quickly lost his shirt, borrowed from Susan, and got back in. After that he bet more cautiously, watching the money shift between Curly Larson and Rabi. The physicist knew more than anyone at the table about hands and odds, but Curly could bluff. The two skills seemed to be on a par. At no time did Grady or Antony come close to even, but it was good entertainment.

Late in the afternoon of August 6, Stode came by and said, "That's it. Go home." It was their first knowledge that the bomb had been dropped. No one told them the target.

They flew home in Antony's plane, more slowly this time. They didn't speak much, and they barely looked at the sights that had so fascinated them on the way out. At sunset Grady, with the wind whistling against the canopy and the Mississippi a calm, flat band below them, actually fell asleep; Antony had to wake them when they landed at the Dwarfworks. Antony, dead tired himself, drove Susan and himself to Providence. Grady slept through the first part of the drive home with his head against Susan; then they shifted and he slept with Susan's head on his shoulder.

Grady woke at noon the following day to find Antony already gone. Grady called work, only to discover that Stode had already called Plimstubb Furnaces. Susan,

Antony, and Grady had taken emergency leave to perform government business. All of them had received paychecks from the U.S. Army. Susan had already picked up hers, Talia informed him. She seemed awfully happy about something.

He bicycled to the plant and came in through the shop door, not bothering to stop for a cigarette. The floor looked remarkably normal. All the damage had been cleared away, the dents hammered out of the workbenches. The lathe and the brake shear had both been repainted. Flash was back at work with one of the electric welders. Grady looked at it uneasily.

A grinning Hammer Houlihan stopped Grady on his way into the front office. "Did you hear about Hastings?"

"What about him?" Grady demanded, hoping no one had seen them leave with Warren.

"He took off in the company car with a couple hundred bucks from petty cash. They found the company Cadillac on a side road in Connecticut. No sign of Hastings." Houlihan looked Grady in the eye and said shrewdly, "Me, I figure that's not the whole truth. Hastings was one smart bastard, but not as smart as he thought he was. I figure whoever tore up the plant last month had something on him, and he tried to skip out but didn't make it."

Grady nodded thoughtfully, "I could believe that."

Houlihan snorted. "You'd better believe it."

The next person Grady met was even happier. Grady was having a much-needed cup of coffee when Joey Cataldo bounded up and said, "Did you hear the news?"

For a moment Grady wondered dizzily if Joey meant that the war was over. Then he realized that was news he'd hear from one end of Plimstubb to the other. "What's up?"

"I am." And he was, a man in his fifties bouncing up

and down like a child of five. "Talia Baghrati's going to marry me, that's who."

"Hot dog!" Grady grabbed his hand, pumping it up and down. "That's just swell, Joey. When did this happen?"

"Just this morning. Not two hours ago." He said proudly, "I propositioned her in the reception area."

"How 'bout that." Grady considered. "How did you propose?" He sipped at his coffee.

He reached into his pocket and pulled out a jeweler's box for a ring, showing that it was empty. "I went down on one knee, I held out the ring, and I asked her to make me the happiest man in a woman."

Grady choked. Joey went on, "She wants me to write a letter to her son and introduce myself."

"Really?" Grady said with interest, "Say, that's great, Joey, just great. Say, just to make sure you get the spelling right when you send that one, why don't I go over it for you?"

"You'd do that?" He was touched. "Thanks. You're a good man, Grady."

He waved a hand. "Ah, it's nothing. Listen, I gotta go congratulate Talia." He hurried off, reflecting that even without interference by dwarves and gnomes, humans were pretty fascinating.

Grady, appalled, thought that his desk looked like a file cabinet had thrown up on it. Nobody had been here to read the mail for sales, and no one in the plant had the authority to pull a sales rep in from the field to cover a desk. He scanned some of the deadlines for quoting on new projects and paled. For him, at least, quiet days at Plimstubb were over for a while.

After sorting through it, he went out to the shop. "Roy?"

Roy Burgess said with a grunt, "Welcome back. Did you bring Antony with you?" That was a great improvement over calling him "Shorty" or "the little shit."

"He's had to work at the other plant for a while." He looked around. "This place looks great, considering."

Roy said with obvious pride, "We cleaned it up pretty fast." He added, "Not before your buddy Renfrew showed up with a barbershop quartet of Feds in suits."

Grady felt a chill. "Feds?"

"Uh-huh. They went through the plant from end to end making notes, they wrote a report, and they sent a copy to the state."

"The state?" Grady had uneasy visions of Rhode Island State Troopers investigating Plimstubb and, particularly, him. "Who?"

Roy glared at him and recited by rote, "The Rhode Island Occult Labor Benefits Program. What the hell did you get us tangled up in?"

Grady said evasively, "I never heard of an occult labor benefits program—"

"Nobody does. Maybe it's some kind of New Deal thing. That's why they send checks, to shut people up when something happens. Some guy named Lovecraft wrote the state a letter in the thirties and suggested setting it up." He shook his head. "Typical state program. I asked Renfrew, 'Who gets that cushy job?' and he said, "Ghosts from assemblymen's families, it's all political.' " He snorted. "He could've said 'I don't know.' "

"Where's the report?"

"I didn't want it, Chester didn't want it, and that left you. It's on your other desk, in the manager's office." Roy smiled, for once looking kind. "Since Warren ran out and you're the only in-house salesman left, that makes you the new manager of the Sales Department. With any luck, you'll keep the job when old man Plimstubb comes back. Congratulations," he added with what might have been respect.

Grady, barely absorbing what that might mean for his future, went to Warren's office and took the report back to his own desk. The report was one page. The title was "Summary by the War Department Subcommittee for Reviewing Nontechnological, Thaumaturgical, Revenant-Inspired and/or Occult-Related Damages to a Wartime Supplier." It described damages, eliminated the possibility of arson, vandalism, or natural causes, and recommended compensation for Flash, Hammer Houlihan, Benny Behind, and Plimstubb itself. A copy of the report had been sent to someone named Hector Delagardie, head of Occult Labor Benefits for the state of Rhode Island.

Grady reread the report. Then he put it in a folder, labeled the folder, and put it on his shelves between *Astounding* and *Weird Tales*. Then he set to catching up on three weeks of ignored requests for quotation, follow-ups on leads, and equipment costing on Warren's desk. By five o'clock he was wondering how much easier his life would have been if more people had known that Warren had fired him.

The following weekend he returned to the Dwarfworks with Antony's check. On the way he didn't see a single convoy. It was as though everyone in America were holding still, waiting for news.

The hill over the Dwarfworks looked as it always had. The fields near it were ready for a second cutting of hay. The field the gremlins had used for an airfield was empty and showed no signs of landings or of a crash. Antony's plane was safely out of sight once more.

Inside the Dwarfworks, not much had changed. The shop floor was busy but not hurried. Kirsten was at her desk, head down and writing furiously. Beside it was a small shed, like the kind a construction company might use to store tools or dynamite.

He tapped his cane on the desk. She brushed the cane aside impatiently and finished her sentence, concentrating. The tip of her tongue stuck out as she wrote, and momentarily she looked less like a seasoned warrior and more like a small child trying to draw.

Then she looked up, startled. "Oh! I didn't expect you." She tried to look happy to see him but stole a furtive look at the new shed.

Grady glanced the same way and heard a sound that hadn't registered before: muted, regular snoring, coming from behind the shed door. He jerked a thumb toward it. "Warren?"

Kirsten nodded. "We had to put him somewhere."

"Why on the shop floor, for God's sake? Why couldn't you lay him out behind a stalagmite and forget about him?"

She frowned. "We can't. He's our charge. He needs water, feeding, and bathing. He turns over regularly, so bed sores aren't a problem. I change the bedding once a week. Gretchen made a nightgown and I put it on him. In twenty years we'll put his clothes back on and leave him outside against a log, and he'll wake up."

Grady was impressed. "You've done this before."

"I haven't, and I didn't want to," she said frankly. "It smacks of dirty fighting. Pieter's done it before, and only to protect the secrecy of the Dwarfworks or to save a life."

He put his hand on her shoulder. "It did save a life, Kirsten—Warren's. Klaus would have tortured him for decades." He shivered. "Maybe centuries. You did what you had to do."

"Everybody does," she said. "I hear your war is nearly over."

It startled him to hear it called "your war" when for so much of his adult life it had been everybody's war. "Yep. Pretty soon now."

"Congratulations." But she didn't seem happy.

He leaned far forward, putting the foot of his cane out for balance, and kissed her on the cheek. "Thanks for teaching me how to fight."

"You knew how to fight," she said. "You just never knew how to do it with weapons."

"Where's Antony? I have a check for him."

"At his cottage." She was looking at him strangely. "He has a guest, but he'll be glad to see you."

Grady pounded on the door, realizing that he'd never entered here. A distracted voice said, "Sure, why not?" Grady opened the door.

He glanced quickly around, recognizing the quarters the way he recognized Antony. A watercolor of a Spad XIII greeted him. To the right of the fireplace was a framed box of ribbons and metals, including a decoration from the Austrio-Hungarian government. There was a photograph near it of a biplane, Antony in uniform, and a second soldier who might have been the young Curly Larson. Antony looked no younger than he did now.

On the bed was a naked human figure. Grady could see the bedclothes through the figure.

His outline was irregular, as though he had been drawn by someone with shaky hands; it took Grady a moment to realize that the irregularity was a series of charred gouges, as though in flesh. It took longer to identify the light patches on the body as the flaming echoes of the dark patterns on some long-gone silk print shirt. The ghost was burning, a sickly yellowish-green flame that would have been invisible by daylight. "Help me please," he said mechanically, politely. "Help me please."

"He's been saying that for two days," Antony said. "I think it's the only English he knows. Or maybe it's the only English he wants right now. It doesn't matter; we can't help him."

He squeezed water out of the cloth again; it passed right through the figure, which shifted uncomfortably and said again, "Help me please."

Grady stared at the outline. "What happened to him? Did it kill him?"

"I think he was a ghost before it happened. Japan has a lot of ghosts, because of all the ancestor veneration I think. Anyway, he showed up here a day or two ago, burning like that, and the only other words we've gotten out of him are 'Hiroshima' and '*pika-don*.' " He smiled tiredly. "We asked some friends, and it turns out that '*pika-don*' means 'flash boom.' What do you think happened to him?"

Grady remembered the force of the light in the desert. "Will he die?"

Uncharacteristically, Antony said, "Jesus, I hope so." He reached through the figure, laying the damp cloth on the pillow. "He's fainter every day. I don't know how you can kill something already dead, but maybe it's happening." He turned away from the bed. "Anyway, he's better off than most. Remember what I said about magic? It's a whole lot safer than science, because with magic you know what's gonna happen. We've helped let loose something stronger and scarier than anything the dwarves or the gnomes ever made. Who knows what's gonna happen now?"

In a complete non sequitur, Antony said, "By the way, kiddo, she finally said yes."

When Grady figured that out, he whooped and pounded Antony's shoulders. "Terrific! When did you ask her?"

Antony grinned. "The first time? Between the Spanish-American War and the Big One. But I asked her again just before you and I and Susan went barnstorming together. When I came back, she said 'yes.' " Antony braced himself. "Grady? I know there have been some awkward moments among you, me, and Kirsten—"

"Like being despised, shunned, and beaten up?" But Grady was smiling.

"You're not gonna make this easy, are you." But Antony knew he had to say it. "I'd like you to stand up for me at the wedding."

Grady hadn't been sure he'd be invited. "It's an honor," he said slowly. "Is it a problem that I'm human?"

The corner of Antony's mouth twitched. "It's been known to be." He spread his hands. "But after all that's happened, how could I keep you and Susan and Sonny away?"

"Thanks." There was another problem, an embarrassing one from Grady's viewpoint. "Will I have time to buy a new suit? And—ah, hell, we're friends. Antony, what other expenses are there? I'm broke." Even with his father's and brother's service pay, keeping up two households and the occasional war bond took every dime he made.

"Don't worry about expenses. You're my guest. It's a wedding tradition." Antony made a note to warn Kirsten about the "tradition" he had made up. "Anyway, the wedding's not scheduled yet. The courtship took thirty years. I'm hoping this won't be a long engagement."

"I hope not, too. I want to be able to stand up when I stand up for you." But he sighed.

Antony didn't miss it. "What's up?"

He told Antony about Joey Cataldo and Talia. "I'm happy for them. It just seems like—"

" 'They're writing songs of love, but not for me,' " Antony sang. "You take Gershwin too seriously, kid. She'll come around. I know her, and I know you. All you're worried about now is time."

The figure on the bed, which had stayed quiet, now said politely, "Help me please."

Antony pulled the damp cloth off the bed and soaked the cloth in water again. "Believe me, kiddo, time is the smallest problem in the world."

Grady left Antony's check on a chair and tiptoed out.

• • •

On Monday morning Talia gave Grady a letter, jointly addressed to Grady and Susan. There was no return address. He took it to Susan's desk.

Susan took it away from Grady to open. Grady, unsurprised, said only, "If any part of it is really for me, why don't you tell me how I should answer it, too. . . ."

He trailed off. For once, Susan was stunned into silence.

She handed the letter over without saying a word. It was badly typed, though it was on White House stationery.

Dear Mr. Cavanaugh and Miss Rocci,

A source who would know swears that you were a lot of help at the last minute on a certain project. I know him, and I know what he was working on, so I'm writing to say that your country thanks you. He thinks you will keep the story to yourselves. I appreciate that.

I don't know if the recent bombings bothered you in any way. They were my decisions, and I'm damned proud that I made them. Don't ever take it on yourselves; you served your country, and I ran it.

Written beside that in the margin, in blue ink, was a hasty note: "I won't ever drop a third bomb. You have to think about all those kids."

The letter closed:

It's been a long war, and we saw it to the end. My source says that you acted from the best of motives. Make sure you always do. The country is always better when you do, even if people disagree

*with what you do. Thanks again for all you did
for America.*

Yours sincerely,
Harry S Truman

*P.S. Sorry about my typing. Normally a secretary
does it, but I could do my own office work when
I was a haberdasher and I can still do it when I
have to.*

They looked at it together. Grady said shakily, "Toss
you for it."

Susan goggled at him. "A coin toss? On something
like this?"

"It's all just probabilities, right? Schrödinger says the
cat's either dead or alive. Call it."

He tossed a quarter. Susan said "Heads." Grady
flipped the coin over to his other wrist as though he had
meant to all along. "Heads it is. Keep it where I can
look at it, that's all I ask."

Susan held it, marveling. "We're holding history."

"We *are* history. We don't notice while we move
through it." Grady left for his desk, marveling at how
easy it was to give away the most amazing letter in his
life to Susan. He genuinely did love her more than he
did fame and fortune.

At his desk was another letter, dropped off by Talia,
and brief and to the point.

To: Grady Cavanaugh
Subject: Recent military work

*I found your work satisfactory. Susan Rocci's
work was as well. This is to inform you that I will
be transferring to a civilian job of sorts.*

>   *Do not attempt to reach me through any pre-*
> *vious address.*
>
>   *Yours,*
>   *Drake Stode*

Underneath was written, in block letters, a phrase Grady had seen in photographs and would see again and again in the weeks to come, "WELCOME HOME. WELL DONE."

At a little after 7:00 P.M. on a warm August night in 1945, Tom Garneaux's car screeched to a halt in front of Grady's house. Susan waved from the backseat. Tom honked the horn impatiently, then slammed his fist down on the hood. "Hop in the car."

Grady said, "What about your wife?"

"She hates crowds," he said easily. "Besides, she always wants to be around to bail me out. Someday when you have the time, let me tell you about the great woman I married."

Susan said, "And before you ask, my mom wanted to go over and be with Julie. She took dinner over and for once a bottle of Chianti. They'll be fine."

Grady said with relief, "Then I'll be fine." He got in the car, noting that Susan's eyes were shining. He felt sure that his own were.

They'd gotten half a mile from downtown from before abandoning the car and walking.

Tom had insisted on walking up to the cathedral first. It was even fuller than Grady had seen it for concerts or for victory over Hitler. It was packed with people who had prayed for victory, prayed for safety for their families, and finally, in the weakness we all share, prayed for the safety and homecoming of their own loved ones above all. The last day of the war was here, and all the prayers were being answered one way or another.

The noise in the square in front of City Hall was deafening; some of the noise was Grady's and Susan's. The square was crawling with servicemen. Ten or twelve had climbed onto the equestrian statue and were waving a flag. The street was littered with confetti, ticker tape, and broken bottles.

"This," Tom Garneaux said with satisfaction, "looks like a party."

Grady heard a window smash and turned. Down the street from him, the front of a store was wide open, people handing out clothes and shoes through the jagged opening.

A woman in a red dress kissed Grady on the lips and handed him something, saying, "Have one on me, kid. Courtesy of the store on Exchange Street." Grady kissed her back and dazedly took the champagne. In her wake, men and women grabbed at liquor bottles and ran into the street and disappeared, obscured behind a kick line of men and women on Washington Street.

Grady forced the cork out with his thumbs and passed the foaming bottle around to Tom, and to Susan, and to strangers. "It's over," a blond woman said as she grabbed the bottle. "My God, it's finally over." She took a mighty gulp, kissed Grady firmly on the mouth, and passed the champagne back to him.

Susan, watching, laughed. "It's over."

The people around her echoed it, and a man added, "I'll tell the world."

A tiny, rational part of Grady was intrigued that no one seemed to be saying "We won." He had some more champagne, and the tiny rational part went to sleep.

The dancers from Washington Street had made it to the mall. Susan, watching them, threw her arms in the air and shouted happily, "I can't stand it!" She leaped off into the kick line of laughing, shouting men and women, then leaped out of it in a mass of frenzied people embracing, breaking apart, and embracing again.

Grady leaned on his cane and watched, wishing he could dance but too happy for her to feel sorry for himself.

Susan was weaving in and out of the crowd, sometimes joining the kick line, sometimes breaking away and running back and forth. Watching her was as exciting as dancing would have been. Whenever she disappeared, he stood on tiptoe to try to find her. Whenever she reappeared, his heart tugged at his chest.

Anonymous strangers lit fires in the streets. Periodically, a sailor or a soldier would kiss an escorted woman and get socked; the resultant fight would disappear into the crowd. Grady was sure that the fights and the arrests would be as understandable and as meaningless as the initial kisses.

The kick line grew wilder, seeming to drive everyone's pulse faster. Grady watched Susan as she threw her head back and sang in a wild way she never had in the choir, and he gaped as she skipped across the street to kiss a lonely Marine, a complete stranger, on the mouth, and she pulled away and lurched back into the street toward Grady, and kissed another with her red-lipped mouth, and Grady thought she must have kissed forty sailors before she spun, laughing, back across the street into Grady's arms and she stumbled and he caught her and they were kissing harder than either of them had in their entire lives.

They pulled part, staring at each other before Susan smiled at him and began dancing again. Grady looked after her for a long time before taking a pull from the champagne bottle and getting back to his own party.

The next day was a state holiday, and it was probably just as well. The morning after that, Grady's bicycling was wobbly and he still winced every time he rode over a bump. Still and all, he felt awfully good. He strode to the back door, pulling a pack of cigarettes from his shirt pocket and looking around for Susan. After five minutes, he gave up waiting and went inside.

Susan was at her desk. The pictures of Marie Curie and Einstein were up. The picture of Vince Rocci next to his plane, *Sassy Susie,* looked exactly the same and somehow not the same. No one was flying planes like that in combat anymore.

He said, "Better break out the peacetime designs you've been working on. We're going to need them."

She had them out already and was sorting through them on her desk. "Plus the glass-to-metal sealing you wanted for RCA and the Pacific. I'll bet we'll still build vacuum tubes after the war."

He raised an eyebrow. "What do you mean, 'we'? I thought you were going back to school."

She avoided his eyes. "Did you hear about Betty, out on the floor? They asked her to work in Accounting. She said 'no.'"

"She's quitting?" Grady was sorry. Betty had a raucous laugh and infectious good humor, and she even got along with Flash and Roy Burgess.

"Who said she's quitting? She's staying on the floor."

"But you said—"

"I said she wouldn't work in Accounting. She loves welding, and she's an old friend of Plimstubb's daughter Gloria." Susan was smiling. "So if she wants to stay, she can."

Grady wouldn't be distracted. "And if you don't want to stay, you can go back to school."

"No, I can't," she said tiredly.

"Of course you can."

She slammed her hand on the desk. "Don't kid me about this; it hurts. If I quit my job, who takes care of Ma?"

Grady said, "I want to marry you."

Susan looked down, saying nothing. Grady went on, "The war's over, and my brother and my father will come back, and I love you." He bit his tongue too late.

But she only smiled, thinking how to say it. "I love you," she said, "and the war's over, and my father won't ever be coming back, and I have to take care of my mother."

"I could help. I could send you back to school—"

"I have to take care of my mother." She said more softly, "And you heard Dr. Fermi; there isn't going to be much peacetime physics anymore. It's all going to be about boys making bombs."

Grady said, "Now we're all sons of bitches."

Susan looked up at him, and her eyes were full of tears. She grabbed his hand, first squeezing it painfully tight and then caressing it. "We don't all want to be. I'm sorry I'm not saying 'yes'—"

"Then don't be sorry and say 'yes.' "

"Grady, I *can't*." The panic forced her voice high. "I've got to learn all the things my father used to do for the family—not just put them off, the way we've done for years—I don't even know what's going to happen to me yet."

He said softly, "I could give you some clues."

"And maybe you can someday. For now, I've got to stay here and work, and think more about my mother than about me."

Grady was silently impressed. As much as he loved Susan, he never expected to hear that from her.

She held her other hand out to him and said as he took it, "Be patient with me."

Grady thought of Kirsten. "Antony's waited thirty years."

Now she grinned at him. "Don't be that patient." She kissed him, then let go of his hands and left abruptly for the shop, leaving him wondering what exactly she meant.

He turned to see Tom Garneaux watching him. As always, Tom was unembarrassed. "I told you someday you'd be a great salesman, kid. Start selling."

"Optimism and confidence," Grady said. "It's not enough, Tom."

"They're pretty good, though," he answered. "And if they're not working, try optimism, confidence—and patience."

Grady went back to his own desk, promising himself he would never again kiss Susan at work. He meant it so firmly that he kept to his word until 2:35 P.M., and only broke it seven more times before four o'clock.

At four-thirty he leaned into the treasurer's office to make a joke to Chester. It died before he could say it; Chester was staring down at a blizzard of telegraphs.

He lifted them up in two hands, holding them toward Grady. "Cancellations. Pratt & Whitney, Lockheed, Thomson Aircraft, Motorola, you name it."

Grady was horrified. "They can do that?"

"They can do that. Some of them have to pay a penalty, but it's worth it to them. They don't need us anymore; the war's over." He smiled weakly. "We won."

Chester went back to sorting carefully through the telegrams, clipping them to canceled contracts and noting the revenue loss in the Plimstubb account book. Grady watched him and turned away, shaken. Maybe Susan was right about how complicated things were going to be.

At five Grady watched Susan stride away home. She was wearing a light summer dress, and he couldn't help but watch her until she was nearly out of sight. Then he stepped away from the plant, looking up and down the street.

Scrap paper blew against the curb; he automatically bent to pick up the paper and then let it go. Just that one small act told him how large the letting go of the next few months would be for him; he leaned against the comforting solid bricks of Plimstubb, trying to understand it.

He had no idea what his plant would be making or for whom. He had no idea what he could sell from here.

He had no idea what his father or his brother would do for a living when they came home.

Everything he had lived for, worried about, stayed awake for through the past forty-odd months no longer mattered. It was done, and soon most of the things that had absorbed him—ration cards and scrap and blood drives and winning a navy "E" and blackouts—would all seem quaint and inconsequential.

An airplane buzzed overhead. Grady squinted upward at the silhouette, but for the first time in his adult life he wasn't anxious about identifying it.

"Change is good for me," he said quietly. "And I am not afraid."

That night he and Mary and Julie had dinner at Mrs. Rocci's house. At ten, he and Susan slipped to the back porch to kiss. He opened an eye from time to time and stared up at a sky without a single patrol plane or searchlight in it, and he knew that, after all, he was not afraid.

And change would be very, very good.

Sharon Shinn—————————